"I think we should get married. Don't you?"

"But…that's ridiculous. We don't even know each other." Plus he hadn't even asked her. Not that a ring and a bended knee would make any difference, but at least she wouldn't feel like a problem he needed to sort out. She folded her arms and glared at him.

Nico raised one lazy brow. "Rosalind Anne Marlowe," he drawled. "Twenty-four years old. Your parents own a well-thought-of light aircraft manufacturer, which your sister, Imogen, now runs. You have two more sisters, one a pilot, the other a celebrity journalist who is in a relationship with Javier Russo, a friend of my cousin, Alessandro."

"Yes, but…"

He carried on as if she hadn't spoken. "You went to train to be a ballerina when you were eleven and graduated into a company where you spent the last five years as a member of the corps de ballet until your unexpected sabbatical this summer. No one knows if you plan to return to dancing or if you have other plans, but your sabbatical has caused quite a stir—you have shown no interest in anything except ballet your entire life. You share a flat with two other dancers, have had a handful of boyfriends although no relationship lasted more than three months and you met them all through work. How am I doing so far?"

"You had me investigated?"

His eyes darkened and he took a step nearer. "I know you like to dance on the beach ~~even when there~~ audience there to see you. ~~I know you like the sea~~ ater on your b~~…~~ ake your r~~…~~ nch when ~~…~~ en I touch ~~…~~"

Summer at Villa Rosa

Four sisters escape to the Mediterranean...
Only to find reunions, romance...and royalty!

Villa Rosa holds a very special place
in the hearts of Posy Marlowe and her three sisters,
filled with memories of idyllic summer holidays on
L'Isola dei Fiori. And her recent inheritance of the
beautiful but fading *palazzo* from her godmother, Sofia,
couldn't have come at a better time for them all!

Now, this summer, they all escape to L'Isola dei Fiori
and rediscover Villa Rosa again.

Don't miss all four books in this fabulous quartet:

On sale June: *Her Pregnancy Bombshell*
by Liz Fielding (Miranda's story)

On sale July: *The Mysterious Italian Houseguest*
by Scarlet Wilson (Portia's story)

On sale August: *The Runaway Bride and the Billionaire*
by Kate Hardy (Imogen's story)

On sale September: *A Proposal from the Crown Prince*
by Jessica Gilmore (Posy's story)

Only in Mills & Boon Romance.

And Jessica Gilmore brings you an exciting online
read—a prequel to **Summer at Villa Rosa**.

Available now at millsandboon.co.uk

A PROPOSAL FROM
THE CROWN PRINCE

BY
JESSICA GILMORE

MILLS & BOON

First Published in Great Britain 2017
By Mills & Boon, an imprint of HarperCollins*Publishers*
1 London Bridge Street, London, SE1 9GF

© 2017 Jessica Gilmore

ISBN: 978-0-263-92328-5

23-0917

Printed and bound in Spain
by CPI, Barcelona

A former au pair, bookseller, marketing manager and seafront trader, **Jessica Gilmore** now works for an environmental charity in York, England. Married with one daughter, one fluffy dog and two dog-loathing cats, she spends her time avoiding housework and can usually be found with her nose in a book. Jessica writes emotional romance with a hint of humor, a splash of sunshine and a great deal of delicious food—and equally delicious heroes!

To my very own hardworking ballerina.
I hope one day you really will be a tree
in Covent Garden xxx

CHAPTER ONE

POSY'S CHEEKS ACHED but her smile didn't waver, nor did she flinch as a bead of sweat rolled down her forehead, another trickling slowly down her back. Her muscles screamed for release but she kept perfectly still, one leg bent, an arm outstretched, head high, eyes fixed on the cheering crowd. They were on their feet, shouts of 'bravo!' reverberating around the auditorium as bouquet after ravishing bouquet were carried onto the stage to be laid reverentially at her fellow dancer's feet.

What must it feel like to be Daria, Posy wondered as Daria kissed her hand to the ecstatic audience, to know that all this rapture was for you? How did it feel to star in a brand-new ballet, choreographed just for you, and to have London at your feet? She and Daria had started ballet school together years before, had once stood side by side, the only two girls from their year to make it into the Company—but now Daria shone right in centre stage while Posy remained firmly in the heart of the Corps de Ballet.

But there was still hope, the promotions were yet to be announced. Maybe this year she would finally make Artist and be given some of the smaller featured roles—

and then First Artist to Soloist and on and on until she reached the exalted rank of Principal. Maybe...

But at twenty-four, five years after she'd graduated into the Company, it was getting harder and harder to keep hoping. Of course, she reminded herself as another bead of sweat trickled down her cheek, thousands of people would kill for the opportunity to be doing exactly what she was doing, would consider being able to dance in nearly every production of the most prestigious ballet company in the world enough in itself. But it wasn't enough; she wanted more.

Posy stayed backstage longer than usual after the curtain finally fell, standing quietly to one side of the cavernous room as the rest of the dancers exited chattering excitedly and the stagehands began to move the scenery back into its designated space. There was always an extra buzz after a Saturday night's performance, adrenaline mixing with the sweet knowledge there was no class on a Sunday so the dancers could flock to their favourite Covent Garden haunts, filling the tables vacated by the tourists as night drew in. But Posy couldn't shake her flatness and so she waited until the backstage area had cleared before making her way out. When she finally reached the dressing room she shared with several other girls it was empty apart from the usual bottles of make-up and brushes scattered on the dressing tables, discarded tights and pointe shoes piled in the corner and costumes hanging on rails, waiting for the costume department to collect, clean and mend them before the next performance.

Posy sank into her chair with a sigh, avoiding her own gaze in the brightly lit mirror. She didn't want to see the sweat-streaked stage make-up accenting her eyes, cheekbones and lips, the dark hair twisted into the bun she had worn every day for years, slim but muscled shoulders and arms, the clavicles at her neck clearly visible. Her make-up itched, felt too heavy, claggy on her skin, her shoulders ached and her ankles twinged. As for her feet, well, she knew all too well that it was her job to smile and look effortless while *en pointe*, that it took as much practice to smile through the pain as it did to perfect a pirouette, but tonight her shoes pinched more than usual, the ribbons too tight around her ankles. It took a few moments to undo the knots and slip them off, pulling off her toepads to reveal the bruised and blistered feet of a professional ballet dancer. She winced as she flexed her feet. Every twinge was worth it. Usually...

'You look *triste, chérie.*'

Posy jumped as a voice floated over from the door; she'd assumed all her friends had left. She forced a smile and turned to greet her fellow Corps ballerina. 'Hi, Elise. No, I'm fine. Just end-of-season blues, the usual.' The principals and soloists were heading out on an Australian tour before stepping into a series of lucrative guest artist appearances but the summer always seemed longer and emptier for those without international reputations. She usually filled her break with stints teaching at summer schools, extra classes and courses and trying to find opportunities to perform wherever she could. She knew she was luckier than many ballet dancers—at least she was paid over the summer months—but she still felt lost at the thought of weeks without her usual routine of classes, rehearsals and performances.

The diminutive French girl sauntered into the room

and dropped gracefully into the chair next to Posy's. 'Me, I'm looking forward to the break,' she said. 'I thought you were too. Don't you have a holiday home to visit?'

Posy shrugged. She knew she should be more excited about the house her godmother had left her but her recent visit to the rambling pink villa on L'Isola dei Fiori for her sister Miranda's rather sudden wedding had left her filled less with the thrill of home ownership than with panic. The villa was huge and had obviously once been beautiful but now it was dilapidated, the garden still overgrown despite her sister Immi's best efforts, with walls literally crumbling down. It was going to cost a fortune to put right—and a fortune was something she most definitely didn't have.

'I am planning to go there at some point over the summer, but my sister's there at the moment and I'm not sure how long she's planning on staying.' The villa did have an immediate use—it had been a bolt-hole for all three of her sisters; first Miranda, then Portia and now Imogen had all fled there to try and regroup in a year that seemed full of upheaval. Posy knew she was being silly, there was no reason she couldn't stay there at the same time as her sister, but years away at ballet school had left her feeling very much the outsider in her own family. It didn't help that the sisters nearest in age were twins, neither of whom had wanted to spend much time with the baby of the family when they were growing up.

'If I had a villa on the beach I would be heading straight there and possibly never coming back.' Elise eyed Posy keenly. 'Unless there's another reason you're staying around.'

Posy shifted in her seat, unpinning her hair so she didn't have to meet Elise's gaze. 'I don't want to be too far away. People are ill on tour, they need emergency understudies; I'd hate to miss out because I'm not here.' She just needed the opportunity to stand out. If they would just give her a solo, one small role, then they would see what she could do.

Elise didn't answer for a long moment; instead she swept the discarded hairpins up from Posy's dressing table and began to bend them back into shape. 'Posy, you and I have danced together for how long now? Three years?'

Posy nodded, her chest tightening at Elise's unusually serious tone.

'In that time neither of us have been asked to do anything extra, to be featured in any way while girls who joined this season, last season, have been getting duets, solos, character parts.'

Posy closed her eyes. It was all too true. 'It doesn't mean we won't get there...'

'*Non,*' Elise contradicted her. 'It does. And I for one did not become a dancer to spend my life being nothing but beautiful scenery.'

'What do you mean?'

'I'm leaving. I'm joining a tour company.'

Posy spun round and stared at her friend in disbelief. 'You're what? Cramped dressing rooms, digs, a different small town every day, no paid holiday? Instead of here, instead of all this history, the reputation? Why?'

'To dance,' Elise said simply. 'I will go in as First Soloist, if I do well then I could be Principal by this time next year. I have been promised a chance to dance Clara and Aurora this autumn. There's even a chance of Odette/Odile if I work hard. I deserve this. I've paid my dues here, Posy. As have you. Why don't you come with me? I know they would jump at the opportunity to have someone with your training.'

But Posy was already shaking her head. Here was where she was meant to be. This was the stage she wanted to conquer—not a different stage every night. 'I can't. But I wish you all the luck in the world if this is what you really want.'

'What I want is a handsome prince to whisk me away from all of this, but if it won't happen in real life at least I'll get to dance it. Posy, there's a whole world outside. Remember that, you have choices…but come, it's Saturday night and we are free for such a short while. Do you want me to wait for you? There's a table at Luigi's with our name at it.'

'You go ahead. I'm still not changed and I left my jacket in the studio. I'll see you there, okay?'

'Okay. Don't be too long. It's not good to be alone when your thoughts are sad.'

There's a whole world outside. Elise's words echoed through Posy's head as she headed away from the dressing room and up the staircase that led to the rehearsal studios and break rooms where she spent much of her day. There *was* a world outside but this was all she had ever wanted from the moment she first put a ballet shoe on. She had sacrificed friends, romance, higher education, even her family to be able to walk along these corridors, rehearse in these studios. To step out onto that stage. How could she give up on her dream when it was still attainable? Impossible.

She'd expected the dancers' area to be dark and shut up but to her surprise the lights were on in the wide corridors. She stopped to look at the familiar space, at the sofas lined up along the wall facing the huge windows with their views across Covent Garden and the wider city skyline, encouraging the dancers to sit and rest between their gruelling routine of class and rehearsal. Windows above the sofas looked into the large studios, each wall covered with mirrors and barres, capable of holding forty or so dancers. She spent nine hours a day, six days a week in these corridors and studios; they were more home than the narrow bedroom she rented just a few streets away.

She'd left her jacket slung on one of the sofas and she picked it up, suddenly impatient to be out of the building and away from her worries. Elise was right, maybe being alone when she was sad was a mistake. She'd be better off at Luigi's with a glass of wine and a plate of pasta, her usual Saturday night treat. As she turned she caught sight of two people in the studio and froze when she recognised the ballet master, Bruno, and the formidable company director, Dame Marietta Kirotsova, deep in conversation.

Her heartbeat speeded up. Here was her chance, handed to her on a plate. She could go in there and ask them just what she had to do, what she had to work on, how she could distinguish herself enough to finally take her rightful place as a featured artist. She inhaled, apprehension creeping through her. She was used to criticism, to rejection; she had to be. But this time it mattered more than it ever had.

'Just move, Posy,' she admonished herself, but for the first time in her life her feet wouldn't obey. Maybe she was a coward after all, maybe it was better to hope than to know that there *was* no hope.

And then all thoughts fled as she heard her name, loud and clear through the partly opened door. She tried to speak up, to let them know she was there, but her voice had dried up, her limbs incapable of movement.

'Rosalind Marlowe? Oh, you mean Posy?' Bruno's voice, still heavily Italian even after several decades in London, carried easily through the still air. Posy swallowed, wishing she were anywhere else.

'She's danced with us for five seasons. Do you think she's ready for a featured part?'

Posy squeezed her eyes shut, wishing with all the fervour of a small child for the right answer, that her worries would all be over soon.

'No.'

And just like that her world ended.

'She's an excellent technical dancer, maybe the best we have. I can see her as *coryphée* one day—and she would be a wonderful teacher. But she doesn't have the fire, the passion to step outside the corps. I never look at her in character and believe this is a woman who has loved, who has lived. It's a pity but as I say she is almost unsurpassed technically and a great asset to the company...'

Posy didn't wait to hear more. Somehow she regained control of her legs and began to back quietly away. She had her answer. She would never be a soloist, never stand in the spotlight, never see the crowds jumping to their feet for her. Worse, she would never dance the steps she knew and loved so well. Would never be Juliet or Giselle. She was fated to watch other girls live out the tragedies. She had failed.

CHAPTER TWO

NICO MIGHT—AND DID—tell himself that he would rather be anywhere in the world than stuck here on L'Isola dei Fiori but even he had to admit that right now he was as contented as an imprisoned man could be. Maybe it was the soft summer evening light, the way the brilliance of the sun had dimmed to a glowing warmth, the sea breeze a cool accent to the heat. Maybe it was the scent of night-blooming jasmine mingling with the salty tang of the sea or maybe it was the way the green cliff tops rolled across the horizon dipping suddenly into the azure blue of the sea punctuated only by the curving perfection of fine white sand.

So, maybe L'Isola dei Fiori felt like a prison but at least it was a beautiful one and as he strolled along the cliff path towards the Villa Rosa it was easy to forget all the reasons he didn't want to be here—and all the reasons why he was tethered to his island home.

Although the nearest beach was technically open to anyone, like all the beaches on the island it was Crown property; the only known path to it led from the fading pink villa, majestically poised on the very edge of the cliffs looking out over the sea. The only known path to those who didn't know every inch of the island by heart, that was. And Nico did. Whether he liked it or not every path, every bend, every slope, every blade of grass and grain of sand was emblazoned on his heart, in their own way as binding as his obligations.

The way was hidden by two boulders, seemingly impenetrable unless you knew the exact turn—a smart right, almost turning back on yourself, a squeeze and then the path lay before you—more of a goat trail than a formal path, a steep, twisting scramble down to the beach. Nico stared down at the overgrowth covering much of the rocky path. How many times had he raced Alessandro down here, half running, half slithering onto the beach below, only to return bruised, scraped and exhilarated from another forbidden adventure?

His eyes burned. No, he wouldn't think of Alessandro. But it was hard not to when every corner held a twist of nostalgia, a memory to cut deep. Two years on and time had healed nothing. Grimly he increased his speed, the adrenaline of the fast clamber down chasing away his grief in a way no other attempt at solace had until he finally half leapt, half fell down the last vertical slick of rock onto the sand below. Nico kicked off his shoes, the soft sand beneath his toes anchoring him firmly back in the here and now.

It had been over a decade since he'd last visited this particular cove and nothing seemed to have changed. Nico had travelled to more than his fair share of stunning places but on an evening like this the secret cove was hard to beat: small but perfectly formed, the sand curving in a deep horseshoe partitioned by a graceful arch of craggy rock. The waves lapped gently on the shore and Nico knew from experience that the currents were kind, the water deepening gently, several long strides before a bather found himself thigh deep.

The summer breeze was lessened down here, the steep cliffs providing a natural shelter, and Nico realised how warm he was, his T-shirt sticking to his torso. He eyed the sea, already feeling the coolness of the water against his heated skin. It wasn't that late and the fierceness of the day's sun would ensure the water was a pleasurable temperature—not that he and Alessandro had ever cared about the time of year or day, as happy to night swim in winter as they were in summer, the sea their eternal playground, until Alessandro had grown up, grown into his responsibilities and put their boyhood adventures firmly behind him. For all the good it had done him...

And now it was Nico's turn to shoulder the burden, to take his responsibilities so seriously he would no longer be able to sneak away for an evening swim. Really he shouldn't now; the sensible thing would be to turn around and go home. He clenched his fists. *No*, he had a lifetime of making sensible decisions ahead of him, a lifetime of duty first, self last. Tonight belonged to him. To the memory of two young boys sneaking away from tradition and responsibility to bathe by the light of the moon.

His body decided before his mind was fully made up, shucking off his damp T-shirt and stepping out of his shorts and boxers, leaving them in a crumpled pile on the sand as he walked naked towards the welcoming sea. It was only as his toe touched the refreshing water that he remembered the main reason why this was a bad idea. Nico paused briefly then shrugged the thought off. If a paparazzi was so enterprising as to follow him here then he or she would get the shot of a lifetime. His mouth curved as he pictured his uncle's reaction. It would almost be worth it…

The water was every bit as revitalising as he had hoped, the waves not too strong, the temperature warm at first, turning more bracing as he headed out into the deeper waters. He struck out with strong, sure strokes, out, out and further out until, when he turned to float lazily on his back, the beach was just a smudge of yellow. He stayed there for some time, happy to just scull gently in the water as the waves broke over him, rocking him from side to side, the late, sinking sun still warm on his salt wet face. It was hard to imagine ever being this free again when tomorrow he would formally take up his duties, his future one of ceremonies and meetings, a hidebound, indoor, rigid existence.

And, sooner rather than later, a wife. A family. A suitable consort chosen for him.

At the thought his buoyant mood sank quicker than a pebble thrown into the water and he was back on his front and striking back to shore, not with the bold freedom of his earlier strokes but with a precise, weary determination, fighting his own instinct to flee as much as the outgoing tide.

He was closing in on the beach, his pile of clothes coming into focus, when he saw her. Nico stilled, swearing under his breath as he slowed to tread water.

She was on the other side of the arch that bisected the beach into two, standing near the narrow jetty and the natural thermal pool that made the beach so famous. He couldn't see her boat but, seeing as she had just stepped off the jetty, he was betting she had moored on the other side. If he was careful then Nico might be able to make his way to shore and grab his clothes and be out of there before she noticed him. Or he could stay here, bobbing up and down like a seal and wait for her to leave. Neither option appealed but action would always win out over inaction. So stealthy approach it was.

His mind made up, Nico looked over at the girl again. She was too far away for him to make out her features. All he could see was a petite, very slim frame topped with a mass of long dark hair. She kicked along the beach, hands in pockets, staring down at the ground. Everything about her suggested despair and Nico felt a pull of kinsmanship. He was about to move off when she stopped, straightened and flung back her hair, curving one elegant arm above her head and executing what seemed to him to be a perfect pirouette on the beach. She paused and then spun round again and then again, hair flowing, like some beach naiad performing her evening rites.

Nico sensed that he was intruding on something intensely personal yet he couldn't look away, transfixed by the grace and agility so unselfconsciously displayed, and by the time she drew her white dress over her head in one fluid movement and dropped it on the beach it was too late to turn away, to swim away. She wasn't wearing a bra and it took less than two seconds for her to step out of her knickers and walk into the sea with the same grace she had displayed as she had danced.

She must be a naiad or a siren and he, like Odysseus, was caught, too mesmerised to retreat. All he could do was wait and hope that she wouldn't see him. A futile hope—Nico knew the moment she spotted him because she stopped dead in the water, spluttering as a wave caught her unawares. It was his cue and he swam a little nearer, not too close, not enough to alarm her any more than he already had. 'Nice evening for it.'

If looks could kill he would be shark meat, his dead body right now slipping underneath the waves. 'I thought this was private property.'

His mouth curved appreciably. Her head was held high as she trod water, her dark eyes fierce. 'The sea? Are you Poseidon's princess to claim ownership over the waves?'

She swallowed, visibly fighting for control. 'The beach. The beach is private property.'

'It's not, you know,' he said conversationally. 'It's property of the Crown, open to all, and even if it wasn't you, mysterious naiad, aren't a Del Castro.' That he was confident of; he knew every member of the most distant branches of the royal family tree.

'But there's only one way down and that *is* private property.' She tossed her head as she spoke, triumph in her voice. 'And I know you didn't come by boat.'

'There's always another way, if you know where to look.'

'Were you watching me? Just then?'

'Not on purpose,' Nico admitted. 'The beach was empty when I got here so, really, I should be the offended one. You intruded on my privacy, not the other way round.'

She didn't answer his teasing smile. Instead her brows shot up in rejecting disdain. 'A gentleman would have drawn attention to his presence.' She managed to convey affronted dignity despite the hair floating around her pale, naked shoulders, the drops shimmering on her eyelashes.

'Ah. But I'm no gentleman. Ask my uncle. Besides,

I didn't want to draw attention to my presence. I am also…erm…in a similar state of undress.' His smile widened as her cheeks flushed.

'I think you should leave immediately.'

'But I don't trust you not to peek.'

She glared at him. 'Believe me, I've seen it all before.'

'This is a predicament.' Nico moved closer. He was enjoying himself more than he had believed possible. If she'd shown any real signs of anger or fear he would have swum out of there with an apology but, for all her outraged words, there was a spark in her eyes that told him she was enjoying the verbal sparring as much as he was. That maybe she too relished the opportunity to forget her worries, to feel alive. She was younger than he had first thought, early to mid-twenties, her creamy skin a contrast to her large dark eyes and almost-black hair. She wasn't exactly beautiful but there was something arresting about her features, a striking dignity that made him want to look twice and then again. 'You and I here, our clothes there. I'm really not sure what our next move should be.'

That wasn't entirely true. He *was* sure what he wanted to do—but not if he should. He wanted to swim closer, next to her. He wanted to see if those eyes darkened even more with desire, wanted to taste that plump bottom lip. He wanted to forget that tomorrow he would be presented with a list of suitable wives and expected to pick one with as much thought as he gave buying a new phone. He wanted to lose himself in another human being of his own choosing while he still could. He wanted to live on his last night of freedom.

* * *

She should be outraged. Possibly scared. Definitely wary. This man had plainly been watching her—watched her dance, watched her strip, watched her wade naked—*naked*—into the water. He'd lounged here insolently invading her privacy. And now, instead of apologising and leaving her to her evening swim, he was looking at her as if…well, as if he wanted to eat her.

She s*hould* be outraged but the clench deep down wasn't fear; nor was the tingling in her arms and breasts. Posy took a deep breath, her legs suddenly weak, treading water as she fought to hold onto her composure. 'Our next move?' she managed to say, keeping her voice level. 'There's no "our". You are going to swim back to your clothes, I will swim back to mine and neither of us will turn around or acknowledge each other in any way. Understand?'

His smile didn't waver, a confident, amused grin, which infuriated her almost as much as her body's traitorous reaction to the play of muscles across his shoulders and to the heat in his navy-blue eyes. 'If you insist, naiad.'

'Don't call me that.'

'But what else should I call a fair maiden dancing on the shore before slipping into the waves? A mermaid? A siren—or are you a selkie? Waiting for me to leave before slipping into your seal skin?'

'Don't be so silly and you don't need to call me anything…' She paused, embarrassed that she was reacting so strongly to his teasing, her innate good manners forcing her to add, 'But if you did need to, then my name is Posy.'

'Nice to meet you, Posy. I'm Nico.'

'I wish I could say the same but I didn't actually want to meet anyone tonight.'

'Me neither,' he admitted and, startled, she looked directly at him, her prickles soothed by the lurking smile in his eyes. 'This is a place one comes to for solitude, isn't it? I didn't think anyone would be here. If I had I would have packed some trunks.'

'Yes.' She wasn't sure what she was agreeing with—the joint need for space and to be alone or that swimwear was a good idea. 'Okay then. Now we've been introduced let's call an end to this impromptu meeting. I propose that you go that way, I go this.'

'Deal. I hope you find it, whatever you came out looking for tonight.' He paused, his eyes intent on hers for one long moment, before turning and with a graceful dive, which gave Posy a glimpse of a tanned, lean torso and a decent pair of legs, he powered off towards the opposite side of the beach. She lingered, watching his strong body cut through the waves for one guilty second before turning and kicking off in a more sedate breaststroke back to the beach, glad of the cool water on her overheated flesh.

Posy was no stranger to gorgeous male bodies—she spent most of her time with physically perfect specimens clad in Lycra and tights, every single muscle perfectly defined. She was used to being lifted and held, spun and moved, her partner's hands moving with sure possession over her body. That was why when she dated, she dated within the company. Men from outside could never understand that when her partner's hand clasped her inner thigh the last thing either of them was thinking about was sex. A dancer's body was public property; there was no room for coyness. She was used to nudity, to being nude—or as good as. To react so strongly to the knowledge of another person's nakedness was foreign to her. She hadn't been able to see much. They'd both been cloaked by the evening sea. But she'd known, she'd reacted—and that discombobulated her.

Also, she was a fool. She should have swum away the second she noticed him. She was lucky he wasn't some kind of maniac who lurked in deep water waiting for unsuspecting night swimmers. Maybe he just waited for said swimmer to return to the beach lulled into a false sense of security instead…but when she checked he was clearly heading to the far side of the beach, not even looking in her direction. As they'd agreed. Which was a good thing. And she wasn't even the teensiest bit disappointed.

It was far less pleasant pulling her dress back over her wet body than it had been to shuck it off. She'd hoped that an evening walk and swim would distract her from an ever-lengthening list of questions and worries. She stifled an unexpected giggle; to be fair her plan had worked, although in a very unexpected way. She hadn't thought about bills or her future once in the last ten minutes.

Posy took a few steps along the beach, heading for the jetty, almost hidden on one side, which led to the private path up to the villa, via the natural thermal pool. The pool might be famous but, like much of her godmother's legacy, she would gladly swap it for a roof that didn't leak in places, a new boiler and some idea of how she was going to pay the bills over the next few months whether she stayed here or not. What on earth would she do if she stayed here—and where would she go if she didn't?

Posy stopped as panic overwhelmed her, almost crushing her chest so she could barely breathe. She wrapped her arms around her torso, as if by squeezing tight she could push the terror out. Stay here or leave, she had nowhere to go, no purpose. Without dance who was she? What was she? How would she get up each day?

'Posy? Are you okay?'

It took a while before the words penetrated through the grey mist. Posy looked up to see Nico—still on his side of the arch—looking at her, concern etched on his face. She forced a deep breath, dragging the night air into her lungs. 'Yes. Thanks.'

He didn't move. 'That didn't look okay to me.'

She forced herself upright, forced her arms to loosen in a pose of defiance and strength she didn't come close to feeling. 'What happened to straight home no looking?'

His mouth quirked into a half-smile. 'I just wanted to check on you. Turns out there's all kinds of strange people lurking in this bay nowadays.'

She should go. She meant to go. Yet once again her limbs, usually so obedient, used to being kicked up high and held in gravity-defying positions, refused to move a single step. 'There are. Very chivalrous of you to think of me.'

'I'm a chivalrous type.' The sun had almost set behind him, casting a red glow over him, making him otherworldly, the cove a place of magic and mystery. He was taller than she had realised, lean to the point of slimness but with a coiled strength apparent in his stance, in the definition in his arms and legs. Casual in a grey T-shirt and khaki shorts, his dark hair, wet from the sea, falling over his eyes, he still radiated a confidence and purpose she coveted. Barely aware of what she was doing, she took a step closer and then another. He didn't move but his eyes tracked her every movement. Posy was used to feeling graceful, assured in her every gesture, but right now she didn't know what to do with her limbs, every part of her body a stranger.

She knew his name, nothing more—no, that wasn't quite true. She knew that he had craved an hour's peace and solitude. Knew that she couldn't tear her gaze away from his, knew that every fibre in her body was aching to be given a purpose, a meaning. She was a creature of movement, she belonged in the dance, in the pairings of a duet or the exhilaration of many feet and arms all placed in exactly the right way at exactly the right time. For so many years that had been enough. Or so she'd thought.

But it wasn't. Pouring her body and soul into her craft had left her lacking. She had no fire; she hadn't lived. Those overheard words had burned through her, the truth of them hurting the most.

With the sunset blazing behind him Nico looked like a fire god personified, Mars come to earth blazing. Could some of that fire touch her? Warm her? Bring her to life?

Posy took another step. He leaned against the arch, watching her every move. She swallowed, the dryness in her throat a mixture of apprehension—and anticipation. 'Not too chivalrous, I hope.'

He stilled. 'Depends on the task.'

'If I was a selkie, would you hide my seal skin, just for the night?'

'I never thought that was playing fair. I'd prefer the selkie to come to me of her own free will.'

'Would she?'

'I think so.'

Another step. He was close now, close enough that, even as the dusk drew in, Posy could see the heat in his eyes, the tension in his stance for all his supposed nonchalance, the muscle beating in his cheek. He felt it, this connection. He wanted her. 'I think so too. Just for one night.'

He nodded, understanding her every meaning. 'You can't trap a wild creature.'

Her entire life Posy had put ballet first. Her few relationships fizzling out, hardly mourned, they were so unimportant compared to her career. Bruno might feel that she lacked passion but everything she had was poured into her work. Without it she had no outlet, her emotions, her physical energy pent up, her worries needing an outlet. She'd thought a swim might help. She'd been wrong. But Nico might. If she let him.

If she let herself.

Posy Marlowe did not go skinny dipping. Posy Marlowe certainly didn't flirt with strangers in the sea, on the beach. Posy Marlowe would never tug her dress off and stand naked in front of a complete stranger as the sun dipped below the horizon, the only sound the hush of the waves on the shore. With shaking hands she clasped the fabric and tugged, letting the cotton slither onto the beach as she stood before him. His intake of breath emboldened her. 'You might tame it for an evening, though.'

'Not too tame, I hope.' He stepped away from the arch as he spoke, stepped close and looked into her face for one long moment, searching for truth, for consent, for surety. She appreciated it even as impatience surged, her hand reaching for his chest, tracing the lines of his muscles. She knew muscles, their purpose, look and feel. She'd never quite appreciated them before today as he quivered ever so slightly under her touch before capturing her hand with his even as his head bent towards hers, his mouth firm and sweet, his touch knowing and sure as he took control. Posy knew all about being led, the steps in a duet, and she sank into his kiss, into his touch, into his arms. Living. For one night only.

CHAPTER THREE

Nico bowed smoothly in his uncle's direction before backing out of the Great Hall, working hard to keep the irritation off his face. He'd lost his temper too many times in the past and it had never got him anywhere. His uncle made a toddler in the middle of a tantrum seem reasonable, which meant rational debate was as unlikely to work as anger. When King Vincenzo V made his mind up it was well and truly up and neither logic nor reason could shift it. In the past Nico had simply circumnavigated his uncle's wishes but things were infinitely more complicated now.

'Dammit, Alessandro,' he said softly as he finally made his way out of the double doors and into the opulent hallway. 'You could always handle him so much better than me.' The guards standing smartly to attention either side of the open doors, hot and ridiculous in the full burnished splendour of their dress uniforms, didn't betray that they had heard his words with as much as a flicker of an eyelid. Maybe he should take lessons from them.

The hallway was wide enough for two cars to drive down it with ease, the vaulted ceiling at double height, the marble floor kept so highly polished Nico doubted it had ever been subjected to a health and safety risk assessment. As small boys he and Alessandro had skated along here under the disapproving eyes of ancestors frowning down from huge portraits, careering along, narrowly missing the spindly chairs and occasional tables that were dotted along like valuable obstacles in their headlong race. At intervals discreet doors were set into the ornate panelling, leading to suites of offices, other function rooms and rooms that Nico had discovered no discernible use for. He had his own suite now, one here for work, meetings and audiences as well as his private rooms, in the west wing. At least they hadn't tried to give him Alessandro's rooms yet. It was hard enough to feel at home in the high-ceilinged formal rooms without mementoes of his cousin scattered around his living quarters.

Not that he'd ever really felt at home here. He'd spent too much time alone in the family suite while his parents had jetted off to Paris, to London, to New York and even when they'd been resident in the palace they'd barely seemed to notice he was there, too busy enjoying the luxuries and privileges of royal life to settle for anything as mundane as private family meals or playing with their son. Luckily he'd been a firm favourite of his grandmother's—and he'd idolised his cousin, two years older yet with plenty of time for his younger shadow. They were all the family he had needed. And now one was gone and the other fading fast.

'Your Highness?'

It still took a few seconds for the title to register in Nico's brain and for him to respond. In a way he hoped that never changed, that he wouldn't supplant his cousin so easily. He stopped and allowed the harried official rushing along the corridor to catch up with him.

'Your Highness.' She was breathing hard, swaying in her too-high heels. Every official dressed as if they were being judged on their power dressing skills, aggressively cut suits the unspoken palace uniform; Nico's own faded jeans and checked shirt were a pointed contrast. 'Her Grace would like to see you at your earliest convenience.'

Which meant now. Nico's grandmother, in her own way, was just as stubborn as his uncle. 'Thank you.'

The official hesitated; obviously she had orders to bring him then and there but Nico had no intention of being ordered around by anyone, not even Graziella del Castro, Dowager Queen. 'I'll be along shortly,' he added. She didn't look too placated but nodded and marched away, her heels perfectly balanced on the marble floor. Nico paused, his mini rebellion feeling as paltry as it was. It wasn't his grandmother he was angry at—nor even his uncle. It was fate. Fate for snatching away his cousin and landing him here in this unwanted spot with this unwanted future. He pivoted and caught up with the official in three long strides. 'Don't worry, I'll head there now.'

She gave him a startled look; palace officials were never worried—at least they were well trained not to look it—but nodded as Nico headed off in the direction of his grandmother's rooms.

Like her son, the King, and Nico himself his grandmother had two sets of rooms, her formal receiving and business rooms in the main part of the palace and her own private suite in the west wing, compromising her bedroom, her sitting room, dining room, study and roof terrace. Up to a year ago she would usually be found downstairs during the day, sitting erect at her desk in her office or on the ornate chair in her receiving room, refusing to slow down despite having achieved her seventieth birthday a few years before. But since Alessandro's death she tended to spend more and more time in her private rooms and it was towards these Nico headed, up the grand staircase, along the balcony that overhung the famous hall, the oldest part of the original castle, and through a discreet—at least it would have been if it weren't for the two heavily armed soldiers guarding it— door that led to the royal family's private apartments.

The door led into another corridor, as luxurious as the main hallway that bisected the palace in two, but less ornate. These rooms weren't designed to impress and, although Nico personally found the rose velvet and cream a little cloying, it was a refreshing contrast to the pomposity of the gilt and purples in the public parts of the palace. His own rooms were on the top floor but his grandmother's were on the first, and it only took a minute before he was rapping gently on her door to hear her voice bid him 'Enter'. He did as he was told, sweeping a low bow before her and taking her hand in his and raising it to his lips. 'Your Grace.'

Graziella didn't look at all impressed by his display of manners. 'Don't humbug me, young man.'

Nico rocked back on his heels and grinned unrepentantly down at her. Her silver hair was in its usual elegant chignon and she was dressed with her customary chicness but the shadows under her eyes—and the shadows *in* her eyes—were new. No wonder, she had lost her husband, youngest son and grandson in the space of five years.

His grandfather's heart attack had come as no real shock, the warning signs had been there for years, but Nico's own father's untimely death in a helicopter crash followed shortly by Alessandro's sudden collapse had rocked the family—and the island—to the core. Nico still didn't understand how a man as healthy, as strong as Alessandro could just drop down dead—and none of the reading he'd done on Sudden Arrhythmic Death Syndrome could convince him that he couldn't have done something, anything, to prevent it if only he'd known.

In that way he was still well and truly stuck in the first stage of grief—denial. He could have held several medical degrees and been right there and still he couldn't have done anything to save his cousin.

The remaining members of the family still all suffered, still all grieved, but his grandmother had been the slowest to return to some semblance of normality. Nico tried to hide his concern as his smile widened. 'Not humbugging, just showing respect.'

'Hmm, and did you show your uncle the same degree of respect?' She waved him towards the uncomfortable-looking sofa that sat at right angles to her own chair and Nico obediently perched on the edge of the slippery satin.

'Of course. At least,' he amended, 'I refrained from calling him a fool in public.'

'Nico, he doesn't like change, you know that.'

She might closet herself away in her rooms but she still knew everything that went on in every hidden palace corner. 'Grandmamma, we have no choice. Change will come whether we like it or not. Better that we control it rather than let it control us.'

'But tourists, Nico.' His grandmother couldn't have

sounded more disgusted if he'd suggested tearing down the ancient woodlands to build a nuclear power station. 'With their noise and their litter and their shorts and all they can eat. It's never been our way.'

'It depends on the tourists, Grandmamma.' He'd already made exactly these points to his uncle. Nico took a deep breath and re-embarked on the speech he'd prepared. 'We already get a few who make the journey here *because* we're unspoilt, to walk or swim or relax. We just need more of them. We won't be able to compete with the established Mediterranean resorts and nor should we, but if we market ourselves to honeymooners and couples as a luxury holiday destination and to the thrill seekers who will love our mountains and lakes then we won't need to change too much. Invest in some new hotels, enable our cafés and restaurants to cater for more people, improve our transport links. Nothing too scary, I promise.'

'But…'

'Our people need jobs. Our schools and hospitals need investment. Our youth need a reason to stay. We don't want them all heading off the island to start their lives elsewhere.'

As he had done.

'But why, Nico? You've only just come home. Why shake things up now with your consultants and plans? Give your uncle some time.'

'There is no time, Grandmamma.' He paused, unsure how much to tell her. 'Look. You know I spent the last year at Harvard doing an MBA. As part of that I studied our finances really carefully.'

The island monarchy wasn't purely constitutional and the royal family still took a very active role in government. Once Nico had begun to comprehend how much rode on his new position as heir to the throne he'd realised how ill equipped he was for such a responsibility and so had given up his research position at MIT to study business at Harvard instead. It hadn't taken him long to realise how much work he had ahead of him. A lifetime's work.

'I loved my grandfather, you know that, but he was a lavish spender, his father too. Look at how they redecorated the palace—all that marble imported in. And the rest: planes, cars, villas, ski lodges…'

'And an apartment for every mistress, an annuity for every mistress, jewellery for every mistress—and there were a lot of mistresses.' Bitterness coated his grandmother's voice for one unguarded second.

'For two generations the island was ignored in favour of jet-setting and pleasure. L'Isola dei Fiori needs a lot of careful managing to make up for fifty years of neglect.'

'And you think tourism will do that?'

'I think it's a start. We need more, some kind of real industry as well but that's a whole other step. One day I would like to see the island a beacon of innovation for renewable energy and other forms of eco-friendly engineering. Expand the university, bring in the expertise, offer the right companies, the right entrepreneurs the right deal so they settle here, build here and create jobs here.' That had always been his dream. That was why he had put in the hours at MIT, made the right contacts, had worked towards his PhD, never giving up hope that, even if he couldn't persuade his uncle to throw the weight of the government behind him, he could still return in his own time, at his own will, to start up his own research company.

But the current crisis needed a quicker fix and his own dreams had to be set aside, just as he'd set his research aside.

'Tell me how I can help, Nico.'

He patted his grandmother's hand gratefully. 'You're a key part of my strategy, Grandmamma. First of all I need you to work on my uncle. I know he's done his best to put things right but selling the odd yacht and ski lodge isn't enough. He needs to give the tourism campaign his full backing and ensure the rest of his ministers do as well.'

'What did he say today?'

'The usual. That I'm too young to understand, that I've been gone too long, that I think fancy degrees from fancy universities make up for my own lack of sense.' He grinned at her. 'Nothing he hasn't said a million times before.' It didn't stop the words from stinging though. He was thirty-two, not twenty, and he was proud of his degrees. He'd worked damn hard for them. But his uncle preferred to believe the rubbish in the papers than the evidence before him. Nico had been labelled a playboy Del Castro in his teens, like his father and grandfather before him, and his uncle had no intention of challenging that narrative.

Graziella drew herself up. 'I'll speak to him.'

'Thank you, Grandmamma. There are another couple of things. I need to marry...'

'Yes?' Her eyes lit up. This was exactly the kind of project she relished.

'And I need you to choose me a bride. I know you have a list of suitable names and that's fine. Better to find a girl who has been raised to manage this kind of life than throw some hapless innocent into the circus. I just have one request…'

'Just one?'

'I need a bride who is willing to be wooed. Publicly. The marketing consultant thinks a royal wedding is the perfect international showcase for L'Isola dei Fiori and we should milk it as much as possible. You know, boat rides into the grottos, horse rides through meadows, a royal ball…' He grinned at the revolted expression on her face.

'I had no idea you were such a romantic, Nico.'

'I'm not a romantic. I'm a realist. There's nothing people like better than a royal love story. So pick me a girl who will play her part and I'll marry her. The papers follow me around anyway. I might as well make use of my reputation.'

As a young, unattached prince he'd attracted the gossip magazines like wasps flocking around a sweet drink at the tail end of summer. If he'd lived quietly they might have left him alone eventually but he'd hung out with a young, moneyed crowd, enjoying time away from his studies at parties in New York, summer houses in the Hamptons, winter breaks in the Bahamas, on yachts, in clubs throughout Europe. At first it had been an exquisite relief, freedom after the strictures of a childhood at court. At some point it had become habit.

His grandmother nodded. 'Everyone loves a reformed playboy, I suppose. I'll find you a suitable bride. But, Nico? Just be discreet, when you find other amusements.' And for a fleeting second she looked so vulnerable Nico felt a surge of anger against the grandfather who had put that look on her face—and emptied the palace coffers to do so.

'No need. When I marry I'll be faithful. It might be arranged but that's no reason to treat marriage like it's meaningless. I hope I'm better than that.' As he said the words a fleeting image passed through his mind, a slim girl on the beach, hair tumbling around her breasts, eyes on his. He'd known then it was his last act of freedom, a sweet goodbye. Something to carry him through the years of duty that lay ahead.

'And the other thing?'

He winced. He knew she would dislike his next proposal. 'If we're going to start the campaign soon we need a few places ready for the tourists we're hoping to attract. There's a few decent city hotels, a couple of beach places and some lovely guesthouses but none of the boutique hotels that the kind of holiday makers we want to attract prefer. The consultant has suggested that we invest in several now, do them up over the winter ready for next season.'

'And?'

'And one of the places she suggested is Villa Rosa.'

His grandmother didn't answer but she drew herself up, her mouth tight. Nico watched her sympathetically. Until early last year the villa had been occupied by an aging beauty who, had been involved in a very public and very steamy affair with his grandfather, who had visited her, semi discreetly, by sailing around to the cove at night. The owner had died recently and the villa, as far as he knew, lay empty. His grandmother had always behaved with a dignified ignorance where his grandfather was concerned but installing a mistress on the island had pushed even her resilience to the limit.

'It has a certain notoriety that will draw people in: the parties that were held there, the famous people that stayed there—and of course the thermal pool and the secret beach.'

'I see.'

'I'm sorry to bring it up, Grandmamma, but I think the consultant's right. It is the perfect location and the Villa Rosa markets itself. Plus the lawyers say it's likely that my grandfather shouldn't have gifted the villa away in the first place; because it is so close to the cliff top and because it has access down to the beach it's situated on Crown land and therefore…'

'Therefore it can't be sold or owned by a private individual.'

'Or inherited,' he confirmed. He hesitated. 'I know you keep tabs on everything that goes on around here. I wondered if you know who owns it now? I could ask around but I don't want word to get out that we're interested.'

His grandmother shrugged. 'Apparently that woman left it to a niece or something but it's been empty or used as a holiday home since she died—they tell me it needs a lot of work. What are you going to do? Serve her notice?'

Nico shook his head. 'No. I'll offer her money to sell. We don't want the delay or cost of going to court—nor the publicity. But we can pay a fair price, tied up in a lot of legal documents that will hopefully persuade her to say yes sooner rather than later.

'Do you know anything about this owner? Where she's from?'

His instincts had been right. His grandmother knew everything. She tilted her chin. 'England, but I believe she arrived on the island a week ago. By public ferry, coach class, one battered bag.'

Which meant she had been there when he and Posy... an unwelcome thought hit him. He hadn't, had he? 'What's her name?'

'Marlowe. Rosalind Marlowe.'

Relief flooded through him. Not the same woman after all. And coach class with one bag? That added up to one cash-strapped Englishwoman. She'd be putty in his hands. The sooner he got his tourism project up and running, the sooner he got married, then the sooner he could work on his ideas and create something real, something sustainable in his homeland. And then this whole Crown Prince deal might start to feel less like an unwanted burden and more like something he could live with.

It was time to pay the owner of the Villa Rosa one very official visit.

CHAPTER FOUR

POSY CROSSED THE courtyard and eyed the garages curiously. They were in pretty good nick, their roofs sounder than that of the house itself. They would, with new doors, a new floor, heaters and a sound system, make pretty awesome studios.

Just a quick DIY job then. Posy mentally totted up the possible costs, wincing before she got to the sprung floor, mirrors and barre. Converting wasn't going to be that much cheaper than building from scratch and right now she was more geared up for a 'lick of paint and a good clean' type budget.

Of course, she could always sell the stylish vintage car that she'd inherited along with the villa to pay for the work. Her sisters would never forgive her—she'd already had to hear rhapsodies about engines and paintwork and rpms—but unlike the rest of the Marlowes Posy's interest in transport was limited to did it work and would it get her where she needed to go? Hanging onto a vintage car for the sake of it when it could be turned into cold, hard cash would be utter folly.

Maybe she should offer Miranda and Imogen first refusal though...for a reasonable price because goodness knew she needed the money.

She pivoted and looked closely at the villa in all its faded glory, trying not to glaze over the imperfections. Thanks to Immi the gardens were looking a lot more manageable and her sisters—and their various husbands and fiancés—had all helped make the inside more home-like, but there was no way she could even consider opening to paying guests until she had fixed the roof, put in a new boiler and pulled the kitchen into the twenty-first century. Then she'd have to make sure the bathrooms were all in decent enough condition for non-family use and check each bed for broken springs or damp. She'd need bed linen as well. And she still needed actually to qualify as a Pilates and ballet teacher…

She sighed. The way she saw it she had two choices. Either she sold the villa or she stopped it being a liability and turned it into an asset. And it could, with some work—okay, a lot of work—be a very considerable asset. The island was famed for its hot springs, the rock pool offered a natural bathing experience all year round and the view and the gardens were tranquil enough to soothe any stressed city dweller. She had bedrooms to spare, more bathrooms than she could use if she bathed in a different one every day and plenty of nooks where people could settle with books or just to doze.

She had the space, she had the contacts, she had the knowledge and, if she sold the car and ransacked some of the contents of the villa, she might be able to muster up enough money.

Posy blew out a frustrated breath. Her other choice was to sell. That would solve the money problem but left her with no idea what a twenty-four-year-old ex-ballerina with one good GCSE to her name could do for the rest of her life.

And the Marlowes were famously long-lived.

Of course there was nothing stopping her jumping on a plane and returning to London either. When she'd falteringly handed in her notice Bruno had taken a far too keen look at her before telling her to keep in shape and exercise and if she changed her mind within the year there would still be a place for her in the company. For all her resolution to start again, when she lay awake in the middle of the night the prospect of slinking back and resuming her place in the Corps de Ballet was far too tempting. But if she returned to London would that make her a double failure? Prove that she didn't know how to live?

But she'd lived last night…

Heat flared in her cheeks, an answering warmth in her breasts and low deep in her stomach and she fought the urge to hide behind her hands like a small girl caught out in a misdeed. What had she been thinking? Taking her clothes off in front of a complete stranger? Allowing him—no, wanting him—to touch her like that in public? She had never behaved so recklessly, so provocatively. It was all too easy to blame the moonlight, the sea, the need to feel wanted. But she was the one who had wanted. She was the one who had initiated. Not that she'd kept that control for long…

She shivered as flashbacks of deep, sweet kisses, long, torturous caresses, whispered endearments overwhelmed her. She had never known it to be like that, at once so wild and urgent and yet so tender. It had taken every inch of resolution to walk away, disappearing before midnight because every fairy tale reader knew not to stay beyond the witching hour. They'd agreed on just the one evening but she'd taken her time as she'd moved along the beach, just in case he called after her, asked to see her again.

She'd been half disappointed when he hadn't, the feeling intensifying when she'd reached the jetty and turned back to find him gone. Okay, more than half disappointed.

Posy wandered back towards the house, the day stretching before her, empty and meaningless just like the day before and the day before that. She'd mechanically stretched and gone through her exercises earlier that morning, keeping her muscles warm and her body supple, but her books sat unopened, her crochet hook lay unused and the colouring books were still pristine. Turned out she wasn't much good at relaxing and doing nothing.

Maybe she should start going through the house— she had a list of contents somewhere along with valuations. Whether she sold up or sold enough to convert the villa into a retreat she still needed to know what was where and if she wanted to keep any of it—not that her tastes ran to shelves filled with vases, ornaments, boxes and the numerous other knick-knacks that filled the villa. When she had come to visit her godmother as a child she'd loved to play with them all, creating intricate games and scenarios for the various china animals. Now they were just clutter, gathering dust.

The double doors that led into the grand double-height conservatory stood open, the sun reflecting off the panes of coloured glass randomly interspersed with the plain glass. It must have been gorgeous in Sofia's, her godmother's, heyday, filled with climbing plants winding their way up the leaded panes, providing much-needed shade and contrast. Sofia had held parties in the room attended by movie stars, European aristocrats and millionaires; if Posy closed her eyes she could still see the glittering jewels around the throats and in the ears of the women, the long, elegant cigarette holders, the cocktails circulating on silver trays. If rumour was to be believed Sofia had had her own share of diamonds and other precious stones but all that was left was paste and crystal, pretty but worthless. Sofia had sold them all as her looks had faded and her lovers had melted away.

She'd still been a consummate hostess though. Posy had loved coming here. Sofia had always treated Posy and her sisters as if they were small adults, not children. Posy had never known what to expect from one day to the next—they might get dressed up in some of Sofia's old couture gowns and hold a party, canapés and mocktails at three in the afternoon for just them. Or Sofia might decide they needed to redecorate the dining room, or teach them to snorkel, or take them into the town for oysters and champagne. But mostly she allowed them freedom to swim, sunbathe and run free so that they returned to the UK tanned and relaxed. Posy treasured the visits even more once she had started at ballet school, her holidays no relaxing time off but filled with residential courses around the country. The two carefree weeks she managed to snatch at Sofia's were a welcome contrast to the rigid, disciplined life she had chosen. The rigid, disciplined life she was trying so hard not to miss.

She jumped as the bell tolled solemnly. Who could that be? The house had been empty since Immi left a month ago and no one apart from her family knew she was here.

She didn't have to answer it. If she stayed quiet they would probably just go away.

The bell tolled again, low and commanding. 'Don't be such a coward,' she scolded herself. After all Imogen's fiancé, Matt, had lived on the island for several years. It would be just like Immi to get a friend of Matt's to check up on her. She knew her sisters were worried about her decision to move into her money pit of an inheritance, to leave London, to quit her hard-fought-for career; of course they'd send in an intervention.

Well, the intervention could just intervene right out. She was fine. Almost.

The bell tolled for a third time as she moved briskly through the hall, a room large enough to hold a ball in if the conservatory was otherwise engaged, and she wrenched open the front door, indignation buzzing through her veins. 'Hold your horses. I'm here. Oh!'

Her hand tightened on the door. 'Nico?'

She wasn't sure at first. The expression in the blue eyes was a mixture of surprise and determination, the dark hair slicked back, the broad shoulders and narrow waist covered by a perfectly cut light suit. But her body knew him instantly, every pulse beating rapidly as he looked straight at her.

'Hello, Posy.'

Any thought he might have come looking for her, that this was the start of the kind of whirlwind romance she'd read about but never experienced, evaporated in the late morning sun. There was no flirtatiousness in his voice, no seduction in his eyes. Whatever Nico wanted here it didn't include a re-enactment of last night.

That was fine. She didn't expect anything else. Hoped maybe, in that first flare of surprise, that he

might be pleased to see her but two could play at the
'polite strangers' game. She forced her hand to relax,
her face to remain still, her highly trained muscles obey-
ing in instant precision. 'How can I help?'

'I'm looking for Rosalind Marlowe. Is she here?'

'You're talking to her. I'm Rosalind,' she clarified
as his forehead crinkled. 'Rosalind shortened to Rosy,
my family called me Rosy-Posy and then when I started
to dance, they kind of lost the Rosy in a *Ballet Shoes*
Posy Fossil way.' She was babbling. Great. 'Not that
that matters. What do you want?'

The mask had slipped a little; Nico was looking uncomfortable. 'Can I come in?'

'I don't know,' she said honestly. 'I didn't expect
to see you again after last night and now here you are
looking for me but not knowing it's me. I don't want
someone who makes me uncomfortable in my house.
So probably not. Whatever you want to say to me you
can say right here.'

Nico narrowed his eyes. Two minutes in and already
this whole situation was slipping dangerously out of
control. It was his own fault. He should have heeded
the warning bells clanging loudly the instant his grandmother mentioned that the villa had passed to an Englishwoman. There was a reason Posy had sprung
straight into his mind. She was the logical choice, appearing on the beach the way she had last night, her
conviction that he was trespassing, her surety that she
was safe to swim naked—but the difference in name
had allowed him to ignore his premonition. Big mistake.

None of this would matter if he hadn't given in
to temptation last night; this was a lesson, if ever he

needed one, not to engage in *al fresco* fun and games with complete strangers. Maybe it was a good thing he was about to be safely and dutifully married.

Posy held onto the heavy oak door as if it were supporting her—and as if any moment she might swing it shut in his face. Nico suppressed a smile—he couldn't remember anyone refusing him entry before.

She was casually dressed in soft grey yoga trousers and a matching vest top, her gorgeous dark hair twisted up into a messy bun, her face make-up free, emphasising the disparity between them. He'd wanted to wrong-foot Rosalind Marlowe, to impress her with his title, his designer suit, his offer. He didn't want to wrong-foot Posy, dark-eyed naiad of the night before. He should have called first, given her a chance to put her armour on just as he had his.

Either way he needed a sharp change of tactic. 'In that case will you take a short walk with me? Just along the cliff top,' he added as she stared at him doubtfully. 'There's a matter I really need to discuss with you.'

'Is it to do with last night?' Pink blossomed on her cheeks as she asked the question but she held his gaze defiantly.

'Last night? No. I didn't realise you lived here.'

'Where did you think I lived? There's no other house for a mile.'

'Secretly I thought you really had come from the sea—or more prosaically that you'd sailed round. Not many people think they're allowed to stop off at the beach but those who do know that they're almost guaranteed to have the beach to themselves and that the jetty makes it a safe mooring.'

'We always assumed it belonged to the Villa Rosa.

The beach, I mean. We never saw anyone else on it when we were kids. It was our own playground.'

'We?'

'My sisters and I. There's four of us.'

'Four? Are any of them here with you now?'

'They've all been and gone. The villa's been a bit of a godsend this year. I don't know what we'd have done without it. I didn't expect Sofia—my godmother—to leave it to me and I'm not entirely sure what to do with it but I'm grateful we all had somewhere to come when we needed it.'

She wasn't entirely sure what to do with it—there, that was positive. Better focus on that than the glow in her eyes when she had mentioned how grateful she was to own it.

'Look, Nico, we can't keep talking like this. Come on in. I didn't mean to be rude but you startled me.'

She held the door open and Nico stepped into the large, light-filled hallway. The panelling was painted white and hung with bright abstract paintings, the floor covered in white tiles; a glass-sided staircase curved along one wall onto the landing above. Doors on either side stood ajar; through one he glimpsed a huge dining table capable of seating at least twenty, through another a room filled with vintage furniture, the plastered walls covered in delicate murals. But for all its sumptuousness the famed Villa Rosa felt shabby and a little grubby, cobwebs coating the plasterwork, lines of grime in between the tiles.

'I know, it's kind of ridiculous for one person, isn't it? Far too much to look after.' Posy read his thoughts with unerring accuracy. 'Of course, when she first lived here, Sofia—my godmother—filled the place with visitors. She didn't really live on her own until the mid-eighties. And it must have been so expensive to keep up—some rooms are just covered in dust sheets and shut away. This way. Do you want a drink?'

'No. Thank you.'

Nico's eyes widened as she took him through another faded, but lavishly decorated and ornamented, hallway and into an impressive, if in need of urgent repair, conservatory. He was right. This place would make a superb boutique hotel.

It was also disconcerting. His grandfather's influence was stamped all over the place, in the hunting prints hung along one wall to the cushions flung casually on a wooden bench, embroidered with King Ludano's own personal seal. The parties held here were legendary—parties his grandfather had funded and attended rather than concentrating on improving the lives of the people who lived and worked on the island that gave him his title and their loyalty.

Nico rocked back on his heels and stared up at the roof. He'd been so busy mourning the loss of the future he had been working towards, so busy mourning his cousin, so busy bitterly resenting the title and responsibilities due his way that he'd forgotten what it all meant. Forgotten what he owed every man, woman and child born on this island or who chose to make their home here. A monarchy might be absurdly old-fashioned but that was what they had and it was up to him to make the best of it.

Duty, honour, service.

He turned and smiled at Posy, pushing his sympathy for her to one side. 'I'm afraid there's a problem with the villa. It doesn't look like your godmother was entitled to leave it to you after all.'

Duty, honour, service. They might be worthy but they weren't particularly nice. The memory of the stricken look in Posy's eyes when he'd explained the situation to her was very hard to shake—and even the very generous under the circumstances settlement he'd mentioned hadn't lifted her spirits.

'I can't think. I need to, I need to talk to someone,' she'd said, clutching the deeds and official settlement in her hands. 'I'll be in touch. You have to give me time— unless you're planning to throw me out straight away?'

He'd reassured her that she had all the time she needed—within reason. 'But we do need an answer fast. The settlement offered is dependent on a swift, uncontested acceptance,' he'd warned her and walked away, leaving her standing alone in the vast conservatory, the papers twisted in her hands.

He had only just returned to the castle when he saw the same, harried-looking aide waiting for him, still teetering on the same uncomfortable heels, heels matched by the look on her face. She didn't want to summon him as much as he didn't want to be summoned. 'Sir, Your Highness…'

Nico supplied the rest. 'My grandmother?'

'Yes, if you would be so kind. She said it was of the utmost importance.'

'Then it would be rude to keep her waiting. Thank you.'

She managed a quick smile of relief before rushing away on whatever other errand his grandmother had devised. Nico paused. He really didn't want to discuss

Posy with his grandmother and she probably wanted to see him to elicit more information about the new owner of the villa. He needed a deflection and what better way to deflect a doting grandmother than with a potential bride? She'd sent him away with a terrifyingly thorough dossier on some of Europe's most eligible young women for him to shortlist candidates from. Perfect.

Ten minutes later and armed with his grandmother's dossier, Nico tapped on her door once again. He expected the usual faint murmur and to let himself into the room. Instead the door was flung open and his grandmother stood there, eyes blazing and her usually pale cheeks flushed. 'It's unfortunate that you take after your grandfather in looks, but to take after him in actions too? Are you planning to bankrupt what's left of the island's economy while you're at it?'

Nico's lips tightened. 'Nice to see you as well, Grandmother, especially on your feet and so animated. Do you mind if I can come in so we can have this interesting discussion in private or would you like us to invite the TV station in and broadcast live to the nation, not just to the palace?' He kept his voice as normal as possible but his grandmother took a chastened step backwards, leaving the way clear for him to walk into her room, closing the door firmly behind him as he did so.

She wasn't alone. Her private secretary was perched on the sofa, hands clasped and mouth pursed disapprovingly. Nico nodded in her direction. There was clearly not much point in turning on the famous charm. To his surprise Anna, the marketing consultant, was also sitting down; a tablet and a laptop lay on the table in front of her. She could barely meet his eye. What was going on? Had his uncle interfered already and shut down his plans?

'It's a little late to worry about broadcasting to the nation, Nico,' his grandmother said peevishly. 'After everything you said this morning as well.'

Nico stared. 'Would you mind just explaining what's going on here?'

Anna picked up the tablet and handed it over, still without meeting his eye or saying a word. Nico took it and touched the screen to bring it to life. He blinked. 'What the hell?'

'That's not the worst of it.' His grandmother sniffed. 'Not all of them are pixelated.'

'What?' He stared at the screen in utter disbelief.

Splash! screamed the headline. *Prince Nico and mystery brunette steaming up the sea!*

Somehow the photographer had zoomed in to show Nico in the water facing Posy, their shoulders naked, the look on his face unmistakable. Lust. Interest. Desire. 'Dammit.'

'It gets worse,' his grandmother said, snatching the tablet from him and swiping. She wasn't exaggerating. Shots of them kissing on the beach, just a few pixels concealing their nudity. Then today, Posy at the door of the villa, her face set, watching him walk away. *Lovers' tiff?* the shot was captioned.

Nico turned away in disgust.

'Ghouls.'

'Yes—and you fed them,' his grandmother retorted. 'What were you thinking? No, don't answer that. You clearly weren't thinking. Who is she, Nico? Is she related to that woman?'

'Not exactly. She is her goddaughter, though, and the

current owner of the Villa Rosa. Look, Grandmother. This was last night, I had no idea who she was…' He stopped. He wasn't sure his explanation was making the situation any better.

'It's not so much *who* as *where*,' his grandmother said tartly. 'In the sea? On the beach. Where anyone can see?'

Despite himself Nico's mouth curved as he remembered the first sight of Posy on the beach, the unselfconscious way she'd danced, the smooth lines of her lithe body. He should be sorry but he couldn't quite bring himself to regret much of the night before. 'You said yourself everyone loves a reformed playboy,' he said with a shrug. 'You know how deserted it is up there. I didn't see anyone when I arrived and, yes, I did check before deciding to go for a swim. It's unfortunate and a gross invasion of what little privacy I have left but it'll soon be forgotten.'

Anna stood up, her mouth tense. 'Nico, you're supposed to be wooing your bride over the next few months.'

His grandmother nodded. 'What will people think when they see you strolling hand in hand on a beach with your intended? They'll be wondering if you went skinny dipping and then rolled around in the sand, that's what they'll think. You said that we were supposed to be selling the island as a romantic destination, not an eighteen to thirties resort! Romance, Nico, not sex.'

'The two aren't mutually exclusive.' He couldn't help himself.

'Nico!'

Anna shifted her feet. 'I'm sorry, Your Majesty, but I agree with His Royal Highness.'

Nico turned to his grandmother. 'See, Grandmamma, nothing to worry about. This will soon be yesterday's news.' His thoughts flew to Posy, her defeated look as he'd walked away. She was all alone in that villa, no one else around. Vulnerable.

Anna interrupted his thoughts. 'I'm sorry, I agree that romance and sex are not mutually exclusive, not that this will be quickly forgotten and I don't think hastily bringing one of the other girls to the island and rushing into a relationship will serve as enough of a distraction. But if we could supersede these images with a whole host of positive others we control then we might be able to relegate them to a footnote.'

Nico searched through the jargon to come up with a translation. New images? 'What kind of others?'

'What kind of girl is she?'

Nico stared, bewildered. 'Posy? In what way?'

'Parents, money, lineage, education, history?'

'I don't know. We met last night, in the sea. We didn't get round to swapping business cards.'

'I'll find out because right now she's our best hope of turning this fiasco into a positive story, of taking back control and selling you, the island and this relationship as one positive package.'

'What do you mean?' his grandmother asked.

'This wasn't a one-night stand, it was an expression of love. Nico and this girl—Posy did you say her name was?—have been dating secretly for months but he didn't want to impose the rigidity of a royal relationship on her. But their love was too strong and she has come to the island to see how their relationship works in the public eye. Last night was supposed to be the last privacy you had before presenting her to your family, the island and therefore the world's media. This way we can still play out the love story as we intended and salvage this situation.'

His grandmother sat down, her face pale. 'That woman's heir? In my house?'

'That's part of the reason they had to keep the relationship secret. A Romeo and Juliet scenario. They knew you wouldn't accept Posy.' Anna sniffed. 'That will never do. Does she have a middle name?'

'She's actually Rosalind. Posy is a nickname.' Nico's mind was racing. He had to get engaged to someone after all. At least he and Posy had attraction working for them. And, much as he usually laughed at his playboy image, these pictures had shaken him, the way the captions turned something beautiful into something sordid. A rush of protectiveness overwhelmed him—he was used to the media spotlight but Posy was an innocent. How would she manage when she was doorstepped and papped every time she set foot outside? How would she cope when every future friend or date had potentially seen such an intimate side of her? He couldn't turn back the clock but he could make amends. He had accepted his life was now full of duty; he would start here and now. 'Do you think this would work?'

His grandmother grabbed his hand and the weakness of her clasp alarmed him. The righteous anger had disappeared and with it her sudden return to health. 'Are you seriously considering this, Nico?'

He patted her hand, the bones fragile beneath his palm. 'I don't know,' he said slowly. 'I need a convincing love story and if she agrees then this could be just what we're looking for. If we play out an engagement over the next few months then these pictures will hopefully be forgotten, the tourism campaign ready to roll…'

'Culminating in a royal wedding in the spring,' Anna said enthusiastically.

His grandmother paled. 'The thought of a relative of that woman…'

'She's not a relative, not as far as I know. And the Romeo and Juliet idea could be powerful, you know. Drawn together but knew it couldn't work because of family history. Let's find out as much about Posy Marlowe as possible and we can convene later and make a final decision then. But if we are going to try and change the direction of this story we need to move fast. Time is running out.'

And either way he needed to get back to the villa and get Posy out of there. He knew what it was like to be in the eye of a media storm and this one was definitely a Category Four.

CHAPTER FIVE

ONE OF THE things Posy loved best about the villa was its isolation. The sole building in the beautiful national park, it was a complete contrast to her home in London. There she shared a tiny flat with two other dancers, living in a building crammed with studios and small flats, the paper-thin walls ensuring intimacy with all her neighbours. She stepped straight outside onto a grey pavement flanking a busy main road and walked through streets thronged with people to the tourist Mecca of Covent Garden. She was surrounded by noise and bustle and humanity twenty-four hours a day, the chorus of shouts, chatter, traffic, car alarms, sirens and music so consistent she barely heard it at all.

Here she looked out across the sea on one side, the other had a view of distant mountains rising from the flower-filled meadows. The nearest village was at the edge of the park, a twenty-minute walk if she needed bread, milk or help but otherwise she was all alone, the waves crashing on the rocky shore below and the plaintive cries of the gulls the only sounds. There was no Internet, mobile signal was so patchy as to be nonexistent and although the old-fashioned dial phone with its long curly cord still lived in the kitchen it had been discontinued years ago. The first few days she was here she'd liked that she was cut off from everyone and everything, that she couldn't see her fellow dancers' social media accounts full of excited chatter about classes and costumes and industry gossip.

But today she couldn't help being horribly aware of just how isolated she was. Just how alone she was.

Posy picked up the document Nico had left and read it through for what must have been the fortieth time, but the dense legalese still made no sense. The document was in English, not the Italian spoken by most islanders, but it could have been written in Elvish for all the sense it made. Nico might be pushing for a quick decision and the money he'd mentioned dependent on her just walking away but, unworldly as her sisters called her, she wasn't a total fool. She knew she needed advice. 'You were always planning to sell anyway,' she murmured. But that had been before. When she had a career that left her with no time to look after a villa a plane and ferry ride away. Now she had nothing *except* the villa she was suddenly loath to let it go.

But even if she had some means of contacting the outside world who could she ask? All her friends were dancers, and her parents had only recently returned from a year travelling the world and were now fully occupied in their aviation business. And much as she loved them Posy had never run to them with her problems. It wasn't that they wouldn't have listened or cared—it was more she didn't trust them to understand. Because as supportive as they had been of her dancing career, as proud as they were of her, her father still didn't know a *pas de chat* from a *chasse* and her mother worried more about Posy's lack of a love life than she did her lack of career progression.

As for her sisters, Miranda was pregnant and Not to Be Worried, Miranda's twin, Immi, had decided to emulate her parents and was also travelling with her new fiancé, Matt, and their eldest sister Portia was blissfully, disgustingly loved up with the gorgeous actor Javier Russo. And she was happy for them all. Goodness knew they deserved some good luck and love. It just made her even more alone, more apart from the family than usual.

She scowled at the document as if it was responsible for all her troubles—which in a way it was.

'Mrs Eveslade!' Posy dropped the paper on the table in her excitement. How could she forget? She had a lawyer. Well, Sofia had had a solicitor who had taken care of all the probate and other legalese to do with Sofia's will. Mostly she had sent Posy piles of paper Posy hadn't got round to reading, a terrifying bill that was thankfully settled from the estate, tax documents and probate certificates and lots of other paperwork all piled up in a shoebox in the bedroom still called hers at her parents' house.

But one of things she remembered was the valuation and all the work associated with that. It had taken months before the villa was put into her name and she was sure that part of the delay had been because the solicitor had been establishing ownership and land boundaries and other things that she really should have paid more attention to. But, she distinctly remembered the solicitor saying how important it was to make sure it was all done properly, as if Posy had intended to sell it was better to make sure everything was in order at the

outset. So if there was any discrepancy in land ownership or entitlement surely that should have been high-
lighted then?

Either way she needed someone with more qualifica-
tions than a D in GCSE maths to double check Nico's
claim. She might decide to take the money and walk
away or she might not, but she wasn't going to be bul-
lied into anything. Of course, that meant calling Mrs
Eveslade, which wasn't the easiest of propositions. Either she walked into the village and hoped that if she
fed enough coins into the antiquated phone box she
might manage an international call or she could charge
up her phone and walk along the cliff top until she hit
a sweet spot.

She barely had any coins and she was pretty sure the
island phone boxes didn't accept anything as modern
as credit cards. Sweet spot it was. If only the darn spot
would stay in one place and not keep moving around
like a restless spirit.

Half an hour later, phone charged, Posy left the house
by the small gate at the very back of the house. Hidden by a riot of clambering plants, it wasn't an obvious
way in—which was probably the point. Sofia's royal
lover had installed several discreet entrances into the
villa although the whole island and European media
had known exactly what their relationship was. This
door made it easy to slip away onto the coastal path and
take the back way to the village or to the jetty without
being seen. Or in Posy's case it simply meant a scenic
walk straight along the cliff path rather than tramping
down the hot dusty road. Plus it was easier to lock the
back door rather than wrestle with the imposing front
door locks.

It didn't take long to skirt around the back of the house and join the cliff path on the other side, leading away from the village straight along the cliff tops and into the heart of the beautiful national park. The park was full of paths and trails perfect for hikers and climbers but Posy had seen very few during her stay and, although she appreciated the tranquillity, she couldn't help but think it a shame that the island didn't attract more tourists. It was so hospitable, the food wonderful and the climate sublime, to say nothing of the breathtaking scenery. It was just a little too off the beaten track to appeal to the masses—which was no doubt a good thing—but there was a happy medium between a trickle and a deluge and she knew plenty of adrenaline junkies who would have adored scaling the mountainous peaks towering in the distance or cycling up the foothills at top speed or walkers who would love the trails and paths.

She switched her phone on and left it to power up as she walked slowly along the path. Below the waves purred rather than roared but summer was fast approaching its end and she knew the island in autumn and winter was a less forgiving place than the dreamy, sun-drenched summer idyll. Even if the villa was hers, did she really want to stay on year round? She turned, looking out over the green plains dotted with brightly coloured flowers and low trees leading inexorably to the craggy mountains, and breathed in air untinged by car fumes, cigarettes or cooking smells. There were worse places to be.

The problem was all this choice. Posy had never had a choice before—she'd had a compulsion. From that first baby ballet class she had been on a path with only one destination and no deviations. School had been an unwelcome distraction until finally she had worn her parents down and they had agreed to allow her to audition for ballet school. Her mother had admitted later they knew how hard it was to get a place; they hadn't really considered what they would do if Posy got in. But she *had* got in and she'd stayed in despite some major culls as she'd progressed through the school. On to upper school, into the company—and there her path had halted. Leaving was the first major decision she had made since she was eleven.

And she still wasn't sure she'd done the right thing. It wasn't that she missed dance. That didn't even begin to convey how it was not having ballet in her life. She ached with loss, was sluggish with lack of purpose, empty without the daily discipline and routine. Would travelling or setting up a studio fill that emptiness? She doubted it. Maybe she should settle for technically perfect and no solos. A future as the head of the corps. There were worse things. Maybe that was growing up, accepting your limitations.

With relief she saw the bars on the top of her phone flicker into a faint life. She still had the solicitor's number and, thanks to the time difference, it could only be early afternoon in London. She'd make the call and then at least she would have done something decisive before heading back to curl up in the small snug where she ensconced herself of an evening to watch Cary Grant films on Sofia's ancient VHS player. It was *An Affair to Remember* tonight. Maybe not, with her own too brief affair all too memorable for all the wrong reasons.

With purpose she angled the phone away from the sun, ready to scroll through her contacts until she found the solicitor's number, only to stop and stare as her missed call alerts began to flash incessantly. Unknown numbers, her mother's mobile, all three of her sisters, friends, more unknown numbers. Her voicemail alert was also going crazy. What was going on? An accident? Had the baby come early? She frantically counted back. No, it was far too early. Please no. Her fingers stumbled as she struggled to retrieve her voicemail and her mobile fell to the ground; she bent to retrieve it, uncharacteristically clumsy in her haste, stumbling as she stooped.

'I wouldn't listen to that if I were you.'

Posy started at the voice, falling back onto her bottom, hardly aware of the stones digging into her tender flesh as she pushed herself back up into a sitting position. Clasping her errant phone in one hand, she glared up at the smiling Nico. How did he manage to be in the wrong place at the wrong time every time? Begrudgingly she took the hand he held out to her and allowed him to pull her up.

'Where did you come from?'

'The path. I saw you leave the villa and followed you.'

She should have been annoyed, or even scared at his words but she wasn't. Nico wasn't the charming tease or the sweet seducer of the night before, nor was he the serious suit of earlier that day. Instead he seemed thoughtful, a determined set to his shoulders as he took the phone from her hand.

'That's mine. Give it back.'

'In a minute. I need to tell you something—ask you something first.'

She made a grab for it, fear filling her, not because she was alone with a near stranger and with no way of getting help—but because of the odd look on his face.

A sixth sense whispered to her that his odd behaviour was all mixed in with the missed phone calls and a dim part of her knew that somewhere, somehow, everything had changed. 'No. I have to call my sisters. Something's happened and I don't know what. Give it to me.'

But he held the phone just out of reach, compassion in the dark blue eyes. 'In a minute. Posy. Listen to me. I know what's happened.'

His calm words hit her and her hand dropped unsteadily to her side, tension competing with fear. 'You know, but how? How would they know to call you? I don't even know I know you so how would they?'

He closed his eyes briefly. 'Posy, listen to me. I haven't been entirely honest with you.'

A snort of disbelief escaped her. 'Haven't been entirely honest? Which part exactly? When you seduced me on the beach or when you marched up to my front door and told me I'm not entitled to my home? Is this all some part of an elaborate plot to what? Con me out of the villa? What kind of lawyer are you exactly?' She knew she was babbling again, but it was easier to allow the words to bubble out than hear whatever it was he had to say, find out just why the world, his wife and their cat were so desperately trying to get hold of her.

Nico held up a hand and she came to an abrupt stop, the words drying up in her mouth, and she stared at him. 'Listen to me, Posy. This is important. I'm not a lawyer. I don't represent the royal family, the Del Castros. I *am* one. I'm Nicolas Del Castro.'

'Nicolas Del Castro?'

She knew that name. How did she know it? 'You're a member of the royal family? Like, a prince or a duke or a…' She paused. What else were royals? Kings, of course, but she'd seen a picture of the current king and she couldn't remember him being drop-your-clothes-in-the-sand hot. Or indeed hot at all.

His mouth tightened. 'A prince? Yes. The Crown Prince.'

'The Crown Prince?' She stared at him, no doubt looking as stupid as she felt. 'But yesterday, today…'

'That's why I am here. Look, we were seen. Last night. That's what everyone is trying to tell you.'

Posy blinked as the world swirled to a nauseous stop and she swayed. 'Seen? When? Who by?' But she knew the answers. It was all too clear. Her phone was red hot and he was a prince—a crown prince. The answer was unlikely to be a shepherd minding his own business who'd decided to ignore the whole proceedings.

Nico's answer confirmed her thoughts. 'A photographer.'

'And it's all over the Internet, isn't it? How bad is it?'

'It's pretty explicit.'

Posy swallowed, a laugh trying to inappropriately bubble up. She'd wanted some direction, something to change. *Careful what you wish for, Posy.*

'Why are you here, Nico?'

'To bring you to the palace until we get this situation under control.'

She wanted to stamp her foot at his calmness. 'Under control? What do you mean?'

He looked at her, his face unreadable. 'I think we should get married. Don't you?'

CHAPTER SIX

POSY BLINKED, THEN blinked again. Yep, he was still here, still with that determined set to his shoulders and the same shuttered look on his face. 'You think we should what?'

'Get married.'

This was a joke, right? But there was no hint of amusement in his hard eyes.

'But…that's ridiculous. We don't even know each other.' Plus he hadn't even asked her. Not that a ring and a bended knee would make any difference but at least she wouldn't feel like a problem he needed to sort out. She folded her arms and glared at him.

Nico raised one lazy brow. 'Rosalind Anne Marlowe,' he drawled. 'Twenty-four years old. Your parents own a well-thought-of light aircraft manufacturer. You have three sisters, one a pilot, another a celebrity journalist who is married to Javier Russo, a friend of my cousin, Alessandro's.'

'Yes, but…'

He carried on as if she hadn't spoken. 'You went to train to be a ballerina when you were eleven and graduated into the Company where you spent the last five years as a member of the Corps de Ballet until your unexpected sabbatical this summer. No one knows if you plan to return to dancing or if you have other plans but your sabbatical has caused quite a stir—you have shown no interest in anything except ballet your entire life. You share a flat with two other dancers, have had a handful of boyfriends although no relationship lasted more than three months and you met them all through work. How am I doing so far?'

'That,' Posy said, trying not to shudder at the bald facts of her life laid out before her, 'is worse than a naked picture. You had me investigated?'

'Of course. The future Crown Princess of L'Isola dei Fiori can't have any skeletons in her closet and your closet is squeaky clean. Not as much as a knucklebone.'

Twenty-four and squeaky clean. No wonder she'd been dismissed as having no fire, no life. 'So you know where I went to school? Big deal. My parents' job? So what? That doesn't mean you know anything about me. You don't know my favourite book or colour or food or film…'

His eyes darkened and he took a step nearer. 'I know you like to dance on the beach even when there's no audience there to see you. I know you like the feel of cold, salt water on your bare skin and the barer the skin, the better. I know the look on your face when you make your mind up to do something and the way your hands clench when you're nervous. I know the look on your face when I touch you. I know the way you sigh, the way you moan…'

She put a hand up, warding him off, telling herself that his words were meaningless, that they weren't sinking into her, swirling through her veins. 'That's not what I meant and you know it. My sisters have all fallen in love this year and that's wonderful but I didn't feel jealous of what they have. I *don't* feel jealous. Marriage has never been my goal. Why would I marry you? Why would I marry anyone?'

'What are your plans, Posy?'

She gaped, thrown by the sudden change of subject. 'What?'

'When you leave here. Once you've escaped the paparazzi who will very soon be at your door—if they're not already—when you've got off the island and away, where will you go? Back to London?'

'I don't know. I'm on a sabbatical, remember? I'm trying to figure things out.'

'I'm offering you a job for life. It has its perks: a nice salary, a home—several homes—good holidays. You'll have to work, that's the bit the fairy tales leave out. It's not all balls and white chargers. There's a lot of opening things and state occasions and smiling while your feet hurt but as a ballerina I think you're more than qualified.'

That last bit was true; she was an expert at smiling through sore feet. 'A job for life. How romantic.'

She turned and began to walk back to the villa. There was some of Sofia's sherry in the kitchen and if that wasn't strong enough she was pretty sure there was a dusty bottle of absinthe in one of the covered rooms. It couldn't make her hallucinate more than she clearly already was.

'There's no room for romance in my life,' Nico said soberly as he fell into step beside her. Despite all the craziness of the last few minutes Posy couldn't help but be aware of his height, of the warmth of his arm as the path pushed them together, of the way she felt his every move, his every look deep inside, the tension in her stomach, in her thighs, at his proximity. 'Look what happened when I took a chance on a night's adventure. Everything I do, everywhere I go I am scrutinised and any woman unlucky enough to be linked to me goes under the same intense spotlight. Men like me marry women who know the score. Women prepared for this world.'

An unwanted flicker of sympathy warmed her momentarily. It sounded lonely. Almost as lonely as a loveless marriage full of duty. 'Why me? Why now? And no, don't give me the photo story. It's embarrassing, sure. But.' She flicked him a sidelong glance. 'Men usually get away with this kind of thing much easier than women. I don't think this is going to make a huge impact on your life—just make sure the next viral photograph shows you being adorable with a puppy and the world will be at your feet.' She swallowed as the impact of her words sank in, heaviness descending, blanketing and choking. There was no way she could get back on stage in the foreseeable future, knowing that everyone would be whispering, speculating, knowing…what reputable company would want someone so notorious?

'Maybe, maybe not. You're not no one. You're the goddaughter of my grandfather's mistress. We were photographed on the beach they used to throw parties on. Pictured standing outside the villa he gave her. That makes you a story, makes us a story and I think it'll take more than puppies to change this narrative. Look, Posy. I know this seems drastic but you've lived a life of discipline, I don't think life as a royal would be as chafing for you as it would for many other women, the way we have to live, the lack of privacy and freedom.'

Posy swallowed. 'You're serious. You actually think this is a real, viable option? I'm on a sabbatical, but that doesn't mean I'm ready to give up my dreams for good. I'm a dancer, not a princess. Yes, I can stand for long periods of time and curtsey in heels but even if I was crazy enough to consider agreeing—which I'm not— there's got to be more to being a princess than that.'

'Posy, I'm just trying to find a way out of this mess that works for both of us. Either you go down in history as the dancer who romped naked with the Prince or you can be a princess. Your choice.'

Posy shivered despite the balmy afternoon sun. Ballet dancers were for the most part free from the downsides of fame, their private lives unknown to the outside world. But her sister Portia was an entertainment journalist and Posy had seen how easy it was for her to tear people down, people who were famous for much more laudable reasons than a fling with a prince. She'd seen how Javier spent his life as a headline, the truth an incidental compared to the possible scandal. 'I don't want to be famous,' she half whispered. 'Or notorious. Yes, I want to be loved and admired for my dancing but once the spotlights dim I don't need or crave attention.'

'Then this has got to be hard for you but you don't have time to dwell on it. You need to decide now.'

'What's in it for you? If I say yes?' She couldn't believe she was even asking the question, asking any questions instead of marching back to the villa, packing her bags and hightailing it away from the villa and away from Nico. But hadn't she run away from obstacles just a week ago? Look how that had panned out.

'What do you mean?'

Oh, that blank look wasn't fooling her. 'I agree and

I get a job for life, as you so romantically put it. I get a PR team doing their best to make sure those photos are forgotten and buried. But what about you? What do you get out of it apart from a loveless marriage?'

There was no answer for a long minute and when he did speak his voice was toneless. 'My cousin died unexpectedly the year before last. He was supposed to be the Crown Prince, the next King.'

Of course. How could she have forgotten? 'I heard, I'm so sorry.'

'Thank you. He was raised to it, to duty and country first. As the spare, a cousin at that, expectations weren't so high for me and I may have taken advantage of that.'

'May?'

For the first time that day his mouth quirked into a smile and Posy felt an answering pull. Prince or not, she doubted many people turned Nico down when he smiled in that particular way, charm mixed with devilry and a certain *aw, shucks* frankness. 'That was the narrative. Alessandro was the obedient heir and I was the wastrel always getting him into trouble. Truth was Alessandro loved trouble as much as any boy, but he loved his country more and he knew his duty. I didn't expect to be standing here, heir to an old-fashioned constitution and a dependent country, but here I am—and I love my country too. L'Isola dei Fiori needs a stable succession. It needs an heir settled down with a wife and children, the one thing Alessandro failed to do. If he had…' the smile intensified '…you and I would be having a very different discussion right now.'

Posy wasn't sure if the jolt in her stomach was in answer to that wolfish smile or the casual mention of a wife and children. That was what he'd meant by duty, wasn't it? Not just making pretty speeches and cutting ribbons but bearing his children, future princes and princesses. The begetting of those future princes and princesses. Surely, *surely* this had to be some kind of joke…

But although Nico was smiling there was still little humour in his face. She shivered, pulling her battered mind back to the matter at hand, utterly ludicrous as this whole conversation was. 'But he didn't marry and so you need a wife. Any wife.'

'That's about it. Apart from the any wife part. My grandmother went to a lot of trouble to put a shortlist aside for me.'

'I'm guessing I wasn't at the top of that list.'

'It's doubtful but you've been catapulted right up there. It seems,' he clarified, 'that recent events make it hard for me to court any of these eligible young ladies in an approved fashion.'

'Oh.' She chewed on her lip, a habit she'd thought had been trained out of her along with slouching and bad turnout. 'You don't sound too heartbroken.'

He shrugged. 'I haven't even looked at the list. I got…sidetracked.'

Her toes curled at the dark meaning in his voice. It was a good thing she wasn't even entertaining this crazy idea because Nico Del Castro was definitely a bigger bite than she could comfortably chew.

'So you pick a wife, she agrees gratefully and bang, happy ever after?'

'Not quite. Before we get married there is a nice, public falling-in-love period to go through. What do you think, Posy? Ready to be wooed and wed?'

* * *

It stood to reason that nothing about this process was going to go smoothly and, by the pursed pinch of her lips and the cloud on her brow, his intended bride was the biggest obstacle of them all. She hadn't spoken one more word since Nico had brought up the whole public wooing part of the plan. To be honest he couldn't really blame her—he had agreed to the idea but it was still far too sickly for him to easily stomach.

But the more he considered it, the more he was convinced Posy could be the right candidate for the royal role. She had poise and dignity, which were always assets, she didn't want to be Queen, which meant she had no expectations ready to be dashed, often a danger with a royal bride, and she came with no baggage. She didn't have a title or a fortune to bring to the table, no scheming relatives or concession-demanding lawyers, just a Cinderella stroke Juliet stroke Goose Girl vibe, which had the marketing consultant salivating into her forecast spreadsheets.

So all he needed to do was convince the lady herself. She had to have an Achilles heel; he just needed to probe until he found it.

'Why ballet?'

She darted a surprised look up at him. 'What?'

'Why did you want to be a ballet dancer? The tutus?'

'How old do you think I am? Three?' Her face relaxed into a soft smile. 'Maybe a little bit the tutus, at the beginning. No, it was Sofia. She was my grandmother's best friend. They met at boarding school and, even though they lived such different lives, were such complete opposites, were fast friends. She was like an aunt to my mother—an indulgent, impulsive, glamorous aunt—and Mum wanted to let her know she was part of the family and asked her to be my godmother. She said, Sofia, that a godmother's purpose was to spoil the child and so she did. She took me to London every Christmas for a matinee and afternoon tea at Fortnum's.' Her smile widened. 'My sisters were so jealous. It's not easy being the youngest. They all did their best to squash me so I did rather boast about my good luck.'

'And Sofia encouraged you to dance?'

'She took me to my first ballet. The Nutcracker. I was only five—Royal Opera House, a box, expensive chocolates. My mother was really doubtful I'd sit still for that long. I was rather an energetic small child, never still if I could move, but as soon as I saw the lights and the stage and the seats filled with people all dressed up and expectant I was hooked. And then the music started...' Her voice died away, her huge dark eyes glistening before she resolutely wiped a tear away. 'That was it. I wanted to be Clara floating on an adventure through a fantasy world. Yes, it was partly the tutus, but mostly the way the dancers seemed to soar. How graceful yet strong they were. I begged and begged my mother for ballet lessons and as soon as I set foot in that studio, all serious in my pink leotard and tiny ballet shoes, I knew I'd come home. I always felt that way, no matter how hard it got, how tired I was, how painful my feet. Like I was home.'

'So why are you here and not there? Dancers don't have a very long shelf-life, do they? Can you really risk a sabbatical?'

Posy brushed away another tear. 'It stopped being home.' She didn't say any more and, after a quick look at her averted profile, Nico decided not to push any fur-

ther. He didn't need to. He had his information. Posy
Marlowe was at a crossroads—all he needed to do was
show her the right way.

They rounded the curve in the coastal path and Villa
Rosa came into sight. The famous pink villa was surrounded by a high wall on three sides, the front of the
villa overlooking the beach and ocean. The coastal path
diverted from the cliff tops to ensure passers-by gave
the villa a wide berth, wild meadows running rampant
between the walls and the paths, 'Keep Out, private'
signs dissuading hikers from taking a short cut through
the long grass. Posy had trampled a narrow path from
the wall to the path and she set off back along it. 'Sofia
would never let us walk through the meadow in May
and June,' she said. 'It belongs to the poppies then. We
had to take the long way round, through the gates and
along the road until it met the path and then turning
back on ourselves. Sofia always said it was a sin to step
on a wild flower.'

But not a sin to sleep with another woman's husband.
Nico stopped the acerbic words before they reached his
lips but, he realised, he was going to have to warn Posy
not to mention her godmother in front of his grandmother. He might be envisioning a star-crossed lovers
narrative for the pair of them but that didn't mean Lady
Montague had to befriend Lady Capulet even beyond
the grave.

Ivy hung over the faded pink walls, so thickly Nico
didn't see the gate until Posy pushed the dark green
leaves to one side and revealed the discreet, slim door.
Images of his grandfather slipping furtively out rose ir-
resistibly in his mind and Nico was torn between laughter at the ridiculousness of the King sneaking out of

the villa like some kind of burglar and icy anger at his grandfather's betrayal, not just of his Queen, but of the whole island. He paused, one hand on the door. Would marrying Posy be worth reviving all that old gossip? Or would their carefully orchestrated happy ever after finally put it to bed? Only time would tell—if she agreed.

The door led into the gardens, now overgrown, faded and crumbling like so much else in the villa. To one side were the garages and in front the famous conservatory with its jewel-coloured glass. The driveway was at the side of the house so that the front had a clear view of the ocean, unhindered by anything as mundane as a path or a driveway or the impressive wrought-iron gates. Gates that had been standing wide open when he had visited the villa earlier today.

'Posy, did you close the gates after me? This morning?'

She started, still lost in a world of her own. 'No, why? I haven't closed them at all. They're so heavy and the lock's stiff. Besides, this is L'Isola dei Fiori. There's practically no crime here.'

'No,' he said grimly. 'But there are photographers. Wait here.'

As boys he and Alessandro had often played at being spies, slipping through the palace as stealthily as possible, searching out the hidden corridors that they knew must be somewhere if they just looked hard enough. Of course they hadn't practised being spies in a creaky house, full of furniture with ludicrously large windows exposing them on every side.

Nico opened the conservatory door and stepped as quietly as possible onto the tiled floor before crossing the vast sunlit room to let himself into the shabby kitchen. He didn't need to go any further. He could hear the noise from here. Banging on the door, voices echoing in through the letter box.

'Miss Marlowe, we just want to talk.'

'Is Prince Nico here?'

'Posy, we are prepared to offer big for an exclusive tell all. My card's on your mat.'

Nico swore under his breath. 'Dammit.' He'd hoped to have had a little more time. It was a good thing he'd made plans for this very situation. Retreating as silently as he had come, he made his way swiftly back to the garden and a wide-eyed Posy. She stood next to the fountain, her dark hair falling out of its loose bun, her legs long and strong in denim cut-offs, the oversized white shirt emphasising her air of fragility. It was just an air, he suspected, remembering the way she'd moved on the beach, the lines of her body twisting and turning, the way she stood poised, balanced, one leg high in the air, the way she cut through the water with clean, strong strokes. But would she be strong enough for what awaited her?

'They're here,' he said brusquely. 'We need to leave. Now.'

CHAPTER SEVEN

Posy sent a nervous glance Nico's way. He hadn't said a word beyond a curt 'careful' since he'd hustled her away from the villa and down the steep path to the jetty, where he'd helped her into the boat. Posy was torn between admiration that he was one step ahead of the paparazzi by electing to sail to the villa, not drive along the narrow road where they would undoubtedly have found themselves hemmed in by the scarily large pack of photographers and paparazzi—and irritation that he was one step ahead of *her* right up to orchestrating their quick getaway.

She shivered despite the late afternoon sun. Her own sister was an entertainment journalist, used to celebrities and cameras and hustle—and since being linked to Javier had become a paparazzi target in her own right—but this kind of attention was beyond anything Posy had ever experienced.

As for Nico and the crazy plan he had come up with… Suddenly it didn't feel quite so crazy and that scared her more than anything. When a fake love affair and an arranged marriage seemed logical it was a sure sign everything else had turned upside down.

Whoa. Her mind skidded to a stop. Did that mean

she was considering agreeing? Of course she wasn't—couldn't—but everything was all happening so fast. Too fast, rapidly skidding so far out of her control she had no idea how she was going to get her life back on track.

She swallowed, willing her voice to come out calm and assertive, not plaintive and wobbling. 'Where are we going?'

Nico barely turned to look at her, all his attention on the wheel as the boat ploughed smoothly through the blue waves. 'The palace.'

'The palace? Is that wise?'

'You'll be safe there.'

L'Isola dei Fiori was a small island and during her childhood holidays Posy had been to pretty much all of the limited and often old-fashioned sights. She'd sailed out on the old sailing ship, toured the grottos and sea caves, eaten *gelato* at Giovanni's—still renowned as the best ice cream in Europe by those in the know—and spent hours at the old-fashioned fair in the centre of San Rocco, the quaint capital city. Sofia had loved the carousel, riding the faded wooden horses with as much straight-backed grace as if she were on an Arabian steed.

But Posy had never set foot inside the palace even though parts were open to the public, never seen the famous paintings, the celebrated romantic architecture, the graceful spires and spiral stairs more like a fairytale castle than a living, breathing building.

Sofia had kept them away from anything and anywhere to do with the Del Castro family. Not for them the feast days and carnivals celebrated with such enthusiasm by the rest of the island or the parades and parties. For the first time Posy realised just how limited her godmother's seemingly glamorous life must have been. Everyone knew who she was and yet she could never be publicly acknowledged.

While Posy herself had suddenly become all too public.

'Maybe I should have stayed put. They'd have gone eventually. If I go to the palace with you then we're making a statement, aren't we? It's as if I'm agreeing to your...' She searched for the right word. She could hardly call it a proposal. 'Your suggestion. But I haven't had a chance to think it through.'

'What do you want, Posy? If this hadn't happened, if we hadn't met, what were you planning to do next?'

She looked down at the water, stirred up into white froth by the boat, and wished for a moment she could dive in and just float there until this was all over. 'I don't know,' she confessed. 'All I ever wanted to do was dance and I haven't decided yet whether I'm ready to stop. I can't make that decision, such a final, life-changing decision, not yet. It's too soon. I might be on a sabbatical but I'm not sure I'm ready to walk away for good.'

'Then give me three months. Three months to convince the world we're falling in love. If after that you decide this isn't for you we'll plan an exit strategy.'

Plan. Exit strategy. Marriage as a boardroom presentation. 'Three months? And then I can walk away?'

'You'll still be linked to me but hopefully we can turn the story around, make you someone people want to be, not someone...'

'Not someone people are giggling about?' It made a crazy kind of sense. 'How would we end it? If I agree?

And what about the villa? Will you still pressurise me to sell it to you?'

'We have three months to figure it out. But, Posy, I want you to promise something. If you decide to try, then please really give this engagement a chance. It might not be something you want, something you've ever considered, but it could give you a way forward. You love this island too. Why else would you come here? The island needs some good news, some positive publicity, someone to help me look after it and lead it. You could be that person. Think about it.'

Posy nodded, unable to speak. He was right. The island did have a hold on her heart. It was the place she'd instinctively turned when she had nowhere else to go, nothing to hold onto, no one to turn to. Maybe she could have a purpose here. It was better than no purpose at all.

Three months. It wasn't that long a time. She'd be free before Christmas. Maybe she could give him that. Give herself that. After all, it wasn't as if she had anything more pressing to do. She looked at him, at the set of his jaw, the way his eyes focused on the horizon, the muscles playing in his arms as he kept the boat steady. She'd taken a crazy chance on him once before. Trusted him. Okay, it had all gone horribly wrong but not because of anything he had done—and here he was, trying to make it right.

'Fine, I'll do it. I'll give you three months. But if I do this then you have to be honest with me as well. If it's not working for you then say. After all, you have an entire dossier of other potential wives to choose from.'

He shot her an unreadable look. 'Deal.'

She shifted in her seat. The wind whipped the strands of hair that had fallen from her bun around her face.

Posy breathed in, the sea air tasting like freedom. She'd better inhale it while she still could. 'So, what happens next? We announce our engagement straight away?' An unexpected giggle burst from her as she pictured it. Would he stand there and say 'whatever love is' while she stared coyly at her hands?

'Not immediately. First, first we fall in love. Obviously, publicly, and as photogenically as possible. I hope you're ready for your close-up, Miss Marlowe. We're here.'

Any inclination Posy still had to giggle disappeared as Nico expertly steered the boat in between two high, narrow rocks and the boat emerged into a wide bay, the palace perched on top of the cliffs. Guards manned the parapets looking out to sea—not that the island had been invaded during the last two hundred years or so. Before that, however, it had fallen prey to several different empires, which was why, although the official language was Italian, there were Greek, French and the odd bit of British influences across the island.

'Couldn't anyone just sail in?' she asked as Nico headed towards a small harbour on the opposite side of the bay. Several boats were already moored there, including the surviving royal yacht—there had been three but the current King, Nico's uncle, she realised, had sold two—some fancy-looking cabin cruisers and catamarans as well as some more modest boats and dinghies like the one Nico was currently guiding in.

'Technically but the only way up to the palace is heavily guarded and the harbour and beach are monitored and patrolled. We do get the press coming in occasionally but there's very little for them to see here so they can usually be persuaded to leave without too much bloodshed.'

As he spoke Posy saw several smartly dressed soldiers stepping smartly along the harbourside. A welcoming party. 'Oh, no, I'm a mess.' She quickly smoothed back the wisps of hair and pulled her shirt down. 'You should have let me bring some clothes. We had time to pack.' Not that she had anything suitable for a palace. She spent her life in sweat pants and vest tops. Hardly royal attire.

'Don't worry, I called ahead. It's being taken care of.'

'Oh.' One step ahead again.

The boat glided against the dock and Nico threw the rope to one of the soldiers, who caught it in one hand and looped it around a pole. Nico jumped smartly up onto the dock and extended a hand to Posy. She took a deep breath. It was time.

His hand was warm and firm and oddly comforting as he pulled her onto the dock. Posy had an urge to keep hold of it, an anchor in this strange new world. 'Okay?' he asked.

'I think so.'

The soldiers fell in step around them. She could do this. It was just like a ballet, everyone knowing their steps and their place—except Posy, but she was an expert at finding her feet. Nico slanted a glance at her. 'A room's been prepared. I'll take you straight there to wash up and change.'

'And then?'

'And then you meet my family.'

Great. Straight into the lions' den. 'Meeting the parents on the second date.' As she said the words she remembered that his father had died three years ago in a helicopter crash. There had been some whispered scandal; a woman's body had also been uncovered from the wreckage.

Nico seamlessly covered her gaffe. He must have had training: *How to Speak to Tactless Commoners for Beginners*. 'My mother isn't here, you'll be relieved to hear. She lives in France now, splitting her time between Paris and the Riviera. Just my uncle and aunt and my grandmother.'

'Just the King, Queen and Dowager Queen. Nothing I haven't dealt with one hundred times before. No, wait. That's those girls in your grandmother's dossier.'

He laughed at that. It was the first time she'd heard him laugh. It transformed him, lit him up. It would be nice to make him laugh more often…

'Just call them all Your Majesty and defer to my uncle's wisdom and you'll be fine.'

'Is that what you do?'

'I manage the Your Majesty bit, the other I have a hard time with,' he confessed. 'They can be a little intimidating but it's in everyone's interests that this works out so don't let them worry you.'

It was hardly the most reassuring speech Posy had ever heard.

She'd expected hordes of interested onlookers but it was eerily deserted as the guards escorted them past the checkpoint and into the tiled tunnel cut into the cliff, through two sets of security doors, and saluted them as they stepped into a plush lift, just two accompanying them up to the palace. Posy tried not to think about how the lift shaft must be cut into the solid rock as the lift smoothly rose upwards at a stately speed. It was equally deserted when the doors opened into a marble vestibule and they passed through another set of security doors and into the corridor beyond. Either people had been told to keep away or nobody knew she was accompanying Nico back to the palace. She didn't care which one it was, she was just grateful for these last few moments of privacy.

Not counting Nico and the two guards, of course.

She was escorted through a maze of corridors, treading over highly polished marble floors, waxed wooden floors and plush carpets, some passages papered with intricate wallpaper, others painted and edged with intricate plasterwork. No two were the same and as they turned yet another corner Posy knew that she would never ever be able to find her way around here without a ball of thread to mark her way. She walked mutely, following Nico into another lift and along more corridors until he halted outside a white-painted door.

'This wing is the private family wing,' he said. 'We all have rooms here. My uncle and aunt occupy the ground floor, my grandmother's rooms are on the first floor and I am on the floor above you. So you have some privacy. I hope these will suit.' He opened the door as he spoke and stood aside to let Posy precede him in, the guards taking up station on either side of the door as he did so.

Eying the guards nervously—were they really planning on being there all the time and if so what exactly were they there for? To guard her or to keep an eye on her?—Posy stepped inside and stopped still, aware her mouth was hanging open in a most undignified way. 'OMG,' she muttered.

She'd had no idea what to expect—had had no time to consider it—but if she had pictured the private rooms in the old palace she wouldn't have come up with this. She stood in a long, light room, the opposite wall punctuated with four sets of French doors opening out onto a spacious terrace overlooking the sea, the outside space filled with huge flower-filled terracotta pots, a small table and chairs, two loungers and a swinging hammock. The room itself had simple white walls brightened with some huge landscapes and a couple of mirrors and was furnished with a comfortable-looking grey corner sofa and matching love seat, both heaped with red and purple cushions. The seating area was arranged around an open fireplace, a television discreet against the far corner. Tall, filled bookcases took up the far wall, another comfortable-looking love seat sat opposite the windows and a round dining table and four chairs upholstered in a bright flowered pattern were positioned in front of the bookcases. Every available shelf and occasional table held a vase filled with flowers.

The room was bigger than her entire London flat and more luxurious than any hotel room she had ever stayed in. Posy swivelled, eyes wide.

'Like it?'

'It's okay, a little cramped but I'll try to manage.' She did her best to sound nonchalant but knew her wide grin gave her away.

'Your bedroom, dressing room and bath are through there.' He nodded at a white panelled door by the bookcase. 'Your study is through there.' This time he indicated a door by the love seat. 'If you want to change the configuration at all that's fine, just talk to your secretary. You're sharing my grandmother's until we can appoint a permanent one for you.'

'A secretary?'

'To organise your schedule and administrative duties. My grandmother and aunt also have personal ladies-in-waiting but I'd suggest waiting until you know your way around before appointing your own. It can be a political minefield and you don't want to be stuck with a wrong choice—the housekeeper will assign maids to help you until then. The two guards outside your door are part of your bodyguard detail. You'll be accompanied by two at all times.'

Her smile wavered and disappeared. Bodyguards? Ladies-in-waiting? 'I don't really need…'

'Yes. You do. You'll be glad of the help. Dinner is at eight. It's formal dress. Do you want me to ask someone to help you bathe or dress?'

To help her what? 'No. I think I need some time alone.'

His eyes softened. 'I know how it seems. It was always a shock returning home from MIT to all this formality and pomp. You'll get used to it, I promise.'

Posy couldn't imagine ever getting used to guards outside her door but she nodded mutely. Nico strode to the door and paused, gaze intent on hers. 'It's in both our interests to make this work, Posy. If you need anything just let me know.' And then he was gone, leaving Posy alone in a room that she was rapidly realising was more like a luxurious prison cell than a home.

She crossed the room and opened one of the French doors, stepping outside onto the stone terrace, relieved to feel the evening sun on her face, the soft sea breeze on her arms. The terrace stretched out in both directions. It must be accessible from each of her rooms, she realised. She was glad she was on this side of the palace, looking out to sea; it meant she couldn't be overlooked.

A buzz from her pocket startled her. Of course, her phone. She must have a mobile signal here. She pulled it out and sighed. Her phone had picked up the palace wi-fi and it looked as if her inbox was as full as her voicemail. She'd deal with that tomorrow. She couldn't actually face any of it now but she couldn't keep her family waiting any longer. But where to start? What could she say? She took a deep breath and pressed play on her voicemail.

As expected, worried messages from her sisters and her parents, several offers of interviews and representation, which she promptly deleted, and, to her surprise, supportive messages from her flatmates and from a couple of other friends. Posy listened, blinking away tears. She wasn't as alone as she had thought; there were people who cared. She quickly texted Portia, Miranda, Imogen and her parents.

I'm fine. Don't worry. Sorry for everything. Will let you know everything soon. P x

That would hardly put their minds at ease but she simply couldn't talk to them right now. Not until she knew how she felt, could convince them that she was okay. Was less numb. Of course, she hadn't actually seen the pictures yet. She took a deep breath and pulled up her browser and typed in her name.

'Oh, my God.' She sank onto the nearest lounger, putting a hand down for support. 'How could they?'

It was all there. Nico wading naked into the water. Posy dancing, holding a perfect arabesque in the surf. The moment she pulled her dress off. The first kiss. The two of them lying on the sand, naked limbs wrapped around each other. Each picture seared itself onto her retina. How could this be legal? It was so wrong to intrude on something so private and send it out into the world.

There was only one person who could help her right now. Posy closed the browser, wishing she could unsee the images as easily, and pressed Portia's name, relief flooding through her as the call connected.

There was an odd sense of kinship between herself and her oldest sister despite the three-year age gap. Partly it was because Immi and Andie were twins and had always had each other, leaving Posy and Portia together on family days out. Partly it was because Portia, like Posy, had little interest in aeroplanes, the all-consuming family business and passion. She had built a life away from Marlowe Aviation as a successful journalist in LA—and she'd just married a bona fide A-list film star, which in this day and age almost trumped bagging a prince.

'Posy? Are you okay? Listen to me. Talk to nobody, do you understand? We will be with you tomorrow. Javier's PR person is going to handle everything.'

'Hi, Portia.' To her horror Posy could feel her throat thickening, her chin wobble. *Keep it together, Marlowe,* she told herself sternly. 'I'm so, *so* sorry. Are Mum and Dad furious?'

'You haven't spoken to them?'

'I haven't spoken to anyone. You know what the phone reception is like at the villa.'

'All too well.' Her sister's voice sharpened. 'So where are you? Has anyone seen you?'

'I'm fine, don't worry. I'm...' She paused, aware that once the words were said they couldn't be unsaid, that she would be definitely set on this path. 'I'm with Nico. At the palace.'

'With who? Hang on.' Portia's voice became indistinct as she must have moved the phone away, but Posy could hear the deep rumble of Javier's famously sexy Italian voice replying. 'I'm back. Javier is going to talk to Nico. They're old friends. So what's the plan?'

'Nico wants us to fall in love. I mean, he wants us to look as if we're in love.'

'Interesting. Are you in love with him?'

'No! I mean, I barely know him…'

'Barely seems to be the operative word here. I've seen the pictures.' Portia's voice was dry. 'Why a fake relationship? It all seems a little drastic. My advice is say nothing, keep your head down and return to work. If you're at the palace pretending to be in love then the Internet is going to explode. Are you sure you know what you're doing?'

'He needs to get married, now he's the Crown Prince, and he was planning an arranged marriage anyway so…'

'Rosalind Anne Marlowe. Are you engaged to a prince?' Her sister's voice had risen in pitch to a decibel only bats could comfortably tolerate. 'That's it, I am on my way. You have obviously taken complete leave of your senses.'

'No. Don't come, not yet and, no, I'm not engaged. Yet. I promised to consider giving him three months. To see if we could live together, be married. That's all.'

'That's all? Posy, I don't understand. Four months ago you were almost too busy to come to your own sister's wedding and now you're not dancing, you're living on the island even though I know you should be back in training and you are seriously contemplating marrying a man you don't know. A man you slept with despite not knowing him, which is not like you. What's going on?'

They were all too valid questions. Posy closed her eyes and swallowed. When she said the words out loud then they would be out there. Not just her private shame any more. 'I'm not good enough.' Her voice cracked.

'What do you mean? Of course you are, you're incredible. What makes you say that?'

The tears were freefalling now. 'I wasn't moving on. I should have had solos by now, you know that, but I just wasn't getting picked. I decided to ask for advice and I overheard them say. They said…' She gulped, the sobs tearing out despite her best attempts to swallow them back down.

'Said what, Posy? Darling, try and calm down. You're scaring me.'

Posy took a moment, dashing the tears away with an impatient hand. 'That I had no fire. No life. That I would always have a place in the Corps but I'd never be anything more. I didn't know what to do but I couldn't stay there, Portia. My dream was always to be a soloist, you know that. So I came here to think and when I met Nico I just… I just wanted to prove them wrong. Show myself that I could live. That I had fire.'

'And you got burned. Posy, I have to say when you decide to do something you do it all too thoroughly. Do you really not want me to come right now? I can be with you tomorrow, honey.'

Posy shook her head, forgetting her sister couldn't see her. 'Not yet. Let me figure this out. I appreciate the offer though.'

'If you change your mind…'

'I know. You'll be the first person I call. Thank you, Portia.'

'Do you want me to call Mum and Dad and the twins? They're all pretty worried.'

'Would you? Tell them I'm fine and I'll speak to them as soon as I can. Portia?'

'Yes?'

'I don't want anyone to know. None of it. About why I left London or about the relationship not being real.'

'That's your choice, Posy. But what about Mum and Dad? They'd understand.'

Posy pictured her parents at Andie's wedding, remembering how relaxed her father had looked, ten years younger than when she had last seen him. They'd all been so worried about him after the terrible accident that had killed Rachel, Cleve's pregnant wife, who had been flying one of Marlowe Aviation's new prototypes when she died. The inquest had cleared Marlowe Aviation completely and now Cleve was happily married to Posy's sister, Miranda, their first baby on the way, but the whole incident had left her father badly shaken. How could Posy be responsible for stressing her father when he needed nothing but relaxation and peace?

'I don't want to worry Mum and Dad, and you know how protective Cleve is about Andie now she's pregnant. I can't tell Immi if I'm not telling Andie. They hate keeping secrets from one another. So it's just you. Is that okay?'

'I'm an entertainment journalist, Posy. I know far more secrets than I ever exposed. If you want me to stay quiet then of course I will. They'd all understand but I do see why you want to keep this one quiet for now.'

'Thank you. Love you.'

'Love you too, Rosy-Posy.'

Posy finished the call and collapsed onto the lounger, the sun sore on her swollen eyes. But despite the tears still wet on her cheeks and the ache in her throat she felt better, unburdened. Maybe she should have spoken to someone earlier about her crisis of confidence. If she had then she might not have ended here, lying on a lounger that looked as if it belonged in a high-end fashion shoot and about to change for dinner with a real life King and his family. But it was a little too late to worry about that.

She swiped her eyes again. She had less than two hours before said dinner and she must look an absolute state; she'd never been able to cry prettily. Time to explore the rest of these lavish apartments and get herself ready for tonight. If there was one thing she understood it was the importance of costume and tonight she was going to need every piece of skill she possessed.

CHAPTER EIGHT

DINNER WAS STILL half an hour away but Nico was ready early. He was pretty sure Posy would need a fortifying drink before the ordeal awaiting them—and he was definitely sure that he did. He pulled at his tie, already hearing his uncle's sarcastic tones. He didn't need reminding that Alessandro would never have messed up in this way. He knew it all too well.

The two guards at Posy's door stood at attention, Nico's own bodyguards waiting at the end of the corridor. If he hadn't dismissed them last night, hadn't snuck out on his own… Was it really only last night? So much had happened in the twenty-four hours since then.

Pushing the dark thoughts from his mind, Nico rapped on the door. None of this was Posy's fault. At first he'd wondered if this was all some kind of elaborate set-up, some kind of trap, the chances of them both skinny dipping on the same deserted shore, the chances of her turning back and propositioning him, the chances of the photographer being there—but her shock had been all too real. She was a victim here, more so than him. And he knew all too well if it weren't Posy here this evening making her formal introduction to his family it would be some other woman a few weeks hence. Better the devil he was getting to know.

'Come in.'

He turned the handle and opened the door, stepping in with a carefully prepared sentence ready, the offer of a drink and a polite compliment, only to stumble to a halt as she turned, illuminated by the last of the summer evening's light pouring in through the windows.

No longer the bare-legged urchin of the day, or the sea-drenched naiad of the night before, Posy personified elegance in a full-length blue cap-sleeved dress, the silky material hugging her shoulders, moulding itself to her small, perfect breasts before gathering just underneath her bust and falling in graceful folds to the floor. She'd left her cloud of silky dark hair loose, simply twisted at the front and fastened back with two silver clips, and her feet were slipped into high-heeled silver sandals. He'd not seen her wear make-up before; it was artfully understated except for the deep red lipstick, accenting every curve of her full mouth.

Posy smiled shyly and gestured at her dress. 'Hi. Will I do? You said formal and this was in the wardrobe but seriously this feels more ball gown than dinner gown to me.'

'You look beautiful,' he said softly.

'Not too much?'

'My aunt wears a tiara to lunch.'

She stared at that. 'Too little? Should I bling it up? Not that I have any bling...'

'No, you look perfect.'

'I had some help, thanks to whichever elves stocked that wardrobe. It's a little creepy to find several outfits, all in my size, waiting for me but as I don't think your uncle and aunt would have appreciated me turning up in yoga pants and a crop top I'm ignoring creepy and going for thankful.' She smiled straight at him then, gesturing to his dinner jacket. 'You scrub up nicely as well.'

'It's a family requirement. We're a little early but I thought you might appreciate a drink before meeting my family.' He held out an arm, feeling more like a character playing a part than he'd ever felt before. 'Shall we?'

Nico devoted the next half-hour to putting Posy at her ease, noting with some relief the colour returning to her cheeks and the sparkle to her eyes. His family wouldn't go easy on her just because she was unprepared and ill at ease; in fact they seemed to scent fear like a pack of wolves and were more than happy to go in for the kill. His father had thrived on the cut-throat atmosphere but his mother had always hated it; no wonder she'd cut and run, moving to France a mere month after being widowed. She'd have been a lot happier if his father had agreed to move there a long time ago, but like a true Del Castro he had refused to leave L'Isola dei Fiori permanently. Just one of the many ways in which they had failed to find a compromise. If his uncle's marriage was a perpetual uneasy truce, his parents' had either been a battlefield or a honeymoon—and Nico had never known which to expect: flying crockery and bitterness or finding them half undressed on the sofa. Either way he had been completely superfluous to their requirements, a spectator to the melodrama of their marriage.

'Your Highness, Miss Marlowe.' A footman was at the door of the small salon to which he had escorted Posy. 'Dinner will be served in five minutes.'

'Thank you,.' He smiled reassuringly at Posy, who had risen to her feet at the words. 'Ready?'

'No, but I don't suppose that makes any difference. Do you do this every evening?'

'Dine in state? No, thank goodness, only when we have guests, which is far too often for my liking, special occasions or when the family needs to meet, but we're just as likely to dine informally in our rooms.'

'Thank goodness. I'm not sure I can eat much in this dress, it's so tight. I'd fade away if I had to dress up like this every night.'

'My mother said formal meals here were the best dieting technique she'd ever found. If it was a busy week with too many dinners then she would usually order a supper in her rooms afterwards.' As he finished speaking they reached the double doors heralding the entrance to the dining room. Footmen stood at attention on either side and, after a respectful nod, one stepped forward and opened the doors. 'His Royal Highness Prince Nicolas and Miss Rosalind Marlowe.'

Posy's grip tightened on his arm but that was the only outward sign of any concern as she moved in perfect time with him, her face relaxed, smiling politely. She had this, thanks to years of stage training. No matter how nervous she was she knew how to perform. Something his tempestuous mother had never understood.

The tension in his chest lightened. Posy might not have been the obvious choice for his consort but maybe his moment of madness might just work out after all.

The vast dining room was as intimidating as it could be, every chandelier lit and blazing, lighting up the green walls, which were hung with grim still lives mostly featuring dead poultry artfully arranged by a jug or bowls of rotting fruit. Nico and Alessandro had never understood why such off-putting pictures had been hung in a room where people ate—Alessandro had always sworn that when he was king every still life in the palace would be donated to a museum far, far away. The light picked up the gilt edging on the ceiling plasterwork, throwing the various rioting cherubs into hideous relief. Not that things got any better at floor level. The long table was fully made up, crystal candlesticks clashing with the gold cutlery and plates. His family sat like glowering statues at the far end. His uncle upright and unsmiling in the throne-like chair at the head of the table, his aunt at his left and his grandmother to his right.

Nico wasn't sure whether or not to be relieved that they were evidently dining *en famille* this evening. There would be no one outside the family witnessing Posy's first encounter with the Del Castros—but at the same time all gloves would be off. He halted a few steps into the room and bowed stiffly, Posy, less than a second behind him, falling into a graceful curtsey. 'Your Majesty.'

'Sit down, Nico. Next to your aunt. Miss Marlowe, please.' His uncle gestured to his right and a footman pulled out the chair next to his grandmother. Posy hesitated for one moment and then with a nod let go of his arm and walked over to the chair, seating herself smoothly with a polite nod and a quiet but clear and steady, 'Good evening, Your Majesties. It's nice to meet you.' Impressive. His admiration for her courage shot up another notch.

The first few courses went surprisingly well. Posy had excellent table manners and, although she was hardly talkative, she answered any questions put to her with a quiet confidence Nico hadn't expected and the conversation remained on general lines, probing a little into Posy's family and evolving into a discussion about ballet, luckily one of his grandmother's passions. It wasn't until the fruit, cheese and biscuits were served and the footmen waved away that things took a more personal turn.

'So, Nico. I see you behaved in your usual headlong fashion.' His uncle peered at him disapprovingly. 'Am I to understand that you plan to marry this girl?'

'It seems the best option.'

'Hardly the behaviour of the future Queen of L'Isola dei Fiori, is it? Romping naked on the beach with a perfect stranger. I am right in thinking you didn't know each other before yesterday?' His uncle had turned purple. He'd obviously been suppressing his feelings throughout the meal and now, typically, he was erupting with rage.

Posy flushed scarlet and his grandmother set down her cheese knife decisively. Beside him his aunt continued selecting grapes as if nothing was amiss. This was how it always was, the pair of them living parallel lives, never allowing the other to affect them in any way. Nico had never known what was worse—the passion between his parents, which had swung such a fine line between love and hate, or this icy politeness. He'd just known he'd wanted neither. Del Castros weren't known for their happy marriages.

'No. You're not right. Posy and I have known each other for some weeks now.' Nico ignored his grandmother's raised eyebrows and Posy's hastily muffled splutter and smiled pleasantly at his grandfather. 'Her sister married Javier Russo earlier this year. You remember Javier, don't you, Aunt Katerina?'

'Of course. Such a nice boy. He was always such a good friend to Alessandro.' Unlike Nico, she managed to imply without as much as a look in his direction.

His uncle glowered in a way that showed he was still to be convinced. 'What? Where? Thought you were in Boston all spring and summer.'

'I was but I headed to London for a few days.' This was true and luckily Javier and Portia had been there at the same time. His old friend had phoned him a couple of hours ago and, once he'd got his quite considerable feelings about the situation Nico had put his sister-in-law in off his chest, he and Nico had concocted a story that would hopefully stand up to scrutiny. It was quite plausible he and Posy could have met earlier this year. 'We were introduced then and…erm…fell in love. Didn't we, Posy?' He raised his glass to her. She narrowed her eyes at him while picking up her own glass and matching his toast.

'It seemed impossible though. Not only does Nico have his duties here but we were both so busy, Nico in Boston…'

'Finishing my MBA,' he supplied and she thanked him with a swift smile.

'And of course dancing is so all-consuming, we didn't think we would be able to see each other again. But we kept in touch and Nico persuaded me to take a sabbatical and spend a few months on the island as I already own a house here. So we could see if what we had was strong enough. Especially with the, ah, personal connection, we knew any relationship between us would cause some upset.' She shot an apologetic look at Nico's grandmother Nico could swear was genuine. 'Unfortunately we were outed before we could talk to our families. I'm sorry for any embarrassment my actions have brought on the family. This was exactly the kind of situation we were trying to avoid.'

'Our feelings were just too strong,' Nico said helpfully, enjoying how quickly Posy had taken his story and run with it. There was a flicker of that same smile again before she lowered her eyes, the picture of contriteness.

'You'll have to behave with perfect decorum from now on,' his aunt said. 'All eyes will be on you, waiting for you to slip up. Vincenzo and I have worked hard to stop the Del Castro name being a byword for scandal and profligacy. I would hate for all our work to have been in vain. This is exactly the kind of situation which could have been avoided. It's your grandfather all over again. Or your father. If he'd shown some sense and decorum then he'd be here right now, but even in his death he brought shame on the family and on your poor mother.'

Nico sensed his grandmother tense and his grip tightened on his wine glass. His uncle got angry and said exactly what was on his mind no matter how offensive, but Nico would rather that than listen to his aunt's colourless voice dripping poison. How she had managed to birth and raise a sweet-tempered, warm-hearted boy like Alessandro he had no idea. All he knew was that since her beloved son's death she was worse than ever, especially where he was concerned.

He swallowed. 'We have no intention of behaving in any other way,' he said tightly.

'The PR department are all over it,' his uncle cut in. 'The two of you have a full diary of engagements designed to show you in love and committed, some personal, some formal, including the September ball in five weeks' time. We will announce your engagement that evening.'

Posy's surprised gaze flew to meet his at the pronouncement. Nico tried to smile reassuringly at her but it was hard to muster the enthusiasm. He could feel the bars closing in, smothering him. Duty, country, family. Everything he was, everything he wanted irrelevant—and he'd be dragging the elfin girl opposite down with him.

'So we're in love, are we?' Posy kicked off the too tight heels with an inward sigh of relief and turned to glare at Nico, who was leaning against her wall, arms folded and navy eyes gleaming with sardonic humour.

'Madly.'

'It was a good save,' she admitted. 'It would have been nice to have had a heads-up though.'

'You didn't need it. That was a very impressive show you put on there.'

'Good to know all those character, improvisation and mime classes came in handy. When did you speak to Javier?'

'Just before I escorted you to dinner. He and Portia had planned it all. They were just checking dates to make sure we wouldn't get caught out. He texted me while we were at dinner to let me know it was a go. I would have warned you it was a possibility only I didn't want to raise your hopes. I didn't expect my uncle to be quite so direct. No, that's not quite true, I did expect it. I just hoped he might show some better manners.'

'No, he was justified in what he said.' Posy realised how very tired she was, the adrenaline that had kept her alert draining away and with it all her energy. She collapsed onto the sofa, the folds of her dress frothing up around her. 'I did behave badly. I don't know what came over me. I've never done anything like that before.'

'You didn't act alone. And, Posy. Don't let anyone make you feel that last night was wrong or sordid. The person who sold those photos is the one who should be ashamed.'

'Right up until I saw those photos it was the most beautiful moment of my life. The one and only time I acted on instinct, without thinking.' Had she just said that out loud? She cringed, more exposed than when she had seen him in the water and realised she wasn't alone in the evening sea.

Nico didn't respond immediately, his face carefully blank, and Posy searched for something to say to lighten her statement. Beautiful moment? What had she been thinking? He pushed off the wall and walked purposefully over to her, taking her hands in his.

'We're in this together. It's not what either of us wanted but I won't let you face it alone. And not just because your brother-in-law thinks he's a Hollywood hard man.'

Posy inhaled, the pressure of his fingers entwined in hers a strange comfort. She looked at him, at the sharp lines of his face, the long-lashed eyes, and her stomach folded. He was the most glorious man she had ever seen, strong and solid with a mouth made for sin. And he was both hers and not hers. Possibly, if she agreed, her partner in a *pas de deux* for life and yet it would always be for show, every step a fake. 'How can you face it? An arranged marriage? Don't you want to fall in love?'

'Do you?' he countered.

'I don't know,' she said honestly. 'I hadn't really thought about it before my sisters married. My life was so full, so busy. Love was a distraction.' But it was a whole other thing to take it completely off the table, to promise to be faithful to a man who didn't want her love, who didn't love her.

'It's all a gamble, Posy. My parents married for love, my aunt and uncle because she had the right name and the right fortune but they had no shared interests, nothing beyond a tepid liking. Neither couple managed anything close to happiness. It's not easy, life here. Common goals, a common duty, these are the ways to survive a life in the spotlight. It's hard enough without adding emotion into it. But I think we might have respect. Liking. Attraction.' His eyes darkened on the last word and her chest tightened. 'We have that, don't we?'

It was too late for coyness, for denial. She felt him with every part of her whenever he was near her; she tingled with awareness of him. Her mouth remembered the taste of him, salt sweet on the tip of her tongue, her hands knew the feel of him, the play of muscles under her hand, the strength of him. Her breasts ached with the memory of his touch, his kiss. Her throat was thick with need, with wanting. He was the one constant, the one bridge between the Posy she was and the Posy she was going to have to be and she wanted to hold on, to lose herself in him.

'Yes,' she whispered. 'I think we do.'

'We have to play at being in love.' His thumb was moving, caressing the sensitive spot at her wrist, and a jolt shot through her at the contact. 'We might as well enjoy it. Put on a good show.'

'I think we already did that.' It was hard to formulate the words while his thumb made those lazy circles, while his eyes smiled at her with such intent.

'You'll have to hold my hand, kiss me, laugh at my jokes. Gaze at me adoringly.'

'Luckily I'm a good actress so I might manage that.' She gasped as his hand slipped lower, his thumb caressing her entire forearm now. How could one touch on one small area of skin set her whole body alight like this? Sparks were fizzing around her veins, fireworks going off with each swirl.

'We might want to practise.'

'The laughing?' Posy had no idea how she was managing to speak when all her mouth wanted to do was find his.

'The kissing.'

She couldn't answer; all words were gone. She was incapable of thought, of anything but feeling as his hands slipped up her arms to her shoulders, one feather-light touch stroking her throat, and she arched like a satisfied cat before finally his mouth was on hers, as warm and demanding and sweet as she remembered, his body pressing on hers with a glorious heaviness. Posy's hands buried themselves in the nape of his neck, pulling him even closer until she wasn't sure where she began, where he ended, pulling impatiently at layers of clothes, wriggling out of that darn, tight-as-a-glove dress until finally there was nothing separating them. Finally she could surrender to his hands, his mouth, the demand of her body as she soared higher than she ever had before, all memories obliterated by the here and now.

CHAPTER NINE

IT WAS ONLY early September and already change was in the air. The sun was setting a little later, the evenings were that little cooler, the wind whipping their faces and ruffling Posy's hair had an unexpected bite unthinkable even a few days earlier.

Nico steered his sports car around one of the island's famous hairpin bends, the mountains rearing up on one side, the sea a dizzying drop below on the other. Posy leaned back in her seat, a relaxed smile on her face, her eyes hidden by huge sunglasses—and if her knuckles were a little white then that was only to be expected. The mountain drive could test the hardiest of nerves.

It was a good thing he was keeping his eyes on the road and not on the enticing dip in her sundress. His own test of nerves.

They were supposed to be in love and, Nico supposed, lust came close. He hadn't expected this to happen, even after the circumstances of their first encounter. He'd told himself that Posy needed time to adjust to their situation, that it would be wrong to let her think he could or would give her more than affection and respect. He'd reminded himself how much less experienced she was than him and that he absolutely mustn't take advantage of that—but she'd looked so lost, so alone, so vulnerable when she'd told him that their night together had been beautiful, that he'd ached to comfort her the only way he knew how. He might still have held back, done the right thing, if she hadn't looked at him with need in those big eyes, if her skin hadn't been so soft under his touch.

He didn't know if the physical intimacy made things easier or harder. He did know that now they'd started it seemed silly to stop. Everyone in the palace expected him to spend the night in her rooms. It would cause unwanted gossip and speculation if he stayed away.

So he didn't. And although he still didn't know her favourite food or book or movie he did know the way she liked to be kissed, to be touched. He knew that she slept splayed out like a child, somehow managing to take up far more than her fair share of both bed and covers; he knew the way she eased into the day, a minute at a time. He knew how she looked in the middle of the night, eyes closed, lips parted, totally relaxed.

It was unnerving, knowing so much about a person. Even more unnerving to realise she must know the same things about him. That there must be times when she watched him sleep, saw him vulnerable and unaware.

Everything he was trying to avoid.

The days were a little easier. He had his work: meeting with consultants, tour companies and investors, as well as the more ceremonial side of his role and the other demands the palace loaded onto his increasingly heavy schedule. Posy was still a guest in the palace but, once the September Ball was held and their engagement announced, she would have a few carefully selected and managed public appearances. For now her stay in the palace was being treated as a 'family affair'. Not that she was on any kind of holiday. The time she didn't spend with him on an orchestrated 'date' she spent being educated in everything from the correct way to address a diplomat's mother to Italian lessons to an intensive course in L'Isola dei Fiori history, geography and customs.

She bore the intense workload without grumbling— as she explained to him she was used to early mornings and to being in class at least eight hours a day. As long as she wasn't expected to stay still for too long she could cope with hours of instruction and when it got too much she, like him, escaped to the gym. More than once he found her there, engrossed in her stretches and exercises, completely unaware of his presence as she moved her body through routines she obviously knew as instinctively as language. The first time Nico came across her he watched for a while as she stood, straight-backed, feet apart, one hand steadying itself on the rail, the other curved in front, balanced on one impossibly slim, impossibly strong leg, the other raised at an impossible angle.

It felt even more intimate than watching her sleep. He'd moved soundlessly away to pound out his energy on the running machine and made sure to avoid the gym when she was there.

'So what's the plan?' Posy's soft voice interrupted his reverie and Nico roused himself, glad to shelve his thoughts for the time being.

'Plan? We're having a spontaneous day out on one of the island's most famous beauty spots where we may just get photographed having fun, and the photos sold to both demonstrate how respectably in love we are and, conveniently, what a romantic destination the island is.'

'Two-in-one day trip.'

'The best kind.'

Over the last couple of weeks he and Posy had visited several picturesque spots, the palace PR ensuring that friendly photographers were tipped off as to their whereabouts. He'd taken Posy out to visit some of the enchanting rocky islands that lay less than a mile off L'Isola dei Fiori's coast, the two of them all too visible on the small sailing boat as they sunbathed, picnicked and kissed. They'd spent a day in San Rocco's enchanting medieval old town, where they'd wandered hand in hand through the colourful market. Nico had bought a peach from a delighted stallholder to present to his lady before enjoying the rides at the small carnival, which might keep knuckles unwhitened but held such olde worlde charm. A photo of them embracing by the famous waterfall, said to have been formed from Venus's tears, went viral almost instantly. The PR team were constantly monitoring all references to the pair and in just over a fortnight the mood had turned from prurient to curiosity and romance. The public were buying it.

Not only that, but enquiries for accommodation on the island for the next season were already up significantly on this year. The plan was working.

And in less than a month their engagement would be announced.

Posy's whole family had been invited to the September Ball; not only were her parents taking time out of their busy schedule to attend, but all three of her sisters complete with their husbands and fiancés would also be there. 'We'll have to fake it like never before,' she told him when the news was relayed to them. 'Portia's the only one who knows the truth and I want to keep it that way. One hint that we're not in this for real and they'll whisk me away before you can say royal wedding.'

'You're an adult,' he'd protested. 'They can't make you do anything you don't want to do.'

'I just don't want them to be disappointed in me.' But it wasn't her words that rocked him back on his heels. It was the wistful look in her eyes. She'd agreed to give him three months and he sensed she would keep her word but she was still unconvinced about the marriage, even if she was enjoying some of the benefits of royal life, including a knockout wardrobe. Every time she was photographed looking immaculate it triggered another delivery of clothes. On his aunt's advice she accepted a few; the rest were sold off to benefit the Del Castros' chosen charities. But not even the most exquisite dress had made her happier than a box that had arrived from London this morning, a box filled with pale satin shoes with blocked edges. 'My own shoes,' she'd gasped, her eyes suspiciously wet. 'Look, Nico. Pointe shoes.'

He had managed not to point out that she would have little use for them now. 'Surely you have hundreds of pairs,' he'd said instead as she'd picked one of the slender slippers out of the box and cradled it.

'These were made just for me. This is the make I prefer and they're the perfect fit. We always get several pairs at a time so we can break them in, sew ribbons on, darn them.' She'd turned the pale satin shoes over in her hands, her fingers caressing them.

'You have to darn them?' He wasn't entirely sure what darning even was. 'Don't you have people to do that for you?'

She'd swatted him away, appalled. 'Every dancer sews and darns her own shoes, no matter who she is.'

Unnecessary work, antiquated customs, a rigid hierarchy? No wonder she fitted in so well at the palace. Even his grandmother had conceded that Posy had pretty manners, although she was still wary of Posy's close connection to her great rival.

Posy shifted in her seat, a sure sign she was about to say something she was unsure would be well received. 'Nico, I'm arranging for my parents to stay at the Villa Rosa, my sisters too.'

He kept his eyes on the perilous road. 'We have plenty of space at the palace.'

'An entire wing's worth of space, I know. But the Villa Rosa is really special to all my family, all of my sisters stayed there this year, we all love it and, no matter what happens with us, you and me, the villa won't be part of that. If we...' She paused. She did that a lot, he'd noticed, happy enough with the present-day deception but unable to talk about their possible future together. 'If things go the way you're planning,' she said instead, 'then I won't need the villa. And if we don't.... If after the three months we decide it's not working then it would be a little awkward for me to come here to the island for a while, let alone live here. So you can have the villa for your hotel. It needs more spending on it than I could manage and it's too beautiful for just one person to own. If it's a hotel then many people will get the opportunity to fall in love with it. But I want one last time there with my family around me.'

'You're planning to stay there too? Is that wise?' The island still teemed with journalists and photographers, all eagerly covering this most scandalous of royal relationships, and although that was exactly what Nico had hoped would happen it did mean Posy had no privacy and was followed everywhere she went.

'I think I'll be okay. It was built to keep out prying eyes, after all, and with my family, my sisters' partners, Javier's bodyguards and my own bodyguards I think I might be able to sleep soundly at night. The only thing is...'

'What is it?'

'If we were to go ahead and marry then the villa can be my engagement gift to you,' she said in a rush. 'I have nothing else suitable. I mean, what do you buy a man who has everything he needs?' The words shot through him piercing and cold. Everything he needed? Materially yes. Physically Nico knew he was blessed with good genes, a strong body, better than average brains. But everything? He'd put his research aside the day Alessandro died. And, he realised, there was no one who cared if he lived or died save what it meant to the island's succession. After all, his own mother hadn't seen him in two years.

'But if we don't you want compensating? That seems fair.'

'Thank you. I wouldn't ask but the villa is all I have.'

'You could sell your story. You'd make your fortune.'

She turned to face him then, eyes wide with indignation. 'I could *what*? I can't believe you would even *think* that I would do that to you.'

'You wouldn't be the first.' Nico could hear the bitterness coating his voice and forced himself to lighten up. 'Or even the second.'

He started as she laid a cool hand on his arm. 'Who?'

'It's probably easier to tell you who didn't,' he said,

keeping his voice light. 'There's quite a list, starting with the first girl I slept with, my first girlfriend at MIT, several of the girls I dated since. More than several.' The latter didn't matter. Once Nico had worked out that it was his name, his title that attracted the girls the later betrayal was inevitable. It was the first two that really had got him. He'd thought that they were real, that they saw beyond the image, beyond the Prince.

'Oh, don't look so horrified,' he said, glancing over with a grin. 'It goes with the territory. A family with my reputation is always in the headlines. Might as well make sure it's for the fun we had rather than the fun we didn't have. Why do you think we investigated you so thoroughly? Made sure there was nothing in your past to hurt you? The last thing you needed was the *I deflowered Princess Posy up against the ballet barre* headlines. Luckily your relationships were not only brief but you chose well. None of the gentlemen concerned are at all interested in speaking to the press.'

'It wasn't against the barre, thank you very much,' Posy protested and, as he'd intended, she stopped looking at him with soulful, sad eyes.

His relief was short-lived.

'Who was she?'

'Which one?'

'The first?'

'It was a long time ago,' he said, hoping she'd take the hint, but although he steadfastly refused to look at her and she didn't speak he could feel her gaze, compassionate and curious. He sighed. 'She was French, a friend of my cousin's on my mother's side. She was a couple of years older than me, a model, had acted in a couple of films in a semi-unclad love-interest way. I was sixteen. Obviously I was besotted. She went back to France, released a single and made sure she got all the publicity she needed.'

'What did your family say?'

'My grandfather called me a true Del Castro, my father mentioned he'd have liked to have known her better himself, my uncle told me I was a disgrace and a reprobate. All the women pretended it had never happened. A standard Del Castro scandal.'

'What did Alessandro say?'

Nico's chest tightened as the heaviness of grief descended once more. Even after two years it was never far away. 'That he was sorry this had happened to me.'

'Me too, although she sounds like a right cow and you were definitely better off without her.'

He couldn't help smiling at the indignation in Posy's voice. 'I know that now, I knew that when I was seventeen, but at sixteen? Then I thought my heart was broken.'

Not broken, just cracked a little. Then cracked again and once again until he'd simply hardened it so no betrayal could ever hurt him again.

'What about Alessandro?'

'What about him?' he asked warily.

'He was a Del Castro too. Did no one he ever dated or slept with sell their story? I mean, he was what? Thirty-one, thirty-two when he died and single? There must have been something scandalous.'

'No, not really.' He paused, inhaled and then said the words he had never said to another living soul. 'Alessandro fell in love when he was seventeen and as far as I know was completely faithful until the day he died.'

'He…he was? But why on earth wasn't he married? I

mean, if a complete commoner like me is an acceptable wife then surely…' She stopped and when he risked a quick look she was staring at him, comprehension on her face. 'It wasn't a she, was it?'

'Guido,' he confirmed. 'He's a Captain in the Guard. I'll introduce you. You'll like him.'

'Who knew?'

'Me. No one else as far as I know. Guido knew that if it got out he'd lose his job, Alessandro that the scandal might be too much even for L'Isola dei Fiori.'

'Scandal? I can see it might have caused a stir…'

'This isn't London, Posy. This is a small, religious, deeply conservative island. It's improving, becoming more tolerant but we don't yet have equal marriage— that's something I hope to change one day. So the chances of them accepting a gay king? Right now that's inconceivable.'

'What was he planning to do?'

'He was hoping to abdicate.'

'What was stopping him? I can see your uncle would have been upset but surely that was better than living a lie?'

'Me,' he said bleakly. 'I was stopping him. He knew how much I hated the duties and responsibilities that come with being a Del Castro, knew that the last thing I wanted was to be King. He kept steeling himself to break up with Guido, to marry and get an heir to let me off the succession hook but he always found a reason to put it off for another year. I knew how miserable he was at the thought of marriage but I never told him it was okay, never accepted my role as his heir.' His smile was tight. 'Ironic, isn't it? Here I am anyway and yet he never had that peace of mind. I never *gave* him that peace of mind. Now Guido mourns, unacknowledged and alone, and I'm Crown Prince anyway. Alessandro's sacrifice was for nothing.'

CHAPTER TEN

POSY SEARCHED FOR words of comfort and came up blank.
This was beyond her world, beyond her knowledge.
She'd been a guest at several gay weddings, attended
christenings for the offspring of same-sex parents; it
was easy to forget that not every couple, every person
had that acceptance, that in some families, in some
places, who you loved could still be considered a sin,
was still thought wrong.

'I'd love to meet Guido.' It was all she could think
of to say and it was nowhere near enough. Poor Alessandro, caught between duty and the man he loved—
and poor Nico, knowing that a word from him might
free his cousin and yet unable to utter it, to take on that
burden willingly.

'I'll organise dinner in a few nights' time.'

'Good.' She stared out at the scenery, heart aching.
In a few minutes they would pull up somewhere beautiful and hold hands, laugh, gaze soulfully at each other,
kiss…usually she quite enjoyed it. Nico was fun to be
with, attentive—and lovely to kiss. It wasn't exactly a
chore, more a perfectly choreographed performance.
But right now the thought of the pretence sickened her.
'Can we do something else?' She turned to him, not

even knowing what she was going to say until the words came out. 'Something you love? Something for us, not for the cameras?'

Something for us. She cringed inside as the words echoed through her brain in all their neediness but Nico didn't comment, just gave her a quick hard look then nodded.

Posy sat back and stared out at the scenery but, even though the sun reflected off the impossibly blue sea and a company of gannets rose high in the distance before plummeting deep into the watery depths, she barely noticed the wild beauty.

Nico had just shared something of himself with her.

Her stomach twisted and she turned to stare fixedly out of the window, hoping her face didn't betray her thoughts. She'd known him for just over a fortnight, plunged straight into this unnatural intimacy, all their spare time spent together, their nights.

Heat pooled deep down and her hands tightened their grip on her bag. Oh, dear God, the nights. Nothing in her admittedly limited experience had prepared her for those...

She'd only had a few brief relationships, unwilling to spend frivolously time that could be used to improve her dancing, and had met them all through work. She'd liked them well enough but once the first 'butterflies and speeded heart rate' stage had passed she'd had little incentive to keep the relationships going; and nice as the physical side had been it hadn't compared with the adrenaline rush of being on stage. *Nice.* Such a telling word. And nothing about this situation was nice.

It wasn't that Nico was ever anything but polite and attentive, because he was both of those things. It wasn't that she didn't feel attracted to him because—oh, my goodness—she really was. But polite and attraction weren't enough to stake her life on. Her future.

She'd agreed to the three months. Agreed to keep an open mind as to their future and she'd meant it. She had no other pressing options so why not see how a permanent role on L'Isola dei Fiori worked out? But open-minded or not she hadn't really—didn't really—expect that at the end of the three months she was going to say yes. Because that would be insane.

And that was an easy decision to make and keep to while Nico stayed being perfectly polite—even if just the thought of the sex made her toes curl and her throat close up. But when he opened up, revealed something personal, confided in her? Well, that shed a new light on everything, on him, on the darkness inside him, a light Posy desperately didn't want or need. Because she could survive this, she could walk away head high, as long as her heart was intact. But she was a mere novice at this game and too many conversations like the one they'd just had, too much intimacy? That would make things very difficult for her indeed.

'We're nearly there.'

'Great.' She grimaced as her voice came out more like a squeak than the casual, relaxed tone she'd been aiming for. She straightened and looked around. Nico had taken her inland, back into the national park although it wasn't a part she recognised, wooded and far nearer the mountains than the Villa Rosa. He pulled off the road and drove down the kind of unmade track that would be uncomfortable in a four-by-four but was teeth-rattling in a low sports car. Posy hung onto the door and gritted her teeth, blowing out a heartfelt sigh of relief when he finally pulled to a stop under some trees. They were in a car park of sorts, grassy and un-marked, but several other cars were parked there in an orderly fashion and a definite path led off from one side.

Posy opened her door cautiously, searching for a clue as to where they were or what they were there to do. Nico's whole demeanour seemed lighter, freer, as he swung himself out of the car, eyes lit up with excite-ment, more like the teasing, carefree man she'd met in the sea rather than the dutiful, honourable Prince. Her heart stuttered. 'Careful, Posy,' she muttered. That teas-ing, carefree man had led her into trouble once before…

The four-by-four that held her two bodyguards and Nico's own detail pulled into the car park behind them. It was funny how quickly she forgot to notice them, not even aware of their constant presence on their tail. Nico held up a hand to tell them to stay where they were and to her surprise they obeyed with no more remonstration than a sharp look. Obviously this was somewhere Nico came often. Somewhere considered safe.

'This way.' He paused only to lock the car before setting off at a pace down the grassy track. Posy had dressed with care for the day's visible date wandering through one of L'Isola dei Fiori's picturesque villages, purchasing some souvenirs from the wood carver and lunch in the village square, and so was wearing an or-ange silk skirt that flared out to her knees and a white, sleeveless, broderie anglaise blouse, block-heeled san-dals on her feet. Hardly an outfit for a woodland walk. She paused for a moment and then followed him. A ruined pair of shoes was a small price to pay for a day away from the cameras.

She was horribly aware that if she wanted to avoid

another opportunity to get to know the real Nico then the last thing she should be doing was playing hooky with him, asking him to choose something for them to do. But as she fell into step beside him, as her arm brushed his, as he gave her a quick grin she couldn't find it in herself to be sorry or to suggest they went back to the original plan. One day and then they would be back on schedule, back to playing their parts. What harm could one day do?

The track was in better shape than she'd expected, the grass mown down and the ground smooth under-foot. The trees on either side cast a much-appreciated shadow over her as she walked, relieving some of the oppressiveness of the hot late summer's day. The path curved away in front of them and as they followed it a clear blue lake came into view, a few small wooded islands breaking up the smooth water. It didn't seem to be a huge lake, less than half a mile across and an-other half a mile to one side; the other end was still out of view. It was very attractive, the edges ringed with golden beaches, the trees a green backdrop behind. 'Oh, how pretty. Almost too pretty to keep to ourselves. This is exactly the kind of place you want potential tour-ists to see.'

'We can come again with cameras,' Nico assured her. He shot her an amused glance. 'And appropriately dressed as well.'

Posy shook her skirt out with a flounce. She might not be in full on trek-proof walking gear but she was more than adequately dressed for a wander around a lake...

Or not. She came to a standstill as the rest of the lake and lakeside opened up before her, wider and longer than she had imagined—and instead of the quiet walkers' paradise she had been expecting the lake was filled with sails and crafts, from small sailboats only big enough for one to kayaks, paddleboards to windsurfs. Two long jetties jutted out, boats bobbing alongside attached by short ropes, and kayaks were pulled up high on the beach. A low, long building was positioned behind the jetties and behind that a larger car park, this one full of cars. Picnic tables were dotted all around the building and the smell of fried food wafted enticingly from a serving window, a queue snaking back several feet.

Nico turned with a grin of anticipation. He looked as if he'd come home. 'Like it?'

Posy stared. 'I guess. I mean, everyone looks like they're having fun.' She hadn't expected people, especially not so many of them.

'So, what do you fancy? Pick your ride.'

'Erm…what do you usually do?' she hedged.

'If I'm feeling lazy I might take out a paddle board, if I don't want to think I usually pick a sail boat because that keeps me pretty occupied and if there's some issues I need to work out I'll kayak. I belonged to a watersports club in Boston,' he clarified. 'I like climbing as well but this was right on the river, easy to do after I'd finished in the library so a great way to work out. In winter I skied, obviously.'

Obviously. How, in two weeks living at close quarters with him, had she not realised he was an adrenaline junkie? *Come on, Posy,* she scolded herself. He was skinny dipping the first time you saw him and even if you didn't expect to get caught he must have known full well there was a chance he'd be followed. Of course he's an adrenaline fiend.

'I don't ski. Or climb. Or do any of these things. I've always had to be careful of torn muscles or broken limbs.'

'But you must kayak. All those summers at Villa Rosa. That beach is perfect for water sports.'

She shook her head. 'Petrol head sisters, remember? If there was anything that needed steering, revving or manoeuvring then they were there first. At first I was too little to care and then I was too worried about muscles in the wrong places so I didn't mind sitting back while they rowed or steered. And since I joined the company it's not been an issue. I've not been near a lake or beach except to sunbathe or walk or have a sedate swim.'

'So what do you do to relax?'

She took a deep breath, the lead weight back in her stomach. 'I dance.'

The words hung there for a moment and then she added, 'But I'll need something else now, I guess, and I don't need to worry about developing the wrong muscles so what do you suggest?'

'A kayak,' he said promptly. 'Let's test your balance. And we can get a double so you don't go drifting off across the lake and need rescuing.'

'I admire your faith in me. The only thing is, I know these clothes were free but I still don't want to waste the designer's generosity by taking a silk skirt into the water.' Not to mention the certainty that her blouse would get see-through the second it was wet. Just because they hadn't arranged for a camera to be here didn't mean there wouldn't be any candid shots leaked and Posy was quite sure the world had seen quite enough of her nipples, thank you very much.

Nico nodded towards the shack. 'They have a shop. Go get yourself kitted out. I have an account.'

Twenty minutes later Posy had been kitted out in a bikini, which she wasn't entirely sure covered much more than the nothing she'd worn just over two weeks ago, a pair of tiny board shorts and a cropped T-shirt. If she'd been able to fit in them she would have preferred to choose from the men's baggier and lengthier range but the one T-shirt she'd tried had dwarfed her and the smallest shorts had slid right off. The appreciation in Nico's eyes went some way towards mitigating her feeling of exposure but not much.

'If I become Queen I am going to decree that everywhere should sell clothes that cover women properly,' she said, pulling the T-shirt down and realising she was either exposing her bare stomach or her cleavage but there was no way of hiding both.

Nico's eyes slid over her approvingly. 'I'll immediately rescind it,' he said. 'In fact all women should dress like this all the time.'

'Hardly practical. I've been here on the island in February before and it may not be London cold but it's chilly. Ugh, this is ridiculous, I feel like I'm dressed for a swimsuit-calendar photoshoot.' She tried tugging the shorts up and, when they still didn't budge over her hip bones, started stomping towards the beach, resisting the temptation to wrap her arms around her torso.

Nico watched her, obviously bemused. 'Posy, you're a dancer. I've seen pictures of you in outfits far scantier than that, flesh-coloured leotards, carnival costumes all glitter and sequins and nothing else. I agree it's wrong not to give women the choice to cover up and not everyone is comfortable in such clothes, but why are *you* so het up?'

It was a good question and Posy paused on her way down to the water, her newly acquired flip-flops uncomfortable on her feet. 'Maybe because all those leotards are just costumes. No one looks at me in those and sees my body as anything but an instrument. I was always proud of my body.' She looked down, at her taut stomach, muscles clearly defined, at her strong legs. 'I worked hard at it, to shape it, to make it move the way I needed it to. But that night, when they took those photos, it stopped being something I was proud of.' It had become something shameful instead. She gulped, barely able to say the words.

'I just don't want to be photographed like that again. Exposed like that again.'

She bit her lip and looked down again. She'd been angry, at first, and from there whirled into this ridiculous over-the-top life of fake courtships and language lessons and never having time to think or be alone. There hadn't been time to really process what had happened, time to admit how violated she felt even to herself. But as she stood here, in the ridiculously tiny shorts with an even tinier bikini underneath, the fear of being photographed like this, leered over, laughed at, judged, chilled her.

Nico stood stock-still then turned and went back into the shack. He was only gone a short while, a minute at most, before he emerged wearing one of the bright surf T-shirts, holding his short-sleeved shirt in his hand. 'Here,' he said, handing it to Posy. 'Wear this.'

The shirt was a little crumpled, warm from the sun

and his body heat, and as she drew it on she could smell his scent, the slightly salty, musky essence of him. It was large on her, baggy as she knotted it across her stomach. It was comforting. 'Thank you,' she said huskily.

It was a sweet, thoughtful gesture. Posy shivered. This day was proving to be full of surprises and every one pulled her in deeper than she'd had any intention of going.

'Here.' Nico broke into her thoughts as he tossed a life jacket over to her. 'This will cover you up even more nicely.'

She took the luminous orange bulky inflatable and shrugged into it, glad to have something to occupy her hands, a reason to bow her head so he couldn't see her face. 'Okay, Captain,' she said. 'I'm ready.'

If Posy hadn't been sitting in front of him, paddle clumsy in her uncertain hands, digging away at the water with more enthusiasm than skill, then Nico would have set out at top speed, pushing every muscle to the max as he forged through the water, burning every regret, every second thought away with sweat and searing muscles. Instead the pace was as sedate as a maiden aunt on an afternoon stroll, his attention focused on keeping the boat upright as Posy pushed it this way and that, squealing as she did so. 'Sorry!' 'Oops!' 'My bad!'

'I thought a ballerina would have perfect balance,' he said. Unable to resist teasing her.

'I have. It's this boat that's off...'

'Yeah, yeah. Blame the boat.'

He tried to concentrate on the stroke, on matching her efforts, but instead her earlier admission rang in his head, the picture of her downcast eyes as she'd practically whispered her words, the knowledge she no longer celebrated her beautiful, perfectly honed body but sought to hide it instead. The way she'd tugged at that ridiculous T-shirt as if somehow with sheer force of will she could make it bigger.

Before him she had loved her body, what it could do, how it made her feel. Now she was ashamed. And he'd had no idea.

The last couple of weeks had been such a whirlwind and she had slotted into the role assigned to her with such grace and ease it was easy to forget it wasn't a role she had applied for at all. She hadn't complained once, had shed no tears as far as he could see, had borne with good grace any off-colour remarks or questions thrown at her by the pursuing reporters. He'd had no idea she was struggling, that that night had left scars that were still all too raw.

He should have known. He knew what it was like to be vulnerable, exposed. And yet watching her pose for the cameras, the way she prettily flirted with him in public, the way she gave him space in private, the way she welcomed him into her bed—or on the sofa or floor—he'd had no idea she was hurting at all. He'd promised himself that no matter what he would be a good partner. Less than a month in and he was failing already.

But how could he have known? What was normal to him was impossible to anyone else and it was so easy to forget that he was the one whose life was off kilter. He lived in a family where divorce was impossible, admitting to your sexuality even more so. He lived in a family who thrived on affairs, on scandal, whose every move was examined in tabloids across the world. Those photographs for him had been annoying, sure, but more because of the timing, less the subject matter. He had already been exposed in public in every way possible. 'Sweet, enthusiastic but clumsy' his first girl-friend had dismissed his early love-making efforts as, for all the world to read. Five years later some nearly forgotten woman had upgraded him to 'blissful'. He'd barely noticed.

But Posy hadn't grown up in this world, in his world, and just because she hadn't made a fuss about the pho-tos evidently didn't mean they hadn't hit her hard. She might have made the first move that night on the beach but she had had no idea who he was, no idea of the risk she was taking, the risk he was letting her take. If she married him she'd harden; she would have to. The pro-cess had already begun. And he hated himself for the role he had played, was playing, in the painful process.

He pushed the thoughts away, upping the pace to Posy's evident surprise, guiding the kayak through the clear water towards the furthest island. 'That's it,' he told her. 'Keep it at that angle, let the paddle slide in, deeper than that. Well done, Posy, that's great.'

'It's harder than it looks,' she panted. 'Although we do seem to be going a little faster than everyone else.' She gave a longing look at the kayak they passed, the girl reclining in the front smiling up at the boy lazily paddling them sedately over the lake. 'Look, they're taking time to enjoy the view.'

'I thought you were fit.'

'I *am* fit, different muscles, that's all. Remind me to challenge you to a workout contest some time.' Nico wasn't sure he wanted to take her up on the offer, now when he could see the play of muscles in her back through the thin fabric of his shirt, the flex in her arms.

As he'd hoped, the furthest island was free of all habitation, most paddle boarders and kayaks preferring to explore the cluster of islands nearer the jetty, moving from one to another, while the sail boats tended to head to the other end of the lake. He swung himself out of the kayak, extending a hand to Posy before pushing the small boat up onto the small beach.

'Our very own island,' Posy said appreciatively as she waded in. 'Shall we build a modest hut and live off coconuts and fish?'

'We'd soon starve. This is barely a hundred metres wide. One dwelling and a few fires and we'd be out of trees. Plus I hate to break it to you but there's a distinct lack of coconuts.'

'No coconuts? What will we do?'

'Luckily I am a trained hunter gatherer.' Nico reached into the kayak and retrieved the bag he had stuffed in at his feet. 'My lady, a feast awaits.'

It was hardly palace standard. No blanket or chairs, just the grainy sand to sit on. Bottled water and a grilled panini apiece stuffed with mozzarella, grilled vegetables and pesto. A dish of olives. But sitting there, the sun beating down overhead, feet in the warm water, Posy by his side, Nico felt something he hadn't felt in a very long time. He thought the word might be content.

CHAPTER ELEVEN

'You need a cause.'

Posy peered up at Melissa, the private secretary she was sharing with the Dowager Queen, and tried not to yawn. Last night Nico had kept his word and introduced her to Guido, Alessandro's partner. Usually on the nights she didn't have to endure the formal dinners, she ate in her rooms, either alone or with Nico, still struggling to come to terms with the knowledge she could order anything she liked whenever she liked and it would be prepared and delivered to her. She'd had a couple of useful conversations with the head chef and as a result he made sure he always stocked her favourite ingredients, creating delicious salads full of wild salmon, avocado, quinoa and all the other foods she filled up on to keep her body at optimum strength and fitness.

Of course now she could binge on pizza three times a day but old habits held hard. She might not be in class for eight hours but she stretched religiously and spent at least an hour on the old familiar exercises on the makeshift barre, in the centre, on pointe. She didn't ask herself why, didn't want to examine her motives too clearly, but she knew deep inside she hadn't quite given up on her dreams no matter what she told herself.

Last night had been the first time she had set foot in Nico's rooms. A similar size and layout to hers, they were decorated in a stark white and dark wood style, the furniture almost aggressively modern with its sharp lines and lack of decoration. He'd ordered a selection of the small tapas dishes so popular on the island, taking their influences from the cuisine of all the larger nations that had colonised it over the years, so plates of grilled vegetables, arancini, bruschetta, cheeses and rich meaty stews had all jostled for attention on the large glass table. Posy had warmed to Guido immediately and they had stayed up long into the night, drinking the rich red wine so typical of the island and eating until all they could do was lie supine and groan. He was a good conversationalist with a huge knowledge of the island's myths and traditions and, although Posy knew how hard it must be for him, to have no formal recognition as Alessandro's partner, no way to mourn publicly, he showed no bitterness or anger.

'They say,' he'd told her, 'that anyone who kisses under Neptune's Arch on the beach under the Villa Rosa will be in love for ever. Alessandro and I would sneak away there sometimes. It was a risk, a crazy risk but it was his way of committing to me. I knew what I was getting into, that we could never really be together, but I know he loved me and he knew how I felt. In the end that's all that matters.'

Posy hadn't been able to look at Nico as Guido had talked. They had kissed under Neptune's Arch—under it, against it, a lot more than kiss. But it hadn't been love that lured them there. 'We used to watch couples sneak onto the beach when I was a kid,' she'd admitted. 'It was a tradition for newly engaged couples to come out to the arch by night and kiss there to bring good luck to their lives together. Sofia always knew but she never tried to stop them. She was a big believer in love.'

What would she say if she knew Posy was even contemplating tying herself into a loveless marriage? She'd be horrified. She'd preferred to live alone and in love than settle for any of her wealthy, adoring admirers.

'Miss Marlowe?' Melissa's sharp voice brought Posy back to the far too early morning and she blinked, taking a long sip of her coffee as she did so. 'Yes. A cause. What do you mean?'

'It's the September Ball in two weeks.'

Posy nodded, holding onto her temper as best she could. She knew it was the ball in two weeks; after all, Melissa only mentioned it one hundred times a day.

'Your engagement will be announced along with an honorary title...'

'Hang on.' Posy held a hand up. 'A what?'

'An honorary title. It's customary when a Del Castro marries a commoner...' she practically sniffed the last word '...that the said commoner is given a title until the wedding when they then assume their spouse's title. I believe you will become a Contessa.'

Posy swallowed a giggle. A *what*? 'Is that really necessary?' What would happen when she walked away? Would she get to keep the title, a unique souvenir of her engagement? She'd have to get a new passport; she'd bet that it would guarantee upgrades on every flight.

Melissa didn't see the joke. 'Yes. It's the custom. I told you.'

'Oh, well. If it's the custom.' Posy managed not to roll her eyes. There were many customs she was ignorant of and Melissa loved to enlighten her, whether it was the right way to wear her hair when she attended church in the royal pew or which pastry she should eat for breakfast on which saint's day.

'The King will announce your title and then you need to launch your cause, what you will be patron of. The Dowager Queen is patron of a literacy programme and the Queen a charity to alleviate child poverty on the island.'

Child poverty? Just a couple of the Queen's necklaces could probably solve that far better than a letterhead and a charity but Posy wasn't going to say that out loud. L'Isola dei Fiori was an island of contrasts, the two cities and many villages prosperous, as were many of the bigger farmers, but there were still far too many subsistence farmers eking out a meagre living from their small patches and the slum areas around the cities were as poor as any Posy had seen in places like Marseille or Naples. Nico was working hard to bring in the money to raise educational standards across the island and to introduce free health care but the old feudal systems were engrained and any change looked on with suspicion.

What on earth could Posy contribute—and what was the point if she wasn't staying?

'I'll think about it,' she said, but the doubts remained. She was twenty-four and all she knew was dance. She had no other skills.

The idea still preyed on her mind as she and Nico returned from a date adorably riding adorable horses against an adorable backdrop of rolling hills and the sea. Luckily Posy's horse was both adorable and placid and when Nico put a steadying hand on her bridle it looked more lover-like than restraining. Horse-riding was one

of the many things she had never learned to do for fear
of injury and using the wrong muscles. And yes, she
was enjoying these new outdoorsy skills, testing herself, her body. But, oh, how she missed the discipline
of the studio.

Nico had been less talkative since their kayaking trip.
It was as if having opened up once he was reluctant to
do so again. On one hand Posy appreciated his return
to polite and agreeable, it made her resolution not to
continue this charade past the promised three months
easier, but on the other it just reinforced how isolated
she was in the palace, the disapproving Melissa her most
constant companion. Guido could be a friend, but they
would have to be circumspect. She didn't want to inad-
vertently betray his secrets with too close a friendship.

Usually she filled the silences with chatter. It was
easier to talk inanely than to brood about her future and
the opportunities she'd missed in the past, but today she
couldn't put her lack of skills out of her mind. Obviously
she wouldn't be here to figurehead a cause so it was all
speculative anyway, but if she were here she wouldn't
want to just hold meetings and fundraise, she'd want
to be involved, properly hands-on. But how? What did
she have to contribute?

'You're very quiet.'

'I thought you might appreciate the peace.'

He glanced over at her. 'Don't stop on my account.
What's on your mind?'

Posy glared. 'Just because I'm quiet doesn't mean
there's anything wrong.'

The corners of his mouth quirked into a smile.
'Maybe not but as you managed to talk while kayaking, while horse-riding, you even manage to make con-

versation with my aunt, it is out of character for you to sit worrying in silence.'

'I'm not worrying exactly,' she said with as much dignity as she could manage. 'I'm just wondering what I'm good for. No, not that…' she scolded as his gaze automatically dropped to the vee in her dress. 'Eyes on the road, Your Royal Highness. I mean what could I be a patron of? I wouldn't want just a ceremonial title. If I'm to champion something I want to get stuck in.'

'Isn't it obvious? The arts.'

'Yes, but do you have any arts? I know there's folk dancing and folk songs, but beyond that? There's not even a theatre on the island, is there?'

'Not open. My great-grandfather—or was it my great-great-grandfather?—commissioned one. He was a great lover of the theatre—well, of actresses mainly, but it had the same result. But it closed down several years ago, longer maybe. It was mainly used by amateur groups and got too run down even for them.'

'Really? There's a theatre?' Posy was gripped by a homesickness so intense she clutched her stomach to try and stifle the pain. A stage, spotlights, curtains, wings. 'Can we visit it? Now?'

'Really? That's how you want to spend your first free afternoon in nearly three weeks?'

'Yes. Unless… You don't have to take me. You must have things you want to do. I'll see if one of the guards can, if that's okay, I mean. I won't be trespassing?'

'No, no, you won't be trespassing and, yes, I can take you. If that's what you really want to do.'

'It is,' Posy said, immeasurably cheered up by the prospect. 'I can't imagine anything else I'd rather do. I still don't see there's much scope to be a Patron of the

Arts here but I always think best on stage. Maybe it'll spark a bright idea.'

It didn't take too long to get there. The theatre was near the centre of the island's capital, San Rocco, on a side street in a vibrant bohemian neighbourhood filled with cafés and restaurants, not far from the university. The front was boarded up but it wasn't hard for Posy to see the potential in the building. It had been built along art nouveaux lines, the lobby a graceful, marble introduction to the small but perfectly formed auditorium beyond, complete with stalls, a dress circle, upper circle and balcony. The royal box wasn't to one side as was usual but in the very centre of the dress circle, all the better for Nico's ancestor to watch the actresses and dancers from.

Posy stepped inside the auditorium, staring around in wonder, and took in a deep breath, regretting it almost immediately; it was very dusty. 'Look at this,' she managed, despite the dryness in her throat. 'It's perfect.'

Nico raised a sceptical brow. 'You are easily pleased. Dingy and in need of disinfecting, I would say.'

'It's not dingy,' she protested. 'It's full of character.' Okay, the velvet on the seats was threadbare, the great stage curtains were moth-eaten, the glass on the chandeliers smeared and dim. But the bones of the theatre were there. It wouldn't take a huge amount to clean it up and repair it. Possibly.

There were wooden steps at the end leading up to the stage. Posy walked up them carefully, feeling with her foot for any sign of rot or damp, anything that would make the stage unsafe, but it felt completely sound. 'I agree it's a little shabby,' she called down to Nico, who stood at the back of the stalls, watching her. 'But there doesn't seem to be anything structurally wrong. What a shame it hasn't been used for so long, you'd think someone would have tried to restore it.'

'It relied on royal patronage and neither my grandfather nor uncle cared for the theatre. The amateur groups kept it going for a while but when it started to need more than TLC they gave up too.'

'Poor old lady,' Posy murmured, and could have sworn the theatre answered her back with a dignified sniff.

She wandered into the wings and inhaled. No one had been here for a long, long time and yet she could still smell it, smell the anticipation, the sweat, the excitement. How many girls had stood here, stomachs tumbling with nerves, before stepping out onto that stage? How many times had she stood in the wings, rosin on her shoes, smile ready on her face, waiting for that moment when she ran onto the stage, doing the only thing that made her feel alive? How had she walked away from that?

She flexed a foot, pointing it instinctively, the stage calling to her louder and more enticing than a siren's song. It needed to be used, trodden upon, brought back to life. Before she could remember all the reasons this was a bad idea she pulled her phone out of her pocket and selected a piece of music, slipping off her shoes as she did so. The music would reach no further than her ears, she would be dancing barefooted in a fifties-style sundress but she had no choice. There was a stage and Posy had to dance.

She'd come home. The instant Nico had wrestled the last lock off the side door and ushered Posy inside she had changed, every atom in her alert, vibrant, positively buzzing with happiness. She didn't see a lobby caked in dirt, dust and graffiti; she saw a stately, welcoming space. To her the bar wasn't chipped and stained but ready and waiting for patrons to stand and drink. The seats weren't rusty and sagging but in need of some TLC, the chipped and faded plasterwork easy to fix with a coat of paint. Her smile grew wider with each step, her eyes brighter. This dark, dusty, cavernous space lifted her, sent her spinning with joy.

Literally.

The faintest strains of music reached him as Posy set her phone on the stage, a violin's melancholy note. She stood, leg pointed, arms raised, perfectly and utterly still. And then as the music swelled, as much as music played tinnily through a phone's speaker could swell, she began to dance. Nico stood, immobilised, as if each movement she made wound a spell around him, and one blink, one step would break the magic. He'd seen her move before, her prayer-like exercises, the arabesque on the beach, but he'd never seen her here in her natural environment.

As she danced the magic spread. He could see the seats as they should be, plush red velvet and filled with excited people, the chandelier gleaming, the freshly painted cherubs above blowing golden trumpets for eternity. And Posy herself: it was as if there were two, the girl in the pink dress, barefooted, hair flowing down her back, and the ballerina with her tight bun and layers of white tulle.

Nico had spent a lot of time in various theatres in various capital cities, watching various plays, ballets and operas. He had probably seen Posy dance before, sitting in a hospitality box in Covent Garden, taking no notice of the dark-haired girl in the Corps de Ballet, so used to watching genius at work he barely appreciated it any more. But not one of the exquisite performances he had watched moved him the way this dance did. She was music brought to life, a lyrical poem in motion, dancing for herself, for this old, forgotten theatre, for the life she had left behind.

He just couldn't understand why she had left it. He had loved his research, the logic mixed with experimentation, and had felt a pang when he had left it behind for the drier but eminently more sensible MBA. He was still interested in the subject matter, still read widely, still planned to lure the right people to the university, for his legacy to his island to be a healthy economy and a reputation as a market leader in using and developing clean energy. But he didn't yearn for research the way Posy yearned to dance. He'd always had a full and varied life whereas she was totally dedicated; nothing else really mattered. And he was no connoisseur but it seemed to him that the girl in front of him was full of life, burning with passion, every movement so evocative of loss and yearning it almost hurt to watch.

'I'm sorry, that was indulgent of me.'

He realised with a shock the music had stopped and Posy was standing at the edge of the stage, looking out at him. 'No, it was beautiful. What was it?'

'Giselle. I've danced it many times but always as a *willi*, a spirit. Never the title role. I always wanted to and here was my chance. The peasant girl saving the life of her Prince. I never thought I'd live it rather than dance it.'

'Live it? You plan to save me from being danced to my death by the ghosts of scorned women?'

'Maybe. It depends if you deserve saving or not. I was thinking more of the peasant girl and the Prince part rather than the whole supernatural and betrayal bit.'

'That's a relief. Is that the part you wanted to dance most?'

'Or Juliet.' She laughed, a little self-consciously. 'I always liked the really tragic roles best. But yes, it's a dancer's dream, to go from shy girl to falling in love to the whole mad scene at the end of Act One and then the tragically noble Act Two with that gorgeous *pas de deux*…not that it matters. That's not my role any more, not my life.'

No. She was quite clear about that. The thing Nico couldn't understand was why. Why if she danced like that?

Nico had to get married; he knew that. He knew that compatibility and respect were the best he could hope for and in the last few weeks he had believed it could actually happen; that he could marry someone he could be content with. He hadn't been able to believe his luck that he'd stumbled on her, on the safe partner he needed. With Posy there would be no huge dramas, no cold wars. She was diligent and disciplined, realistic and hardworking. She'd led a narrow life but she was intelligent and a quick learner, an easy conversationalist, good with people. Everything on his 'how to be a good queen' wish list personified with the added bonus of a sweet sensuality that heated his blood.

She deserved more than he could offer. Deserved more than life in a gilded cage. Deserved to dance the roles she craved. Deserved a man who loved her for all those qualities he had listed, not one who merely esteemed her for them.

She deserved better than him.

'You're right…'

He jumped as she came up beside him, wondering for one moment if he had spoken his thoughts aloud. 'I usually am.'

'You're going to make an insufferable king. But in this instance I'll let you have it. I should choose the arts. I should try and get enough money to restore this theatre and get touring companies to come here. That would be great for tourism but I'd want discounted tickets for locals and performances for schools. At the same time I could champion dance, music and drama for people of all ages.'

'That sounds like a great idea.'

'I don't really know how to go about it,' she confessed. 'But I know plenty of people who do. Maybe this is what I'm meant to do. If I can't dance myself I could inspire others to, show people how important music and drama and dance are.'

It was perfect. A working theatre with performances by some of Europe's touring groups would do wonders for tourism, offer visitors the culture they would expect when visiting a capital city. At the same time Posy's idea tied into his own plans to raise the level of education on the island, including more opportunities for adults. And if she was thinking so far ahead she must be considering staying past the end of their three-month agreement. Which was exactly what he wanted. Wasn't it?

CHAPTER TWELVE

WHEN POSY HAD been little and unable to decide what to do her mother had always made her write a list. 'You know the right path somewhere deep inside,' she would say. 'Write a list of fors and againsts and the right path will appear.' And it always had. Posy hadn't needed a list for a long, long time, her path had been so straight-forward. Until it had suddenly twisted and the way she'd fled she'd chosen purely on instinct.

And look where instinct had brought her: away from her career, onto the front pages and about to get for-mally and possibly, probably, temporarily engaged to a man who didn't love her. Poised on the brink of, sur-really, and hilariously, becoming a *Contessa* before—even more surreally—a princess. One day a queen.

Maybe. If she decided that was what she wanted.

She definitely needed a list.

Okay. Points in favour of staying: she would have a purpose. The idea of taking over the theatre and intro-ducing an educational arts programme to L'Isola dei Fiori filled her with more excitement and hope than she would have believed possible a couple of months ago. She would be protected from the paparazzi, who cur-rently had her firmly in their sights. She could make a life with Nico, whom she liked, whom she was attracted to, who seemed to like her. Who needed her...

Posy closed her eyes. Needed her for *what*? To provide romantic photos and lure the tourists in? To act as a hostess? To provide him with heirs? None of that was something only she could do. Nico didn't need *her*, he needed a wife, any wife.

Okay. That was the first item on the 'against' list. What else? When she'd walked away she had thought she would probably never dance again but marrying Nico would ensure that actually happened. Had she really given up on her dream? She would live her whole life in the spotlight. Nico didn't love her...

Posy's stomach twisted. It wasn't as if she were actually looking for love, but neither had she consciously *not* been looking for it. She was only twenty-four. Was she ready to give up any chance of really falling for someone? Of someone really falling for her?

It was hard to imagine settling right now when she was surrounded by so much loved-upness it almost made her ill. Thanks to a sterling effort by some of the palace staff enough of the rooms in Villa Rosa were both clean and secure enough for her whole family to stay there and Posy had moved back in yesterday to welcome them to her home for the last time. It had been an emotional reunion, even though it wasn't that long since they'd last all gathered together here at the villa for Immi and Matt's engagement celebration barely two months before, but knowing it was the last time they would be able to call it their second home had provoked more than a few nostalgic tears.

'After all,' Miranda had said, hand in hand with her new husband, Cleve, 'the villa was a refuge when we needed it. It brought us love and happiness. It seems right to share that with others but it won't be the same. Not for us.'

It was as if they all had agreed to make the most of this last stay. The summer hadn't yet broken and so the family had spent the day swimming and sunbathing, wandering along the cliff tops and revisiting their favourite haunts in the villa for a nostalgic wallow.

The evening had drawn in and, after a feast sent over by the palace chefs, they were all relaxing in the sitting room separated into pairs, apart from Posy all alone in the love seat. She couldn't help a sad, wistful sigh for when they had been a family of six, not nine. It wasn't that she didn't like her sisters' various husbands and fiancés, she really did, it was just they were their own families now. Little complete units of two—soon to be three in Miranda's case. Everything had changed irrevocably. For her as much as any of them.

'Why so sad, Rosy-Posy?' Her parents were just as bad as her sisters, curled up together on the sofa, actually holding hands. At their age! This year out had brought them closer together than ever. Not that Posy was complaining. After several weeks of watching Nico's uncle and aunt ignore each other it was lovely to be back in her parents' all-encompassing loving circle.

'I'm not sad. I'm thinking.'

'That explains it, then.'

'Careful, Posy, you'll hurt your brain.'

Miranda and Imogen were sitting at opposite ends of the room, Andie lying next to Cleve as he absent-mindedly massaged her growing tummy, Immi and Matt cuddling up together on the window seat, but her twin sisters still managed to insult her in unison. Maybe nothing too much had changed after all.

The only person not to smile at their joint offensive was Portia, who looked penetratingly at Posy. The sole member of the family who knew the truth, she'd been trying to get Posy alone all day—and Posy had eluded her at every turn. She didn't know why; it should have been a relief to stop acting the happy bride-to-be for one moment, to stop laughing good-naturedly at all the Princess Posy jokes, to allow herself to drop her guard. But she was more than a little scared that if she stopped pretending even for a minute she wouldn't be able to carry on at all. And it was lovely seeing her parents so happy and proud, so relaxed, the last thing she wanted was to be the person to change that.

'Isn't Nico joining us?' Javier, Portia's handsome film-star husband, asked.

'Yes, when am I going to meet my future son-in-law?' her father chimed in. Posy had dreaded seeing her parents, knowing that they had seen the pictures of her and Nico, but they had fallen over themselves to reassure her of their support. Her father had made it clear that he blamed Nico entirely for the whole fiasco. Posy hadn't known whether to be relieved or not when Immi had loyally pointed out it was the photographer at fault, leading Portia to defend the freedom of the press, and the whole discussion had become a heated one about body shaming and double standards. Normally she would have loved to join in the debate but today she'd sat quietly, all too aware the body that had been shamed was hers.

'We're not actually officially engaged, Dad, and you'll meet him tomorrow,' she answered, feeling Portia's investigative gaze on her. 'Before the ball. I wanted you all to myself tonight.'

'What's he like?' her mother asked. 'You know him, don't you, Javier? Is he good enough for Posy?'

'You thought so when you introduced us,' Posy said meaningfully in case Javier had forgotten the story he and Nico had concocted.

Javier smiled at her reassuringly. 'I was a couple of years older than Nico when I lived here, so I didn't see much of him outside of lessons. I was always friendlier with Alessandro. Nico had a reputation as a wild boy, he hated the restrictions of the palace, but he's grown up to be a steady young man. He cares a great deal about L'Isola dei Fiori's future and how to ensure it thrives.'

'It's Posy's future I'm concerned with,' her father growled and Posy was overcome with a rush of love for her parents, who had always supported her, even when they didn't understand her. 'I hate that you've given up ballet, Posy. Why the rush to marry? Can't you wait a couple of years?'

'Nico needs to take on his duties here now, Daddy. He had a couple of years after Alessandro's death to take his MBA so he could help manage the economy with confidence, but he can't put off joining the government any longer. And I need to be with him, helping him. I'm looking at ways to make dance part of my life here.'

'That's all very well and good but what's he like as a person, not a prince? What do you love about him, Posy?' Since when had her sensible and capable mother got so romantic?

'Yes.' Miranda shifted with an audible huff, her hands automatically moving to cradle her stomach.

'Tell us about him. He must be pretty special to lure you away from the stage.'

Posy stared at her family, searching for the right words to convince them. 'Erm… Well. He's really handsome…'

The twins immediately made gagging noises and Posy threw a pillow in Imogen's direction, remembering in time that Miranda's pregnancy gave her immunity and contenting herself with glaring instead. 'He is. He's always winning Europe's Hottest Prince in *HRH Magazine*'s polls. His eyes are the darkest blue I've ever seen and when he smiles it's like you're the only person he sees…' Where had that come from? She shifted, picking up another cushion to cuddle and hide her embarrassment behind as her mother heaved a romantic sigh.

Better stop dwelling on his looks before she moved on to his shoulders and forearms and hands… 'He's clever. Properly clever. He was studying for a PhD in some kind of engineering and then switched to an MBA when Alessandro died. He loves being active. He finds it hard, palace life, because he really likes being outdoors pushing himself. Rock climbing and skiing and things like that.'

'Impressive CV, Posy, but beyond the hot body, action-man hobbies and big brains what's he really like? What made you fall for him?' Imogen laid a hand on Matt's knee and smiled up at him. 'Apart from the title, that is.'

Posy glared, needled by her sister's words. 'There's lots of things, actually. He has this absolutely huge sense of duty. I mean, people don't see that, they see the motorboats and the girls and the parties and the rest but he's always put the island first—that's why he switched to an MBA. He knew he couldn't govern the island without that kind of knowledge. He has such big plans. He wants to make L'Isola dei Fiori a tourist paradise while keeping the heart of it intact, to improve the health and education for everyone, to expand the university to make it a world leader in technology, especially renewables. And he's loyal. He doesn't let many people in but if he's on your side he'll defend you to the end, do anything to protect you.' As he was protecting her with the best weapon he had—his name. 'He's thoughtful and really kind. He carries the world on his shoulders but pretends it doesn't weigh anything. He's the best person I know and that's why I'm marrying him,' she finished defiantly.

There was a moment's silence. Posy's whole family were staring at her.

'I can't wait to meet him, darling,' her mother said at last and the others chimed in. All except Portia, whose expression was troubled.

Posy hugged the cushion tighter. Where had all that come from, that torrent of words? Of emotions? Worst of all she'd meant every word.

Did she feel like that because she had spent so much of the last few weeks with Nico? Was it simply Stockholm Syndrome? Or was it the sex twisting her brains and emotions with all those feel-good hormones?

Or was she actually falling for Nico? And if so what on earth was she going to do when he'd made it all too clear that emotions weren't part of their deal at all?

It should have been a relief, this small respite from looking after Posy. Nico had never appreciated before how difficult life in the palace could be for someone not bred for it. Not only did Posy not know her way around, not know the customs or etiquette, she didn't speak the language. Nor did she have any friends or acquaintances on the island. Oh, she had bodyguards, tutors, maids and the private secretary she still shared with his aunt, but otherwise she was completely dependent on him.

He had obviously anticipated spending some time with his chosen bride aside from the official 'dates'— he wanted his marriage to work as some kind of partnership, after all. He just hadn't expected to spend *this* much time, to find himself so responsible for another human being.

Nor had he expected to find it so easy.

Nico paced around his sitting room. Soon he would have to steel himself to move into the much larger suite traditionally lived in by the heir and his family. Alessandro had lived in all those rooms alone, never changing the décor chosen for him when he was twenty-one, décor that represented the man the palace wanted Alessandro to be, not the man he actually was. Nico intended to give Posy free rein to redecorate the rooms any way she saw fit, to give her one piece of this old, formal place that could really be hers. Would that be enough to keep her, a place of her own?

He turned and looked at his sitting room. He'd only been here a few weeks so it wasn't that surprising that, although it had been furnished with his own furniture, shipped over from Boston, he hadn't personalised any of his suite yet. There were no books on the dark wooden shelves, no pictures on the white walls. But then there hadn't been a great deal of personal stuff in the Boston apartment either and he'd lived there for five years. He had one photo of Alessandro, a candid shot of his cousin out on a boat, laughing as the spray hit him, on his desk but he displayed no pictures of his grandparents or his parents. No ex-girlfriend special enough to deserve a lasting place anywhere—no ex-girlfriend special enough to deserve a temporary place. He didn't buy art or ceramics or anything that showed his personal taste and all his books were textbooks, his magazines research journals and he read most of those electronically anyway.

By contrast Posy had already personalised her rooms with little more than a sprinkle of fairy dust. She'd arrived on the island with a backpack and a small hold-all and half of her things were still at the villa and yet photographs of her whole family—and a much-loved and deceased golden retriever—sat on her bedside table. Books and magazines were strewn across her coffee table and haphazardly piled onto her bookshelves. She had raided some of the unused rooms so that cushions were piled high on all seating and lamps cast warm glows from every nook. Her sewing basket sat on the floor, usually open with a pair of unfinished shoes on top—what she planned to do with all the darned pointe shoes once she'd worked her way through the box, he wasn't quite sure. She collected gifts and souvenirs everywhere they went and examples of the lacework, pottery and glass ornaments presented to her as they toured the island were proudly displayed on every available surface. She'd kept the vases filled with flowers and added glass bowls with pebbles and shells she'd collected, and scarves and throws decorated every chair. The main rooms of the various royal suites were large affairs, acting as sitting/dining rooms informally and private reception rooms more formally, big enough for small parties. They were grand, purposefully so, luxurious but not usually cosy. Somehow Posy had made hers so. Made herself a home even if it was temporary, something Nico had never really had.

He'd grown up here, son of the second son, a spare whose use was supposed to be temporary. No one wanted a spare to feel too much at home in a place where they had no real purpose, just a drain on the royal purse. He'd liked Boston a lot but that had never been home either, the city so busy, the winters so very cold and long. He'd always intended to return to L'Isola dei Fiori armed with a purpose, with a way to make his own life, one away from the palace. Then he might have thought about putting down roots, buying some art, a photograph or two. Maybe.

He'd never envisioned anyone else living with him. Never met anyone who might have persuaded him otherwise, anyone he could have trusted. Maybe he'd been looking in all the wrong places. Maybe it was easier to look in the wrong places and know he'd be disappointed than look elsewhere and risk actually being really hurt. Maybe.

Damn but it was quiet. He'd been looking forward to the peace but the quiet just seemed eerie, his bed too big, his rooms too stark, every meeting duller than the one before.

He was relieved when the shrill ringtone interrupted his introspective pacing and he was conscious of a lightening of mood when he saw Posy's name lit up on his phone's screen. Unwilling—or unable—to analyse why that might be, he snapped, far more curtly than he intended, 'Yes?'

'Oh, hi, Nico.' He'd thrown her, he could tell. 'Is this a bad time?'

'No.' He tried to soften his tone, aware that his irritation with her was completely irrational. Why did she have to be so damn reasonable? 'It's fine.'

'Oh, okay. It's good news. You know I emailed Bruno, my old ballet master, to see if he could put me in touch with some people to advise me on the best way to go about starting the Arts programme? Well, he's come here. For the ball. And he's brought some third-year students to perform as well. Isn't that amazing?'

'He's just turned up here with some students?'

'Well, no, not exactly. I mean, I invited him. They like to give the third years performing opportunities but it was such short notice and he's so busy, I didn't think for a moment he'd actually come.' Posy was breathless, the words tumbling out of her in her excitement. This man, Bruno, clearly meant a lot to her. Nico was conscious of a tension in his shoulders, his grip on his phone too tight. 'He knows everyone, from philanthropists to musicians, and does loads of educational work on the side. If he's willing to advise me then I'm so less likely to make mistakes.'

'That's great.' It was. Posy was clearly fired up about restoring the theatre, which meant she was likely to want to see the project through. Not that she actually needed to be married to him to accomplish that. 'Is there time for them to perform tonight? My aunt has spent a lot of time putting the timings together.' He had no idea why he was being so dampening, why Posy's news was sending out danger alerts when it all seemed so possible.

'She's delighted. I've never heard her sound so pleased. She actually called me Rosalind rather than Miss Marlowe, which is a major step forward, I reckon. There's loads of space in the ballroom, enough for an entire company, not just a quartet. I thought you'd be pleased.'

'I am. It's great, well done.' He tried to muster some enthusiasm into his voice, aware he was overdoing it and sounding more like a children's entertainer. 'Are you planning to show him the theatre tomorrow?'

'He has to get straight back to class so there isn't time. We're popping over there now and then straight back to the palace for rehearsals. There's just about time.'

'You're cutting it fine.' He glanced at his watch. Two p.m. 'The ball starts in six hours. Don't you have to get ready?' His mother and aunt usually started getting ready around lunchtime for the September Ball, massages and manicures, hairdressers and facials.

Posy laughed. 'There's six hours yet. It'll take me twenty minutes. Actually, make that forty if I have a quick shower. I'm used to dressing up, remember? That's why you've hired me.'

She was joking but her words twisted in his gut all the same. He had hired her, hired, bribed, persuaded—the word didn't matter—to do a job. And it was a huge job. She was only twenty-four, her whole life still ahead of her. Did she really want to limit herself to this narrow life on a small island? Was he really willing to allow her?

'Forty minutes? It'll take me longer than that.' He tried to inject some humour into the conversation. 'So you're heading to the theatre now?'

'That's why I'm calling. Do you want to meet us there, meet Bruno and explain some of the history of the theatre to him?'

'That sounds great but I can't, meetings, you know.'

'Of course, I should have thought. I'll see you later, at the reception. My family's looking forward to seeing you. I think they were hoping you'd have had time to make it over to the villa. I warned them how busy you are but they never listen to me, perils of being the youngest.'

Was that hurt he could detect in her voice? He had meant to visit the villa yesterday to welcome the Marlowes to the island—and to formally ask Mr Marlowe for Posy's hand, despite Posy's cross reminder that she was a grown woman and quite able to speak for herself. But he'd known how much Posy was looking forward to having all her family around her, to being just a Marlowe girl again, not a Prince's paramour or a tabloid sensation, and he hadn't been able to bring himself to intrude.

Plus he didn't know how to be part of a big, cosy family and he'd had enough of being the outsider. 'I'm sorry, it's been so busy.'

'No, it's fine, don't worry. I guess I'll see you at the reception.' There was a wistful question in her voice, which Nico ignored.

'See you then. Enjoy the theatre.'

He put the phone down and stared unseeingly at the white walls, the wistful sound in Posy's voice still echoing in his ears. He'd known her five weeks. Just five weeks. And already she needed more than he could give her; she'd probably deny it, even believe her own words, but he knew.

He just didn't know what he was going to do about it.

CHAPTER THIRTEEN

'I STILL CAN'T believe they were just left here to stand empty.' Bruno, the Ballet Company's irascible ballet master, stood, hands on hips, and looked disbelievingly at the studio. Posy had already toured him through the theatre itself and onto the stage before showing him the maze of backstage rooms she had discovered: offices, dressing rooms, rehearsal spaces and, best of all, two huge studios, barres and mirrors still in place, the floor perfectly sprung.

'They were filthy,' she said. 'But I had them cleaned up and I've been using them for exercises. It's not far from the palace and, although there's a gym there I can use, this floor is just so much better. The only problem is the temperature. It's still warm enough, just, but give it a few more weeks and it won't be any good for my muscles, far too cold. But there's so much to do here, fussing about heating in here feels silly.'

Bruno nodded. He didn't ask why a future princess, a girl who had given up dance, needed a professional studio at the right temperature and Posy knew she wouldn't have had an answer for him. Just as she didn't know why she had put all her energies over the last couple of weeks into cleaning up the studios rather than the offices or something else more practical. Why she darned so many shoes. Why she put herself through a class every day, even though there was no teacher, no other students, just the music and the comforting repetition of barre and centre work.

'So, I was thinking it seems a shame to waste this gorgeous space.'

His eyebrows snapped together. 'You want to set up a ballet company?'

'No.' She paused, momentarily seduced by the idea before dismissing it. 'No, L'Isola dei Fiori is far too small to sustain one, I think if we could attract some of the better touring companies we'll be doing well. Besides, a theatre like this needs variety: plays, operas, concerts. It's the only way to make it viable. No, I was thinking summer retreats for professional dancers and summer schools for children. It ties perfectly in with Nico's tourism idea—the whole family could come here for a holiday, drop aspiring ballet-mad child here for the day and they can go off and explore the island knowing they're leaving their child in expert hands.'

'Your hands? I always thought you'd make an excellent teacher.'

Ouch. It was a compliment but it stung harder than his harshest critique. What did they say? Those who could do…she'd always thought she could.

'No, not me. I won't be able to train or get the experience needed in time. To get the right kids—and the right fees—I'll need high-calibre teachers with workshops from some of the big names. Workshops from people like you, from some of the soloists, not just ours— yours—but from Paris, Rome, a really international school appealing to an international audience. Realistically we're more likely to attract Italian tourists, maybe Spanish and French, than people from the UK so we need to cater for that.'

'And this will fulfil you?' Bruno's eyes fixed on her, the exact same expression on his face as when he focused on a poorly turned-out foot. 'Organising summer schools, fundraising for the theatre, getting the arts into schools here? This is how you see your life now?'

Posy turned away so he couldn't see the yearning on her face. 'No one can dance for ever, Bruno. We all need a retirement plan. And you just said I'd make a good teacher. This is an extension of that.'

'One day you'll make a great teacher. Not now. You're twenty-four, Posy. You have your entire career before you. Don't you remember when you were in Year Three and I brought you to dance an exhibition, just like those children out there are doing?' He waved a hand in the direction of the other studio where the four young dancers were practising for the evening. 'That was… what? Five years ago? I promoted you and Daria straight into the Company that week. How can you walk away?'

Posy swallowed. She couldn't admit to him that she'd eavesdropped, overheard his damning words. He saw the Company as a whole, wouldn't understand her motives, would think she'd walked away because of a selfish need to shine. Right now, back in the studio, still sweating from the class he'd taught, she didn't understand her reasons either. 'Life has changed for me, Bruno.'

'Is he worth it? Your Prince?'

'I think so.' She pushed Nico's brusqueness earlier out of her mind. He must be stressed with the big announcement later, the prospect of meeting her entire family. She knew how he felt. Every time she thought of the all too public engagement announcement she felt nauseous, like stage nerves amplified one hundred times.

It didn't help that she hadn't slept last night, her mind a whirling mass of confused thoughts, all of them centred on Nico. On the things she'd said to her family about him. Trying to analyse her feelings until she was almost crying in frustration. One thing was all too clear: she was in too deep now to just walk away. Her life was more and more embedded here on the island. Maybe she should just accept the inevitable and admit she was planning to stay. That it made sense on many levels: she'd be protected; she'd have a purpose, a role she could really get excited about. The only real problem was Nico himself. Because if she *was* developing real feelings for him…

If? Funny how she still tried to fool herself. But how could she really admit there was no 'if' about it? Maybe it was a good thing he'd been so offhand earlier. She'd missed him so much, had been so relieved to hear his voice that she'd been on the verge of telling him she didn't need the three-month grace period, that she was in. That she had a purpose here—and she wasn't sure she could walk away from him either. No, she couldn't tell him the last part. Not yet. It wasn't part of their agreement, after all. One step at a time.

'So what are you dancing this evening? We have time for some coaching. You still represent us, Posy, whether you wish to or not.'

'Me?' She turned in surprise. 'I'm not…'

'Of course you are. You want to launch this scheme,

then you need to show why it's important. What will it be?'

Posy stood stock-still. For the last five years of her life she had wanted this man to single her out for a solo. And now he had it was the wrong time, the wrong place, the wrong reason and simply too damn late for her.

'I hadn't thought there would be any need to.'

'Well, think now. Quick, we don't have much time.'

There was only one real answer. 'Juliet?'

He nodded. 'Yes. Do you have the music?'

She always had the music. The studio didn't have a working sound system but she'd brought in some speakers and so she slotted in her phone and pulled her shoes out of her bag, glad that she'd joined in with the class Bruno had just conducted for his students. She was warmed up and supple, even if she had only been managing an hour, two hours tops, over the last few weeks rather than the eight hours she really needed to meet Bruno's standards.

She finished tying the ribbons on her pointe shoes, took a deep breath and took her position in the middle of the studio. She was Juliet, young, at a ball in her honour, her life before her. She could do this...

Nico froze. The studios had long viewing windows and so, from the dark, dingy passageway, he could see everything inside them both. In the first studio two serious-looking young men and two equally serious-looking young women were painstakingly going over and over a short routine. There was nothing glamorous about the loose buns, legwarmers and battered shoes; this was very clearly work.

As was the scene in the next studio. Posy was also

wearing a leotard. She had paired hers with a long wrap skirt, her hair bundled up so the nape of her neck, her shoulders were clearly visible. She looked delicate, like a wisp—or she would have done if it weren't for the play of muscles in her legs, her back. There was a lot of power in that slim build. She was listening intently to a whippet-thin man, probably in his early fifties, who gesticulated a lot as he talked, pausing to demonstrate a move, a pose. Nico froze when the man held Posy, manipulating her into place. *His* territory, his body whispered, *his*.

'Once more,' the man said. 'You're fourteen, remember? Filled with anticipation, with happiness. Now go...'

She nodded, took up a pose—and then as the music started she began to move. Nico had seen her dance before, on the beach and on the stage, but here she was in the studio, her natural element, up on the tips of her toes, the blunt edge of her shoes making her look as if she were floating, balancing on the merest edge and yet able to make it look effortless. He stayed stock-still, watching until she finally spun to a stop and held her pose. It looked so easy somehow and yet her skin shone with perspiration and her chest heaved with exertion. But she was grinning, clearly as exhilarated as he was after a long mountain-bike ride, after scaling a sheer rock face or riding the rapids. All things he could no longer do. Had she felt as caged as he, without her usual outlet? More so, he suspected. Dancing wasn't just her pastime; it was her entire life. She'd tried to explain but he'd never understood before.

Now he understood all too well.

'Yes, that's it,' the man said. 'I don't know what's happened to you, Posy. You're a little out of practice and your technique isn't quite as spot on as usual, all of which is to be expected after a break of a few weeks... but there's a quality to your dancing, Posy, a poignancy, a maturity I have never seen before. A fire.'

Posy hadn't moved but Nico could tell she was struggling to contain herself, to keep that poise she prized herself on. The poise he prized in her. The poise that made her such a perfect choice to be his bride. 'Thank you, Bruno. From you that means everything.'

Everything. Such telling words. Nico swallowed hard. His chest seemed to have petrified, his heart heavy within it. He hadn't felt this kind of physical emotional pain since, well, since he was sixteen and found himself a front-page laughing stock. Only that had been a deliberate betrayal. This wasn't a betrayal at all, just a realisation...

No. He'd known all along that Posy wasn't for the island. Wasn't for him. She'd played her part brilliantly, was prepared to carry on playing it.

The question was for how long—and how long would he let her?

Bruno's voice brought Nico back to the here and now. 'Look, Posy. I know you have left us but I meant it when I said the door was open for you to return at any time. I admit, I saw a role for you as *coryphée*, maybe as an assistant to me one day, but if you dance with the emotion I saw just now? Then there may be another role for you. No one knows yet but Isabella is pregnant. She'll be cutting down on her work soon and that leaves a space for a soloist. I don't see why that couldn't be you. Why you couldn't get that chance to prove yourself.'

Posy froze, her eyes wide with hope. 'A soloist? Me?'

'You should have been there years ago but somehow you never quite made that leap. Now may be your time. You're finally ready if you want it enough. I can keep that door open for you for three weeks at the very most but I'll need a decision by then. Earlier if possible. I'm sure your Prince is very nice but you can marry any time. You can't say the same about dance. Think about it.'

'I will.'

Just two words. But as she said them Nico realised with a physical pain that he hadn't managed to encase his heart in stone at all and somehow, without his even being aware, Posy had snuck in through his defences and lodged herself there. Which put him in the uncomfortable situation of doing the right thing.

Nico turned and walked away. He had some thinking to do but he already knew what his decision would be.

'Hello, stranger.' Posy turned and smiled shyly at Nico as he walked into her room. 'Are you ready for tonight?'

Nico's hand brushed his pocket, feeling the solid bulk of the two boxes he had concealed in there; the larger held a diamond necklace, begrudgingly unearthed from the vault by his aunt, who didn't see why, just because there was going to be a new Crown Princess, she should give up the heirlooms she had enjoyed for years—no matter that, as Queen, she had access to plenty more.

The other held a ring. Not an heirloom, a diamond flanked by two sapphires the colour of the sea. A ring he had bought himself, knowing it was perfect for her. All he had to do was give it to her.

The box was leather, lined with satin, and yet it weighed him down as if it were lead.

'As ready as I'll ever be. You look beautiful, like a prima ballerina.'

'Thank you. Luckily I had already chosen this dress so no costume changes needed.' She had opted for a simple cream gown, ballerina style, fitted to just below her breasts the skirt falling softly to mid-calf length. The cream was shot through with gold thread so she shimmered as she walked. She'd pulled her hair back, a heavy dark coil on top of her head, wrapped around with gold thread. Small cream and gold pins twisted in the shining mass.

'You're looking forward to dancing?'

'It's a dream come true. I know it's not a full-length ballet and I'm in the middle of the ballroom, not on a stage, but I'm finally dancing Juliet in front of an audience. Everything I've spent my life working for is happening right here. I'm equally thrilled and terrified but I'm ready for this. I've been ready for a long time.'

'Yes,' he said heavily. 'You deserve it.'

She turned then, concern on her face. 'Are you okay? You've been, I don't know, maybe a little preoccupied all day. Can I help?'

He took a deep breath. It was time. 'Posy, remember when you agreed to help me out?'

'Agreed to…you mean the relationship?' Her eyes were wary. She knew something was up.

'Yes. You agreed to three months before deciding either way. Time enough to showcase the island and to get the press to change the story. To give you time to work out whether you could live this life and figure out an alternative if not.'

'I did, but…'

'It's unfortunate that the September Ball is halfway

through that three months, unfortunate that my uncle wants our engagement announced tonight. An engagement is a bigger thing than a love affair, especially when it's an engagement to a Crown Prince. Ending a relationship is one thing but an engagement is quite another. It could cause quite a scandal, reignite interest in you.'

'I hadn't thought of that. You're probably right. But…'

'Remember what you said that afternoon, when I offered you a three-month trial and said you could walk away at the end? You said I could do the same, if I wanted to. You gave me the same get-out clause. Told me that if this wasn't right for me then I needed to let you know, that you wouldn't hold me to this engagement.'

Her eyes widened but she tilted her chin so she was looking right at him, as if she could see into the heart of him. But she couldn't; he'd made sure of that. 'Say the words, Nico.'

'I'm invoking that clause, Posy. I don't think we should get married and I won't be announcing our engagement tonight. You're free.'

'I see…' she said tonelessly. She was the same girl in the same dress but it was as if all the light had gone out of her.

'It's not you…'

She stepped back at that, colour high in her cheeks. 'You don't need to say it, Nico. This isn't some grand love affair—you don't have to worry about my feelings. Of course it's me. You don't care who you marry as long as she looks right and acts right and isn't as emotional as your mother or as cold as your aunt and needs nothing from you but is prepared to pretend she adores you and bears your children. Right? So I must be failing in one of those criteria, which means it is very much me.'

His hand fell to the ring box again. 'I thought you'd be relieved.'

'When my whole family is here expecting me to announce my engagement? The palace is full of people expecting it! I didn't used to care what people think but turns out, after being plastered over the front pages, I'm a little more sensitive than I realised. I don't want people to gossip about me any more.'

Of course. The only reason she'd agreed to this whole engagement was because of the gossip—that and because she had no idea what to do with her life. One of those things was solved; he would take care of the other. 'I'll tell your family we are taking things slowly, that although we're still secretly engaged, in light of your promotion at work we've decided not to make it public yet to give you time to return to London for a few months. I'll let my family know the same thing. We'll then announce your appointment as Patron of the Arts, starting with your intention to renovate the theatre and introduce a programme into schools—we'll make sure everyone goes away thinking that's the announcement planned for tonight.'

'So I won't be a Contessa after all? I can't say I'm sorry, although I was looking forward to being upgraded on flights.' She was trying to smile but her mouth trembled and Nico had to take a step back to stop himself from kissing her until she trembled for a whole other reason. 'Then what? I just walk away?'

If only it were that easy. He needed a clean break but he had to think of her and the best way to manage her exit strategy. Somehow it was easier if he coated it in business speak. 'I'm sorry but I think we need to carry on this charade for a while longer.' It took everything he had to keep looking her full in the face, to keep his voice casual, even a little bored. 'It would be great if you do actually take on the patron role for real. You have a platform now. It would be a shame to waste it. If you could come over a few times to work on that and the tourism project...'

'So that's what we're calling it now? You mean being photographed with you? Pretending we're together.'

'Yes, and I'll come to London. And then next spring we can issue a press release saying we've drifted apart. Perils of a long-distance relationship.'

'Meanwhile you've perused your grandmother's dossier and picked out the perfect bride.'

There was no sugar-coating his answer. 'Yes.'

'I see. You have it all worked out.'

'Posy. I am really grateful—'

'The villa,' she cut him off. 'You still need it, I suppose?'

'Can you afford to keep it?'

Her eyes glinted then, defiant. 'No, but Javier could without even noticing the cost. He loves it too. I could sell it to him.'

A wave of tiredness swept over Nico. That ridiculous pink villa. If he hadn't been drawn there, hadn't thought it would make the perfect hotel, then they wouldn't be standing here now, staring at each other over a newly opened chasm with no way across. And sure, he had been the one to shake the ground but it didn't make any of this easier. Not that Posy could suspect that. He knew her all too well. If she suspected for one moment he wasn't for real, if she had any idea that he...that he loved her, goddammit…then she would insist on staying, Throw her one chance away out of misguided loyalty and an overdeveloped sense of honour. Out of pity.

Would it make any difference if she did love him back? No. Giving up on a dream was an awful lot to ask of another human being. He would never be worth that kind of sacrifice.

'Do what you want. I'll give you fair market price.'

She sagged then, defeated, just for a moment but it was enough. 'Fine, have it. I'll talk to my solicitor.'

'Good. Posy, this is for the best. You're meant for the stage, for dance. You need to go back to London and shine, not spend your life here shouldering burdens that were never yours to shoulder.'

She straightened and turned away to gaze out of the window. 'You may be right. Nico, I need a moment. I'll meet you downstairs.'

It was his turn to pause before bowing and turning away, the ring box still weighing him down, taunting him with its forbidden promise. But he knew with utter certainty it was the right thing to do. Better end it now rather than in a couple of months when letting her go would hurt more and she'd lost her chance at the promotion. Better let her go now than marry her and watch her regret her choice more every passing day. He hadn't done the right thing for Alessandro and he regretted it every single day. Hated himself for being too selfish to free Alessandro to live his life. But he could free Posy. And maybe one day, when it stopped hurting, he'd know that he'd done a really noble thing for once in his life.

CHAPTER FOURTEEN

POSY STARED AT her hands and tried to formulate a co-
herent thought, a way of framing what had just happened, but the words slipped out of reach. Last night
she had come to a realisation, this morning a decision.
And sure, Bruno's offer had thrown her, seduced her
because she would always, *always* be a ballerina, but
the last few weeks had shown her the possibility of a
different kind of life. Not a normal life, sure, not a free
one, but a life with purpose.

It wasn't an easy life. She didn't like the stuffy traditions and frosty atmosphere and customs and bodyguards and the press following her everywhere she
went. But she liked it when Nico smiled with those
navy-blue eyes and she knew he had her back, when
he grazed her arm with the back of his hand and she
trembled with sheer lust. She liked it when he noticed
she was uncomfortable, whether she was trapped in a
dull conversation or out of her depth socially, and he
came to her rescue so smoothly no one noticed. She
still had his shirt, hidden in her wardrobe, crumpled
and unwashed, smelling of him, a reminder of when
he had understood her, protected her.

And it wasn't one-sided. He confided in her, relaxed

with her; she knew he let down some of his defences with her. She'd felt needed. More fool her.

Sure she'd missed dancing, was lost without the ritual of it, but the theatre was a way of combining old Posy and new Princess Rosalind and changing lives for the better. There was no denying she'd have liked her Odette/Odile moment first but she was ready to choose a new path.

But Nico didn't want her to. He wanted her to return to London with Bruno and take the promotion, and of course he was right but...

He wanted her to take the promotion.

She hadn't *mentioned* the promotion.

So how did he know?

The only other person who knew about the offer was Bruno and he was busy putting his hapless students through their paces until they were perfect—and even if Nico had bumped into Bruno she couldn't imagine Bruno saying anything. It simply wasn't his style.

But hadn't she asked Nico to come to the theatre? What if he had? What if he'd overheard her conversation with Bruno?

Or maybe she was delusional, clinging onto some ridiculous hope. He'd made it clear: her usefulness was at an end, her exit planned. And she would walk away with a promotion and money in her pocket. Things actually were going to work out for her. It almost seemed too good to be true...

Selling Villa Rosa would enable her to buy a small flat in London, the promotion would mean more money plus more teaching and sponsorship opportunities. She'd be a fool to not grab this chance with both hands. Who knew? Maybe in ten, twenty years' time she'd look back at this interlude with nostalgia, her few weeks of being an almost-princess. Maybe she'd see pictures of Nico in the papers and tell her children about her romance with a prince, her very own fairy tale.

Only this wasn't a fairy tale and Nico was no Prince Charming. She didn't love him because he was perfect—she loved him because he wasn't.

Posy turned and looked at the rooms; somehow they had come to feel like home. She still felt a little uncomfortable when she came in to find her bed made, her bathroom cleaned and her laundry miraculously done and she wasn't sure she'd ever get used to being tailed by two six-foot-something unsmiling men in dark suits, but she loved the old palace with its maze of corridors and twisty staircases. Her Italian was coming on and she only unknowingly ignored some archaic custom three times a day now, rather than ten or twenty.

And Nico was here.

Would he tell his perfect princess bride about Alessandro? Would he host small, intimate dinners with his bride and Guido where all etiquette was cast aside and they acted like the family they so very nearly were? Would he take his bride kayaking away from the bodyguards and onlookers, buy her a picnic to eat on the beach? Would he kiss her under Neptune's Arch until her knees buckled and she didn't even realise how itchy sand could be until the next day when her flesh ached for him?

No, he wouldn't. He wanted a bride he could keep at arm's length. She had got too close. Was that why he was running?

She folded her arms. 'Running never solves anything, Nico Del Castro.'

She'd run away once before and, if it hadn't been for Nico, she'd probably still be sitting in Villa Rosa staring out to sea and mourning her lost life. But Nico had made her see a world that existed outside class and discipline; he'd given her the new ingredients Bruno saw in her dancing. Life. Fire.

The truth was she'd been a coward. She saw that now. Too scared to confront her fears, her failure. If she'd just gone to Bruno in the first place maybe he'd have suggested a change of scenery anyway, helped her find a way to improve, and she could have spared herself all that heartache and uncertainty. But she'd been too lost, too heartbroken to risk opening up, to allow herself to be seen in all her vulnerability.

Not again.

No more regrets. She was going to tell Nico how she felt and if he didn't like it, didn't reciprocate, well, she'd lived through a broken heart before, she could do so again. But she wasn't going to just give up. Not this time. This time she was going to fight.

'You look ready for battle, Posy.'

Posy did her best to relax, unclenching her fists and remembering to smile, but she clearly wasn't fooling her family.

'I thought you were dancing Juliet, not Boudicca,' Immi teased.

'I'm just a little nervous.' She put on her most winning smile and beamed round at her family, who had been collected from Villa Rosa by palace drivers and were now gathered in one of the grand salons for an informal audience with Nico's family before the ball officially started. 'Don't you all scrub up nicely? Dad, you look so handsome in a tux.'

'I keep expecting someone to mistake me for a waiter,' her father confessed, pulling at his tie.

'If someone hands you a tray of canapés, then keep them,' Miranda told him. 'I'm starving. Will there be food later, Posy?'

'We already ate,' Immi reminded her twin, but Miranda just snorted.

'Hours ago so we could get ready for tonight and some of us are eating for two.'

'Don't worry, there are copious amounts of canapés and a whole room groaning with buffet food,' Posy assured her. 'The baby won't go hungry.'

She shifted, her nerves too tight to allow her to stay still. When could she get Nico alone? There were the family introductions to get through, after which they were heading straight to the September Ball, where Nico would be on the receiving line as a dutiful Crown Prince should, welcoming the island's great and good to the palace. Then, after the opening waltz they would announce her role as Patron of the Arts for the island and she would perform her solo, followed by Bruno's students. The chances of her speaking to Nico before midnight were slim but every second she didn't her fears and doubts grew. Was she just going to make a colossal fool of herself?

'It doesn't matter,' she reminded herself. 'It's time you learned to take a risk, remember?' But taking a risk was one thing, the slow build-up another, just like the agonising crawl up, up and up on a roller coaster, the eternal wait at the top of the loop with a sheer drop before you, knowing any moment now you were going to fall but with no idea when. Her stomach clenched with fear, her legs wobbled. She really needed to calm down somehow before she danced.

She wasn't sure how she made it through the next hour but despite her nerves it went surprisingly smoothly. Nico's mother had elected not to attend the ball so Posy was spared that particular introduction, and Javier's presence meant the usually haughty Queen was almost warm, unbending enough to make polite conversation with Posy's mother. The King, it turned out, had an interest in aviation and soon he and Posy's father were chatting away like old friends, joined by Cleve, Miranda and Imogen. The Dowager Queen had been frosty on introduction, obviously all too aware that these people knew and loved her greatest rival, but Portia used all her interviewing skills to break the ice and was soon entertaining the irascible old lady with outrageous titbits of Hollywood gossip.

Only Nico stood aloof, one hand on the ornate mantelpiece, looking more like a Regency hero than a real flesh and blood man, his features carved in stone, eyes set. Posy took a deep breath. They still had a job to do, people to fool, a relationship to fake. She walked over to him, smile steady and hands only a little shaky. 'I didn't imagine they would all get on so well.'

He didn't reply for a moment, the muscle in his cheek the only sign he was actually flesh and blood. 'Your family are lovely.'

'They have their moments,' she said thoughtlessly and winced. It was true they'd had their worries, her father's health this last year, Immi's troubles in her teen years, but they were still loving and supportive no matter what. Something Nico had never had. Something he was determined not to want, to need.

But no one could go through life alone.

Not even Nico.

You could say one thing about his timing: it totally sucked. Obviously he had had little choice. He needed Posy to accept the promotion as soon as possible, had to ensure his uncle didn't say anything about an engagement tonight, but playing the happy couple in such intimate surroundings, Posy's family clustered around them, was almost physically painful. The only thing he could do was turn off his feelings and detach himself from the whole situation.

Standing and watching the two families make their way through the stately dance of introductions, Nico felt more like an observer watching a play. Posy was coping better than he was—she was probably relieved the decision about her future had been made for her. She seemed a little nervy, her hands fluttering as she talked, her words a little fast, but that was to be expected. No doubt she was excited about her solo, about her future. Her freedom.

He'd have to keep an eye out, get tickets when she performed. Incognito, no royal box this time.

His uncle had frowned when Nico had informed him that they weren't planning to announce their engagement tonight and that Posy would be leaving L'Isola dei Fiori to take up her career once more, but had accepted the news with unexpected calm. 'I hope you haven't driven that girl away,' was all he'd said. 'She's far too good for you.'

'I know she is.' He'd left it at that. When his uncle

found out the engagement was never going to happen he'd have the satisfaction of telling Nico that he'd told him so. Who was Nico to deprive him of that?

That detached feeling continued through the early stages of the ball. He took his place in the line, grief stabbing him as he did so. This was Alessandro's place. As the spare, Nico had escaped the ordeal, using his time when he was younger to raid the buffet table, later on to chat up the prettier female guests. His parents, on the other hand, had always insisted on being included, needing that validation of their status. More fool them. An hour of shaking hands, remembering names and smiling at inanities left him with a headache and an urge for a strong drink. Instead he had to dance the first waltz. With Posy.

As she approached, shimmering in that dress, a goddess brought to earth, reality crashed back. His heart hammering, he took her hand, every nerve on fire where their flesh met. Her mouth was so soft, inviting, but not for him. Not any more.

But no one out there could suspect that they weren't in love, and so he made a sweeping bow, and allowed himself a teasing smile. 'My lady?'

Posy took his extended hand as she curtsied with her usual grace. 'My Lord.' She paused. 'You can waltz, can't you? I don't want to dance Juliet with a bruised foot.'

'Waltz, foxtrot and tango,' he assured her. 'Part of the essential princely toolkit.'

His uncle and aunt had taken their place in the centre of the ballroom floor, his grandmother allowing a bristled field marshal to lead her out. Custom dictated that the first few turns would be made by the royal family alone, the rest of the guests joining in afterwards. The ballroom glittered, every chandelier lit, the sparkling lights reflecting off a thousand diamonds and other precious stones, myriad sequins and crystals on the gorgeous, jewel-like dresses of the assembled guests. Champagne was served in crystal flutes, the black dinner jackets of the men the only sombre note—although many were wearing waistcoats as gorgeous as any of the ladies' dresses. The September Ball was a time for colour, for celebration, and the island was known for its bright fabrics.

Posy's hand was cool in his as he put an arm around her waist and drew her in close. He closed his eyes as he touched her supple curves, felt the heat of her through the thin fabric and inhaled her scent, a warm, spicy perfume. They had this one dance. He should make the most of it, a gift to himself, something to remember in the long years ahead.

'Are you having a nice time?' Oh, the inanity of that sentence. But what else could he say? I was wrong? Please don't go? Marry me, stay with me, love me. His jaw clenched.

'Not really.' Posy was still smiling, her voice low and intimate. For all the people watching them knew they were whispering love words to each other. They both knew how to play the game to perfection. At that moment the first chord swelled and the waltz began.

Neither spoke again. Nico knew he had been taught well and Posy was a dream to partner; she understood how to be led, how to respond, to follow his twists and turns with confidence and trust. The room fell away, the voices drowned out by the music until it was just the two of them in perfect time. Her hand in his, her breasts against his chest, hip to hip. It was all he could do not to pull her even closer, crush that soft mouth and claim her as his. Only his.

They should finish as they started. With a kiss. Only this time a goodbye kiss, a memory to keep him company through the years of duty and ritual that lay ahead.

Just one kiss…

The floor was filling up, laughing, smiling couples allowing themselves to be caught up in the romance of the moment. Nico navigated Posy around an elderly couple dancing in stately dignity and, without allowing himself to consider his actions, whisked her behind a curtain into a certain private alcove he had made good use of in years gone by, a low light and a small sofa making it the perfect secluded spot. They came to a stop, both breathing heavily, Posy's eyes glazed. 'What? Where? Why are we…?'

He didn't allow her to finish, couldn't allow her, pulling her closer as he had wanted to from the minute he'd seen her and kissing her with a force, a passion he hadn't allowed himself before. Not the teasing, gentle kisses or the carnal erotic embraces but pure want, pure need. A hard kiss, a punishing one, although who he wanted to punish he couldn't say. She froze for one moment and then her hands were around his neck, tangled in his hair, pulling him even closer.

'No…' She broke free, her hands pushing now so he staggered back, shocked.

What had he done?

'No,' Posy repeated. It couldn't be like this, not like this. Not anger and hurt and denial all mingling together. She had to tell him first, and then he could kiss her or walk away or take her right here against this wall; her knees buckled slightly and she put out a hand to steady herself.

His face whitened. 'I'm sorry. I shouldn't have. Forgive me.' He nodded, turned. And she knew if he went she would lose him for ever.

'No! Nico, don't go.' She grabbed his shoulder. 'Please. It wasn't that I didn't want you to kiss me. I did. I do. But there's something you need to know. I was going to say yes.'

He didn't move, his shoulders set, back rigid. 'I know. You have the chance to become a soloist. Congratulations, Posy, I know you'll be magnificent.'

'No,' she said again, feeling a little like a foolish parrot. 'I mean, yes, Bruno has asked me to return and offered me the opportunity to dance solo roles but I haven't answered him yet. I was going to say yes to you. To staying. To marrying you.'

He quivered then, a movement so slight that if she weren't so finely attuned to him she might have missed it. Slowly, slowly he turned back to face her. The alcove was small, almost oppressive, the thick velvet curtain shielding them from the ballroom. They were in a world of their own.

'Why? Bruno offered you everything you want. Everything you've worked for. Why throw that away?'

It was time. Posy took a deep breath, hands clenched, her nails biting into her palms. 'Not quite everything. He didn't offer me you.'

The silence stretched around them. Nico's gaze was intent on hers, his eyes darker than the sea at midnight. 'Me?'

'Three months ago all I wanted was a solo. I didn't want anyone or anything else. But then I met you.'

He didn't respond. She took a small step closer.

'I've never done anything like that before. That first night on the beach. I told myself it was because I was lonely—and I was—and lost. I was that too but that's not why. I did it because you were the most beautiful man I'd ever seen and I was so tired of being afraid, of not reaching out, of not living. And so I did, and the consequences were catastrophic. I embarrassed my family, your family, turned your life upside down. But you never blamed me. Didn't leave me to deal with the consequences I brought on myself. You were honourable and kind and protected me. Just like you protect the island and everyone on it. Putting yourself last.'

Another step. They were almost back in waltz position, barely a millimetre between them. 'I knew what you were offering, Nico, and it seemed fair. I didn't expect to fall in love with you. I've never been in love before, you see. But I did. I am. And that's why I was going to say yes and stay. I don't expect you to love me back. I know that's not the deal. But I needed you to know that. Before I leave. You're a good man, Nico. My heart is safe with you.'

His expression was shuttered. 'I'm not good or honourable. I let Alessandro down. I let you down. I should have swum away that night, not dragged you into this life.'

'No, no you didn't let me down and you certainly didn't let Alessandro down. Your cousin never expected you to give up your life and dreams for him. Talk to Guido—listen to him. Alessandro would never have abdicated even if you had offered to take over. He was always ready to do his duty no matter what the cost. As for me. You didn't let me down, you saved me.'

She scanned his face. Had she got through? Was he going to walk away, horrified by the emotion? She could barely breathe as he just looked at her.

And then he touched her. One fleeting caress, a hand on her cheek, his finger brushing her mouth. Her skin sizzled where he touched. 'That night I was facing up to the reality of my life here. I'd managed to bury it, the last two years, pouring everything into my MBA, not grieving Alessandro, not allowing myself to think about what being Crown Prince really entailed. And then I found myself back here with a diary full of engagements, an earful of admonishments from my uncle, a realisation that all control over my life had gone. I gave myself one last evening, away from my bodyguards, away from the palace. It was a farewell to my life. And then I saw you... I thought I had conjured you up, a naiad from beneath the waves.'

Posy smiled then, knowing her heart was in her eyes. 'I'm all too real.'

'Yes,' he said hoarsely. 'You are. And you're too good for me. I can't allow you to give up your dreams for me, Posy.'

'Nico, do you love me?'

She couldn't breathe while she waited for him to answer. And then he bowed his head so their foreheads touched, his hands light on her shoulders. 'Yes. I really do. Madly. So much I tried to let you go.'

Tears ran down Posy's cheeks; she hadn't even noticed her eyes filling, the lump in her throat. 'For an intelligent man, Nico Del Castro, you can be very stupid.'

'You're sure, Posy? It's a lot, this life of mine. As Crown Princess, as Queen, you'll always have to put

L'Isola dei Fiori first, never have a life that's truly your own. Can you cope with that?'

'If you're with me, then yes. I can cope with anything.'

He smiled then, suddenly younger, carefree, once more the dangerously sexy man on the beach. 'In that case, Posy Marlowe...' he reached into his pocket and brought out a small, dark blue leather box '...would you do me the very great honour of being my Princess, my future Queen, but, most importantly, my wife?'

EPILOGUE

Ten months later

'READY, POSY? HER father fiddled nervously with his collar. King Vincenzo had invested him with an honorary military title and he was uncomfortably wearing the uniform to match. Her parents had also been granted titles and were now the Conte and Contessa of Baia de Rose, to their slight embarrassment.

'Ready,' she confirmed, looking at herself in the mirror. This was the last time she would be simply Posy Marlowe. In an hour's time she would be Rosalind Del Castro, Crown Princess of L'Isola dei Fiori. She would be a wife. 'I don't think I can add anything else, do you?'

Her dress was probably a little more ornate than she would have personally chosen. She'd been aware that she needed to stand out in the old medieval cathedral, that her wedding wasn't a personal ceremony but a way of putting L'Isola dei Fiori on the map. Posy had decided on a sweetheart neckline, the skirt swelling out just a little, enough to give her some presence, the whole dress covered with delicate pearls. A lacy overdress covered her shoulders for the ceremony and then cascaded down her back and into a train long enough for her six bridesmaids to carry—and crucially she could remove it during the reception so she would be able to dance unencumbered. The Del Castro diamonds adorned her neck, earlobes and wrists and a magnificent tiara held her long veil in place.

'You look so beautiful,' her father told her. 'Even more beautiful than you looked in Giselle.'

Posy squeezed his hand. Nico had insisted that she went back to London for one last year to seize her opportunity to dance some solos and featured roles. A steady winter dancing bit parts had led to the opportunity to dance bigger roles over the spring and early summer, culminating in several matinee performances as the coveted lead including Giselle. She was leaving the stage behind with no regrets, no dreams left unfulfilled.

Ahead of her lay the excitement of introducing dance and drama to the island, into the schools and the newly restored theatre. Their engagement and wedding had pulled tourists to the island in their thousands and she knew she and Nico had an important role in ensuring that they returned and brought their friends and families with them. From next week the first few lucky guests would be staying at the luxuriously renovated Villa Rosa—but for the next few days the cliff-top house would be home to her and Nico alone. Their very own idyll. After all, it was thanks to her godmother's legacy that they had met on that moonlit night nearly one year ago...

'Okay then, let's do this.'

She turned and smiled at her sisters and mother. They were all in blue, the colour of the sea that had brought her Nico, her mother smart in a dress and matching jacket, a huge hat balanced on her head, her sisters in long straight gowns. Her other bridesmaids, including Daria, were already in the first of the three horse-drawn carriages that would convey her and her entourage to the cathedral.

Immi held a beautiful bouquet, but Miranda and Portia were holding bundles far more precious: Miranda's eight-month-old daughter, Daisy, in a gorgeous blue and white dress, ballet slippers on her chubby feet, while Portia cradled her tiny little girl. Just a few weeks old, Isabelle was maybe a little young to be a bridesmaid but there was no way Posy was leaving her newest niece out of the wedding party. Her father looked at his family, his heart in his eyes. For all he joked about being horribly outnumbered by the womenfolk, Posy knew he wouldn't have it any other way. Besides, as Immi pointed out, he wasn't alone any more with three—soon to be four—sons-in-law.

Immi was smiling softly at the babies. She and Matt had decided that they would give IVF a chance and she would be starting treatment soon. Posy hoped it would be successful, but she knew their relationship was strong enough to weather any storm and disappointment.

'We'd better get going,' Portia said a little gruffly, wiping away a tear. 'A bride doesn't get to be fashionably late when there's TV cameras involved.'

'Okay.' Posy embraced her mother and sisters one more time and then she allowed her father to hand her up into the open carriage. The journey passed like a dream, the waving and cheering crowds lining the streets a mirage, and soon she was standing at the back of the long cathedral aisle, her skirt shaken out and adjusted, her train in one perfect line, her father solemn as they began their procession to the altar—and to Nico.

Her heart turned as she saw him, grave and handsome in his own military uniform, the medals glittering on his chest. They were both so dressed up, more like characters in a film than real people. But as he caught her eye, as his own eyes widened in appreciation and a smile spread over his face, he winked. Just a small wink, a reminder that, at the end of the day, they were just two people who loved each other. And as Posy began to recite the vows that would make her his wife she knew that that was all that mattered.

* * * * *

If you loved this book, make sure you catch the rest of the SUMMER AT VILLA ROSA *quartet!*

HER PREGNANCY BOMBSHELL
by Liz Fielding
THE MYSTERIOUS ITALIAN HOUSEGUEST
by Scarlet Wilson
THE RUNAWAY BRIDE AND THE BILLIONAIRE
by Kate Hardy

Available now!

"I didn't file for divorce, Savannah. You did."

Bewildered, she stared into his eyes, seeming to be searching for answers. "I did? Why? Why would I do that?"

"We had a lot of problems we just couldn't seem to work out," he told her honestly.

Savannah covered her face with her hands. In a muffled voice, she said, "I just want to go home."

Bruce moved to her side; sitting on the edge of the bed, he pulled her hands down from her face and tugged her gently into his arms so he could comfort her in the only way he knew how. He ran his hand over the back of her hair, the way she always liked him to, and was relieved that instead of drawing away from him, Savannah leaned against him and rested her head on his shoulder.

"Come home to me, Savannah." Bruce hugged his wife, his eyes closed.

Savannah broke the embrace and studied his face, looked directly into his eyes again when she asked him, "Do you still love me?"

The cowboy answered firmly and without any hesitation, "Yes, beautiful. Yes, I do."

* * *

The Brands of Montana:
Wrangling their own happily-ever-afters

A WEDDING
TO REMEMBER

BY
JOANNA SIMS

MILLS &
BOON

First Published in Great Britain 2017
By Mills & Boon, an imprint of HarperCollins*Publishers*
1 London Bridge Street, London, SE1 9GF

© 2017 Joanna Sims

ISBN: 978-0-263-92328-5

23-0917

Our policy is to use papers that are natural, renewable and recyclable products and made from wood grown in sustainable forests. The logging and manufacturing processes conform to the legal environmental regulations of the country of origin.

Printed and bound in Spain
by CPI, Barcelona

Dedicated to my dear friend Madhu.
An exceptional woman
who recently rediscovered romance.
I love you.

Chapter One

"Hello?"

It was the middle of the night, but for the last week Bruce Brand had been sleeping lightly, waiting for any news from the hospital. Savannah, his soon-to-be-ex-wife, had been in a coma after a near-fatal car accident.

"She's awake." It was Carol, his mother-in-law, on the other end of the call.

Bruce tossed the covers off his body, sat up on the edge of the bed and dropped his head into the palm of his free hand. "Thank God. *Jesus*—thank God."

"She's been asking for you," Carol added after a pause.

Bruce lifted his head in surprise. "Asking for *me*?"

"Yes," Carol confirmed matter-of-factly. "Will you come?"

"I'm on my way."

Not thinking, just acting, Bruce stood up as he was ending the call. He grabbed his jeans, which were draped over a chair in the corner of the room, and tugged them on. With his jeans pulled up but still unzipped, he pushed the pillows off the chair, sat down and shoved his foot into his boot.

"What's going on?" Kerri, the woman he'd been dating for the last six months or so, flipped on the light.

"Savannah's awake." Bruce rose after his boots were on.

In the yellow glow of the lamp, the nipples of her full, naked breasts peeking through her wavy, sun-bleached blond hair, Kerri wore an expression of disappointment mixed with resignation on her pretty girl-next-door face.

"And she asked for you," Kerri stated in a monotone as she pulled the sheet up over her breasts and held it in place with her arms pinned to her sides.

Bruce didn't bother tucking in his T-shirt; he ran his fingers through the front of his silver-laced black hair several times to push it off his forehead before he put his cowboy hat on. He checked to make sure his wallet was in his back pocket, then grabbed the keys to his truck off the top of the dresser.

"I'm sorry. I have to go." When he leaned in to kiss her on the lips, she turned her head so her mouth was just out of reach.

Bruce straightened; he understood Kerri well enough to know that this was the beginning of a fight they were going to have later.

Kerri looked up at him, and he genuinely regretted the raw hurt he could easily read in her eyes.

"If this hadn't happened," Kerri reminded him, "you'd already be divorced."

She was right about that. He'd spent the last two years paying for his lawyer to fight with Savannah's lawyer. He'd received the final draft of the divorce agreement a couple of days before the accident. For now, the divorce was on hold. And, even though they hadn't lived as man and wife for years, legally he was Savannah's husband.

"She's still my wife," Bruce paused in the doorway to say. "I'll call when I can."

The night of Savannah's accident, and every day since, had felt more like a surreal dream sequence than reality. For the last week, when he wasn't working, he was with the Scott family, crammed into the small waiting room designated for families who had a loved one in the critical care unit. Truth be told, he'd never expected to speak to any of Savannah's kin again, much less spend several hours a day in a confined space with them drinking burnt coffee out of a Styrofoam cup and trying to make sense out of the sudden detour his life had just taken.

When he arrived at the hospital, the feeling in the waiting room had changed dramatically from somber to celebratory. Savannah's two sisters, Joy and Justine, were smiling with tears of relief and happiness drying on their faces. The peaches-and-cream color had returned to Carol's plump face, and John, Savannah's burly father, was actually smiling broadly enough so that the tips of his upper teeth, normally hidden from view behind his thick salt-and-pepper mustache and beard, were visible. But there was one person in the room who didn't seem to be happy at all.

"Hi, Carol." Bruce stopped next to Carol and the cowboy Savannah had been dating. He didn't offer his hand when he said, "Leroy."

Beside the fact that the cowpoke was dating his wife, Bruce had a hard time keeping his cool around Leroy. It was Leroy's high-powered muscle car that Savannah had been driving the night of the accident. Leroy had been in the passenger seat and had walked away from the accident with a broken wrist and a couple of scrapes and bruises, while Savannah had shattered the windshield with her skull.

Leroy had a stricken look on his narrow face. "She doesn't remember me."

Carol put her hand on Leroy's arm to comfort him. "She will, Leroy. The doctor said that it may take a couple of days. We just have to be patient and give her some time."

The cowpoke left with his head bent down, and it occurred to Bruce, for the first time, that Leroy was in love with Savannah.

"What's he talking about?" he asked Carol.

The Scott clan closed ranks and surrounded him as if they were worried he would try to escape.

Now Carol's hand was on his arm. "Savannah's neurologist thinks she may be experiencing some…temporary memory loss."

No one spoke for a second, but all of the Scotts were watching him like a cat watching fish in a fishbowl. "How temporary?"

"They don't know." John spoke directly to him for

the first time, instead of communicating through his wife and daughters as was his usual route.

"Bruce." Carol's fingers tightened on his arm. "Savannah doesn't seem to remember the divorce."

Until right then, Bruce hadn't felt like he needed to sit down. Now he did. Wordlessly, he took a couple of steps backward and settled in a nearby chair.

Savannah's family moved as one unit as they followed him, making loud scraping noises on the floor as they pulled chairs closer to him, boxing him in again. Bruce realized now that Savannah's tight-knit family wasn't trying to protect him—they were trying to make sure he didn't leave.

As much as his in-laws knew about Savannah's condition and potential recovery, they shared with him. Savannah was awake and talking; her speech was a little slurred, but she was making sense. But she had lost, at least temporarily, memory of the last several years. As far as Savannah was concerned, there was no divorce, they hadn't spent the last two years fighting through their lawyers and she had never moved out of their home. In her mind, they were still happily married. Now he understood why she had been asking for him. Savannah needed her husband.

Waking up from a coma had felt like swimming up to the surface from the bottom of a seemingly bottomless pool. Savannah had felt tingly all over right before the awareness of the throbbing, stabbing pain coming from the left side of her head along with the achiness and stiffness that she felt all over the rest of her body. She had been petrified, unable to understand why she was in a hospital hooked up to monitors with needles in her arms. She didn't have any memory of the accident; the last thing she could remember was kissing Bruce goodbye as he left to start his day on the Brand family ranch. Her husband, her one and only true love, was the first person she asked for when she had awakened from the coma. Savannah could count on Bruce to make everything okay for her. He always did. So, when she finally saw her husband walk through the doorway of her hospital room, Savannah reached out to him weakly, palm facing up, and the tears of confusion and terror she had been holding back began to flow unbidden.

"It's okay, Savannah." Bruce quickly dried her tears with a tissue. "I'm here now."

She tried to pull the full-face oxygen mask off, so she could talk to him, to tell him that she loved him, but he stilled her hand by taking it into his and holding on to it firmly.

"You have to get your strength back," Bruce told her.

The mask on her face made her feel claustrophobic, and she wanted to talk. Perhaps her memory was fuzzy about the events that had landed her in the hospital, but she had very distinct memories of her family and Bruce and nurses and doctors all talking around her when she was in the coma. She could hear them murmuring, but no matter how hard she tried to respond, she couldn't. Now that she could talk, she wanted to *talk*.

"I love you," she said, her words muffled by the mask.

Bruce looked at her with an expression she couldn't place. Why didn't he respond right away, as he always had before?

Finally, he squeezed her fingers gently, reassuringly. "I love you."

Behind the mask, her smile was frail, her eyelids slipping downward from exhaustion.

"I'd better let you get some rest." The sound of Bruce's voice made her fight to open her eyes.

When he tried to let go of her hand, she held on, moving her thumb over the empty spot where his wedding band should be.

"Ring?" Her voice was so raspy from having a trachea tube down her throat.

Again, an odd expression flashed in Bruce's sapphire-blue eyes as he glanced down at the ring finger of his left hand.

"It's at home."

"My...ring?"

"I have it," Bruce told her after he dropped a quick kiss on her forehead. "I have your wedding ring."

Retrograde amnesia secondary to traumatic brain injury and stroke. Bottom line, according to Savannah's neurologist: Savannah had lost large swaths of her memory. With time and patience, some, or even all, of her memories could return. Until then...

"What are you suggesting that I do, Carol?" Bruce asked his mother-in-law in a lowered voice. "Move her back to the ranch?"

"We've all tried to talk her into coming home with us, but she wants to be with her husband." Carol's eyes were wide with concern. "She wants to be with you."

Bruce held up his left hand to show Carol his wedding ring. "All she's been talking about for the last two days is getting back into her own bed."

Savannah had been moved to a regular hospital room soon after she had regained consciousness. Her appetite was healthy, she was laughing and talking. Her speech was still a little slurred from the dysarthria, her right hand was a little weak after the ministroke she had sustained, and of course, there was the memory loss. But even with all that, the doctors were getting ready to discharge her and continue with her care as an outpatient. Considering her near-death experience, Savannah was making a quick recovery.

"I know it. I know it." Carol's brows furrowed worriedly. "It's gonna break her sweet heart when she finds out the truth."

They had all hoped that Savannah's memory would return on its own; none of them, including him, wanted to be the one to bring her up to speed on her failed marriage. But her discharge date was barreling toward them with no sign that she had any inkling that they were a signature away from being divorced.

Carol seemed to have something on her mind that she had been skirting ever since he had arrived at the hospital. He had a feeling he knew exactly what his mother-in-law was thinking.

"Would it be such a horrible thing if Savannah moved back to Sugar Creek with you?" she asked him after a couple of silent moments.

Bruce knew it was only a matter of time before Carol asked this question. It was a question that had crossed his own mind a time or two. But it wasn't that simple. Savannah hadn't lived at the ranch with him for a long while. And although he hadn't changed much since she had left, she didn't have clothing or personal items at the ranch.

"Maybe this could be a second chance for the two of you," Carol added.

Carol had always wanted their marriage to work, and had always advocated for spending their attorneys' fees on more marriage counseling.

"You still love her. Even after all that's happened." His mother-in-law looked up into his face hopefully. "Don't you?"

"I'll always love her," he admitted because it was true. And even as angry as he had been with Savannah after all of the fighting and money wasted on attorneys fees, seeing her unconscious in critical care slammed home the truth for him: he still loved her.

Carol's eyes welled with tears. She put her hands on his arm. "And she loves you."

Savannah did love him. Again. It felt bizarre to walk into her hospital room and be greeted with that sweet, welcoming smile he'd first fallen in love with, her hazel-green eyes filled with love and her arms outstretched for a hug. In an odd twist of fate, Savannah was back to being the woman he had married. In an odd twist of fate, Savannah was back in his life.

"Now," Bruce reminded Carol. "She loves me now. What happens when her memory comes back and she remembers that she doesn't love me anymore?"

"I just want to *go home*," Savannah complained to her husband. "I'm so tired of being here. All night long, people are barging into my room, taking my blood pressure, pumping me full of fluids! How can they expect anyone to get better in this place if they won't let us sleep? I'm exhausted, and it's all *their* fault."

When Bruce arrived at the hospital after giving directions to his crew of cowboys at the ranch, Savannah was sitting up in a chair next to her bed.

"Can't you bust me out of this place? I want to sleep in my own bed, with my own pillows." His wife pointed to the small, rectangle pillow on the hospital bed. "*That* horrible thing is a brick disguised as a pillow."

Every time he came to see Savannah in the hospital, she said something that made him laugh. Perhaps that was one of the initial qualities he had liked about her the first time he'd really taken notice of her. She was funny—funnier than any female he'd ever known. And although they had gone to school together virtually all of their lives, they hadn't moved in the same cliques. Savannah had been on the honor roll and sang in the choir and was heavily involved with the school paper and the Beta Club for high achievers.

He'd been the captain of the football team, the popular kid, who happened to be going steady with Kerri Mahoney, the head of the cheerleading squad. He could barely remember seeing her in the halls at school when, as a junior at Montana University conducting research for a bachelor's thesis, Savannah came out to Sugar Creek Ranch looking to study the grazing patterns of their cows. He would never forget how she looked that day—so serious with her round-rimmed glasses, loaded down with an overstuffed computer bag, and the ivory skin of her face devoid of makeup. Savannah hadn't been the least bit interested in him. All of her focus was on his cattle. It had been a rare blow to his ego.

"Let's get you out of this room. Go for a walk."

With one hand, Savannah held on to the rolling stand that held her IV drip, and with the other hand, she held on to his arm. He had to cut his stride in half to make sure that he didn't push her to go faster than her body could handle.

"I feel a breeze on my left butt cheek," Savannah told him. "Take a peek back there for me, will you, and make sure my altogether is altogether covered."

Bruce smiled as he ducked his head back to check out her posterior parts. "You're good."

Halfway down the hall, the pallor of Savannah's oval face turned pasty-white. She swayed against him, and he wrapped his arm around her shoulders.

"Whoa—we've gone far enough for today."

She didn't put up a fight when he helped her make a U-turn so he could take her back to her room. He didn't want to wear her out completely; he still needed to have a serious talk with Savannah. Her doctors were ready to discharge her, and she was ready to leave. If she still wanted to go home to Sugar Creek after he told her the truth about the divorce, he was willing to take her back to the ranch with him. But she had to know the truth. It was her right to know.

He'd already discussed the best way to tell Savannah about the divorce with her doctors and her family. They all agreed that he could tell her privately, but that Carol and John would be on standby in case Savannah needed their emotional support. Bruce had never dreaded a conversation like he dreaded the one he was about to have with his wife. He didn't want to hurt her—even when he had been at his angriest with her, he'd never wanted to hurt her.

After he got her settled back in bed, and the nurses had taken her vital signs and administered medication, Bruce pulled a chair up next to Savannah. He took her hand in his, and it surprised him how easy it was to fall right back into the habit of holding her hand.

"What's bothering you?" Savannah asked him.

Bruce ran his finger over the diamond encrusted platinum wedding band that he had just recently slipped back onto her finger. Savannah didn't remember the day she had taken that ring off and put it on the kitchen counter before she left their home for good. That memory was burned into his brain. He only wished he could erase it. After she'd left, he'd held that ring in his hand for hours, plotting its demise. He thought to throw it away, crush it in the garbage disposal, flush it, melt it down or pawn it. But in the end, he'd thrown it into a dresser drawer, mostly forgotten, until the early-morning hour when Savannah asked about it.

"You've lost a lot of time, Savannah." Bruce started in the only way he knew how.

Fear, fleeting but undeniable, swept over her face. She was scared—scared about the memories she'd lost—and scared that they weren't going to come back.

"Once I get back to my own home, surrounded by all of the things that I love, I really think that it'll all come back." Savannah had an expectant look on her face. "Don't you?"

He wanted to reassure her, but he wasn't as optimistic. She'd lost so much in the accident—it was hard for him to believe that Savannah would ever be exactly as she once was.

"I'd like to think." Bruce tried to take the long way around.

"I just need to go home," she restated. "That's all. I just need to go home."

Still holding on to her hand, Bruce cleared his throat. "Well—that's what I'd like to talk to you about."

With her head resting on the pillow, her dark brown hair fanned out around her face, her eyes intent on him, Savannah waited for him to continue.

"There's a lot that's gone on between us, Savannah. A lot that you don't remember."

Savannah's fingers tightened around his fingers, that look of fear and discomfort back in her eyes. "You're scaring me."

He didn't want to scare her—and he told her as much.

"Just tell me what's on your mind, Bruce."

Her entreaty was faint and laced with uneasiness. Savannah had always been a "pull the Band-Aid off quick" kind of person. She didn't like to draw things out.

Bruce had spent the last two years fighting like cats and dogs with this woman, and now all he wanted to do was protect her from the pain they had willingly caused each other. He dropped his head for a moment and shook it. The only way out was forward.

"For the last couple of years, we've been going through a divorce," Bruce finally mustered the guts to tell her. The sound of her sharp intake of breath brought his eyes back to hers. The look in her eyes could only be described as stunned.

Savannah looked down at their hands, at their wedding rings. She swallowed several times, her eyes filling with unshed tears, before she asked, "You weren't wearing your ring. When I first saw you. You weren't wearing it. Are we even…married?"

He held on to her hand even though it seemed as

if she were already trying to pull it away. How many times had he wished for a second chance with Savannah? He hadn't wanted it this way—never this way—but he would be a fool to let her slip away from him a second time without putting up one heck of a fight.

"We're still married," he reassured her. It wasn't important, right at this moment, for Savannah to know just how close they had come to ending their marriage.

"I don't remember..." Savannah stopped midsentence, tears slipping unchecked onto her cheeks.

"It's going to be okay, Savannah." He felt impotent to console her. There weren't words that could make this right for her.

Savannah stared at him hard, with a look of distrust in her eyes. "How can you *say* that? We've split up, but it's going to be fine? Why would you want a divorce? What happened to us?"

When he didn't answer right away, she tugged her fingers loose from his hold.

"Tell me why."

How could he explain the last several years of their marriage in a sentence or two? There were things that they had all agreed that Savannah didn't need to know right now.

"I didn't file for divorce, Savannah. You did."

Bewildered, she stared into his eyes, seeming to be searching for answers. "I did? Why? Why would I do that?"

"We had a lot of problems we just couldn't seem to work out," he told her honestly.

Savannah covered her face with her hands. In a muffled voice, she said, "I just want to go home."

Bruce moved to her side; sitting on the edge of

the bed, he pulled her hands down from her face and tugged her gently into his arms so he could comfort her in the only way he knew how. He ran his hand over the back of her hair, the way she always liked him to do, and was relieved that, instead of drawing away from him, Savannah leaned against him and rested her head on his shoulder.

"Come home to me, Savannah." Bruce hugged his wife, his eyes closed.

Savannah broke the embrace and studied his face, looking directly into his eyes again when she asked him, "Do you still love me?"

The cowboy answered firmly and without any hesitation, "Yes, Beautiful. Yes, I do."

Chapter Two

"So, this is over." Kerri had been sitting across from him at her small kitchen table, not saying a word, arms crossed in front of her body.

Bruce sat stiffly in the chair opposite Kerri. He'd never felt truly comfortable at Kerri's table—the chairs were too small, the table too low. Today, he felt uncomfortable for a whole new set of reasons.

"I'm sorry." He apologized for the second time. His apology may have sounded hollow to Kerri's ears, but it was sincere. If he'd known that he had even a fraction of a shot of winning Savannah back, he'd never have rekindled his old high school romance with Kerri. He wasn't in the business of breaking hearts for the fun of it.

"You're sorry." Kerri made a little sarcastic laugh as

she looked out the kitchen window. "Well, that makes it all better then, doesn't it?"

Bruce stared at the woman he'd cared about for most of his life. Her forgiveness could be a long time coming.

Bruce stood up and grabbed his hat off the table. "I'd better go."

Kerri didn't look at him. She gave a small, annoyed shake of her head, but she refused to look at him even as he opened the door to leave.

"If you ever need me, I'm just a phone call away." Bruce paused in the entranceway, the door half-open.

Kerri hadn't said a word, hadn't looked his way once, and there were tears flowing freely onto her cheek.

"Take care of yourself," Bruce said before he ducked out of the door, choked up at the sight of Kerri's tears. He cared an awful lot about Kerri. He always had. But Savannah was his heart.

"Home!" Savannah exclaimed as she walked through the back door of the modest log cabin they had designed and built together. "I'm finally *home!*"

Bruce had never thought to hear those words come out of his wife's mouth again. He followed her into the mudroom, carrying in each hand two heavy suitcases packed by her family. They were greeted by three dogs, mutts all, tails wagging, barking excitedly. Savannah immediately fell to her knees and hugged the large dogs around their necks, calling two of the dogs by name, and laughing as the rescue mutts knocked her backward while fighting for the chance to lick her on the face.

Bruce dropped the suitcases with a loud thud so he could intervene. "Whoa, sit, boys!"

"I'm okay." Savannah reassured him, now sitting cross-legged on the wood floor, her arms still wrapped around Buckley's furry neck. "I've missed you guys so much!"

Savannah had never shied away from the dogs giving her a tongue bath on her face, not since the first day she had come out to Sugar Creek. Bruce decided to join in on the reunion instead of trying to control it. He rubbed Buckley between the ears, his favorite spot, while Savannah showed some individual love and attention to Murphy.

With a happy laugh, Savannah turned her attention to the dog he had rescued off the side of the road. "And who are you?"

"That's Hound Dog."

"It's nice to meet you, Hound Dog." His wife smiled at the tan-and-black dog with long floppy ears before she turned her eyes his way. "How long have we had him?"

Bruce stood up and held out his hand to help his wife onto her feet.

"I haven't had him for all that long. Six months, maybe. Found him on the side of I-90, dehydrated, half-starved. An infection in one of his paws so bad the vet thought we might have to amputate."

Bruce rubbed Hound Dog's head. "It shows you what a little love can do."

Savannah gazed up at him with an appreciative look in her eyes. She tucked her hand under his arm and leaned into his side. "You've never been able to ignore an animal in need."

Instinctively, his body tensed. Yes, he had become used to holding Savannah's hand in the hospital, and, yes, he still loved her. But he was having a difficult time accepting all of those little intimate touches that were a part of married life. It had been years since Savannah wanted to touch him; post-accident, Savannah seemed to want to touch him all the time, like she had when they were first married. It was unnerving.

Bruce tried not to be obvious when he took a step away from her. "Let's get you settled."

Once in the master bedroom, he hoisted the two suitcases, one at a time, onto their queen bed. Savannah had opened the door to the cedar-lined walk-in closet and strode inside. He found her standing in the center of the closet, quietly staring at all of the empty rods and shoe racks on what had been her side of the closet.

"Everything okay?"

The color had drained from her face; her arms were crossed tightly in front of her body. Her slender shoulders were slumped forward, and she seemed to be emotionally swallowed up much in the same way her torso was swallowed up by the sweatshirt she had insisted on wearing home. "I really left."

It was a statement, even though there was a question in her voice. She wanted to know what had happened—she wanted to know why she had left. But they had all agreed—her doctors, her family—that it would be better on Savannah to wait a couple of weeks before that subject was broached.

"Hey." Bruce wanted to distract her before she started to ask the next inevitable questions. "Why don't we tackle this later? I'm starved. How 'bout you?"

Savannah shrugged noncommittally. "If you're hungry, I'll try to eat."

Bruce held out his hand to his wife, palm facing up. After a moment, Savannah shut off the closet light and slipped her hand into his. At least for now, he had diverted her from the inevitable conversation about the reason behind their split. For now, he had his wife back.

Her first night out of the hospital was a strange mixture of joy, relief, confusion and discomfort. As much as Bruce tried to act "normal" around her, his body language didn't lie. He felt uncomfortable having her back in the home, and she knew it by the little nervous laugh he would make after trying to explain the changes in their home. At first glance, the house had seemed the same. But after the initial blast of relief subsided, Savannah started to notice little differences. She loved to collect refrigerator magnets, and all of her magnets were gone from the simple black refrigerator in their galley kitchen. Her favorite "chicken and egg" salt and pepper shakers she had picked up in a yard sale had been replaced with generic shakers from the grocery store. How could all of those little touches make such a big difference in the feel of the home? It was as if she had been deliberately erased.

For a moment, she closed her eyes, pushing back a wave of sadness. What a cruel trick, this head injury. She could remember the early part of their married lives together, but couldn't remember what led them to separate. She couldn't remember ever being apart from Bruce. It was so…unfair.

"D'you get enough to eat?" Bruce broke her train of thought.

Savannah opened her eyes and put her hand on the spot on the fireplace mantel where their mismatched compilation of family photos had once been kept. She nodded her head, not turning to face him. Suddenly, the excitement of being home and the realization, if not the actual memory, that she had left the home she had built and loved, struck her like another blow to her head. Her fingers tightened on the rough-hewn mantel that Bruce had crafted by hand; she felt herself sway and the room began to spin.

"Whoa!" She heard Bruce's deep voice, felt his large, warm hand on her elbow to steady her. "What happened?"

Savannah closed her eyes and swallowed back the feeling of nausea. "My head is killing me."

"We overdid it."

"Yes." Her response was weak, more from sadness than loss of strength.

Bruce put his arm around her shoulder for support. "Let's get you to bed."

She nodded her agreement. Bed was exactly what she needed. She wanted to snuggle down into her own bed, with her own mattress and pillows, and pull the comforter up over her head so she could shut the world out for a bit. Savannah left Bruce and the dogs in the bedroom while she got ready for bed in the bathroom. She had never shut the door on her husband before when she moved through her nightly routine, yet tonight felt different.

"Let me know if you need anything," Bruce told her through the closed door.

"Okay," she said after she spit toothpaste into the sink.

After she was done digging out her toiletries from her small carry-on bag, Savannah sat on the edge of the tub and stared at her reflection in the mirror. She tried to tuck her longish bangs behind her ear so she could lightly touch the large, rectangular bandage on her forehead. The right side of her face was still puffy with green-and-yellow bruising around her right eye and cheek. Small cuts and scratches on her nose and chin, already on their way to healing, had scabbed over. In her opinion, she looked like a hot mess, but not just because of the bruises and scratches and bandage. She didn't like her hair at all; sometime during the lost years, she had decided to go with bangs, blond streaks and layers. Three of her most hated hairstyle don'ts! What had possessed her to do that? It looked *awful*.

After a long inhale and exhale, Savannah pulled a face before she stood up cautiously and opened the bathroom door. In her favorite flannel long-sleeved pajamas, she faced the four males in her life. Buck and Hound Dog had already staked out their spots on the bed, while Murphy, the dog that had always favored her, was waiting patiently just on the other side of the bathroom threshold. Bruce was standing on the far side of the bed—her side of the bed—waiting for her. He seemed awkward and stiff to her, and there was a concerned look in his striking blue eyes.

She spoke to the concern she saw in his eyes as she bent down to pet Murphy on the head. "I'm okay. Just really tired."

Bruce had pulled the sheets and comforter back so she could easily slide into bed. As she walked by him, he held his body stiff and away from her. Her husband gave her a dose of her medicine, redressed the bandage on her head and then pulled the covers up to her chest after she lay back on the pillows.

"I haven't been tucked into bed since I was a kid," she mused, her eyes intent on Bruce's face.

"I won't do it anymore if it bothers you." Bruce switched off the light on the nightstand.

"No," she said faintly. "It makes me feel…"

Loved by you, cared for by you—

"Safe," she finished after a pause.

In the low light from the hallway, Savannah saw the smallest of smiles drift across Bruce's handsome face.

"Sleep well." He turned away from the bed.

Savannah had slipped her hand out from beneath the comforter to catch his hand.

"I love you." They had never gone to bed without telling each other that they loved each other—not that she could remember, anyway. It had been their promise to each other—never go to bed mad. Never go to bed without saying "I love you."

Bruce turned back to her, his eyes so intent on her face. After a squeeze of her fingers, Bruce replied, "I love you more."

After tucking Savannah into bed, Bruce went through the motions of cleaning up the kitchen, starting the dishwasher and letting the dogs out one last time. Normally, his three canine companions would stick to his side like glue, following him from room to room. Tonight was different. All three dogs opted to return to the bedroom, to get back into bed with Savannah. He'd felt so lonely after Savannah had left him, that he often found any reason not to be inside the house until he was ready to fall into bed. And he had counted on the dogs to fill some of the void left by his wife.

Now, sitting on the couch in the living room, the only light provided by the three-quarter moon glowing in the purple-black sky, Bruce felt more alone than ever. Having Savannah's energy back in the house, when he thought to never have it back, had been more of a shock to his system than he had expected. Even though it had felt like the heart had been hollowed out of the house, he supposed he had grown accustomed to it.

He hadn't discussed the sleeping arrangements with Savannah—he assumed that she understood that they wouldn't be sharing a bed. He'd turned the second bedroom into a storage room, so his only option was the couch. He had moved his necessary toiletries into the spare bathroom, and that was where he prepared for bed. Wearing only his gray boxer briefs, Bruce lay back on the couch, stuffing two of the couch pillows beneath his head. With a tired sigh, he pulled the blanket draped over the back of the sofa down over his torso. The blanket smelled strongly of wet dog; Bruce pushed the blanket down to cover his groin, and far enough away from his nose not to be distracted by the smell. He'd wash the blanket tomorrow.

Arm behind his head, the cowboy stared up at the vaulted ceiling of the log cabin, his mind racing with "what if" scenarios revolving around Savannah and her missing memories. It was a good long while before he could finally close his eyes and fall into a fitful sleep. But this sleep, as restless as it was, didn't last long. At first, he thought that he had dreamed the sound of dogs barking in the distance; it wasn't until he felt a dog licking him on the side of his face and mouth that he began to awaken.

"What?" Bruce asked Murphy as he sat up while at the same time wiping his hand over his mouth to clean away the dog's saliva.

Murphy disappeared back into the bedroom and joined the other two dogs barking. Bruce stood up, expecting to go tell the dogs to be quiet so they wouldn't awaken Savannah, but then his wife cried out, the words muffled by the barking.

"Savannah!" Bruce rushed to his wife's side.

"Can you hear me! Can you hear me!" Savannah was sitting up in bed, crying, her head in her hands. "*Why* can't you hear me!"

Bruce switched on the light near the bed, and guided the dogs away from Savannah so he could sit down next to her on the bed.

"Hey." He made her lift her head so he could see her face. She looked terrified, sweat mingled with tears on her flushed cheeks, her eyes wide.

Still crying, Savannah lurched forward and wrapped her arms around his body. "I was screaming and screaming and screaming and no one could hear me. Not you, not Mom, not Dad. *No one.*"

Bruce rested his head on the top of hers and let her cry it out on his shoulder. "You're safe, Savannah. It was just a bad dream."

After she took a couple of deep, steadying breaths, he leaned back so he could see her face. Bruce brushed the sweat-dampened hair off his wife's forehead, then held her face gently in his hands and wiped her tears away with his thumbs.   .

"Please, stop calling me Savannah," his wife said,

her face crumpling as if she were about to start crying again.

Savannah pulled back from him a little; he dropped
his hands from her face.

"You only call me Savannah when we fight," she
added when he didn't respond right away.

It was true—he called her "Beautiful." He had rarely
used her first name during their courtship and their
marriage. But for the last year, he'd called her Savannah exclusively.

"All right," he agreed. What else could he do but
agree?

Savannah went to the restroom while he went to
the kitchen to get her a glass of water. When he returned, his wife was back in bed surrounded by his
traitorous canines.

"Guys, you need to get down," Bruce said to the
dogs. Savannah barely had enough room to sleep.

"No," Savannah said quickly, almost dribbling her
sip of water. "I want them here."

At this moment, he would have granted Savannah
just about anything. He hated to see her cry—it broke
his heart when she cried.

He waited while Savannah finished the glass of
water; he took the empty glass. "Better?"

She nodded, pulling on a loose thread in the pattern
of the comforter. After a minute, she looked up at him.
"Where were you?"

Bruce was about to switch off the light again, but
straightened instead. He sent Savannah a questioning gaze.

"When I woke up, you weren't in bed." Her eyes

slid over to the undisturbed pillows and comforter on his side of the bed.

They hadn't discussed the sleeping arrangement—she hadn't brought it up and neither had he. Perhaps it was sheer cowardice that had stopped him from broaching the subject; he figured that Savannah would assume that he would be sharing their marital bed as usual. He'd known all along that he intended to sleep on the couch.

Bruce swallowed hard and pushed his hair back off his face. "I think I should sleep on the couch for a while."

Savannah couldn't hide the hurt she felt, and he closed his eyes for a split second to block out the pain he could see in her eyes before he continued. "I know this is hard for you, Savannah,"

She had dropped her eyes, but raised them when he used her first name.

"Beautiful," he corrected. "I'm sorry. I just need a minute to—" he paused, his forehead wrinkled with his own pain "—adjust."

They said good-night for the second time that night; the three dogs stayed faithfully with Savannah while he returned, alone, to the couch and the smelly blanket. If their first night was any indication of how difficult it was going to be to have Savannah back at Sugar Creek Ranch, it promised to be a tough row to hoe—for the both of them.

Chapter Three

"Well, where the hell is she?" Jock Brand demanded. "Why the hell didn't you bring her with you?"

Bruce arrived at Sugar Creek's traditional Sunday brunch without Savannah, much to the unabashed displeasure of his father.

As Jock's eldest of eight children from two marriages, Bruce had learned to ignore most of his father's bluster and salty language long ago. He leaned down to kiss his stepmother, Lilly, on her soft, light brown cheek, before taking his seat at the long formal dining table.

"I let her sleep in," Bruce told his father. "She needs the rest."

He didn't add that he didn't want Savannah to feel overwhelmed by his family right off the bat; Sunday brunch was the one time when they converged on the ranch. And when the talk turned to politics, as it often did, yelling and fist-banging on the table were as common a fare as eggs and bacon.

"A hearty breakfast and hard work," Jock countered loudly. "That's what she needs."

Jock never used an "indoor voice," and his answer for all things was a good breakfast followed by hard work. And Bruce had to acknowledge that his father led by that example. Jock wasn't a man known for his kindness or his forgiving nature, but he was known for throwing his back into every aspect of his life. Years of working in the harsh elements of Montana were carved into his narrow face by deep wrinkles fanning out from his eyes and crisscrossing his broad forehead. His nose was prominent, strong and slightly crooked, with a hump in the middle from a break that hadn't been set properly. His hair, thin and receding at the temples, had long since turned white, as had the bushy, unruly eyebrows framing the deeply set, sapphire-blue eyes. At one time, Jock's skin had been fair, but decades of work in the sun without any sun protection had given his leathery skin a brownish-ruddy hue.

"She needs her rest," Lilly said in her soft, steady voice as she poured coffee into the cup at Bruce's place setting.

Lilly was Jock's second wife, and the entire family still marveled at the match. Jock was loud and abrasive; Lilly was quiet and sweet. Jock believed in "spare the rod, spoil the child;" Lilly believed in the power of kind words and affection. Jock was a sworn atheist; Lilly, on the other hand, was a very spiritual woman with a deep connection to the land. A full-blooded Chippewa-Cree Native American raised on the Rocky Boy reservation, Lilly Hanging Cloud was an undeniable beauty—kind brown-black eyes, balanced, even features and prominent cheekbones. Her hair, always worn long and straight, was coal black with silver laced throughout. Yes, Lilly was his stepmother, but his memory of his own mother was so faint that Lilly was truly the only mother he'd ever known.

"Morning!" Jessie, Jock's only daughter and the youngest of the bunch, breezed into the dining room, her waist-length, pin-straight raven hair fluttering behind her. Their baby sister was sweet, but had been spoiled by all of them, including him. She had always been too adorable to scold, with her mother's striking features and her father's shocking blue eyes.

Now that Jessie was here, Jock's attention would turn to his favored child, and Bruce would be able to eat in peace for a moment or two.

"Hi, Daddy." Jessie leaned down and kissed their father's cheek; she was the only one of his eight children who got away with calling him "Daddy." All of the siblings, including him, called the patriarch of their family "Jock" or "sir."

Jessie then kissed her mother "good morning," plopped down in the chair next to him and bumped her shoulder into his. "Hi, dork."

Bruce wrapped his arm around his sister's shoulder, pulled her close for a moment and kissed the side of her head. "Mornin', brat."

A steady trickle of Brand siblings filled the empty seats at the enormous dining table. One of his full brothers, Liam, was the first to arrive, followed by their half brothers Colton and Hunter. Shane and Gabe, his other two full-blooded brothers, were missing from breakfast, as was his youngest half brother, Noah. Gabe, a long-distance trucker, was out of town, and no one expected Shane to show. Shane was honorably discharged from the army; diagnosed with PTSD, he was often missing from family events. Noah, a private first class in the Marine Corps, had been recently deployed to South Korea.

As the long dining table filled with his children, Jock presided over Sunday breakfast like a king over his court. Bruce was happy to drift into the background while his siblings dominated the conversation, each one louder than the other, trying as they always did to get the loudest and the last word on all subjects. They were a competitive bunch—but tight as family could be when push came to shove. When the conversation, as it often did, turned to politics, Bruce found his thoughts returning to his wife. The shock of her coming back to Sugar Creek Ranch hadn't worn off; he knew that she must feel the distance between them. He could read the pain in her eyes when he avoided touching her or stiffened when she innocently placed her hand over his. He wanted to open his heart to her again, but he couldn't. Not yet. The first time she'd walked out of his life and into the arms of another man, it had left him feeling like an empty eggshell—cracked, fragile and good for nothing. He had to protect his heart. What other choice did he have?

"Savannah!" his sister screamed over the din of voices.

Everyone at the table stopped talking and turned their attention to the entrance to the dining room.

Bruce had caught the expression on his sister's face, lit up with happy surprise, before he turned his head to look at the doorway to the dining room. Savannah, her slender body engulfed in one of his denim button-down shirts, was standing in the doorway appearing peaked and frail. She had an uncertainty in her body language, a nervousness in her half smile and forward-slumped shoulders that Bruce read right away. Savannah knew in her mind that she had been absent from Sunday breakfast for a long time; it would be normal to wonder about how the family would receive her. And she had some reason to be concerned—several of his siblings were still raw with Savannah and her lawyer, so they weren't ready to welcome her back to the fold with open arms. Their father had no such reservations.

"Daughter!" Jock bellowed as he thrust his seat back and out of his way so he could wrap a possessive, welcoming arm around Savannah's shoulders. Sugar Creek was Jock's ranch—if he said Savannah was welcome, she *was* welcome.

"Good morning, everyone," Savannah said with an unusually shy smile and a quieter than normal voice. She leaned into her father-in-law's embrace, but her eyes had sought out his.

Bruce had stood up at the same time as his father; it was instinctive, natural, to protect his wife—to stand between her and her critics in the room. Even if those critics were his own kin.

"You need something to eat," Lilly observed.

Before his wife could respond, Jock waved his hand over the table. "Everyone move. *Move!* I want Savannah to sit down right here next to me."

"No, don't do that…" Savannah tried to intervene, but Jock's will was the will of the family.

Everyone on the right side of the table, including

him, moved one seat down to make room for their father's most-favored daughter-in-law.

Bruce had gathered up his dishes, swapped them for a clean set and held the chair for his wife to sit down.

"Sorry." Savannah apologized to the table at large.

"Don't you go apologizing for nothing," Jock ordered gruffly. "It's been far too long since we've had you at this table."

The mood at the table changed; the conversation seemed stilted and stiff to Bruce, with his siblings focusing more on their food than talking. Savannah, who used to be a ray of sun shining on Sunday breakfast, had now become a bit of a spoiler. One by one, his brothers finished their meals and dispersed. Liam, his junior by only one year and always the peacemaker, made sure to say a kind word to Savannah, wishing her a speedy recovery, before he left. Jessie was the only sibling who seemed to have made a seamless pivot now that the divorce was on hold; she talked in a stream of consciousness, bouncing from one topic to another, seeming to want to catch Savannah up on the missing years in one sitting.

"Come up for air," Bruce told his sister. "She's not going anywhere."

Had he just spoken the truth? The truth from somewhere deep inside? Or was that hopeful thinking?

Instead of making a quick appearance at breakfast as he had planned, Bruce sat beside his wife while she ate two full helpings of scrambled eggs, a heaping scoop of cheese grits, a biscuit slathered with butter and honey, and drank a large glass of freshly squeezed orange juice. He'd never known her to be much of a breakfast person.

"I'm stuffed." Savannah groaned, her hands on her stomach.

"You sure you can't eat a few more spoonfuls of grits?" Bruce teased her. "I'd hate for those couple of bites to go to waste."

Savannah pushed her plate away and scrunched up her face distastefully. "I may not eat for the rest of the day."

"I haven't seen you eat that much in a day before," Bruce mused.

"A hearty breakfast is exactly what you needed." Jock gave a nod of approval.

Rosario, the house manager for years, and one of her subordinates, Donna, came into the dining room to begin clearing the table.

"Breakfast was good?" Rosario asked, her hand affectionately on Jock's shoulder, while Donna began to clear. Rosario had been with the family for decades, and the house manager had long since become more family than employee.

"It was damn good." Jock tossed his crumpled napkin onto his plate.

"I'm glad." The house manager's eyes crinkled deeply at the corner when she smiled. "It's good to see you at the table again, Miss Savannah."

Savannah placed her neatly folded napkin on top of her empty plate. "It's good to be seen, Rosario."

"We all missed you," Donna said as she reached around in front of Savannah to get her plate.

"Oh…" his wife said, and he could tell by the confused look in her eyes that the memory of Donna had been ripped away, like so many others, by the crash. "Thank you."

"I think I'd like to go home and rest now." Savannah put her hand on his arm.

Bruce gave her a nod of understanding; he said, as he pushed back his chair, "You outdid yourselves as usual, ladies."

Savannah gave Jock a hug and a kiss, said goodbye to everyone in the room, and then, arms crossed in front of her body, she walked into the grand, circular, three-story foyer.

"Hold up." Jock stood up so he could say what he intended to say in a lowered voice.

Bruce waited for his father's next words; the patriarch made a little motion near his mouth. "She sounds kinda funny when she talks. You gonna get that fixed?"

"It's in the works. We're just waiting for insurance to shuffle things around. I'm hoping to get her to therapy starting next week."

Jock gave a nod of understanding accompanied by a single pat on the shoulder.

Savannah was waiting for him on the wide porch that ran the length of the expansive main house. She was sitting on the top step of the wood stairs with their three canines gathered around her; she was staring out at the fields in the distance with the slow-moving herd of cows as they grazed in the early-afternoon sun.

Bruce knelt down so he could greet the dogs. "You all right?"

It took her a couple of seconds to nod "yes," but he didn't believe it. The breakfast had rattled her; being with his family had rattled her.

Her body was curled forward like a turtle shell; it seemed to him like she was trying to disappear into his shirt. Acting, not thinking, Bruce held out his hand to his wife.

"Come on," he said gently. "Let's get you back to bed."

Savannah had turned her head away from him; when she turned it back, there were tears clinging to her eyelashes. She lowered her head and wiped the tears on the sleeve of her borrowed shirt.

"I don't want to go back to bed," she finally said.

Bruce looked down into her face—a face he had both loved and resented. "What do you want to do, then?"

"I don't know." Savannah's eyes returned to the horizon, her arms locked around Hound Dog's thick neck for comfort. "Sunday was always *our* day."

Bruce stood up to full height and slid his hands into his front pockets. Sunday had always been their day—a day they reserved for their relationship. But that had been a long time ago.

"When's the last time we spent a Sunday together?" she asked him without looking at him.

With a frown, Bruce answered her honestly. "I can't remember the last time."

Savannah gave a little sad shake of her head. "For me, it was just last week."

Her husband had offered to stay with her—to reboot their Sunday tradition. But it felt forced to her, so she declined. Bruce had a list of chores he had planned for his Sunday, and she didn't want to keep him from his work. Murphy and Buckley followed behind her husband; Hound Dog stayed with her. Perhaps he sensed that she was new to the dog pack, like he was. She was grateful for the company, now that she was feeling, for the first time, like a stranger in her own home.

Her sisters had always been her solace, so she called her youngest sister, Joy, who had returned to Nashville, Tennessee where she was attending graduate school at Vanderbilt University.

"It was terrible," she recounted for her sister. "Everyone stopped talking when I walked in, half of his brothers looked at me like I'd grown devil horns and a tail—they *hate* me now—*and* I didn't recognize this lady, Donna, who works there who obviously knows me. I felt so nervous that I ate enough food to feed a small army…"

"I'm sorry, Savannah." Her sister, Joy, said in a sympathetic tone. "It's like a bad dream."

Savannah was standing by the picture window, watching Bruce unload wood from the back of his truck and carry it to his workshop.

"It *was* like a bad dream," she said of the breakfast. "Like that dream when you wake up late and you rush to work and everyone is staring at you like you're a freak, and then you realize that you're naked."

"I've never had that dream before."

"Well, I have. It's the worst." She sat down on the couch with Hound Dog faithfully parked at her feet.

Savannah sighed, noticing that her head was throbbing again. "I don't know, Joy. I didn't know it was going to be this way. I don't know what I was expecting…"

"For things to be normal."

She shrugged one shoulder. "Yeah. I guess so."

After a silent moment, her sister probed. "Do you

still think you're ready to find out why the marriage fell apart?"

Before she had left the hospital, she had argued with her family about just this topic. She had been so *certain* that she could handle anything that she found out about her marriage. But now? One awkward breakfast had made her feel so depressed, so disconnected from the Brand family. She used to be a favored sister to Bruce's brothers. Now, the way Gabe and Hunter had looked at her...

Joy added when her sister didn't respond right away, "If you want me to tell you what happened, Savannah, you know I will."

"No," Savannah said with a definitive shake of the head. "I'm not ready. Not yet."

She had sulked for a while after she had placed calls to both sisters and her mother. But then Savannah decided that moping wasn't her idea of making use of a beautiful Sunday. She found her way out to a patch of ground that was her kitchen garden; she loved to cook with fresh, homegrown vegetables picked right out of the garden. The garden was overgrown with layers of weeds; the pretty little white picket fence Bruce had built and painted as a surprise for her was dirty and unkempt. With her hands on her hips, Savannah shook her head. The fence, once her pride, was leaning in places; pickets were broken from animals and weather.

"What a mess."

The garden seemed to be a metaphor for her marriage. Would she ever get used to seeing things so changed, when in her mind, it was just yesterday when her life was perfect? Her marriage had been full of laughter and romance and lovemaking; she'd been a beloved member of Sugar Creek Ranch and her garden had been teeming with fresh veggies, ripe for the picking.

"How do you eat an elephant, Hound Dog?" she asked her companion.

She was going to clean up this garden, one weed at a time. Savannah found her toolshed virtually untouched; she pulled on her gloves, and retrieved hand tools and a sturdy hoe. Armed with her weapons to beat back the weeds and decay, she stepped into the garden, reclaimed the ground as her own, dropped to her knees and began to yank out the weeds. A couple of weeds into the process, sweat began to form on her forehead and on her neck. It felt good to sweat; it felt good to take out her frustration on these stupid, creeping weeds that had ruined her beautiful garden.

"What are you doing?"

Savannah had been deep in thought, focused on ripping as many weeds from the ground as possible; she hadn't heard her husband approach. She sat back on her heels and wiped the sweat from her brow before it rolled down into her eyes.

"Pulling weeds."

Bruce—to her, the most handsome man in the world—had his shirt unbuttoned and his stomach, chest and neck were covered in sweat. Normally—at least the normal she remembered—she would have stood up and wiped that sweat from his neck and chest with her hands, stealing a kiss along the way. It hadn't taken her long at all to figure out that this sexual flirtation wouldn't be welcome. Not long at all.

"You have a concussion, Savannah," he reminded her in a slightly condescending way.

She stared at him in response.

He added, a little less bossy, "The doctor said you needed to rest."

"*This is* how I rest," Savannah argued. She turned back to her weeds. "If I go to bed now, I'll be awake all night. You know that's true."

Silence stretched out between them, and then she heard him walk away. She didn't glance behind her to watch him; she focused on the blasted weeds instead. She hadn't expected him to join her—they didn't spend Sundays together anymore. And yet, he did return. Wordlessly, Bruce came back to the garden with Buckley and Murphy following at his heels. He knelt down in the dirt and began to pull out the weeds in the second row.

They worked like that silently, side by side, until they had completely cleared the first two rows of her garden of the layers of overgrowth. Bruce stood up and then offered his hand to her, which she accepted. Toward the end of the row, she was beginning to feel exhausted and woozy. But she was determined to finish at least one row before she gave in to her body.

"Well," Savannah said, more to herself than to Bruce. "It's a start."

Bruce was staring at her face with an inscrutable expression in his slightly narrowed, bright blue eyes. "Yes," he agreed after a moment. "I suppose it is."

Chapter Four

During the first week that Savannah was back at the ranch, Bruce watched her slowly, day by day, reclaim their log cabin as her own. She had unearthed their framed wedding pictures in one of the drawers in the living room and put them back in their original spot on the fireplace mantel. One of her antique bud vases, a least favorite that she had left behind, was back on the kitchen windowsill with a sprig of wildflowers soaking in the morning sun. The more his wife settled back into their marital home, the more accustomed to sharing the space Bruce became.

He was becoming accustomed to having Savannah's toothbrush, face creams, perfumes and deodorant on the bathroom counter next to his small array of toiletries; he was becoming accustomed to the sound of music playing when he arrived home. It was good to have music back in the house.

"Smells good in here." Bruce hung his cowboy hat on the hook inside of the door.

Today his wife was in the mood for Fleetwood Mac.

Savannah appeared from the kitchen, surprised by his early arrival.

"I wasn't expecting you until later," she said with a small smile, wiping her hands on a dish towel.

Bruce walked the whole way to her side; he had been trying to open up more to Savannah. She had, understandably, pulled away from him once she began to live the truth of their separation, even when her brain wouldn't remember. So they stood, rather awkwardly, a foot apart, without kissing each other in greeting as they always had.

"I decided to knock off a little early today." He leaned down to pet Hound Dog, who was now glued to Savannah's side.

She nodded wordlessly, her smile not completely reaching her eyes.

"What's cooking?"

Now her smile widened. "Guess!"

Bruce played along, looking upward in thought. "It's not… Buffalo Pockets?"

Beef, assorted vegetables and seasonings baked in foil pockets. One of his favorite meals—easy, hardy, but so damn good.

"I wanted to say thank-you—for helping me with the garden." Savannah turned to walk back to the kitchen.

Hound Dog left him and followed behind her.

He wasn't sure how to respond. How many times had he looked out at that garden feeling guilty about letting the elements and the wild animals have their way with it? Savannah had loved that garden, and it was one way, a petty way, to strike back at her.

"I'm gonna clean up," Bruce told her. "For dinner."

On the way into the bedroom, the bedroom he hadn't slept in since Savannah's return, he picked up a pair of socks and a pair of boots—she had never been able to get her clothes in the hamper or her shoes back in the closet. She often just left her clothes where she stripped out of them; it had always annoyed him, and perhaps it still did, but not with the same force as before. How many times had he missed her jeans on the floor after she left? Many times.

What Savannah lacked in housekeeping motivation, she made up for tenfold when it came to cooking. Man, had he missed his wife's cooking, and he told her so.

The good smells emanating from the kitchen had gotten him to speed up his shower, get dressed quick, so he could take his seat at their kitchen table. While Savannah had been gone, this table had been used as a catchall for the mail and any junk he accumulated in his pockets during his workday.

"I love cooking for you." Savannah smiled at him sweetly as she collected his empty plate.

"That was one hell of a good meal, Beautiful." He leaned back, feeling stuffed after two heaping servings. Bruce had been subsisting on frozen meals for a year. Yes, he could have had dinner at the main house, but his father's loud and consistent disapproval over his divorce had deterred him pretty quickly.

"I hope you left some room for dessert," Savannah said as she carried their dishes the short distance to the kitchen. "Lilly and I stopped off at the bakery on the way home."

Bruce followed her to the kitchen, his hands full with as many items as he could carry. Jock had never once helped wife one or wife two in the kitchen, but Bruce had always considered it to be part of marriage. It had always been those little things, like Savannah cooking while he did the dishes, that had made him want to be a married man. And for a while there, he had managed to have a perfect marriage, to the perfect woman for him. For a while there, he had managed to marry his best friend.

"All I have to do is pop them in the oven." Savannah held up a plate of raspberry chocolate turnovers, freshly made from his favorite bakery.

Bruce filled the sink with water and soap and set the dishes in the hot, sudsy water to soak. He wiped his hands off on a dish towel, his mouth watering for the tangy, sweet dessert, but his stomach needed a little extra room before the next course.

He smiled his thank-you. "You know what I love."

Bruce saw a pretty flush of color on his wife's cheeks before she turned away to put the plate on the counter. "Should I heat the oven now? Or wait?"

It had been such a long time since he wanted to pull Savannah into his arms and kiss her. But, oh, how he wanted to kiss her right at that moment. The kindness of her gesture, the sweet blush on her cheeks that spoke of her ability to have a reaction to being in close quarters with him. He felt her attraction for him, just as strong as when they were first married. And in turn, his body, his mind, his heart, were all reacting.

"You up for a walk?" he asked her, not at all sure

that she would accept. Nothing was certain with Savannah. With a nod to the plate of pastries, he added, "I need to make some room for at least three of those."

Walking after dinner had been one of their marriage staples; they both loved to walk in the evening with the dogs, hoping to catch a colorful sunset. Even the rain hadn't deterred their evening routine; they had just grabbed raincoats and gone.

Bruce held the door open for his wife, and then grabbed his hat off the rack as he stepped out onto the porch. As usual, the dogs happily mobbed Savannah, who greeted them as if she hadn't seen them in days, not just an hour.

"Which way?" she asked at the bottom of the steps.

"Cook's choice."

They headed toward the west, toward the setting sun and toward one of the many pastures where some of the herd of black Angus were lying down after a day of grazing. They would have held hands—they always had—but this time, she didn't reach for his hand, and he couldn't bring himself to reach for hers.

Silently, they walked together, side by side, until they reached the pasture fence. With a sigh, Savannah leaned on the fence to admire the view. Perhaps he was biased—most likely he was—but Sugar Creek Ranch was heaven on Earth. A landscape seemingly touched by God's hand, it featured flat pastureland abutted by an expanse of gently rolling hills leading up to the base of royal Montana mountains far off in the distance. Tall grass on the hills swayed, almost imperceptibly, in a calm breeze floating across the hills, and the soft echo of the water flowing over rocks in the wide stream that crossed the ranch like a snake uncurling itself. It was the kind of landscape that would inspire painters like Winslow Homer or Georgia O'Keeffe to unroll their blank canvases and take out their brushes.

"I never get tired of this," Savannah mused. "It never gets old."

"For me, either."

There was much that he resented about his father— Jock was harsh, cold at times and unable to admit wrongdoing or express regret—but he'd gotten it right when he'd bought this land. And though maybe Bruce hadn't gotten everything right in his own life, either, he knew, as he admired his wife's profile in the early-evening light, that he *had* gotten it right when he married Savannah.

"I need to go back, I think."

"You okay?"

She nodded, her arms now crossed in front of her body as she turned away from the view. "I suddenly feel so tired. It's been a long day."

"You overdid it." Bruce fell in beside her. "Cooking me dinner."

A shake of her head. "No. That was fun. It's not that. It's that I seem to be going from one appointment to the next to the next now. I can go years without so much as a cold, and yet now, it seems, that's all I'm doing."

Bruce whistled for the dogs playing in the pasture to follow them back to the house.

"Your limp is less noticeable," he told her. "Already."

The bruises on her face had faded to a light yellow and a faint green, a sign of healing, but her speech was still affected, a little slurred and slushy, and as far as he knew, Savannah hadn't had any memories, not even flashes, of the last several years. All of her childhood memories, the memories of her young adulthood, and even the early years of their marriage were still, thankfully, intact. But Savannah still did not have recent memories about the darkest period of their marriage.

"Don't get me wrong—I'm grateful for the help." She ascended the stairs, holding on to the railing, much more slowly than she had descended. "I just wish I didn't *need* the help."

The first time she mustered the nerve to drive herself into town after she was cleared to drive by her neurologist, Savannah decided to meet her friends from work at one of their favorite spots on Main Street.

"How are you?" her friend Maria, a speech-language pathologist at the elementary school where Savannah had worked before the accident, asked after the waitress took their orders.

Savannah took a sip of her soda, enjoying the burn of the carbonation on her throat and the syrupy sweet taste on her tongue. She put her glass down and then said, "Honestly, I don't even know how to answer that."

Deb, a kindergarten teacher whose classroom had been adjacent to Savannah's, put her hand briefly on her arm. "We've all been praying for you."

"Thank you," Savannah said. "I appreciate that. I do. I just want to…feel *normal* again. But I don't even know what normal is anymore."

"I can't imagine," Maria sympathized. "It must be so hard for you."

"It's messy." She frowned in thought. "It's like trying to make sense of a blurry photograph, but no matter how hard I squint, I can't bring my life into focus. I still can't get my mind around the fact that I've lost *years*." Savannah shook her head and repeated, *"Years."*

"We're so sorry." Deb's sadness for her was easily read in her kind, brown eyes.

"It's the little things that really throw me off," she explained. "Have you ever looked at one of those pictures in the magazine, two side by side pictures, and you're supposed to figure out what's different about them?"

Her friends both nodded.

"That's what it's like. But it's not a picture I'm trying to figure out—it's my life. Everyone looks just a little bit off in my mind, but it takes me some time to figure out why." Savannah turned to Deb. "Your hair is past your shoulders now. But for me, it was just a couple of weeks ago that you were wearing your hair in a bob and thinking about growing it out. That happens time and time again. Everyone looks just a little bit off from my memory of them. And sometimes I find someone staring at me, and I can't be sure if I've met them before and now they think I'm rude for ignoring them, or if I have spinach in my teeth."

"You haven't gotten any of your memories back?" Maria asked.

She shook her head. "But that's not the hardest part. The hardest part," she continued while her friends lent her their listening ears, "is my marriage."

Again her friends nodded to signal that they were listening carefully.

"I know about the divorce, but I don't remember it." Savannah twisted her wedding band. "Bruce told me, once when I was still in the hospital, that he still loves me, but he doesn't touch me. He doesn't kiss me." In a quieter voice she added, "He doesn't sleep in our bed."

"Bruce loves you," Deb interjected. "Everyone knows that. Even when you were getting divorced, we knew that. He just needs some time to switch gears."

"Do you want him to sleep in bed with you?" Maria asked.

Savannah nodded. She really did. Sleeping in their bed, even with the three dogs, felt so lonely. She wanted her husband next to her again.

"Then tell him," Maria encouraged her. "Just tell him."

Her friend's words had rattled around in Savannah's mind all afternoon and late into the evening. The fact that Bruce continued to sleep on the couch was just an accepted fact that neither of them discussed; in fact, they didn't discuss much below the surface. Yes, they were eating dinner together and going for walks. Yes, Bruce had helped her with the garden and taken an interest in her therapy. But they didn't seem to be moving forward together. She resented the divide she felt between them; she resented the figurative wall he had erected as a barrier to keep her at arm's length.

They had already turned in for the night; he went to the couch and she went to the bed. She could hear him snoring lightly from the living room. The more she listened to him sleeping, the more irritated she became with her own silence. Why hadn't she talked to him about the sleeping arrangement? If this second chance at their marriage was going to work, she was going to have to learn how to speak from her heart and tell Bruce what she needed from him. At least, that was what her therapist had told her in her last session. And her therapist's observation seemed to align with Maria's advice.

Savannah carefully pulled her legs out from beneath the sleeping dogs, trying not to disturb her canine bedmates. Barefoot, wearing one of Bruce's white cotton V-neck undershirts and a pair of bikini underpants, she petted the dogs, who'd lifted their heads curiously.

"You guys stay here," she whispered. "I've got this one."

It had been easy for them to put the dogs between them, focus their attention on them, as another way to keep them apart. A distraction from the awkward situation they found themselves in; a distraction from the strange, wounded state of their marriage. Not this time.

"Bruce."

No response, other than a loud snort and a leg twitch beneath the blanket.

She reached down and poked his shoulder with her pointer finger. "Bruce."

That time, her husband's eyes opened wide in surprise, and he sat up, jerking his head back like he was dodging a punch.

"What the heck, Savannah!" he sputtered. "What's the matter?"

"Sorry." She tried not to laugh, but failed. "I didn't mean to scare you."

"I was asleep."

Bruce was always grumbly about being awakened. She was used to it.

"Are you okay?" He squinted at her. "What's wrong?"

Savannah sat down on the edge of the couch, forcing her husband to scoot his legs over to make room for her.

"Nothing's wrong," she started, but stopped herself with a shake of her head. "No. That's not true. Something is wrong."

He waited for her to continue, yawning loudly when she paused to collect her thoughts.

"Here's the thing," she restarted. "I don't want you sleeping out here anymore. I want you to sleep in our bed. With me."

Bruce stared at her in the dim light provided by the glow of the three-quarter moon. When he didn't say anything, she asked, "Did you hear me?"

"I heard you." He pushed his body into a more upright position.

That was all he said; she waited for him to continue, yet he didn't.

"I miss having you in bed with me," she added softly. "I miss my husband."

"It's been a long time."

"I know. I know it has been. For you. But for me…"

Bruce blew out his breath, and then he shrugged his shoulders.

"My back's been mighty pissed off about this sleeping arrangement."

Savannah stood up; that was Bruce's way of saying "yes" without saying it directly.

Her husband threw the blanket off his legs and stood up beside her. His body, naked save his boxer briefs, was warm from the blanket. She could feel the heat from his skin; it always felt so good, so secure, to wrap her arms around her husband and feel that warmth of his body transferred to her own skin. It was hard not to reach out to him now; it would be hard to resist reaching out to him when they were in bed together.

"I'm dead tired," Bruce said sleepily, his pillow tucked beneath his arm.

She led the way back to their bed, a bed they had picked out together, a bed they had slept in and made love in and read the Sunday paper together in. There was so much more she wanted from Bruce—kissing and touching and lovemaking and loving words. But this was a start. Getting her husband back to their marital bed was a very good place to start.

Bruce had been dead tired until he climbed into his side of the bed. He found some free real estate for his feet and legs on either side of Buckley's body. He sighed happily as he slid down into the cool, undisturbed sheets on his side of the bed and put his head down on his pillow. He loved this mattress and he'd sorely missed it. And he had a stiff back to prove it.

Savannah was on her side of the bed, Hound Dog's large body sprawled out between them like a chastity belt. She turned on her side, facing away from him, and said good-night. For her, that seemed to be the end of it. She had gotten him back into bed and now she was asleep. But that wasn't the end for him. Now *he* was the one awake. He'd wanted to hold his ground on the couch for his own good—he didn't need to start thinking about making love to Savannah. They'd had an active sex life—that was the one thing that they could always get right. It had taken him a long time to get over the desire to make love to his wife; it had taken him a long time to get used to the idea of having sex with a woman other than Savannah. If this thing blew up in his face, he didn't want to have to detox his body from craving hers.

"Great," he said in a raspy whisper.

"Are you all right?" Savannah asked him, her head turning back a little in his direction.

How should he respond to that? Should he tell her the truth? The scent of her freshly washed hair, the weight of her body on the mattress, the sound of those little sighs she made when she was getting ready to drift off to sleep—all of those things had made his body respond without his permission.

"Go to sleep," he ordered gruffly. "I'm fine."

"Okay," she murmured in a sleepy voice. "'Night."

Bruce usually slept on his back; tonight, he turned on his side, his back to Savannah. He pressed his face into the pillow and tried to ignore the erection in his shorts. How could he be this weak around Savannah? Why did she always seem to have this hold on him, no matter how much he tried to fight it?

He loved her. Still. And he wanted to love her with his body. With his mouth. With his hands. And day by day, dinner by dinner, walk by walk, it was getting harder for him to figure out why he shouldn't make love to his wife. *His* wife.

Savannah wanted the lovemaking—he could feel the tension building between them. A tension that could only be relieved by bringing their bodies together, skin to skin, mouth to mouth.

"Damn," Bruce muttered under his breath as he slipped out of bed.

His body wouldn't give up, and he couldn't go to sleep with a hard-on. This time, Savannah didn't awaken; she just kept right on sleeping while he took a cold shower. Now that he was sleeping in the same bed with his wife, he was gonna have to stop telling his body "no" and start telling it "yes" if he was ever going to get a second of sleep again.

Chapter Five

Savannah had never needed a shrink before she broke a windshield with her head. But now that she had one, she could see how useful they could be.

"Any memories return since the last time we spoke?"

Savannah was lying flat on her back, head on the couch pillow, legs stretched out in front of her. Dr. Rebecca Kind had told her on several occasions that she didn't have to lie down, but she liked talking about her problems in the prone position.

"Not a one."

"Any images, or scents or sounds?"

"Nope." Savannah shook her head. "You know... Kind is a great last name for a shrink." She looked at the counselor. "I bet you hear that a lot."

Dr. Kind, a woman in her late fifties, with salt-and-pepper long, frizzy hair down to her waist, cracked the smallest of smiles. "Let's stay on topic. How are things going in your marriage?"

For this, Savannah felt she needed to sit upright. "So, here's the thing… I did exactly what you suggested—I told Bruce what I needed. And it worked. Sort of."

"How did it work, and what would you like to see improved?"

"Well, it got him back in bed. That's a step in the right direction."

Dr. Kind, her head down, jotted some notes on a pad.

"But…" she continued. "He still won't kiss me or hug me, and God knows there hasn't been even the prospect of sex."

"And you'd like to be physical with your husband."

"Of course. We used to always make love—that never slowed down, even after we'd been married for several years. Now? I've been totally cut off."

"Have you discussed this with Bruce?"

Hands in her lap, Savannah shook her head. "No. He's hard to talk to. He's always been hard to talk to."

"Has communication always been a problem in your marriage?"

She nodded yes. It had always been a problem. And even though she didn't have any memory of it, the fact that they'd resorted to divorce meant that their communication issues had only gotten worse over time.

Dr. Kind put her pen down on top of the pad of paper and then rested one hand on top of the other. "Have you spoken to Bruce at all about what caused the divorce?"

"No. I'm not ready for that. *We're* not ready for that."

"What frightens you the most about finding out what your mind won't remember?"

Savannah knew what frightened her the most, but it was hard for her to put her thoughts into words, even in this private, safe environment. If she found out what broke their marriage apart while they were so disconnected, then her marriage to Bruce would surely fail for a second time. And no matter what had happened during the last several years—whoever *that* Savannah was—this Savannah was deeply in love with her husband, and she did not want to risk losing him again.

"I have a suggestion." Dr. Kind filled in the silence. "I'd like for Bruce to join us next time."

Savannah's eyebrows popped upward. Bruce didn't mind her going to a shrink, but he didn't believe in paying good money to spill your guts to strangers when you could just walk out to any pasture and tell your problems to a cow for free.

"I don't think he'll come."

"Don't assume. Give him the chance to say yes or no." Dr. Kind looked at her wristwatch and then checked the clock on the wall. "Good. Let's end here today."

"What's on your agenda for today?" Bruce asked his wife after he took a sip of coffee.

Savannah wasn't used to having so much free time during the summer—she always volunteered to teach during summer at her elementary school—so it didn't surprise him that she had been keeping herself occupied by cooking almost every meal for him. They had opted to skip the big family Sunday breakfast; even though he'd had a heart-to-heart with his brothers about Savannah, some of them just couldn't treat his wife like they had before. It made Savannah uncomfortable, and he didn't want to force her to spend concentrated time with his family right now. After his brothers saw that their marriage was going to last—if it did—then things would work out eventually. That was his rationale.

"I was thinking about spending some time with Mom and Dad," she replied distractedly. "What's on yours?"

Bruce leaned his forearms on the table, his eyes drinking in the sight of the simple pleasure of having his wife sitting across from him again. "It's Sunday."

"Uh-huh."

"How 'bout we get back to our Sunday tradition?"

Savannah, who had been answering emails and texts on her phone, finally looked up at him. When she smiled at him, a smile that reached those pretty eyes of hers, it sent a pang into the pit of his stomach. This woman still had the power to wreck him with her smile; he loved to be the one to inspire that smile, and he lived for the moments when he could make her laugh.

"What do you have in mind?"

"Anything you want."

Her smile broadened, and that pang in his stomach grew stronger. He had spent most of his days during their marriage thinking of ways to make Savannah happy—that was his mission, because she had the same mission for him. Maybe it was time for him to risk a little to get a bigger return. Much like her garden, Savannah had been wilting right in front of him. And he had a feeling, a very strong feeling, that he was a big part of it.

"Drinking Horse Mountain," Savannah decided. "Something new."

A cloud entered her eyes when she asked a second later, "It is new, right?"

"Yes," he reassured her. "It's new."

They filled a backpack with water and food, supplies for the dogs, and Savannah called her mom to let her know that she would be spending the day with Bruce.

"Mom wants to know if we want to come over after for an early dinner." His wife held her phone against her body to muffle the sound of his answer.

It was easy for him to read the anticipation on Savannah's face—she loved her family, she loved him—and it would be the perfect capstone on her day if she could see her folks. So he agreed. After hiking, in-laws.

They loaded the dogs into the backseat of his truck, and he held the passenger door open for Savannah and helped her climb into the passenger seat. She had made some progress in physical therapy, but even though the limp was barely noticeable, her leg was still weak.

"Windows up or windows down?" Savannah asked happily when he climbed behind the wheel.

"Down."

"That's what I thought, too."

Bruce lowered the windows halfway in the back seat so the dogs could stick their heads out, as they liked to do, without risking that they would jump out. He cranked the engine, but before he shifted into Drive, he asked, "What are you in the mood for?"

As with everything, his wife put her due consideration into the question of music choice. After a minute of thought, she said with a question in her tone, "Motown."

Bruce scrolled through his phone with a nod. "Motown it is."

On their way off the ranch, they saw Noah riding in one of the pastures. He waved to his younger brother but didn't stop. He did stop when he saw Jock and Lilly rocking on the front porch of the main house.

"Why the hell weren't you two at breakfast?" Jock hobbled down the steps. He wasn't all that old, but his spine didn't seem to know that. His father had a couple of herniated discs in his back that he refused to have fixed. So the rancher and patriarch walked in a side to side motion, often with his hand on his back.

"It's my fault, Dad." Savannah was quick to take the blame. "I was too tired for a big family breakfast."

"Bah." Jock rested his hands on the open truck window. "Where're you off to now?"

Savannah looked at him with an excited smile before she answered Jock. "Bruce is taking me hiking up at Drinking Horse Mountain."

The rancher gave a slight nod, and pushed away from the truck. "Have a good time, then."

Bruce couldn't remember the last time he drove away from the ranch on a Sunday, with his wife next to him, his hiking gear packed, and his dogs ready for an adventure. The day was as beautiful as a day could get, with a clear, cloudless, turquoise-blue sky, and a coolness in the air that made it feel more like fall than summer. Bruce cranked up the tunes, with his right hand on the steering wheel, and let his left arm rest on the open window. The sun would warm the skin on his arm, and then the breeze would cool it of, and his wife was sitting next to him, singing off-key and loudly, as she always did, to Stevie Wonder's "Signed, Sealed Delivered, I'm Yours…"

They didn't speak much on the way to the recreational park—not in an awkward "I don't have anything to say to you" kind of way. It was comfortable. Like it used to be for them. From Sugar Creek Ranch, they drove through downtown Bozeman and then State Route 86 to the figure-eight shaped hiking trail. It was one of the few trails they hadn't visited; they loved to set out together with the dogs and hike the abundant trails in Montana. After their marriage fell apart, Bruce hadn't had the desire to hike alone or with friends. It had been "their" thing, and without Savannah, hiking lost its appeal.

"It's crowded." Savannah had turned down the music as they approached the park. "Oh! There's a spot right there."

"Got it." Bruce pulled into one of the few free spaces just before another truck got there.

He shut off the engine. "Are you sure you're up for this?"

Ever since the accident, she had developed a mild case of social anxiety, and he wasn't sure how she'd feel about sharing the trail with large groups of hikers.

"I'll be okay," she told him, but she had a worried look in her eyes as she took a survey of her surroundings.

Bruce made sure he was at her door to help her down to the ground before he unloaded the dogs and slung the backpack onto his back. Savannah used her standard walking stick, a stick that had pins from most of the trails she had tackled since she was a teenager, as well as holding Hound Dog's leash.

"They have two trail types—we'll take the easy route this time." He shortened his stride to keep pace with Savannah.

She nodded in response because she was too busy admiring the beautiful landscape that encompassed the forty-acre park. "This is incredible. Isn't it?"

"It sure is." They had always agreed on the beauty of Montana. They were both natives, and they both couldn't imagine any other place in the world to call home.

Mindful of Savannah's healing concussion and her leg weakness, Bruce was careful to hold their pace to a slower one than was typical for them. Every time Savannah would speed up, excited to see more of the landscape unfolding before them, he would be the one to remind her to slow down. He got them to take frequent water breaks, and pointed out benches to rest more often than he needed. Her health, her recovery, mattered to him. He couldn't seem to get the image of her lying in the hospital bed, hooked up to every beeping machine in the room, her face swollen, in a coma, out of his head. That was an image that wouldn't wash, no matter how much he tried to scrub it from his mind.

"Let's sit down over there." Bruce pointed to the next bench on the trail.

"Again?" Savannah's cheeks were flushed red, and she had beads of sweat rolling down her neck.

"Why not?" he asked her. "You got somewhere else to be?"

She frowned at him. "No."

He dug a bottle of water out of the backpack and

handed it to her. While his wife cooled off, Bruce took the three dogs down to Bridger Creek so they could hydrate and cool off, as well. Savannah laughed loudly and freely when the dogs, now sopping wet from the creek, descended upon her and shook themselves dry. She was sprayed from three directions and was splattered from her waist to her face by water from their fur.

"You cooled off now?" Bruce joined her on the bench.

Savannah was picking some dog hair off her tongue. "Yeah. I think so."

They sat together, silent, the three dogs at their feet, taking in the brown-and-green mountain landscape before them.

"This is heaven on earth." Savannah sighed.

Bruce looked at her, enjoying the view of his wife as much as the scenery provided by Drinking Horse.

"You know what this reminds me of?" he asked her, gesturing to the mountains.

"What?"

"All those movies they used to show us in school when we were kids about the outdoors."

They decided to eat a snack before continuing on their hike. Savannah finished her last bite of her protein bar, balled up the wrapper and put it in the front pocket of the backpack.

"I couldn't believe that Liam and Cynthia got divorced," his wife said to him. "When did that happen?"

Bruce put his empty wrapper in the front pocket as well, then zipped it shut. "It's been at least a year now."

Savannah shook her head in disbelief. "What happened?"

"I'm not too sure." He flicked a bug off his arm. "Liam doesn't like to talk about it, so I don't push him."

"Does he get to see the kids?"

Bruce stood up and hoisted the backpack onto his back before offering his hand to his wife. "He'll be getting them for a month this summer. But that's about all I know."

He was glad when Savannah dropped the subject— the more they talked about Liam's divorce, the more it made him think about their near miss. They walked the entire trail together, little by little, taking it slow, taking their time. He took pictures of Savannah on the trail for her to text to her family and friends, and a fellow hiker had offered to take a picture of them, as a couple, with the dogs, on the Kevin Mundy Memorial Bridge.

"Send that to me," Bruce said to her after they both looked at the first picture that had been taken of them since her return to the ranch.

By the time they got home, they had spent an entire Sunday together as a couple, and it felt more like old times to Bruce than it had in a long while. They had tired themselves out on the hike, built up a heck of an appetite, and then they'd cooked out at Savannah's parents' house, with Savannah's sister Justine and her fiancé, Mike. The fact that he was back at his in-laws' house, a home he'd loved and in which he had always felt welcome, was like a dream in motion. He'd thought it had all been lost.

"I don't know about you, but I am tired and stuffed." Savannah laughed tiredly.

Bruce shut the front door behind them, hung his hat on the hook and dropped the backpack next to the door.

"I'm right there with you."

Instead of going straight into the bedroom, Savannah turned on the lamp next to the couch and then circled back to him. She surprised him by wrapping her arms around his waist and giving him a quick hug.

"Thank you for today." Savannah dropped her arms, her face upturned.

It would have been so natural to kiss those lips—lips that were small and peach-colored, and always felt so soft beneath his own. She wanted him to kiss her—he knew that look in her eyes—but he just couldn't bring himself to do it.

"You're welcome," he told her as she turned away from him.

"Do you mind if I take a shower first?"

"No. You go on ahead. I'll go after you."

He sat down on the couch, Buckley next to him and Murphy at his feet, in the silence. He didn't feel like turning on the TV or listening to music; he just wanted to sit there and get his mind right. God, how he wanted to trust in his marriage. He wanted to make love to Savannah without any fear that she was going to leave him one day. She'd already ripped out his guts once—how could he give her the chance to do it again?

"Bruce!"

"Yeah?"

"Could you get me a towel out of the dryer?" Savannah called to him from the master bathroom. "I forgot to get one out!"

"Okay!"

Bruce went into the mudroom, opened the dryer and pulled out the towels Savannah had put in to dry before they left. For a split second, he was taken back in time, to another day when he had pulled towels out of the dryer—a day he had tried so hard to forget. He shook off the memory and carried the towels into the bedroom, dropped the pile onto the bed, and grabbed one for his wife.

They had designed the master bathroom shower together—both favoring a roomy shower built for two, with two showering stations at either end of the stall. Two sides of the shower were made completely of glass. Bruce had made it a point not to go into the bathroom when Savannah was showering, because there was no way *not* to see her naked.

"I'll just leave it on the counter."

"Oh, no. I'm so cold. Just hand it to me, would you? Please?"

Savannah was his wife. He had seen her naked thousands of times—and he had enjoyed every moment. In his eyes, she was a lithe, nymph-like beauty, and he loved seeing her body unclothed. Why was he trying so hard to avoid it now? Because he'd have to deal with the hard-on it would surely arouse?

Instead of averting his eyes or trying to avoid Savannah's nakedness any longer, Bruce walked straight over to the shower with the towel.

Savannah had the door of the shower cracked open, and the water was off.

"Thank you." She smiled at him as she hugged the towel to her body. Her right breast was round and full, with droplets of water clinging to the puckered nipple. In moments past, he would have bent down to lick the water from her nipple; he would have taken her, still damp from the shower, to the bed and made love to her.

Savannah caught him staring at her breast, and she didn't cover her body. Instead, she met his gaze when he brought his eyes to hers, and there was an invitation there for him to see.

As much as he wanted to love her—as much as his body wanted to love her—he just couldn't seem to take that leap of faith.

The moment was lost; Savannah wrapped the towel around her body and stepped out of the shower. While he took his shower, she closed up the house, took care of the dogs for the night, and was in bed by the time he emerged from the bathroom.

It had become a pattern for the dogs to create a barrier between the two sides of the bed, his and Savannah's. Bruce turned off the light and lay flat on his back, listening to the sound of Hound Dog licking his private parts.

"Really, Hound Dog?" he complained. "Is that necessary?"

Savannah laughed. "I find it to be oddly soothing."

Bruce turned his head to look at his wife. "Good night, Savannah."

"Good night."

Not right away, but before he drifted off to sleep, Savannah added, "Dr. Kind thinks it would be a good idea if you come to my next appointment."

Bruce didn't respond; he listened.

"Will you think about it?"

When he didn't answer right away, she said, "Bruce? Will you?"

"Yes," he said before he closed his eyes again. "I'll think about it."

Chapter Six

He had gone with her to speech therapy and to physical therapy—he had gone with her to her neurologist, to her internist, and he had dropped her off at her psychologist. But he hadn't imagined that he would be involved in her meetings with the psychologist. Perhaps that was naive thinking on his part.

"Thank you for coming today, Mr. Brand."

"Bruce," he corrected. "You're welcome."

Dr. Kind was wearing a long, flowy skirt with sandals, and her toenails were painted a very deep shade of purple. She folded her hands on top of an open notepad, drawing his eyes back to her face.

Savannah was sitting on one end of the three-seater couch, while he was at the other end. Bruce wondered if Dr. Kind had already made a note on her pad about that.

"Is there anything you'd like to say to start, Savannah?"

Savannah quickly glanced his way; her shoulders were stiff, and she was biting the inside of her cheek, which was a sure sign that she was a bundle of nerves on the inside.

"Um, sure." His wife cleared her throat. "I just feel stuck." She turned her head so she could look him in the eye. "I think that we're stuck. And I want to move forward. I want us to be like we were before."

It took Bruce a second to process what Savannah had said. He thought that he was here for her—to help her with her feelings relating to the memory loss. He wasn't here for marriage counseling. He told Dr. Kind as much.

"Savannah has done a substantial amount of inner work related to her individual concerns. Inevitably, we have to deal with problems related to the marriage."

Dr. Kind continued. "How do you feel the marriage is working?"

Maybe it was the soothing tone of Dr. Kind's voice or the scent of lavender in the air, but one minute he was clammed up and the next he was spilling his guts to a woman he'd just met. Dr. Kind scribbled furiously as he spoke, and when he managed to get himself to shut up, she looked up from her notes.

"Thank you for sharing that, Bruce," the psychologist said. "Let me see if I can recast what I've heard you say. While you understand that, for Savannah, the fighting and the separation and everything leading up to the divorce is not a part of her current memory, for you, every fight, every attorney meeting, every attorney *bill* is very real, and still very raw. Yes?"

Bruce nodded.

"Do you hear that, Savannah?"

Savannah, who hadn't stopped chewing on the side of her cheek yet, gave a little nod.

"What I hear in all that you've shared with me today, Bruce, is that you are afraid to invest in this marriage because you are concerned that Savannah can leave the marriage again."

"I don't know why I left," Savannah interjected; she reached out across the divide and touched his arm. "But I'm not leaving again."

"Do you hear that, Bruce?"

"I hear it," he acknowledged. "But what happens when your memory comes back?" He said this directly to his wife before addressing the therapist. "I personally think that we need to talk about the elephant in the room, about what caused the divorce in the first place. That way we don't have to spend all of this time working on our marriage if all she's going to want is to go through with the divorce."

"Are you ready for that, Savannah?"

He hated the fact that he was the cause of the color draining from Savannah's face.

"No."

Dr. Kind checked her watch. "Okay. We have a couple of minutes left. Bruce, Savannah has made a promise to you that she isn't going to proceed with the divorce. If you want your marriage to work, you're going to have to let go of the pain of these last several years and try to move forward. And, Savannah, you need to be patient with Bruce."

The therapist closed her pad and put it on the table next to her chair. She leaned forward, hands clasped, her forearms resting on her thighs. "Savannah, I want you to sit next to Bruce. Bruce, turn to your wife and take her hands."

Like a robot, he followed her direction. This woman had a way of getting him to do things that he wouldn't normally do on demand.

"Tell Bruce what you need."

Savannah took a steadying breath. "I need you to stop calling me 'Savannah.' You only used to do that when you were mad at me. I need you to hold my hand, and sit with me on the couch and…I need you to kiss me 'hello' and 'goodbye.'"

"Bruce?" Dr. Kind prompted. "What do you need from Savannah?"

He couldn't believe he was in this moment; he hadn't anticipated it. Savannah, her hands in his, her eyes focused so intently on his face, was listening to him in a way that perhaps she never had before.

"Tell me," Savannah said softly.

"Don't ever—" Bruce stared into his wife's eyes "—say that you want a divorce."

"I won't." She whispered the interjection.

"Ever again."

Savannah felt emotionally drained after the session with Dr. Kind. She had imagined that the therapist wouldn't be able to get more than two words out of her husband, but as it turned out, Bruce had a lot bottled inside that he needed to get off his chest. Savannah imagined that no one was more surprised than Bruce himself. He had been quiet on the ride home; when they arrived back at the ranch, he went out to his workshop and she went to her garden.

Dr. Kind had left them with homework to do with a request that they both return the following week. The homework was for them to start dating. Even though they were married, they needed to treat this as a new, fragile relationship and nurture it as such.

"Look up," Jessie instructed, holding an eyeliner in her hand.

Savannah looked up to the bathroom ceiling, trying not to blink as her sister-in-law brought a pointy pencil close to her left eye.

"But I never wear eyeliner," she told Bruce's sister. "A little mascara, a little lip gloss and I'm good to go."

"Keep looking up," Jessie said. "This is Naughty Nutmeg, and it will make your hazel eyes pop right out of your face."

Savannah pulled away and blinked her eyes several times. "Do I want them to pop out of my face? Has fashion really changed that much in three years?"

"Don't wipe them or you'll smear it, and we'll have to start all over!" her sister-in-law exclaimed.

Still blinking, Savannah smiled at her. "That was a little amnesia humor for you."

Jessie screwed up her face. "I got it. Let me look at your eyes."

After a moment, her sister-in-law gave her a smile and a nod of approval before stepping aside so Savannah could see the finished product.

"Well?" Jessie asked impatiently after a moment of silence.

Savannah studied her reflection in the mirror. For her *second* first date with Bruce Brand, she had gone to have her hair dyed a deep mahogany brown; this color was much closer to the color she last remembered. She was growing out those awful bangs—she couldn't imagine what she was thinking with that hair travesty—but at least it could be fixed with time. Jessie had gone shopping with her and "styled" her; her sister-in-law actually convinced her to buy a midnight-blue wrap dress and strappy heels. Jessie had also taken her to the makeup counter to buy new cosmetics.

"I think you made me actually look glamorous."

"That's what I was going for," Jessie said proudly.

Savannah stood up and hugged her sister-in-law. Afterward, she brushed Jessie's long, pin-straight, black hair over her shoulders.

"You're so grown up," she said wistfully. "And so *tall*!"

She couldn't stop herself from remembering Jessie as a gawky, awkward fifteen-year-old who was worried about acne and her breasts not coming in fast enough. Now, she was eighteen, a willowy beauty who had recently graduated from high school and had absolutely nothing to worry about in the décolletage area.

Jessie hugged her again. "I'm glad you're back. I missed you."

"Do you think your brother is going to think I've lost my mind getting this dressed up?"

Her sister-in-law uncapped the new lip gloss on the counter, applied it to her full lips and smacked them together. "Please. He's gonna love the fact that you put in so much effort. What do you think of this color on me?"

"Lovely."

"That's what I thought." Jessie pouted her lips and posed in the mirror, then took out her phone and leaned her head next to Savannah's. "Here. Snapchat."

After the photo op, Savannah took one last look at herself in the full-length mirror on the back of the bathroom door. She pulled at the belt on her dress, then fidgeted with her bra straps. Jessie had managed to cover the puckered red scar on her forehead, and with her hair changed back to nearly its original color, if she squinted, she looked more like the woman she remembered from several years back than the one she awakened to in the hospital.

"Well." She tilted her head. "I hope Bruce loves me in this."

Those were the words that she said for Jessie to hear, but in her mind, she thought—

I hope my husband falls in love with me again in this.

The thirty minutes of waiting for Bruce to pick her up was nerve-racking for Savannah. They consisted of sweating, pacing, sitting back down on the couch, checking her phone, sending texts to her sisters, video-chatting with her sisters and finally landing back in the bathroom to "just in case" urinate and use the hair dryer to dry off the sweat stains under her arms. They had agreed to make this as much like a real first date as possible, so Bruce was getting ready in the main house, while she was to wait for him at their home.

Pacing in the living room, talking to Hound Dog, who was watching her curiously, Savannah wished that she hadn't insisted on getting ready so early. She didn't want to be late for her second first date with Bruce, but by the time the man arrived, she would have sweated through half her makeup.

"Oh, thank goodness," Savannah said to Hound Dog.

She walked over to the window to peek out; Bruce had just pulled up and was about to get out.

"Aw," she told her canine companion. "He washed the truck."

Savannah scurried back to the couch, sat down on the edge of the cushion, smoothed her skirt over her knees and cupped her hands together and rested them on her thighs.

Unexpectedly, instead of just opening the front door of his own house, Bruce knocked. Hound Dog went to the door, his tail wagging. Savannah moved out of her perfectly staged pose on the couch and opened the door for her husband.

"Hello." Bruce was standing in the doorway holding long-stemmed red roses.

"Hi." Savannah accepted the flowers, brought the fat, bright red flowers up to her nose and inhaled the sweetness.

She met her husband's gaze over the top of the flowers; now that she saw him, she was glad she had gone all out for this date. He was wearing a new pair of dark wash denim jeans, his dress cowboy boots and a new button-down shirt, in her favorite color, forest green. If she had a tail, just like Hound Dog, she'd be wagging it for Bruce too.

"I'll just put these in some water."

Bruce followed her to the kitchen; while she cut the ends of the flowers, Bruce located a vase in a cabinet above the refrigerator.

"Thank you." Savannah admired the flowers, now in the vase. "They're beautiful."

As Bruce stood closer to her than usual, the scent of his woodsy cologne, her favorite, mingled with the strong, sweet smell of the roses in the most tantalizing way.

"You look beautiful."

His compliment, so simple, so quietly delivered, brought her to tears, which she quickly pushed back; in every way he could say, without words, Bruce was telling her that he was going to try to make their marriage work. That he was willing to give her—their—life together an honest chance.

"You look handsome." She brushed a piece of lint from his arm.

"Shall we?" Her husband offered her that same arm.

Happily, Savannah tucked her hand into the crook of Bruce's arm. "Where are we going?"

"It's a surprise," he told her. "Is that okay?"

She laughed—for no reason at all other than she felt happy. "Sure. I'm actually starting to kind of like them."

Bruce didn't realize until he shut the passenger-side door to the truck that his palms were sweating. From the time he'd pulled up to his cabin, to the moment he had his wife securely in the truck, he had felt slightly sick to his stomach. He was nervous—nervous as all get-out, actually—to take his wife out on a date.

"The truck looks nice," Savannah said to him. She had always nagged him about using the floorboard on the passenger side of his truck as a trash can of sorts; he'd wanted to make sure that he cleaned the inside and the outside of the truck for their date.

"Any requests?"

"No," Savannah said faintly. "Surprise me."

After Bruce dropped Hound Dog off with Lilly and

Jock, who were already watching Buckley and Murphy, he chose a CD and lowered the volume so it was more like background music.

"Ah," She dropped her head back on the headrest and smiled. "I love Patsy Cline."

"I remember." He remembered everything about his wife—all of those little things that made her his wife. In particular, he remembered the fragrance she was wearing tonight; with some floral and white musk notes, that scent evoked so many memories of Savannah. Always Savannah.

They drove toward Bozeman. As the sun was setting on the horizon in the rearview mirror, the inside of the truck cab was washed with a gold-and-blue romantic light. This was where he always wanted to be—with this woman, by her side, sharing the small pleasures of life and tackling the tough challenges together. Somewhere along the way, things had gone so terribly wrong between them. And yet, here she was, back in his life. It felt like he was being blessed by God, but he couldn't figure out why.

"This is the best night I can remember," Savannah told him softly.

"It hasn't even begun yet." He glanced at her pretty profile.

"Yes, it has." She touched his arm briefly. "And it's perfect."

When Bruce pulled into a parking space in front of the South 9th Bistro, a restaurant that held a lot of meaning for them as a couple, all of the pieces fell into place for Savannah; Bruce was re-creating their first date, from the long-stemmed roses, to Patsy Cline, to the restaurant.

"Bruce…" Savannah unhooked her seat belt. "You're such a romantic."

"I try to be." He took the keys out of the ignition. "For you."

He had reserved their table on the second floor of the quaint restaurant with big-city cuisine. As always, Bruce held the chair for her, making sure she was settled before he seated himself.

"Are you up for a bottle of wine?" he asked her.

In the candlelight of the private table, Savannah couldn't stop herself from speaking her thoughts. "I have always loved sitting across from you at a table. You are so handsome."

That brought out his half smile, a half smile that she had fallen in love with very early on in their courtship.

"And yes—to the wine."

He ordered her favorite merlot, and with every passing moment she felt more spoiled than the next. Although she had believed in the impact of their session with Dr. Kind, the extent to which the session had blown through the barrier that had been holding them back was beyond her wildest expectation. Bruce seemed to be "all-in," and she knew this Bruce—once he locked in on what he wanted, he never gave up.

"Are you hungry?"

Savannah laughed. "You are going to have to roll me out of here, sir. Because I am starving, and I am going to eat like a famine is imminent."

Over their favorite appetizer, escargots, they talked about nothing—and in a way, they talked about everything. They talked about the ranch, and their families

and how she missed her job. They talked about her desire to put a greenhouse in the backyard and his desire
to add a deck to their cabin. It was a lovely moment
and she cherished it.

After the waiter cleared their appetizer plates and
refilled their wineglasses, Bruce smiled at her in a way
that she hadn't seen since before that awful day she
awakened in the hospital.

"Do you remember when we met?" He leaned forward, his eyes locked with hers.

"Of course." She leaned in to the table, as well.
"First grade, Mrs. Coleman's class. As I recall, you
heckled me during show-and-tell…"

"That's a lie."

"I brought my painted lady caterpillar aquarium,
and you heckled me."

"I don't remember it that way at all."

She crossed her arms in front of her chest in feigned
anger. "Even back then you were the most popular kid
in the class. And I was…"

"The smartest kid in the class," he filled in.

"And the nerdiest."

She'd had buck teeth, pigtails, glasses—the works.
And, she had been a precocious reader and had begun
to read the dictionary when most kids her age were
still tackling Clifford books.

"I picked on you because I thought you were cute,"
Bruce added.

"You should be ashamed of yourself, Brand," she
teased him. "You tortured me for years."

"Thank God you have a forgiving nature."

Savannah uncrossed her arms, leaned toward him

and lowered her voice for his ears only. "I thank God for *your* forgiving nature."

Before the tone of the dinner could switch from upbeat to serious, the main course arrived—Bruce had ordered his standard favorite black truffle New York strip steak, bloody in the center. And she couldn't say no to the filet, medium well, with the most delicious cognac-peppercorn sauce. They both took their time, savored the food, savored the company—savored the moment.

"Here's to you." Savannah held out her glass after she had cleaned her plate.

Bruce wiped his mouth, dropped his napkin on his empty plate and raised his glass.

"To us." He touched his glass to hers.

"To us," she agreed.

The waiter swung by their table to clear their plates; he asked the inevitable question, "Did you leave room for dessert?"

Savannah and Bruce locked eyes.

"Are you up for it, Brand?" He issued the challenge.

"Are you?"

Bruce gave a little laugh at her bravado—he knew her eyes were always bigger than her stomach.

"One Black Beast," her husband told the waiter. "Two forks."

Chapter Seven

Bruce held the door for Savannah; she was laughing as they walked out into the crisp night air, and his heart fed on that sound.

"You just had to go for the Black Beast, didn't you?" She bumped into him playfully.

Chocolate torte, dark chocolate ganache, blood orange chocolate mousse and more whipped cream than should be legal, the Black Beast was the dessert that they couldn't resist on their first date, but had wished they had.

"I feel like I need to walk off the Beast and the wine." He admired the way the light breeze was blowing wisps of hair around her face.

Not thinking twice, he moved a wayward strand of hair away from her mouth. His thumb lingered for the briefest of moments on her lower lip.

"Can you walk in those heels?" he asked.

"I think I can hold my own. As long as you let me hold on to your arm every now and then."

An evening after-dinner walk was a part of his plan for this second first date. He'd wanted to show Savannah, without having to say the words, that he wanted to start doing his part to repair their marriage. No, it wasn't going to happen overnight for him. But if he wasn't going to make an effort, put some trust in his wife, risk his heart a bit, then he should let Savannah go right now. *That* he wasn't willing to do.

Bruce wasn't under any illusion that every day would be like this; there were plenty of rough waters ahead. Yet, as he walked down the street with his wife's hand tucked into the crook of his arm, he felt like a king among men. He was proud of his wife—who she was as a person, her values, her choice to pursue her passion of educating children over the amount of money she could make. Her outward prettiness was quirky more than classical—it was the beauty he saw on her inside, once he was mature enough himself to notice it, that made him fall hard for the brainiest, biggest bookworm in Bozeman, Montana.

"Do you remember the first time I kissed you?" On a darkened street lined with mature trees, Bruce asked his wife a question for the second time that evening.

Suddenly, Savannah inhaled when she realized where he had taken her.

"Story Mansion." Her fingers tightened on his arm. "You kissed me first, and then asked me out. Totally backward."

They had both attended Montana State University directly after high school; he had continued with sports and joined a fraternity. Savannah had focused, as she always did, on academic and civic-minded activities. He became the president of his fraternity, Sigma Phi Epsilon, which happened to own and occupy one of the oldest landmarks in Bozeman: Story Mansion.

They both stopped, mesmerized by the historic house built in 1910; it was one of the few remaining three-block mansions in Montana, and for over a decade, the house had been preserved as a public state historical treasure and park after being purchased by the city of Bozeman. Eighty years before the city bought the mansion and saved it from development, his fraternity, SAE, had owned it.

"This brings back a lot of really good memories," Bruce mused. His days living in the Story Mansion, partying with his frat brothers, drinking too much and chasing coeds when he was "off-again" with Kerri were some of the best in his life.

On the other hand, as a volunteer member of the Bozeman Historical Society, Savannah had vehemently opposed the use of an irreplaceable cornerstone of Montana's rich history as a house of depravity for a bunch of oversexed frat boys.

"Uh-huh."

His wife remained unimpressed by his past history with this house that she loved.

"Don't forget," he teased her. "SAE was considered a good steward of this place for over eighty years."

Savannah let that comment slip away into the night without a response.

"Come on." Bruce grabbed her hand and began to lead her down the shadowed path to the front steps of the mansion.

"Wait." This was said in a loud whisper. "It's *closed*."

"We're not going inside."

Bruce led her up the front steps of the mansion, while she continued to protest in harsh whispers. Savannah stopped at yellow lights, never walked on grass if there was a Keep Off sign, while he liked to break a rule every once in a while.

On the porch now, he put his arm around his wife's shoulders, holding her next to him, as they looked out at the view of the street where they were just standing.

"We are *trespassing*."

"This is a public park."

"That's currently *closed*."

"Just stand here with me, sugar." Bruce leaned his head down to hers. "Just for a minute."

His wife stopped protesting and stood very still beside him, as if she wanted to turn into an unnoticeable statue in case a passerby spotted them.

"*This* is where we first kissed," Bruce reminded her. "Right here."

Yes, he had gone to school with Savannah all of his life; but he'd never really known her, other than the immature labels he had assigned her in his young mind: nerd, brain, Goody Two-shoes. But the day that a passionate, self-possessed Savannah lit into him about the impact of his fraternity's debauchery on Story Mansion during a pledge keg party, *that* was the day that they truly met. She had verbally sliced and diced him in a way no one in his life had ever done, and instead of being offended, he'd felt attracted to her fiery, intelligent eyes, her command of the English language, her flushed cheeks and the little gap between her two front teeth.

She didn't care that he was the president of the fraternity, or heir to Sugar Creek Ranch or the captain of the football team. Savannah cared about deeper issues, and he found himself oddly hooked from that day forward. He'd taken her tongue-lashing, found her devotion to an old, kind of smelly house rather charming, and the passion he saw in her hazel eyes sexy. Just as she was wrapping up her ardent plea for Story Mansion, Bruce had kissed Savannah. Right then, right there, without any warning. It had, quite honestly, been a shock to them both. And that unexpected kiss had been the start of their love affair.

"I admit I was a little too zealous back then," she whispered back. "But I just believed so deeply that this beautiful place needed to be preserved for generations to come. This is our history—history that we can see and feel and imagine what life could have been like for the people who came before."

Bruce turned her in his arms as he murmured, "There it is."

In the soft yellow light from the street, he read the question on her face, which he answered.

"That passion I fell in love with." He brushed her hair back away from her shoulders. "Right here on this porch."

This was the place that he wanted to solidify his recommitment to their marriage; this was the spot where he wanted to cross the invisible line he had between himself and Savannah.

Bruce cupped her face with his hands and touched his lips to hers; just that simple light touch wasn't enough. Her lips parted and her arms slipped around his body. His wife, his lovely wife, made a pleasurable little sound as he deepened the kiss. They stood together, holding each other, kissing as if for the first time, surrounded by the brick and stone and wood that had withstood the test of time for over one hundred years.

"I love you." Savannah had her head resting on his chest, her arms around him holding him so tightly.

Bruce closed his eyes for a second, pushing back a rush of emotion. He thought he'd never kiss Savannah again; to have her back in his life, even after all this time passed, still seemed like a dream from which he did not want to awaken.

"And I love you, my beautiful wife." He kissed the top of her head. "I love you."

Bruce sent a text to his stepmother to ask her to keep the dogs overnight. Tonight, Savannah realized, was the night that her husband wanted to be all about them as a couple. Everything he had planned for her, from the roses, to the dinner, to the evening walk and stolen kisses on the porch of Story Mansion—he had pulled out all of the romantic stops. He was wooing her and it had worked. All of the distance she had wanted to put between them, in reaction to the emotional walls he had erected, fell away.

Still a little bit tipsy, Savannah twirled in the living room when they arrived home, making her skirt swing out around her legs. Dizzy, she laughed and fell back onto the couch.

"This was the most amazing night." She smiled at her handsome husband. "Thank you."

Bruce hung his hat on the hook just inside the door; there was a look in his stunning blue eyes that touched her in the most intimate places in her body.

"Is the night over?" he asked her.

Savannah's laugh quieted. "I don't want it to be."

Bruce crossed to her, offered her his hand.

She slipped her hand into her husband's warm, calloused one. He helped her stand and then led her into the bedroom. Tonight, there wouldn't be a canine wall separating them. Tonight, there wouldn't be anything between them.

Savannah sat on the edge of the bed, leaned down to unbuckle the straps on her heels and slipped her feet out of the shoes while Bruce lit candles in the bathroom. The physical side of their marriage had never waned, at least not in her memory; the lovemaking had been just as passionate, and satisfying and adventurous as it had been from the first time they loved each other. The moment she heard her husband running the water in the oversized claw-foot tub, specifically selected because it was roomy enough for two, Savannah knew what Bruce had in mind. Yes, they enjoyed making love in the bed. But making love in the tub, with the slippery, warm water as a natural lubricant, had always been their favorite spot.

She joined her husband in the bathroom; Savannah unbuttoned his shirt, exposing his chest. She ran her hands over his chest, lightly scratching the chest hair and skin with her fingernails. He stood still for her, letting her explore his body, letting her kiss his neck before she slipped his shirt off his shoulders and tossed it on the bathroom counter.

"Hmm." She ran her hand over the bulge in his jeans.

Bruce was ready for her; and without him so much as touching her with his lips or his fingers, her body was ready for him.

Her husband hooked his finger on the belt of her wrap dress and tugged her forward; he kissed her, deep, long—a promise of the pleasure to come. Bruce undressed her then, unwrapping the layers of her dress and undergarments until she was naked before him. No man had ever made her feel as beautiful or desirable as Bruce did. He loved her from the inside outward.

She closed her eyes with a little gasp when he kissed her neck while his fingers stroked the sensitive skin of her breasts and her stomach and the curve of her derriere. Savannah reached between their bodies to unbutton and unzip his jeans.

"You're shivering," Bruce said as he kissed the side of her neck. "Get in the tub and I'll be right behind you."

Savannah sank down into the hot water, sighing at the feel of the water enveloping her body. She turned off the water, not wanting it to spill over the edge of the tub when her husband joined her.

"It's perfect in here." She arched her back to submerge her hair in the water.

Bruce watched her as he stripped off his jeans. Until she'd met her husband, she had never known how much she enjoyed having a man watch her, to admire her naked body. She had discovered her own true sexuality with Bruce.

In the candlelight, her husband's body, to her mind, was a thing of beauty—muscular from a life working on the ranch, with hard, sinewy muscle on his thighs, his arms and shoulders. He wasn't an extraordinarily tall man, but he was an extraordinarily well-built man.

"Do you like what you see?" Bruce asked her, standing unabashed in his nakedness.

Savannah moved to kneel before him in the water; her eyes drifted down to his erection, the proof of his desire for her.

"Yes." She reached for him. "I do."

Cupping him in her hands, she took him into her mouth, loving the sound of his groan, and the feel of his hands in her hair.

"That's going to get me in trouble," Bruce said in a tight voice.

As her lips left him, her hands stroked him. "Then hurry up and join me before the water gets cold."

Bruce stepped into the tub, sank down in the water behind her and then pulled her into his arms. Skin to slippery skin, her husband's strong fingers massaged her breasts while he kissed the water from her shoulder and neck.

"I have missed this—you have no idea," Bruce said in a raspy, strained tone, his hand slipping between her thighs to cover her slick center.

Savannah arched back, pushing into his hand. "Yes," she gasped, "I do."

She spun in his arms, sloshing water on the floor, and hovered above his body, her hands braced on his shoulders. Bruce wrapped his arms around her, hugging her to him, his mouth hot on her breast.

"I need you, Savannah." He grazed her nipple with his teeth. "I need you."

It was too long between moments for them; she sank

down, slipping him inside of her. A perfect fit—so thick and hard, he filled her completely.

With one arm, he lifted her forward, the water swirling around their bodies, so she could sit down completely and wrap her legs around his hips. Her moans mingled with his as their bodies melded together. She took his face in her hands, kissed his lips as he moved inside of her.

"Baby—I've got to come."

"It's okay." She held on to him as he bucked beneath her. "It's okay."

Bruce came with a loud growl, grabbing her shoulders and pulling her body down ono his. As he shuddered beneath her, catching his breath, she leaned into him, loving this moment in his arms.

"I'm sorry," he apologized. "I wanted it to last longer."

Savannah slipped her body free of his with a laugh, and echoed his words earlier. "Is the night over?"

That sexual glint returned to his eyes when he realized that she was ready and willing to go another round. "Not for me."

It was his pleasure to dry off his wife's body and carry her to bed. He laid her down, her skin still a little damp, and indulged Savannah, loving her with his mouth and his tongue, until she was arching her back, reaching for him and writhing with desire. It was the time his body needed to recover, to recharge and to harden. Bruce covered Savannah's body with his and joined them together once again. This time, he loved her slow and long, knowing her body as he knew his own, driving her to climax, one right after the other, until she was screaming and out of breath, their bodies slick with sweat.

They rolled together so Savannah was on top, straddling him, riding him, clawing his chest with her nails. He pulled her down on top of him, slowing them down, not wanting it to end.

"Are you coming for me, baby?"

He could feel her heart beating against his chest, her breath shallow, the little gasps of pleasure so satisfying. He forced himself to wait until he felt that familiar tensing of her legs, that sweet sound of her panting as she began her climb to the peak of another orgasm.

"Yes, baby—yes." Bruce held her tight and kissed her. "You're mine."

Seconds after Savannah peaked, he rolled her onto her back and pushed deep inside of her to find his own release.

The weeks that followed their second first date, their marriage had been a honeymoon state. They made love every chance they got, always taking the bed for themselves for lovemaking, before letting the canine family into the bedroom. They went out on more dates, going to the movies and out to dinner, trying new cuisine as they created a new foundation for their marriage. For Savannah, even though her memory still hadn't returned, remembering wasn't a high priority. Why would she want to go back to the reason why they split up when they were doing so well now? Why rock the boat?

"I'm so glad we could finally make our schedules work," Shayna Wade, a professor at Montana State University, and one of her longtime friends, told her.

"Me, too," Savannah agreed. Spending time with her family and friends had, day by day, made her feel very nearly like her old self—the self before the accident.

After they ordered their food, Shayna put her glass down and said, "I really wish you'd consider going back to school. I know you love being a teacher, but you always wanted to get your PhD. I'd love to have you on faculty with me."

"I'm not ruling it out."

"Good." Her friend seemed pleased with her answer.

"But right now, honestly, I'm just really focused on my therapy and my marriage."

"Your speech is so much better—you sound like you again."

"I've made a lot of progress," Savannah agreed with a smile. "I just want to keep on making progress."

They talked nonstop during lunch, catching up for the time that had lapsed since they last saw each other. After the plates were taken away and they were waiting for the bill, Shayna excused herself to the restroom while Savannah took the opportunity to answer emails and texts.

"Savannah."

A strange chill scurried down her spine; she looked up, and she could feel the blood drain from her face.

"Leroy." The word was said with a waver in her voice.

The cowboy's face brightened; without asking, he took a seat at the table. "You remember me?"

She looked around for Shayna, wishing that she could disappear into the woodwork.

"I…" She met his expectant eyes, so full of hope,

and gave a little shake of her head. "No. I'm sorry. I don't...remember you."

She remembered the lanky cowboy, who appeared to be younger than her, from the hospital, not from any memory before that time. But she did know that they had been dating and that it was his car she was driving when she had the accident.

"But—" his eyes shuttered "—you do know who I am."

Her hands gripped her phone to keep them from shaking. She nodded her response.

The young man's eyes were wet with emotion. "I love you, Savannah."

The only response Savannah could muster was, "I'm sorry."

Leroy stared at her for what seemed like several very long minutes before he coughed, cleared his throat and stood up. He looked down at the wedding ring back on her finger.

"One day you're gonna wake up and realize you're with the wrong man. I promise you, you're gonna remember that you want to marry me."

Those words hurt her heart, and no matter how much sympathy she felt for this man, and she did feel that sympathy, those were words she did not want to hear.

"No. I won't." She shook her head, her body shaking on the inside. "I'm already married."

Leroy turned away from her, almost bumping into Shayna in the process.

"Shayna." Leroy acknowledged her friend before he left the restaurant.

"Hi, Leroy." Shayna greeted the cowboy, then sat

down, a shocked expression on her face. "Are you okay?"

Savannah pulled some cash out of her wallet, handed it to her friend. "Will you take care of the bill? I need to go."

Chapter Eight

"How are things?" Dr. Kind asked her.

"I ran into Leroy yesterday," Savannah blurted out. She'd been keeping it bottled up inside for an entire day and she had been anxious to sit down and talk about it with the psychologist.

"And how did that feel?"

How did that *feel*?

"It felt terrible. The look on his face when I told him that I didn't remember him… He still loves me."

"Are you surprised by that? He hasn't forgotten your relationship."

"Well, I wish he would," Savannah snapped. "I don't want him to love me. I love Bruce. I'm married to Bruce."

"Yes," Dr. Kind agreed. "But you were in a relationship with Leroy. That's also true."

Savannah frowned. It was true—but she didn't *want* it to be the truth. She couldn't change the way she felt about that.

"So, how are things with your marriage?"

"We're in a really good place right now."

"Intimacy?"

"That couldn't be going any better." Savannah smiled. They had just made love that morning before Bruce left for a day of work on the ranch. She didn't want anything to spoil that momentum; losing it was one of her biggest fears.

Dr. Kind took some notes, then looked up thoughtfully. "Does it bother you that you haven't regained your memory?"

"No." She played with her wedding band. "Not like it used to. Why do I want to remember why I wanted to divorce my husband? We're happy right now—that's what matters to me."

"Do you think that's sustainable?"

"What do you mean?"

"Well," the psychologist said after a pause, "up until now, your world has been sanitized. Your friends and family have agreed, with your full knowledge, to protect you from that part of your past with Bruce that triggered the separation, and ultimately, the move to divorce."

It was true. Her friends and family had deleted digital traces of the past several years that might be emotionally upsetting to her. She was aware of it, and she hadn't gone out snooping to unearth images of the past several years. Was she being an ostrich and sticking her head in the sand? Yes. She was. But what was really wrong with that?

"So, I'll ask you again. Do you think this is sustainable? Leroy is just the first reminder of a past you have been actively avoiding. As you go back to work and live your life, pieces of that puzzle will continue to appear."

Savannah didn't have an immediate answer for the doctor, so she remained silent.

"Your body has healed from the accident. You've been cleared to ride horses again, and the neurologist has released you from his care. You have made great strides with both physical and speech therapy, and your marriage is also moving forward. The one place you are refusing to heal is your psychological and emotional health. Don't build your new life on a weak foundation, Savannah. Face what you need to face so you can truly move forward in your life and in your marriage."

"Hey." Bruce found Savannah in her garden at the end of the day. This little piece of ground had always been her salvation and her sanity. If she was having a bad day, if she was having a good day, it was always a day for getting her hands in the earth.

Savannah sat back on her haunches with a smile. "Hi!"

His wife had dirt on the tip of her nose and dirt on her chin. To him, it was adorable.

"Did you have a good day?"

"Uh-huh." She nodded. "I had a good session with Dr. Kind."

"Good."

Savannah stood up, brushed her hands off on her jeans and walked over to give him a hug. "I'm glad to see you."

He gave her a kiss. "I'm glad to see you."

Together, arm in arm, they went into the house, followed by the dogs, to get ready for dinner.

"I'm going to jump into the shower." Bruce shut the back door behind them. "Care to join me?"

Savannah laughed. "It's tempting. But no. I want to wash the veggies and get dinner started. Rain check?"

Bruce smiled at her with a wink. He was happy that the intimacy in their relationship was back and better than ever. They knew each other's bodies; they knew how to please each other. And that had been a big part of their connection as a couple—great lovemaking with your best friend. What could be better than that?

In the bedroom, Bruce picked up some of Savannah's discarded clothes and put them in the hamper along with his work clothes.

"You gonna hang with me, Hound Dog?" He scratched the dog around the scruff and kissed him on the head before he jumped in the shower.

After his shower, Bruce got dressed and was looking forward to a night at home with his wife. He was on the way out of the bedroom when something on the top of Savannah's dresser caught his eye. Something that made him stop in his tracks.

The rancher stared at the Matchbox fire truck—rusted in places, but still recognizable as the truck he had purchased what seemed like a lifetime ago. Bruce picked up the fire truck, memories, unwanted memories, flooding his mind. He clutched the truck in his hand, his eyes closed to push back the tears. It took him several minutes to gather his emotions; with the truck still in hand, Bruce went to find his wife in the kitchen.

"Could you watch this and stir it when it starts to

bubble? I seriously need a shower before we sit down to eat. I stink."

"Yeah. Sure." Bruce nodded, dropping a kiss on her lips as she walked by.

"Hey…"

Savannah spun around. "Huh?"

"Where did you find this?" He opened the palm of his hand to show her the fire truck.

"Oh!" She seemed to have forgotten all about it. "It was buried in the garden. It must've been Cole's, don't you think?"

The fact that Savannah had assumed that the truck had once belonged to Liam's son, his nephew Cole, told him everything he wanted to know. The truck hadn't triggered any memories for her.

He gave her a noncommittal nod, then tucked the toy into his pocket, and wondered how he was going to get through the night pretending that nothing was wrong.

"Damn." Bruce pinched the corners of his eyes to stop tears from forming. He would have thought that he had already cried out all of those tears years ago.

The night Bruce found the toy truck on Savannah's dresser, he didn't sleep. He tossed and turned, and only managed to drop off just before dawn. He awakened feeling hungover from lack of sleep and emotionally shell-shocked. Everything he had spent years suppressing, years avoiding, years ignoring, had suddenly bubbled up to the surface. Like Savannah, he was enjoying their marriage revival; he had his lover back—he had his best friend back. And the idea of rocking the boat by dredging up their past was something he didn't mind putting off.

That morning, Bruce kissed Savannah goodbye and headed off to meet his crew of ranch hands; that morning, he left with that toy fire truck in the front pocket of his jeans.

"I've got some things I've got to take care of in town," Bruce said to his brother Colton. "You good to keep the boys on track today?"

Colton was a die-hard Montana rancher like himself—Sugar Creek was his life.

"Not a problem." Colton gave him a nod.

Bruce climbed into his truck, shut the door and rolled down the window. Almost as an afterthought, he called out to Colton, who was striding toward the day's work.

"Hey, Colt."

Colton turned back to him.

"Go easy on Savannah tomorrow at breakfast. The two of you used to be real tight."

His younger brother's smile dropped. "She did you real wrong, brother. I'm just waitin' to see if she's gonna do it again. That's how I feel. That's how it's gonna be."

"She's still my wife," Bruce reminded him, before he shifted into Drive and drove through the field to pick up one of the many gravel roads that crisscrossed the ranch.

Colton was a carbon copy of Jock—he was passionate, demanding, driven to a fault, and could be unforgiving. While the rest of the family had found a way to make peace with Savannah's return to the ranch, Colt was a noticeable holdout.

Halfway down the main gravel road, Bruce turned onto a dirt road that was overgrown with tall grass.

This was truly a road less traveled on the ranch. His heart started to pound hard in his chest the farther down the road he drove; he felt nauseous as the family cemetery came into view. In Montana, families could still bury their kin on their land, as long as that land was outside of city limits and not near a water source. Jock's first wife, his mother, was the first person to be buried on Sugar Creek Ranch. Jock had already stipulated in his will that, when he was pushing up daisies, he wanted to be pushing up daisies on Sugar Creek.

Bruce shifted into Park and shut off the engine. He leaned his arms on the steering wheel, staring hard at the four headstones in the Brand plot. It took him some time to muster up the determination to get out of the truck and pick his way through the brush to where the unadorned headstones lined up in a row—one large headstone and three smaller headstones.

A wrought-iron fence surrounded the family plot; the stiff gate squeaked loudly as the rancher pushed it open. Slowly, reverently, Bruce walked over to the headstones and stared at the names and the dates carved into the granite markers. He silently acknowledged his mother, wishing now that he had come more often to clean the leaves and the debris off the headstones. The two little headstones next to his mother were his older twin brothers. His mother had nearly died when she miscarried twin boys before she carried him to term. But the headstone he was here to see was the third small marker.

Bruce knelt down next to the headstone—a headstone Savannah had picked out—and brushed dew-damp leaves and dirt off the granite marker. The name carved into the stone, along with the date of death, came into focus. Bruce dropped onto his knees; tears that refused to be ignored poured out of his eyes.

Samuel Jackson Brand.

Beloved Son.

A torrent of memories of the day that Savannah had watched him, along with his brothers, lower their two-year-old son into the ground, memories he had fought to forget, overwhelmed him.

"I'm so sorry, Sammy," Bruce said in a strangled voice.

This was why he had avoided this place—it was too hard. This was too hard.

Bruce took the toy truck out of his pocket and placed it on the top of the headstone. This had been one of his son's favorite toys; he deserved to have it returned to him.

The rancher rubbed the tears out of his eyes, then stood up. How could he even begin to tell Savannah about her son? How could he even begin to tell her that he was responsible for his death?

He left the place that had haunted him—stalked him in his waking moments as well as his dreams. Bruce didn't often feel like he needed advice; he usually knew his own mind. But when he needed counsel, there was one person he sought out, and that was his adoptive mother, Lilly.

He took his time driving back to the main house—he wanted to give himself time to get his emotions under control. When he reached the home he shared with Savannah, he noted that her truck was gone, which meant that she had already gone into town for physical therapy. He parked his truck at their cabin, let the dogs out of the house so they could join him on his walk to the main house.

Bruce found his mother, Lilly, in the sewing loft Jock had built for her. Lilly loved to watch the sun rise and set, so her loft was strategically placed to give her a year-round view of the sun rising in the east and setting in the west.

"Good morning, Mom."

His mother, a Scottish-born woman, had died when he was young; when Lilly came into his life and accepted him so completely as her own, over time, it had been natural for him to refer to his stepmother simply as Mom.

"Son." Lilly reached out her arms for a hug and gave him her usual kiss on the cheek.

Bruce pulled up a chair next to Lilly's workstation, which was stacked high with little plastic boxes of different colors and types of beads.

"What are you working on now?" he asked.

Lilly had always been devoted to her Chippewa-Cree heritage—she was proud of her lineage and was active with her tribe in the preservation of the language, ceremonies and traditions.

"Bracelets." His stepmom held up a bangle that she was hand beading with artistic patterns traditional to her tribe.

"You make beautiful things."

She smiled gently at the compliment. Lilly was a lovely woman who had aged gracefully; her skin, the color of dark golden honey, was finely lined on her forehead and around her eyes, but still held a youthful glow that defied her age. The only giveaways to her real age were the increasingly present strands of silver, which she refused to cover, that stood out in stark contrast to her raven-black hair.

"You're troubled," his mother observed, reading him so easily with her velvety brown eyes.

Lilly was an astute woman, sensitive, kind and insightful. Bruce often marveled at the match between her and Jock.

"I am," he admitted.

"I'm listening." Lilly put the partially beaded bracelet down and turned her body toward him.

Much like the day he had unloaded on Dr. Kind unexpectedly, Bruce unloaded on his mother. He didn't know how to move forward with Savannah without reopening a scabbed-over wound; he couldn't see a way forward in his marriage unless he went back first.

"Isn't it time for you to forgive yourself?" his mother asked him quietly, her eyes full of empathy.

Bruce swallowed hard to keep fresh tears at bay. "I don't even know where to begin."

And if he couldn't forgive himself, how could he expect Savannah to forgive him? She hadn't been able to forgive him the first time around—what would be different now?

"Yes, you do," she disagreed. "You have always known."

These words were followed by a moment of silence. Then, his mother said, "What was once broken has healed back stronger for the breaking."

His mother often spoke in riddles, and he wished she could just talk in a straight line sometimes.

"You are stronger now as a couple. I see you together. This time will be different." She elaborated. "Trust what you feel. Trust that you can weather this storm—together this time—instead of letting it rip you apart.

"It's time, son." Lilly put both of her hands over .his. "It's time to tell Savannah what her mind has forgotten."

After Sunday breakfast at the main house with the family, Savannah couldn't wait to go to the barn and saddle up. Now that she was cleared to ride again, trail riding up to one of the mountain peaks that abutted Sugar Creek was top on her list for their Sunday date. Even Colton's surly mood toward her when she bumped into him in the tack room didn't dampen her happiness.

They saddled two of the ranch's quarter horses and set out together. Up the narrow trail, she took the lead, loving the scent of the wildflowers growing unbidden along the path, and reveling in the feel of the light breeze cooling her face. This was what she had been missing so much; she was so grateful to spend this beautiful day, on horseback, with her husband.

"There's a good spot to dismount up ahead," she called over her shoulder to Bruce.

They were going to have to lead the horses on foot at the narrowest part of the trail just before they reached the peak. At a safe area for her and her horse, Savannah swung her leg over the animal's back and dropped down to the ground. She slipped the reins over her mount's head and gave the horse an affectionate pat on the neck while she waited for Bruce to follow suit.

"We couldn't have a better day for this." Her husband joined her.

She beamed up at him. "I know. It's the most beautiful day we've had all summer."

Bruce looked at her with so much love, so much appreciation, that it warmed her on the inside of her body just as the sun was warming the outside.

"It makes me happy to see you so happy," he said before he leaned down to kiss her lips.

"Being here with you. That makes me happy."

They led the horses single file along the narrow trail; on either side of the path, dangerous, rocky slopes made Savannah cautious with every step.

"I think this is as far as the horses should go." Bruce had taken the lead on this leg of the journey.

They tied the horses with breakaway knots and then carefully climbed their way to the peak of the mountain. There was a favorite spot—their spot—where they would sit together and take in the view spread out before them. On a clear day, they could see for miles.

At the top, a large boulder jutted out from the side of the mountain. This was the target. Savannah loved to sit on that boulder and dangle her legs over the edge. It was like a natural diving board thousands of feet in the air.

"Careful." Bruce held on to her hand as she sat down.

Her husband sat next to her, thigh to thigh, arms intertwined.

"Just look at this, Bruce." Savannah sighed. "It's heaven on earth."

"Yes, it is."

Savannah rested her head on her husband's shoulder, feeling happier in this moment than she could remember.

"I love you." She looked at his strong, hawkish profile.

Bruce leaned over and kissed her lightly on the lips. "I love you more."

Chapter Nine

Their Sunday ended with a quiet dinner that they prepared together, and a movie at home. They didn't see the end of the movie—instead, they let the dogs take over the couch while they went into the bedroom to make love. Sometimes, their lovemaking was hot and aggressive, and other times, Bruce liked to love her slowly, sensually. Either way, it was always passionate.

Naked in the moonlight, Savannah waited for her husband to join her. An unclothed Bruce Brand was a thing of beauty—so muscular and masculine.

"I wish I could take your picture right now." Bruce stopped at the edge of the bed. "You look so sexy."

She smiled at him. "I'm glad you think so."

Bruce started at her feet, dropping butterfly kisses on her ankles, her calves, the inside of her thighs. Savannah moaned with pleasure when he began to kiss that most sensitive spot between her thighs. She threaded her fingers into his hair, and her head dropped back onto the pillow. It didn't take long for her body to want more—to be closer to Bruce, to feel his naked skin against hers, to feel his body fill hers so completely, so perfectly.

With a frustrated little noise in the back of her throat, Savannah let her husband know that she was ready for him. Always responsive to her needs, Bruce dropped a last kiss on her mound before he covered her body with his. She gasped as he slipped inside her, joining their bodies together; he pushed himself up, locking his elbows so he could watch her as he loved her. Savannah held on to his arms, loving the feel of the hard muscles beneath her fingertips, just as she loved the feel of his rock-hard erection moving inside of her.

Every move Bruce made was slow and deliberate—he wanted to have the control, and she was happy to let him. Savannah gasped again, lifted her knees so he could go deeper, take longer strokes as her fingernails dug into his arm.

"Open your eyes," he said in a lover's tender voice.

Savannah opened her eyes for a split second, before she had to close them again as an orgasm forced her to arch her back and lift her hips to take him ever deeper still inside of her.

As she shuddered beneath him, her eyes still closed, her lips parted, Bruce kissed her breasts, her neck, before he wrapped his arms around her and rolled them both to their sides. Her legs were enfolded around his body; she opened her eyes to find him staring at her face.

"How was that?" he asked with a pleased smile.

"Incredible." She took his face in her hands and kissed his lips. "Absolutely incredible."

He ran his hand down her hip, gripped her derriere and pulled her body closer into his.

"Hmm," she murmured. "You feel so good."

Their arms and legs intertwined, Savannah buried her face in Bruce's neck, breathing in that wonderful, familiar scent of his skin. They made love to each other again, their bodies pressed tightly together, their hips falling into a sensual rhythm. By the time her handsome husband growled out a loud, throaty climax that seemed to come from somewhere deep in his soul, they were both drenched in sweat, breathless, hugging each other, and sighing with postcoital satisfaction.

Bruce lay on his back, his chest rising and falling as he caught his breath. He gave a little laugh. "We have always been so very good at that."

Savannah pushed her damp hair off her forehead before she lay down on her back beside him, using his arm as a pillow.

"We really have," she agreed with a smile. "Making love with you just keeps on getting better. I bet we'll still be humping like rabbits when we're in our eighties."

"God willing."

They let their three canine family members into the bedroom and took a quick shower and got ready for bed. Savannah was the first human in bed, while the entire bottom part of the mattress was covered in layers of dogs.

"Really, guys?" Savannah reached forward to pet each animal. "Where am I supposed to put my feet?"

Bruce closed the door behind him and climbed into

bed beside her. He loved to spoon her, wrapping her up in his arms as if she were a giant, cuddly teddy bear. Some nights she was too warm to be cocooned by her husband's usually hot skin, but tonight she couldn't think of another way she'd rather drift off to sleep.

"Comfortable?" Bruce's nose was buried in her hair.

"Uh-huh."

"Good night, sugar."

"'Night." She loved the way her husband smelled right out of the shower. "I love you."

He pulled her even closer to his body and kissed the back of her neck. "I love you more."

One of life's little pleasures on the ranch was to be able to observe her husband from the front porch. She would curl up on one of the two-seater chairs with the dogs and watch her husband do what he loved to do… working in his workshop across the way, or mowing the grass around the house, or fixing fences for the surrounding pastures. Her husband was a Montana rancher to his core, and she loved that about him. She, on the other hand, loved being a Montana woman, born and bred, but she'd had a lot to learn about being married to a rancher at the beginning of her marriage.

Bruce saw her on the porch, said something to the men he had been working with, and then headed her way. His T-shirt was soaked with sweat—on his chest, his stomach and under his arms. For her, Bruce was the most handsome man on the planet. How lucky had she gotten to marry a family-oriented, kind, loyal, sexy cowboy like Bruce Brand? There was a part of her, perhaps more than she was willing to acknowledge, that *wanted* to know what had led to the divorce. But the part of her that didn't want to rock the boat, that didn't want to ruin what was so good with her husband now, was the part that won out time and again. Savannah knew it was wrong, yet she just didn't trust that the tenuous bond she had forged with Bruce could weather the truth.

"Make some room, guys," her husband said to the dogs surrounding her.

Buckley moved so Bruce could sit down on a small sliver of the chair.

"How's it going?" she asked, handing him her glass of sweet tea.

"It's slow goin'," the rancher said before he gulped down the rest of her tea. "But we're getting there."

They sat in silence for several minutes, comfortable in those moments when neither spoke.

"I thought your sister was coming out today."

"She woke up feeling like she was catching a cold."

Her husband nodded, putting the empty glass on the ground next to the chair.

"The vet sent a reminder email." She rubbed the top of Hound Dog's head, lifting up his ears and scratching him around the neck. "It's time to take the gang in for their shots."

Bruce nodded again and looked as if he was going to get up and go back to work.

"Hey." Savannah turned her body toward him a bit. "I've been wanting to tell you something."

"What's that?"

She hated bringing up Leroy—to her, there was this open wound that was trying to heal, and bringing up the topic of a man she'd been dating while they were going through the divorce was like rubbing dirt in the wound. But she had to tell Bruce; she had put it off long enough.

"You know I went out to lunch with Shayna the other day?"

He nodded to let her know that he was listening, but his attention was on his phone and scrolling through texts and emails.

She poked him on the leg with her foot. "Would you put that down for a second, please? This is important."

He tucked the phone back into the pocket of his T-shirt, then looked at her.

"Thank you." Savannah gave a little shake of her head—Bruce had become increasingly addicted to that phone to the point of being annoying. "I don't even know how to bring this up with you, so I'm just going to tell you. Leroy was at the restaurant."

Bruce stared at her for a second, then looked away. "How was that?"

"Horrible."

Her husband looked back as she continued.

"I don't remember him, or at least I don't remember my relationship with him." She crossed her arms in front of her body. "I know he wants me to remember so…"

"…you'll go back to him." The muscle in Bruce's cheek jumped from him clenching his jaw.

He was right—she knew he was right. And it hurt. "I'm glad I don't remember him. I don't *want* to remember."

Savannah had to tell herself not to hold her breath as she stared at her husband's profile. Neither of them wanted to have these conversations; it reminded them that, even though their marriage seemed to be back on track, it wasn't always that way.

Bruce stood up, his eyes shuttered. "I've got to get back to it."

"Okay." She felt sick in her stomach.

He was on his way down the steps when she stopped him. "Hey—where's my kiss, Brand?"

The rancher stopped, turned and pushed the brim of his cowboy hat up with one finger. Wordlessly, he returned to her, bent down and kissed her on the lips.

Savannah grabbed his fingers and held on. "We can't shut down on each other."

"You're right," he agreed with her. "That's not going to help."

Bruce returned to work, swallowing back acid that had started to churn in his stomach the minute Leroy's name came out of his wife's mouth. During the separation and the divorce process, whenever Savannah had talked about Leroy, or he saw the two of them in town holding hands, he wanted to punch the young cowboy in the throat. He knew that Savannah hadn't recovered any of those memories of her relationship with Leroy, but he remembered it all too well. To see his wife, a woman he still very much loved, with another man had made him feel helpless and furious. He'd often found it hard to concentrate on his work or sleep thinking about them. And hearing Leroy's name come out of Savannah's mouth unearthed all of those feelings he had been trying to bury for the sake of salvaging his marriage.

He threw himself into work, the familiar routine of replacing fence boards, a task that relied on muscle memory rather than thinking, giving him a chance to ponder his mother's advice. The relationship between Savannah and himself, on the surface at least, seemed to be stronger than ever, yet he felt like he was standing on shifting sand. Just as Savannah had been worried about telling him about her innocent encounter with Leroy, he too had been worried about opening a Pandora's box by discussing the tragedy that had led to their separation in the first place.

"Coward," Bruce muttered to himself, unmindful of the fact that his brother could hear him.

"What was that?" Colton was a couple of feet down the line, yanking on a stubborn board that wouldn't dislodge from the fence post.

"Nothing," he dodged. Colton, of all people, was the last person he wanted to talk to about his marriage.

But it wasn't "nothing"; he was being a coward. He and Savannah couldn't live in this fantasy bubble forever. They needed to face their past, and because Savannah was happy to leave it "forgotten," Bruce knew that they were heading for trouble. Their past—their mutual tragedy—couldn't be avoided forever. It was inevitable—one day, someone was going to mention Sammy to Savannah. It was just a matter of time, and he couldn't allow that to happen.

He had to be the one to tell Savannah about her son; he had to be the one to tell her about their dear, sweet baby boy, Sammy.

Bruce cut out of work early; he knew that he couldn't spend one more night with his wife without making a plan to face their past. He wasn't sure how to best tackle the subject. Should they be with Dr. Kind? Should they be with Savannah's family? Or should this be a private moment between husband and wife? If there was a right way to handle this, he sure as heck didn't know what it was.

He walked through the door, expecting to be greeted with music and the scent of something cooking in the kitchen. Savannah was on a cooking jag, of which he had been a happy beneficiary. But as he shut the door behind him, greeted by his three faithful dogs, the feeling in the house was off. It was quiet—no music playing—and the kitchen was empty and cold.

Bruce put his hat on the hook, showed each dog some attention, before he called out to his wife. That sick feeling returned to his stomach when Savannah didn't respond. He followed the dogs down the hallway toward the bedroom; he found his wife in the office, sitting at his desk, with an enlarged picture of Sammy in Savannah's lap, his chubby arms around her neck. They were both smiling so broadly, so happy to be with each other; in the picture, Savannah's eyes were sparkling with joy at the simple pleasure of holding their son in her arms.

Fear, pure, stripped-down fear, sent a cold shiver across his body. His heart was pounding, and he was stuck in his spot, unable to speak, unable to move.

Savannah turned in the swivel chair so she could face him.

"Who is this little boy?" she asked him. He could tell by the confusion in her eyes that she recognized that this child in the picture was someone important, but she couldn't remember why. This moment was exactly what he had feared—now there wasn't any way to break the news gently to Savannah. The bandage had just been ripped off without any finesse to minimize the pain she would assuredly feel.

"Samuel." Bruce had to swallow several times before he was able to say his son's name out loud to Savannah after so many years. "Our son, Samuel."

Why she had picked that day to be curious, Savannah couldn't figure. She had sat down at the computer to find a recipe for dinner, but had decided to click on the photo album instead. Bruce had never hidden the photo album—there wasn't a password lock on the computer. She could have looked at the pictures at any time. Until now—until today—she hadn't wanted to look. It had been her choice.

Savannah felt the color drain from her face, felt her stomach clench, when Bruce said the name "Samuel." Somewhere, deep in the forgotten memories of her mind, that name reverberated in the tissue of her body—that name reverberated in her soul.

"Our son..."

She turned back to the picture, one of the few she had found featuring this little boy. Savannah reached out and touched the screen with her fingertips. In a whisper, she said, "We called him Sammy."

"Yes." Bruce's voice sounded choked. "We did. Do you...remember him?"

Savannah pressed her hand to her mouth, the salty taste of her fresh tears on her tongue. She shook her head again and again, unable to speak. All she could think was "our son" over and over, trying to make sense of it. Trying to understand.

"Where is he?" she asked, her voice muffled behind her hand. "Why isn't he here with us?"

When Bruce didn't respond right away, Savannah stood up, her face wet with tears pouring from her stricken eyes.

She put her hand on her heart. "How can I not know that I have a *son*? How can I not *know* this?"

He crossed the divide between them, pulled her into his arms, ignoring her resistance, wrapped her in his arms, his chin on the top of her head.

"Where is my son?" Savannah demanded, her tears wetting the front of Bruce's shirt. *"Why isn't he here with us?"*

As if he wanted to stop her from running away from him, her husband tightened his grip on her body. And then he said the words she knew were coming—she couldn't remember it, but she could *feel* it, in her heart, in her gut.

"God, please help me say it." She felt Bruce's tears fall into her hair. "He died, Savannah. Our son's gone."

Savannah pushed on his chest and twisted her body to make him let her go. She backed away from her husband; the shock and pain and horror felt like a knife slicing at her skin. No words... No words... There were no words.

With a moan of anguish, Savannah pushed past her husband and ran to the bathroom. She slammed the door shut behind her, locked it, and then landed on her knees in front of the commode, retching. Clutching her stomach, she flushed the toilet and stumbled to the sink. The water was ice-cold from the faucet—she rinsed out her mouth and washed the tears from her face.

"Savannah." Bruce knocked on the door and rattled the knob. "Please, let me in."

"Go away," she told him in a raspy voice.

She had a son—a darling little boy with her dimples and Bruce's incredible blue eyes. And she couldn't *remember him*. He had been erased from her brain—erased from her life; it was a cruelty that she couldn't handle. It was a cruelty she couldn't comprehend.

Why can't I remember? How could I not have known?

Savannah stared at her reflection in the mirror—her cheeks and her nose were red, her eyes bloodshot with puffy lids. She put her hands on her breasts—they had changed; she had noticed that. They were a little larger, a little saggier, but it had never occurred to her that it was anything more than fluctuating weight and gravity. Had Samuel suckled them? Had she breastfed her son even though she had never been interested in breastfeeding?

Still looking at her reflection, Savannah lifted up her shirt and pushed down the waistband of her jeans. There were some stretch marks on her stomach, on her hips—hairline, barely noticeable, white marks on her skin. Her hands pressed into her abdomen; she had gotten pregnant, carried a child, given birth to a child, and held that child in her arms. She knew that now. But she couldn't remember the scent of his skin; she couldn't remember what it felt like to hold that chubby body in her arms.

"What kind of mother would forget her own son?" Savannah frowned at her reflection with the smallest shake of the head.

"Savannah." Bruce's voice cut through the door and cut through her own dark thoughts. "Let me in."

All of the emotions she had been feeling seemed

to be pulled out of her body, leaving a gaping, empty, numb hole in their place. Slowly, stiffly, like a robot, Savannah unlocked the bathroom door, turned the handle, and pulled the door open.

On the other side of the door, her husband and her dogs waited for her. Hound Dog was whimpering, his worried eyes on her face. They were so intuitive; they knew, without understanding the words, that something was very wrong in their house.

"Savannah." Her husband's face was ashen. "I'm so sorry. There was no easy way…"

She slipped past him, wordlessly, and went to the kitchen. There, she picked up her keys, her phone and her wallet.

"Where are you going?"

Savannah had trouble looking at him, so instead she looked past him. "I need time."

She was hurting him—she saw the pain in his eyes in her peripheral vision—but she couldn't handle his pain right now. Not right now.

"You said that we can't shut each other out." For the first time, Bruce sounded angry. "That's what you said not two hours ago."

Now she looked him directly in the eyes, her own anger bubbling to the top like magma bubbling up from a volcano. "You don't have a right to dictate how I feel or how I react to this, Bruce. Do you get that? You don't have the *right*."

Chapter Ten

The very thing he was afraid of had indeed come home to roost. He had waited too long to tell her, to soften the blow of Savannah finding out about their son. Perhaps he had hoped, in a way, that her memories of sweet Sammy would return on their own, saving him from the horrible task of telling Savannah that she was a mother and that their son was gone.

Watching his wife leave their home was reliving a scene from his past that he had suppressed for so long. Savannah had walked out on him before, and he hadn't put up a fight. He had been too emotionally raw himself, drowning in his own guilt, that he hadn't believed that he had a right to fight for his marriage. But this time, he was going to be different. He was going to put up one hell of a fight for his marriage.

He spent several hours reaching out to Savannah's

parents, her sisters and her friends. None of them had heard from her, but they all promised to call him right away if they did. It was a relief to have all of them on his side—this time around.

Bruce called her phone, sent her texts, tried to reach her by video chat. Savannah could be stubborn to a fault, and he finally had to accept that he would have to wait for her to return to him in her own way, in her own time. Tired of pacing, tired of not being able to concentrate on any one thing, Bruce finally decided to take a seat on the porch and wait for his wife to come home.

Somewhere along the way, he had fallen asleep on the porch. The sound of the dogs barking excitedly awakened him; he squinted at the early-morning sun and winced at the stiffness of his neck from sleeping upright all night.

The dogs were barking their greeting to Savannah. Bruce watched as his wayward wife parked the truck and got out. She reached down to pet the dogs, but her eyes were on him. Slowly, deliberately, Savannah crossed to the porch. At the bottom of the stairs, she stopped, her arms crossed tightly in front of her body.

"Hi." She had dark circles under her puffy red eyes.

"I'm glad you're back," he told her.

"I'm sorry I left like I did." She apologized in a quiet voice. "You didn't deserve that."

He appreciated the apology, but all he wanted was for her to stay this time—to work through the loss of their son together, something they hadn't been able to do before.

"I'm sorry." He stood up; he wanted so badly to take her in his arms, to hold her, to comfort her. But he was afraid of being pushed away. "I thought—we

all thought—that you needed time to heal before..."
His voice trailed off. Would it always be hard to say
his son's name out loud?

She leaned against the handrail on the stairs, arms
still crossed. "I drove around all night, trying to remember...trying to remember."

Savannah met his eyes, her own eyes damp with a
fresh cycle of tears. "I couldn't remember anything.
Not one thing."

Her next words broke his heart. "Will you..." She
stopped, cleared her throat, and then continued. "Will
you please tell me about our son?"

She waited on the couch, surrounded by her dogs,
while Bruce got his laptop from the bedroom. All night
she had tried to remember her son, but she couldn't.
She couldn't. Her brain had betrayed her, robbed her
of the precious memories of her only child. Now, she
needed to be strong enough to find out about her son's
life—and his death.

"Oh..." Savannah's fingers went up to her lips when
Bruce handed her pictures of her ultrasound. "Look
at him."

Bruce joined her, sitting next to her, but not touching her.

"You were so happy that day. We found out Sammy
was a Samuel instead of a Samantha."

Savannah ran her fingertips over the picture, touching her son's cheek. "He's sucking his thumb."

Bruce cracked a fleeting smile. "In the womb and
out of the womb. We couldn't keep his thumb out of
his mouth. Or his toes, for that matter."

She knew there would be more tears—how could

there not be? She held on to the ultrasound pictures with one hand and wiped the tears from her eyes with the other.

Her husband turned on the laptop; folder after folder was filled with a treasure trove of pictures featuring their son, Samuel Jackson Brand.

"How in the world did you talk me into the name?" Savannah mused aloud. Samuel L. Jackson was Bruce's favorite actor; he'd watched every Samuel L. Jackson movie at least twice.

"It took some doing," Bruce acknowledged. "But you loved it."

Picture after picture, Savannah began to create a three dimensional image of her son in her mind. He was a happy boy, full of energy and curiosity. He had loved all animals and anything with four wheels. Sammy had been an affectionate boy, always hugging someone in the pictures. And that smile—those dimples. He had been...perfect.

Bruce told her about the day they found out she was pregnant—it was a happy accident, an unplanned pregnancy with a rare but possible failure with the birth control pill. They had always wanted a family, but she'd wanted to wait until after she got settled in her career and decided to pursue a doctoral degree. He told her about the day their son was born; she had gone into labor three weeks early on a frosty fall morning. Bruce laughed a little when he recounted how they could see their breath while they were sniping at each other as they loaded into the truck to go to the hospital. He showed her the first pictures of her holding premature Sammy, his tiny pink body curled up on her chest as she smiled, with tired eyes and mussed hair, at the camera.

"I got it," Bruce told her. "Right then, what parents were always talking about. I had no idea how much I could love someone until I first met Sammy."

"I look so happy. In every picture with him. I look so happy."

"You took to motherhood. I think we were both shocked at how much you loved it." Bruce glanced over at her. "You kept on talking about how you wanted ten more just like him. Ten more."

She had so many questions, and he answered every one. Except for the biggest question of all—the one she was afraid to ask.

"Do you need a break?" her husband asked her when she stopped commenting on the pictures.

"No," she said faintly. "No. I don't. I need to know what happened."

Bruce closed the laptop and turned his head away from her.

"Sammy is gone because of me," he told her in a harsh whisper. "I'm to blame."

Savannah became a voracious consumer of home videos featuring her son—from the birth, which she couldn't believe she let Bruce videotape, but now was glad for it, to Samuel's first birthday party and so many more moments, both large and small, of her son's life. She knew his smile now; she knew the sound of his voice, the wonder that always seemed to be present in his wide, bright blue eyes. But she didn't know what it was like to tuck him into bed; she didn't know what it was like to feel his kiss on her cheek. And there was a possibility that her memory would never return, and her only connection with her son was one-dimensional.

That night, Savannah crawled into bed exhausted. She hadn't slept the night before, and the entire day had been spent trying to download every recorded second of her son's life into her brain. Bruce had been able to talk at length about their son's life—but he wasn't able to talk to her about his death. It was as if the words were stuck somewhere deep inside, and he just couldn't get them out. Maybe that was for the best. Maybe she needed some time to reflect on Sammy's beautiful life before she started to mourn the tragedy of his death. So she hadn't pushed Bruce. She didn't push him.

Bruce had stayed up long after she had turned in; when she felt the weight of her husband getting into his side of the bed, Savannah rolled over onto her back. As much has she had tried to fall asleep—as tired as she was—sleep escaped her. And what made it worse was that already they were shutting down, both of them. They hadn't told each other that they loved each other—and even though she obviously still felt it, she couldn't find her way to say the words out loud. It was so easy to see, so easy to understand, why they had ended up separating. Sammy's life had been such a source of joy and bonding between them; losing him had broken them apart.

"Bruce." She could tell by his breathing that he was still awake.

"Yes?"

You have to say the words, Savannah. Say the words.

"I love you."

After a moment of silence, not turning toward her, Bruce said in a clear voice, "I love you more."

Savannah reached out to touch her husband's back. "Will you take me to see Sammy tomorrow?"

Three full heartbeats of silence, and then Bruce said simply, "Yes."

For the second time in a very short time, Bruce returned to the family cemetery. He had worked very hard to push this place out of his mind, to shove aside the emotions attached to the place of his son's final resting place—but the truth was, this little plot of land, with its small marble headstone, was never far from his waking thoughts. The image of it had lurked in the background, haunting him.

"Your parents weren't so sure about burying Sammy here." Bruce shut off the engine. "But we both wanted him to be close. Sammy loved Sugar Creek. Even as young as he was, I could see that this ranch was in his blood."

They met at the front of the truck, and to his surprise, Savannah reached for his hand. Did he deserve this kindness? He didn't think so. But he was grateful for it. Together, hand in hand, they walked on the overgrown path the short distance to the plot of land surrounded by the black wrought-iron fence. They didn't say anything as they made their way over to Samuel's grave, but Savannah gasped when she saw the fire truck that she had found in the garden.

His wife dropped to her knees next to their son's headstone, her finger lightly tracing his name etched into the white marble.

"'Samuel Jackson Brand. Beloved son.'" Savannah read the simple wording on the grave. She had selected the headstone, the font style and the modest wording.

Seeing his wife on her knees beside their son's grave was more than Bruce could stand. He turned away, tears in his eyes, and walked back to the truck. How could he expect Savannah to forgive him if he couldn't find a way to forgive himself? Bruce climbed behind the wheel of his truck and watched Savannah through the windshield. She deserved to take as much time as she needed, to have this private moment at her son's graveside.

The pain he saw in his wife's eyes was the pain he felt in every layer of his body; it never really faded. That sorrow was a pain he had just had to learn to live with; now Savannah would have to learn to live with it again, too.

When Savannah finally stood up and started to walk back to the truck, Bruce hopped out and met her at the passenger-side door. He held the door open for her, his eyes sweeping her face. Her pretty oval face, a face he knew well and loved so much, was wet with freshly shed tears. He took a cloth handkerchief out of the back pocket of his jeans and handed it to her before he gently shut the door.

Savannah was blowing her nose loudly as he got back behind the wheel. He didn't start the engine; he just sat there, staring at their son's headstone.

"I only left him for a minute," Bruce said, still staring straight ahead, not wanting to look at his wife's face. "I promise you—it was only a minute."

Out of the corner of his eye, he saw Savannah watching him, hanging on his next words.

"But one minute was too long," he said with self-recrimination. "One second would have been too long."

Savannah put her hand on his leg, and this show of compassion, this show of support, gave him the strength to continue.

"You were in Tennessee visiting your sister," Bruce told her. "And I was going to spend some quality time with the little man." He laughed a hollow laugh. "I couldn't wait to spend that time with Sammy—I had so many plans. So many plans."

Bruce swallowed hard, choking back tears. "Right before we went to the airport, you told me that you had washed the towels, and all I had to do was get them out of the dryer, fold them and put them away in the bathroom."

He shook his head in disgust. "I have looked back at that moment a million times; why didn't I just take the towels out of the dryer when I got home? What was so important that made me put it off?"

Savannah's hand tightened on his leg.

"That day, I took him to the creek and he chased minnows for an hour. A whole hour. I can remember so clearly how loud he was laughing, stomping his feet in the water, trying to catch those little minnows with his chubby hands."

He glanced at Savannah, who had turned her body toward his. "Sammy loved water. Even when he was a baby, we never had to fight with him to get him into the bath. It was no different that night…" His voice trailed off as the memories, beautiful and horrible, came flooding back to him. "I put him in the tub for his bath that night. I remember he was excited about the new tugboat toy you had gotten for him. We played until that poor kid was all wrinkly from being in the water for too long…"

"But when I opened the cabinet to get a towel—" Bruce's voice cracked on the words, and he sniffed loudly. "I only left him for a minute. Just one minute."

"Oh, no." Savannah gasped as she put the missing, unspoken pieces in place. "No."

He couldn't say the words, "Sammy drowned." He just couldn't. It was his fault that their son was gone— accident or not. If he had just gotten the damn towels out of the dryer before he put Sammy in the tub—their son would still be alive. Their son would still be with them, and they would have never separated, they would have never gone through a divorce, and she would have never been with Leroy.

Savannah didn't yell at him or accuse him. Instead, she moved onto his lap, wrapped her arms around him and held him tightly while years of anger and self-loathing and sorrow poured out of him.

"I'm so sorry, Sammy…" he repeated over and over again. "I'm so sorry."

Bruce held on to Savannah, hugging her nearly breathless, as they wept together, mourning the loss of their precious son for the first time together. After they'd buried Samuel, Savannah had stopped touching him; she'd stopped sleeping in their bed. And, on his part, he didn't want to talk about Sammy. It was too painful. Unlike Savannah, who'd spent hours sitting on Sammy's brand-new "big boy" toddler bed, clutching his favorite stuffed toy to her chest, he'd wanted to strip the room and lock the door. Their grief took them down different roads; their grief had ended their marriage. Only time would tell if their son's tragic death would rip them apart again.

That night, they made love for the first time since she'd found the picture of Samuel. It was a quiet, poignant expression of their love, slow and tender. They held each other, kissed deeply and lingeringly, and mingled breath and sweet words of love. Savannah understood now *why* they had separated and eventually filed for divorce. One of her many flaws was her inability to forgive; she held herself and everyone else to very high standards, and this often led her to fail to forgive flaws in herself as well as others. She had turned her back on Bruce. At the time when he needed her the most—when he needed her to be his best friend and wife—she had walked away.

Yes, it was Bruce's terrible misjudgment that had resulted in their son's death. But wasn't she also culpable? Had she shown her husband some compassion, their marriage would have survived. And she would never have ended up in Leroy's muscle car the night of the crash.

The next day, they went to see their therapist together.

"I'm glad to see the both of you." Dr. Kind gestured for them to take a seat.

They had made an appointment with the psychologist; neither one of them wanted to see their marriage implode as it had before. Bruce didn't hesitate to agree to go back to see Dr. Kind. This was a signal to Savannah that Bruce was "all-in" with their marriage, and that gave her the strength to tackle her emotions

around the death of her son without destroying her relationship with Bruce.

"So, where would you like to start today?"

This time, they were sitting side by side on the
couch, which was an improvement from the last time
they had sat on this sofa together.

"Do you want me to start?" she asked her husband.

He nodded, so she filled the psychologist in on
the events of the last week—learning that she was a
mother, and that her son had drowned on her husband's
watch.

"That's a lot to learn," Dr. Kind noted. "And a lot
for you, Bruce, to relive."

They both nodded. It was, in truth, more pain than
any couple should have to endure.

"And how do you feel, Savannah, now that you
know the truth?"

Savannah hesitated. "I feel…everything. Depressed,
furious, cheated, guilty…"

"Let's explore the guilt," Dr. Kind said "What do
you feel guilty about?"

"The divorce."

"That wasn't your fault," Bruce objected. "We both
had our fingerprints all over that."

"Has any of this jarred memories for you, Savannah?"

"I remembered that we called Samuel 'Sammy.' I remembered his favorite stuffed animal. But that's all…"

"How did Savannah behave toward you after Samuel's death?" the psychologist asked Bruce.

Bruce didn't answer right away; Savannah gave his
arm a little shake. "It's okay. You can tell me. That's
why we're here."

Her husband swallowed hard, his hand clammier to the touch. Then, he cleared his throat and said, "She stopped loving me."

To hear Bruce say that she had stopped loving him had left her temporarily speechless and stunned. He hadn't said it to hurt her; he hadn't said it to be mean or vindictive. He had said it because that was how she had made him feel when she stopped kissing him, stopped holding his hand, stopped making love. She was certain that she never stopped loving Bruce. Not when she had left their marital bed, not when she had moved out, not when she had gotten involved with uncomplicated Leroy, and not when she had filed for divorce.

"I'm sorry, Bruce," she said on the drive back to the ranch.

"You don't owe me an apology."

"Yes, I do," Savannah was quick to say. "I left you when you needed me the most."

"I think there's a whole lot of people in this world who would think that you had all the reason in the world to leave me."

Savannah reached out her hand; Bruce switched hands on the steering wheel so he could take it.

"Maybe so. But they'd be wrong."

Chapter Eleven

That was the first of many sessions that the two of them had with Dr. Kind. It wasn't always easy, and they weren't always happy with each other when they left a session, but they were talking—and they were still together, and that was the goal.

Savannah flopped down on the couch next to Bruce, and tucked her feet beneath her.

"I've decided something," she announced.

As usual, Bruce was immersed in his phone, playing a game—the man was obsessed. Savannah put her hand over her husband's phone and pushed it down.

"I've made a decision."

Bruce never liked it when she covered the screen of his phone. "I was listening."

"I want you to *look* at me."

"Fine. I'm listening." Her husband put his phone

facedown on his leg and opened his eyes really wide as he stared at her. "*And* looking."

"I hope it's not too painful."

"It's never painful looking at you." He winked at her and leaned close so she'd kiss him.

She obliged, giving him a little kiss on the lips.

"So what have you decided?"

"Well," she said excitedly. "I've decided to get a tattoo."

He looked at her like she'd grown two horns and buck teeth.

"Why would you do that?"

Savannah shifted and then hooked her arm around her bent knee. "For Samuel. I want to get a portrait of him on my back." She reached over her right shoulder. "Right here."

It took her husband a short time to get onboard. "If that's what you want, I support you."

Savannah was pleased. "Good. Because I was going to do it either way."

Later that day, armed with the first picture of Sammy she had found on Bruce's computer, Savannah met her sister Justine, her sister-in-law, Jessie, and her friend Shayna at A Touch of Ink Tattoo parlor near the university in downtown Bozeman.

"Isabella is the best tattoo artist *ever*, trust me." Jessie's long, raven's-wing hair swung behind her as she walked with a youthful jaunt.

"Mom and Dad are going to have a baby cow." Justine repeated what she had been telling her sister for a week.

"It's my skin." Savannah loved her parents, but it was her body and her choice to honor her son in this way.

"I would love to get a tattoo," Shayna admitted.

"Get one with me!"

Shayna, a plus-size woman who always dressed in stylish but conservative clothing, shook her head no. "I'm not ready. But I wanted to be here to support you. I love the idea of keeping Samuel with you always."

Savannah felt elated at finally walking into the tattoo parlor, putting her plan into action.

"Welcome." A slender woman who looked like a 1920s pinup greeted them. "Take a look at my portfolio, and I'll be with you guys in a minute."

It was a small shop and surprisingly clean, with hand-scraped wooden floors. Savannah had never set foot in a tattoo parlor before, but Isabella Noble was hot on the tattoo scene. She had graduated from Montana State with an art degree; the walls of her shop were lined with art awards, her degree and enlarged pictures of some of her best tattoo work.

While Isabella finished up with the client in her chair, Savannah and her entourage gathered around the glass counter and flipped through the tattoo artist's portfolio.

"Wow." Savannah was genuinely impressed with the level of talent Isabella demonstrated in her work.

"Told you," Jessie said before she spun away to explore.

"She'll be able to do Sammy justice," Shayna agreed.

Justine kept silent—her sister would give her moral support, but she wouldn't act like she agreed with the idea if she didn't.

"Look at this one." Savannah pointed to a black-

and-white portrait that Isabella had tattooed on a man's arm. "It looks just like a photograph."

They waited for Isabella to finish, and then it was Savannah's turn to talk to the artist about the tattoo of her dreams.

"Who's this handsome fellow?" Isabella admired the photograph of Samuel.

"My son. Sammy."

They discussed the size of the portrait, the position on her body, and whether she wanted the tattoo to be color or black and white.

"I can do it," Isabella told her. "I'll just need some time to draw it up for you."

Savannah left a deposit with Isabella and set an appointment to come back and get the tattoo.

"Thank you, Isabella." Savannah shook the petite artist's hand. "I can't wait."

Savannah hugged her sister and her friend, and then she walked to her truck with Jessie.

"You know what I was thinking?" Jessie asked her.

"No telling."

"I was thinking that you and my brother should have a vow renewal. Wouldn't that be super cool?"

The thought hadn't crossed her mind, yet it wasn't a bad idea. In fact, it was a pretty fabulous idea. Bruce and she could start over—truly start their marriage anew.

"You could get a new dress—I could be one of your maids of honor again, but this time I could wear a bangin' dress. We could have a huge party at the ranch. You should totally do it."

* * *

"How does it look?" Savannah was lying facedown on the bed, naked to the waist. "Do you like it?"

Bruce sat down next to his wife on the bed, amazed at the likeness of his son on Savannah's back. He took the top off some ointment, squeezed a little onto his clean fingers and rubbed it over the tattoo.

"It looks just like Sammy," he told her. "I love it."

"I do, too. It hurt like all get-out, but it was worth it."

Bruce was glad that Savannah had opted not to put his date of death beneath the portrait—he couldn't be sure, but he felt that his wife had him in mind when she opted to just include Sammy's name and "Beloved Son" with the picture.

Savannah rolled over and then sat up. Bruce's eyes, slightly narrowed, admired her naked breasts.

"You are beautiful, my love." Bruce traced the curve of her breast.

"I'm glad you think so."

"I do." He leaned down and took her breast in his mouth.

The moment his mouth touched her breast, that delicate, sensitive core of her body, right at the apex of her thighs, responded to her husband's invitation. Bruce pulled her on to his lap, suckling her breast until she was moving her hips against him, seeking that relief that only he could give her. With one arm, Bruce lifted her up and sat her down on the edge of the bed. He reached for his zipper, but she pushed his hand away.

With a sensual smile in her eyes, she hooked her finger into his waistband and pulled him between her thighs. She unbuttoned and unzipped his jeans like she was unwrapping a present; his erection, so hard, so warm, sprung free as she pushed his jeans and underwear downward so he could step out of them.

She took him in her hands, stroking him in just the way he loved, before taking him into her mouth. Bruce dug his fingers into her hair and moaned. It didn't take Bruce long to change the position—he enjoyed that type of kiss, but he loved being inside of her.

He held out his hand to her, helped her up, and then took her place on the bed. "Come here."

Savannah knelt on her knees on either side of his muscular thighs and then sank downward, taking him in, letting him fill her so completely. With a little struggle, she untucked her legs so she would wind them around her husband. She wrapped her legs and arms tightly around her handsome rancher, kissing his neck, breathing in his scent, while they rocked their bodies in that familiar rhythm as their moans of pleasure melded together.

After the lovemaking, they lay beside each other in the bed, surrounded by their canine family; Savannah was on her stomach so she wouldn't hurt her new tattoo, while Bruce was on his back, one arm behind his head, the other on her derriere. It was dark in the bedroom, cool and quiet. Their eyes had adjusted to the lower light, so Savannah could still make out the expression on her husband's face.

"Jessie had a crazy idea."

"What's that?"

"She thinks…" Why was she so nervous about saying this? "She thinks that we should have a vow renewal."

Her heart started to beat a little faster when he didn't answer right away. Didn't he *want* to marry her again?

"You mean—like a ceremony?"

Savannah pushed upright and sat cross-legged next to her lounging husband. The more she had thought about a vow renewal, the more excited she was about the prospect. It was a chance to recommit themselves to the marriage, a sign that, no matter what, they were a bonded pair for the rest of their lives.

"Yes." She nodded enthusiastically. "The whole she-bang. A second wedding. I could get a dress. You could be in a tuxedo. We could have a reception here at the ranch for all of our family and friends.

"What do you think?" She reached out to hold his hand.

"I think…" he replied slowly, deliberately. "I'm going to have to go ring shopping."

His brother Liam, a strong supporter of his attempts to repair his marriage with Savannah, met him at the Jewelry Station in downtown Bozeman. The fact that he had a second chance at picking out a ring, proposing and having a ceremony with his wife made Bruce feel hopeful for the longevity of his marriage in a way he hadn't before. To pull back from the precipice of divorce, to have a new opportunity to make Savannah his wife for the rest of his life was, quite frankly, a blessing.

"What are you thinking about getting her this time?" Liam, the tallest of his full brothers and a large-animal veterinarian, was wearing the blue scrubs he usually wore when he conducted pre-purchase vet checks on horses.

"I'll know it when I see it," Bruce told him, scouring the rows of glass cases for the exact ring for his bride.

She was such an extraordinary woman, he wanted this ring to reflect that. And he certainly wanted this new ring to be completely different from the single band of diamonds she wore as a wedding band. She had wanted a yellow sapphire for her engagement ring the first time around, which he had agreed to, but this time, she was going to get a diamond.

"Hello, gentlemen." A pretty blonde woman in her mid-forties greeted them. "What are we looking for today?"

"An engagement ring," Bruce told her. "For my wife."

Tiffany was the woman's name, and she spent an hour with him, showing him different engagement rings and wedding sets. Her patience and expertise were exactly what he needed to finally decide on the perfect ring for his bride. He couldn't find it in the cases; instead, with Tiffany's help and creative skills, he designed a custom diamond ring for Savannah. It was going to be unlike anything she had in her jewelry box—it was going to be delicate and sparkly and fit for a princess. It was going to be perfect for her; he couldn't wait to see it finished. In the meantime, he needed to plan the perfect surprise proposal. He had to think of what would make it special for Savannah—how would she want him to propose?

"Thanks for doing this with me," Bruce said to his brother as they left the jewelry store.

"I'm happy to see you making it work with Savannah," his younger brother said. "I wouldn't wish divorce on my worst enemy."

His own divorce was still a sensitive topic for Liam.

"How are the kids?"

"They seem to be happy enough," the veterinarian told him. "But I get real tired of having a relationship with my own children on a screen."

They gave each other a hug before they parted ways. Liam had been through his own private hell, so Bruce didn't say what had popped into his mind when his brother talked about his children. Maybe it wasn't ideal, but it was better that Liam could still see his children, while he didn't have that luxury; if he could have Sammy back but only see him via video chat, he'd take that deal every day and twice on Sunday.

"Is it true that you aren't coming back this year?" her friend Deb asked her while they began the chore of packing the belongings in her apartment. This task was long overdue, and in light of the progress she had made in her marriage to Bruce, and in light of the fact that it was time to renew her lease, Savannah decided it was way past time to give up her apartment and move all of her belongings back to Sugar Creek.

"It's true," she replied while taping up the bottom of a book box.

Soon after she had found out about Sammy—his life and his death—her desire to shape a different future for herself emerged. Yes, she loved teaching. But her soul wanted something else now. She wanted to start a foundation in Sammy's memory, to build awareness about keeping children safe near all types of water, including toilet and tub. She wanted Sammy to have new life, to be remembered always, and to help other parents not experience the same preventable tragedy. In short, she wanted to dedicate her life to Sammy's memory—it made her feel more connected to the son she couldn't remember, the son she only knew through pictures and family stories and videos.

"Well," Deb said with a sad expression, "we'll miss you. But I do understand. And if there's anything I can do to help with the foundation, just let me know."

She worked all day on the apartment, packing up the kitchen and the bathroom and the living room. It was a hard task, not just physically, but mentally. Inevitably, she came across memorabilia of her relationship with Leroy—cards, notes, printed out pictures hung on the refrigerator. One by one, Savannah destroyed those items and threw them in the trash. Leroy wasn't a bad-looking guy; he was just young and a little uneducated and naive. Why in the world had she gravitated to him? It didn't make a bit of sense; she had a feeling that it never would.

"That's it." Savannah taped up the last box.

Deb was sitting on the floor drinking a soda; her friend gestured for her to join her.

"Here's to you and Bruce." Deb first handed her a bottle of soda and then held out her bottle for a toast.

"I'll drink to that." She clinked her plastic bottle to Deb's.

They were both too tired to expend energy on small talk; they had been friends for years, so they could sit in comfortable silence.

Savannah looked around at the apartment she didn't remember living in. "I can't thank you enough, Deb. I'd still be putting boxes together if you hadn't helped. Now all that's left to do is to get Bruce and his brothers to pack this stuff up, then I can clean it and turn in my keys."

The two of them rested and recharged their batteries

before they parted ways. Deb had to make dinner for her three boys, and Savannah wanted to get back to the ranch to see Bruce. She couldn't wait to tell him that she was ready for him to come get all of her stuff from the apartment. On the "undo the mess we made of our marriage" checklist, getting rid of her postseparation apartment, a symbol to the both of them, was about to be checked right off that list.

After dinner, they went for their usual evening walk. This was one of her favorite moments in her day—walking, hand in hand, along the roads of Sugar Creek Ranch, or through the pastures, with their dogs running and barking and chasing each other. It was such an enjoyable way to end their day together, and it also gave them an opportunity to discuss things that they had on their minds.

They reached one of the fences facing west, and Bruce lifted her up and set her down on the top plank. Savannah spun around so she was facing westward, and Bruce, still standing, leaned against the fence beside her.

She reached over to brush his hair, a little on the long side now, off his forehead.

"The apartment is ready to go."

"I'm glad to hear that." Her husband wrapped his arm around her hips. "I'll get the bros together, and we'll get all of your stuff back on the ranch where it belongs."

"I'm ready."

He nodded.

"I also told Deb about not returning to teaching. It feels weird to say that out loud."

She had always had a career—work had always been her joy—but the foundation for Sammy was speaking to her heart now.

"Do you think I'm doing the right thing?" she asked Bruce. "I mean, about starting the foundation?"

"I want you to follow your heart, my love," her husband said earnestly. "I want you to be happy and I want you to be with me. Other than those two things, I'm flexible."

She leaned down and kissed his lips. "Thank you. Sometimes I think I'm being really selfish leaving my kids at work."

"You're not being selfish," Bruce disagreed. "You're being a mother who loves her son. You're being a mother who wants to stay connected to your son, to have Sammy's life touch other parents. That's not selfish. Personally, I'm really proud of you."

This was classic Bruce—he always made her feel good about following her dreams. Would he be on board about the next dream she wanted to pursue?

"I also made an appointment with my ob-gyn today."

Bruce's brows drew together with concern. "Why? What's wrong?"

"Nothing." She shook her head. "I want to talk to her about getting off the pill."

She had Bruce's full attention now.

Savannah turned a bit so she could look into her husband's stunning blue eyes.

"I want to try to have another baby, Bruce."

His expression was inscrutable—she couldn't tell if he thought the idea was crazy or awesome.

"What do you...think about that idea?" she prompted him.

Samuel had been unplanned, but she could see from the pictures that she had reveled in motherhood. She wished she could remember what it was like to "feel" motherhood and remember what it felt like to hold her son and experience that wide, ecstatic smile on her face. Savannah realized that they would never be able to fill the void that Sammy left in their lives, but why couldn't they bring another life into the family? Why couldn't they create another life, a child manifested from their love, their friendship, their passion and their devotion? Why?

"I think," Bruce finally said, his voice gruff with emotion, "that I would be honored to have another child with you."

Chapter Twelve

"You look handsome." Savannah admired her husband.

He was showered, shaved and dressed in dark blue jeans with a black button-down shirt, and the cowboy hat he only wore on special occasions.

"Thank you, darlin'." He tipped his hat to her. "You're lookin' mighty fine yourself."

Wearing new slender-fit jeans and high-heel cowgirl boots, she gave her husband a little spin so he could get the full effect.

"You're a good-looking woman, my love." Bruce hooked his arm around her waist, dipped her and kissed her lips.

Savannah laughed and wiped her lipstick off her husband's mouth. "That lipstick is not in your color wheel."

She grabbed her handbag, and they left for an evening out on the town. One of Bruce's brothers, Shane, a retired marine and more-often-than-not recluse, was making a rare appearance at a bar downtown. Savannah loved all of her brothers-in-law—even Colton, who still treated her like enemy number one—but she had just a little extra special in her heart for Shane. He had always been such a warmhearted, gentle, sensitive young man who poured himself into his music. All of those things that Shane couldn't say out loud, he said with his voice, his lyrics and his acoustic guitar. After being deployed to Iraq four times, Shane wasn't the same young man. The death and the horrors of war had changed him forever.

At a small, round table, Savannah sat beside her husband, waiting for Shane to begin performing. Every available Brand was present—from Jock to Colton to Liam. Only Jessie, who was still underage, and Noah, who was still in South Korea, weren't in attendance. That was something that Savannah could always say about the family she had married into—they were dysfunctional as all get-out, but they stuck together despite the dysfunction.

"Here he is." Savannah squeezed Bruce's arm excitedly. "Here he is."

"He looks real rough."

Bruce was right about that—Shane looked worse for wear. His hair was long and shaggy, and he had an unkempt beard and mustache. His sunglasses, in her opinion, were a way of hiding his hurt spirit and the bloodshot eyes. Too much booze, too much pot, not enough sunshine and fresh air.

"My name's Shane Brand." Sitting alone on the

stage with a microphone and his guitar, Shane seemed more at home in a dive bar than anywhere else. "I'm gonna play for you folks for a minute or two. I hope y'all enjoy it."

Savannah downed the rest of her beer and nodded her head when Bruce asked her if she wanted another.

"Why do I feel so nervous for him?" she whispered to her husband.

"You've got a kind heart, that's why."

She stopped talking then, her attention on Shane's gravelly, haunting voice and lyrics, so raw and honest that it made her catch her breath a time or two. Song after song, Shane played for the attentive crowd. There was something about Shane that grabbed a person's attention and held on to it for dear life. Between songs, Shane reached down to take a swig of the beer that sat at his feet, or take a drag off a cigarette.

"He's so talented," Savannah said sadly. "But, God, he's so screwed up."

After the set, Shane slumped into a chair at Jock and Lilly's table, a cigarette clenched between his teeth and a fresh bottle of beer in his hand.

Savannah waited her turn, but she finally got to hug her favorite brother-in-law.

"Bruce and I are renewing our vows, Shane." She knelt down beside his chair. "Now I know you don't really *do* family events, but I want you to promise me you're going to come."

Shane, still wearing his sunglasses to cover his eyes, blew out a thin line of white smoke before he said, "I'll do my best."

She stood up and touched his arm lightly. "That's all anybody can ask of you, Shane."

The beer was running right through her, so she excused herself to the bathroom. The line for the women's bathroom, as usual, was long and moving at a snail's pace. She finally got into a stall, took care of her bladder and then stopped at the two-sink counter to wash her hands and check her makeup.

"Well, look who it is. Savannah Brand."

Savannah was midway through glossing her lips when a voice from the past interrupted her string of thoughts about trying to figure out how Bruce and she could support Shane, to help him get healthy again.

In the mirror, Savannah looked behind her and there stood the tall, curvy, always a knockout no matter the decade Kerri Mahoney.

"Hello, Kerri," she said as she slipped the wand back into the tube and dropped the lip gloss into her purse.

They had gone to elementary school, middle school, high school and college together. Kerri had always been the most popular, the most pretty, the most everything, while she had been the sort of cute, sort of quirky, brainy geek girl. Kerri didn't have anything to be jealous of Savannah about, except for the fact that Bruce fell in love with her, put a ring on it and then married her.

Kerri stepped out of line to join her at the sink; the blonde smiled at her own reflection and flipped her thick, shiny hair over her shoulders.

"That's some scar," Bruce's ex-girlfriend observed.

Savannah would always have a daily reminder of the accident with that scar; perhaps it would fade over time, but it would never truly go away. Bruce didn't care two straws about the scar, but Savannah hated it. She had tried to cover it with makeup; Kerri had a talent for finding a person's weakness and using it against them. Yes, Kerri was beautiful on the outside—that beauty did not, however, penetrate Kerri's heart.

Savannah turned away from the mirror. "Bruce doesn't mind it."

Hate, genuine hate, flashed in Kerri's cornflower-blue eyes, before she shuttered the emotion. There was no sense wasting time on a woman who didn't wish her or her marriage well. So, she turned to the side to press past the women in line.

Kerri reached out, wrapped her fingers around the upper part of Savannah's arm and squeezed. "Just so you know—Bruce was in my bed the night of your accident."

Savannah yanked her arm out of Kerri's grip. "That's old news, Kerri."

Shaking with adrenaline and anger, Savannah returned to the table, sat down, chugged her beer then slammed the bottle down on the table.

"What's wrong?"

Savannah nodded to the blonde walking out of the bathroom.

Bruce saw Kerri, and that was all the information he needed. "I'm sorry."

"I'm not," she said, her eyes flashing. "This is a real small town. It was bound to happen."

It wasn't her suggestion, but Bruce wanted to leave once he realized that his ex was lurking near his family's tables. They said goodbye to the family, promised to be at Sunday breakfast, and then, holding her husband's hand, she followed him out of the bar and into the warm Montana night.

"It's still early." Bruce opened the passenger door for her. "What's your pleasure, my love?"

"I want to go home. Maybe toast some marshmallows in the fire pit?"

Bruce shut the door behind her. "We can do this."

Seeing Kerri at the bar had brought up some bad thoughts in Bruce's mind. He liked to ignore the past and just look forward with Savannah—would that ever be truly possible with Leroy and Kerri living in the same small town?

"I've got beer and a half a bag of marshmallows." Savannah came out of the house followed by Hound Dog.

Her hair was in a ponytail, she was wearing a ribbed tank top braless, and her cutoff jean shorts showed off her nicely shaped legs. No, she may not be model gorgeous like Kerri, but Bruce only had eyes for his pretty wife with the gap between her front teeth and a brain that rivaled any he'd ever met, man or woman. Savannah, for whatever reason, spoke to him on a soul-to-soul level that went much deeper than just mere outside appearances.

"I like the way you fill out that shirt," Bruce said with a teasing wink as he accepted a bottle of beer from his wife.

Savannah smiled at him flirtatiously. She had taken off her bra as much to please him as for comfort; she knew he was partial to her shapely, perky breasts.

His wife took a seat next to him on the outdoor love seat by the fire pit. She clinked her bottle to his.

"Here's to us," Savannah said, then took a healthy swig from her beer.

"To us."

Bruce had downed one beer and was on to the next, while Savannah toasted two marshmallows, one stacked on top of the other, over the fire.

"Oh, crap!" She pulled the marshmallows away from the pit and blew out the flame.

"Here." He reached over and slid the burned, gooey marshmallows off the stick. "I like 'em charred."

She wrinkled her nose at him. "I worry about your taste buds. I really do."

With sticky marshmallow on his lips, he buried his face in her neck and started to kiss her ear to make her squeal.

"I like how you taste," he said suggestively, looking downward.

Savannah laughed, and how he loved to make her laugh. Her laugh sounded light and airy, like wind chimes blowing in the wind.

"This is so much better than the bar. The smoke was really starting to get to me." Savannah loaded two more marshmallows onto her stick.

"Why don't you just put one there and that way you'll be able to have more control?" he suggested.

She frowned at him playfully. "Are you giving me advice on how to toast a marshmallow?"

"I think I'm onto something."

"I think you need to just sit back, drink your beer and let me handle the toasting."

They sat outside together, drinking their way through a six-pack of beer and eating too many marshmallows to avoid feeling sick later. It was the perfect night at home with his wife; it was the type of night that almost wiped thoughts of Kerri and Leroy and the divorce out of his mind. Almost.

"Wait here." Bruce stood up and swayed a bit from the beers. "I'll be back in a minute."

"I'm not moving from this spot," Savannah said in a singsong voice; she was tipsy, too.

He and a couple of his brothers had moved all of his wife's things out of her apartment; she had cleaned it and turned in the keys, just as she had promised she would. The fact that she was back on the ranch with all of her possessions had made him feel secure and relieved. It made him want to do something equally symbolic.

He returned to his wife and the waning fire in the pit. Savannah was leaning back in the love seat, her legs bent to her chest, her head resting on the cushion.

"I want us to do something." Bruce didn't rejoin her on the love seat.

"What's that?"

He held up the manila envelope for her to see. "I want us to get rid of these."

Savannah pushed herself upright. "What do you have?"

He handed her the envelope. She opened it and slipped the papers out; she glanced quickly over the words, and her eyes widened a bit when she realized she was holding their unsigned divorce decree.

"I don't want them." She handed them back to him.

Bruce held out his hand to her, and she took it.

"Let's burn them together." He held on to her hand.

She nodded; he could tell by the expression in her eyes that seeing the papers had hurt her. They hurt him, too.

Savannah held on to one end of the papers, while he held on to the other end. After a moment of silence, they tossed their divorce decree into the embers. The fire, which had almost died away, began to eat at the paper, burning back the edges of the document and through the center. Bruce wrapped his arms around his wife as they watched the document that had almost ended their marriage turn to ash by the fire.

He couldn't be sure it was the beer, or the thought of how close they had come to destroying their marriage, but he felt, as much as heard, Savannah start to cry.

"Hey…" Still holding her, he bent his head down to look at her face.

Savannah clutched the front of his shirt, the tears from her eyes leaving wet blotches on a favorite button-down.

"We almost lost everything," his wife whispered.

He kissed the top of her head, holding her even more tightly against his body.

"But we didn't," he reassured her. "We're here. Together. Stronger than ever. Aren't we?"

She nodded.

Bruce turned her in his arms, held her away from him, his hands on her shoulders.

"I don't know why I deserve this second chance with you, my love. How did I get so lucky?"

"We both got that second chance."

Bruce looked away, taking a moment to collect his emotions. He looked back to his wife, his eyes taking in the features of the face he loved so much. "I can't seem to forgive myself."

He swallowed hard. "Sammy…"

Instead of pulling away, Savannah stepped closer

to him, wrapped her arms around him and held him as tightly as he had held her.

"You have to forgive yourself, Bruce. You loved our son. You *loved* him."

Bruce rubbed fresh tears out of his eyes. "I miss him. I miss him so much it feels like I can't breathe from it."

Savannah leaned back, put her hand over his heart. "Forgive yourself, Bruce. So we can move on. Forgive yourself—as I have forgiven you."

"Thank you, my love." He took her face in his hands and kissed her lips. "Thank you."

The symbolic burning of their divorce papers was a turning point, a large step forward, in the healing of their relationship. It wasn't perfect, but what marriage was? They had begun to move out of that blissful honeymoon phase, where making love was top on the priority list, and spats were infrequent. Now, it seemed that they were solidly back into the marriage, filled with mundane tasks such as laundry and paying bills and getting the dogs to the vet. They argued more now, but not fights worthy of note. And, they never went to bed mad; they never left a disagreement lingering until the next morning. For Savannah, it was like having her marriage back—just a little bit better, a little bit stronger.

"Good morning, Lilly," Savannah greeted her mother-in-law when she reached the top of the stairs leading up to Lilly's craft loft.

Lilly stood up, hugged her and kissed her on both of her cheeks. "It is a beautiful morning."

Savannah sat down in a chair next to Lilly's crafting table.

"How are the vow renewal plans coming along?" Lilly asked, her fingers nimbly beading a bracelet as she carried on the conversation.

"Great so far."

They had both agreed that they wanted to renew their vows at Story Mansion. They had their first ceremony at Sugar Creek; it had been blue skies and gentle breezes, mountains in the background. They had a lovely souvenir wedding album that they both enjoyed. This time, they wanted something totally different, and they both agreed that getting married at the place where they had first fallen in love *was* that place.

"We're going to have the ceremony at Story Mansion—I've already booked the date."

"What date did you choose?"

"Sammy's birthday."

Lilly looked up from her beading. "That will be a blessing."

"We were worried that some of our family and friends wouldn't understand why we wanted to do that, but in the end, it's really about us. And we want Sammy to be a big part of that day."

"As he should be."

"Do you think that Jock will agree to having a reception here at the main house?"

"Yes, I think so." Lilly nodded. "You are one of his two favored daughters."

Savannah smiled at that. Jock was such a hard man, a difficult man and a flawed man who did not always have the respect of his children. But for some unknown reason she wasn't about to spend too much time questioning, Jock adored her. And he was always kind to her.

"And what shall you wear?"

"That's what I wanted to talk to you about."

She had married Bruce in a simple A-line white lace wedding dress with cap sleeves. She had loved her dress, but in keeping with the "change" theme of their vow renewal, Savannah wanted to wear a dress that was unique, and unusual, and totally unexpected. That was her marriage to Bruce in a nutshell.

"Would you consider making my vow renewal dress?"

Lilly's hands stilled. "You want me to make your dress?"

"I'd like a dress that no one else has ever had. I was thinking of a cross between an American traditional wedding dress and a traditional Chippewa-Cree jingle dress." Savannah lifted her hand. "But only if it wouldn't be considered disrespectful to your tribe."

A jingle dress was a powwow ceremonial sheath, typically made from vibrant-colored fabric, and decorated with rows of shells, metal cones and ornate beading. Savannah had often admired Lilly's ceremonial jingle dresses; it was in her heart to marry Bruce in an outfit influenced by the beauty and symbolism of a jingle dress. Jingle dresses, also called prayer dresses, were considered to be healing garments, and for Savannah, the vow renewal was all about the healing of her marriage.

"I would be so happy to make this dress for you."

Savannah scrolled through some images on her phone and showed one to Lilly. "I think this jingle dress could be made to look like a wedding dress."

Lilly began to sketch some ideas for her daughter-in-law; it amazed Savannah how easily the idea for a dress materialized on Lilly's sketch pad.

"How about this?" Lilly showed her the finished drawing. "When you walk, the dress will sing."

"I love it." She hugged Lilly. "It's so special. Thank you."

Lilly took her measurements and promised to get started on the dress right away. Before Savannah left the craft loft, Lilly selected a bangle she had recently designed and beaded.

"I saw you wearing this bracelet in a dream." Bruce's mother slipped the bangle onto her wrist. "Wear it day and night, and it will bring you much luck."

Chapter Thirteen

"Here she is." Tiffany walked out from the back of the jewelry store carrying a small black box.

The jeweler turned the box around, lifted the lid, and presented the custom diamond engagement ring to him. Inside of the box was a one-carat heart-shaped diamond, surrounded by a diamond halo and set in a delicately embellished white band. It was a Tiffany setting, with the diamond set high up off the band.

"It turned out even more antiquey and princessy than I thought it would."

A small light on the ceiling of the box shone down on the ring, making the center diamond sparkle. For the second time he proposed to Savannah, this was the perfect ring.

"Perfect," Bruce told the jewelry designer. "It's amazing. She's going to love it."

"I know she will," Tiffany agreed. "Do you know when you're going to give it to her?"

"Tonight. We're having dinner with her family, and I'm going to find the right time to give it to her."

"Well—" the jeweler put the ring box into a small, fancy bag with rope handles and gold embossing on the front "—I'm glad that we could be a part of this. Bring her by so we can see how the ring looks on her finger."

"I'll do that."

He wanted the moment to be perfect—Savannah deserved that. Bruce had to admit he wasn't always as romantic as his wife merited, but he did try. All day, while he was out fixing fences and worming the cattle, his mind was on the incredible vow renewal ring he had bought for his wife. It was fancier than she typically liked to wear, a bit flashier than her usual taste. Until he saw her face, until he saw her eyes and her smile, he would be worried that Savannah wouldn't love it as much as he did.

"So, tonight's the night." Colton had ridden up on one of his favorite quarter horses.

"Tonight is the night." Bruce poured some water over his face to cool it off and wash the sweat out of his eyes.

Colton just couldn't move on from the pain Savannah had caused him by leaving the ranch. He understood that; he loved his brother, but this wasn't Colt's decision. This was his decision. And when push came to shove, whether Colton had to fake it to make it or not, he expected his brother to respect his decision and respect his wife.

His younger brother shook his head. "I just don't

get what you're doing here, brother. She left you. She walked. Shacked up with another dude. And now you guys are renewing your vows. You needed her when Sammy died." Colt pointed away from his body. "What did she do? What did she *do*? She kicked dirt in your face, man. I don't care if the whole family wants to act like everything is fine and dandy. That's bull crap, and you damn well know it!"

Bruce let his brother say his piece. That was what brothers did. But when he was finished, he made his point clear.

"She's my wife. I love her. I forgive her." Bruce stabbed his pointer finger into the palm of his other hand. "And God willing, she's forgiven *me*.

"Now…you can hate her guts. That's your right. You *will* treat her with the respect she deserves as my wife, Colt. I don't want to have a problem with you, but we will have a problem if you step out of line with Savannah."

"Mom! Dad! We're here!" Savannah was always happy to be spending time with her family.

Savannah scooped up the family cat and carried him into the kitchen where her mom was cooking up a storm.

"Hi, baby girl." Carol's plump cheeks were flushed from the heat of the stove. "Hi, Bruce."

"Hey, Mom." Bruce hugged his mother-in-law. From the very beginning to right now, Carol had been a big supporter of their marriage. He could always count on Carol to be in his corner.

"Smells delicious, Mom." Savannah smooched

the kitty on the face before putting him down on the ground gently. "Where's Dad?"

"I sent him to the store with a list."

"We could have stopped for you." Savannah snatched a caramelized onion from the pan.

Carol wiped her hand on a dish towel, then hung it over the sink faucet. "I needed to give him a job. I don't know what we're going to do when he retires, Lord help us both. He hovers!"

"Mom." Savannah frowned at her mom.

"I'm not saying that I don't love your father," Carol clarified. "I'm saying that a little space strengthens a marriage. Trust me. The two of you will see when you've been married as many decades as I have."

"God willing." Bruce snuck a couple of caramelized onions out of the same pan.

"All right…okay." Savannah's mother waved her hands in a shooing motion. "Now the two of you are hovering. Go find your sister."

Savannah's sister, Justine, was outside on the deck with her fiancé, high school coach Mike Miller. Savannah was very close to her sisters; they screamed like they hadn't seen each other in years when they got together, and they hugged like they were never going to see each other again. Her strong family values, along with her intelligence that kept him on his toes, were some of the things that made Savannah such a rare find and such a perfect fit for him. He liked that his wife was smarter than he was; he liked the fact that Savannah challenged him to be a better man.

While Savannah and her sister caught up, Bruce excused himself back into the house.

"She's happy again, Bruce," his mother-in-law said plainly. "I haven't seen her smile like that in a very long time."

"When she's happy, I'm happy."

"That's the way family works," Carol acknowledged. "If your spouse is happy, if your kids are happy, you're happy."

"I wanted to show you the ring," Bruce said in a lowered voice.

Carol's face lit up with excitement. She clapped her hands together. Bruce had worn his shirt untucked so Savannah wouldn't spot the shape of the box bulging in his front pocket; he tugged the box out of his pocket and then lifted the lid for Carol to see.

"Oh! Oh!" Savannah's mother's eyes teared up. "Oh, Bruce. It's the most beautiful ring I've ever seen. It truly is."

"Do you think Savannah will love it?"

Carol had her hands on her cheeks. "She's going to feel like the most loved woman in all of Montana."

Bruce hid the ring on the top shelf of one of Carol's kitchen cabinets; the cabinet wasn't often used, so there wasn't a risk of Savannah accidentally finding it.

"You'll give it to her after dessert?" his mother-in-law asked.

"I think so," he told her. "Joy has an early evening class, and I want to make sure we can get her on video chat so she can be a part of it, too."

Carol stopped talking and just started hugging him.

"We are so blessed to have you, Bruce." She used the dish towel to dry her eyes. "Thank you for never giving up on our Savannah."

* * *

It was a festive dinner—everyone was in a good mood, even Savannah's father, who had been slow to accept Bruce back into the fold. A gift of fresh steaks for the grill, straight from Sugar Creek stock, went a long way to ease the relationship with his father-in-law. John cooked the steaks on the grill, taking orders from the family and drinking beer.

They sat down at the picnic table on the deck that they used all summer long in good weather. The center of the table was teeming with bowls filled with potato salad, macaroni salad, hot rolls, green beans, collard greens and mashed potatoes. Carol really knew how to throw together a feast for a family gathering, and Bruce had sincerely missed her cooking during the separation.

"Make sure you save room for dessert," Carol warned the family. "I didn't sweat in that kitchen all day to have my dessert go to waste."

"It's store-bought," John teased his wife.

"Hush your mouth." Carol lifted her chin in feigned outrage. "I would *never...*"

Everyone chipped in clearing the table, stacking dishes in the warm soapy water in the large farm sink; Justine put the coffee on while Carol took the store-bought desserts out of their boxes and put them on serving plates. After the table was cleared and reset for dessert, and the coffee had been brewed, the family converged once again at the picnic table. By now, the sun had set, and a sliver of moon was seemingly floating overhead, a small, yellow slice in a vast, blue-black Montana sky.

"You tell Jock that he can send over steaks anytime."

John had a bit of a slur to his voice. "I missed those steaks while the two of you were separated."

"Dad…" Savannah objected. "That's not even half-way nice."

"It's honest," Bruce said.

"Not polite," Justine added to the discussion. "But honest. Dad, I think that's gonna have to be in the running for your tombstone."

John frowned playfully at his daughters, then to his wife, he said, "You raised a couple of smart-asses, Carol."

Even though they were all stuffed from the meal, every single one of them found something from the pastry assortment to eat for dessert. Savannah finished her chocolate minipastry, wiped her mouth, then tapped her glass with her knife.

"I have a couple of announcements."

Once she had the family's attention, his wife said, "I quit my job."

The joviality seemed to be sucked right out of the air; John's frown was back, and Carol appeared to be both confused, as if she had heard her daughter wrong, and speechless. His father-in-law immediately turned his attention to him—before they were married, he had wanted Savannah to be a stay-at-home wife and mother, while he provided for the family. Yes, it was an old-fashioned model of marriage—a model that he immediately kicked to the curb when Savannah made it clear she wasn't going to play June Cleaver to his Ward Cleaver.

"This wasn't Bruce's decision." His wife was quick to dispel that notion.

"Did you suggest it?" John demanded, that familiar scowl back on his fleshy face. Savannah's father wanted all of his girls to use their brains and stay in school until they received a terminal degree in their field. He didn't care if they gave him grandchildren; he cared that they made something of themselves and stood on their own without the help of a man.

"No," Bruce replied, firmly but still respectfully. He had no intention of starting another cold war with Savannah's father.

"This is—" Savannah gestured to her chest "—*my* choice."

"You love your job!" her sister interjected. "What about your kids?"

"I'm not the only good teacher. They'll get along just fine without me. My heart wants something else now. I want to do something in Sammy's memory."

"Savannah has been exploring the idea of starting a foundation in Sammy's name."

"Well—I *love* that idea," Carol conceded.

"Which brings me to my second announcement."

"How many more of these do you have?" John asked in a caustic tone.

Carol, as she always did, tried to smooth things over between her girls and their father. It was, as far as Bruce could tell, a constant chore.

Undaunted, Savannah smiled, showing her dimples. "A couple more."

His wife reached for his hand, and with a glimmer in her pretty hazel eyes, Savannah announced that they were going to try to get pregnant.

That announcement had the desired impact—Carol and Justine left their seats to give Savannah a hug. A baby was always good for changing a sour mood sweet.

"I'm no longer taking birth control, so..." Savannah caught his eye. "I could be pregnant before our vow renewal."

The rest of the conversation surrounded the plans for the vow renewal, including the date, which elicited a divided response from the family, as well as the venue. After the conversation lagged, the family cleared the table for the final time that night, and everyone seemed to need a break. John went out to his garage with Justine's boyfriend while Justine and Savannah went for a stroll around the neighborhood to walk off some of the calories they had consumed. Bruce helped Carol in the kitchen, rinsing off the dishes and loading them into the dishwasher.

"It's going to take at least two loads," Bruce told his mother-in-law, who was wiping down the kitchen countertops.

"At least," she agreed.

Bruce opened the kitchen cabinet and retrieved the diamond ring. "I think the family has had too much excitement for one night."

"Oh..." she said, disappointed. "I wanted to see her face when she opened the box."

He understood, and he sympathized, but John was pissed off about Savannah quitting her job, and the last thing he wanted was his father-in-law's sourpuss face ruining his proposal. No. He would give Savannah her ring in private; maybe it would be all the more special for it.

"Look at my belly." Savannah was lying flat on her back, surround by canine friends, her shirt lifted up to just below her breasts, her jeans unbuttoned and unzipped. Her stomach was distended, as if she were a couple of months pregnant.

"Total food baby."

Bruce lay down on the bed on his stomach and kissed her belly. "You look beautiful to me."

"I suppose that's all that really matters." She brushed his hair off his forehead with her fingers. "You seriously need a haircut, cowboy."

Bruce captured her hand and brought it to his lips. "Come outside with me for a minute."

"I could stand another walk." Savannah sat up with an uncomfortable groan, then swung her legs off the side of the bed.

Holding Bruce's hand, she followed behind him as they walked out onto the deck. He put his arm around her, and they ambled down the stairs and into their backyard.

"I can't remember a night lovelier than tonight." She marveled at the majesty of the dark Montana sky.

Bruce turned her in his arms, took her face in his hands and kissed her—so softly, so lovingly, that it made her want to cry with joy.

His eyes roamed her face, the way Bruce Brand had always looked at her, as if she were the most beautiful woman in the world, even though all evidence said that she wasn't. She believed that look in his eyes; she trusted the love she saw in those bright, Brand blue eyes.

"I have never seen a woman lovelier than you," he said and then kissed her again. "I can't believe that I've been given this second chance with you, my love. I have no idea what I did to deserve you…"

Before she could respond, before she could tell him

that she was just as lucky to have this second chance with him as he was with her, Bruce did the unexpected and bent down on one knee. There beneath the starless, expansive cobalt-blue sky, her husband, a man she loved to the moon and back, held up a box he had pulled out of his front pocket.

"Savannah Georgia Brand…" Bruce flipped the top of the box open; a strategically placed tiny white light in the box shone down on the stunning heart-shaped diamond solitaire, letting the jewel show off its facets with sparkles of red and purple and blue.

"Will you marry me? Again?"

For a moment, she couldn't speak for the emotion. She didn't wipe away her tears of happiness when she nodded her head quickly, and said, "Yes. Of course. Yes!"

Bruce stood up, took the ring out of the box, and slipped the twinkling diamond engagement ring on the finger of her left hand.

"Oh, Bruce…" Savannah stared at the diamond on her finger. "It's the most beautiful ring I've ever seen in my whole entire life."

"You like it?"

"Are you kidding?" Her voice rose an octave and cracked. "I *love* it!"

"It's a little more…flashy than what you wear… I was worried I'd gotten it wrong."

"No. You didn't." Savannah couldn't take her eyes off her new ring. "It's everything I didn't even know I wanted."

With a squeal of sheer joy, she threw her arms around Bruce's neck and kissed him hard on the mouth.

Her husband lifted her up with one arm, kissed her again and swung her around in a circle.

"We're engaged!" Savannah laughed, her stomach demanding that she stop spinning.

"Married." Bruce let her slide down his body until her feet were firmly back on the ground. "And engaged."

That night, their lovemaking began in the shower and finished in the bed. Now that she had stopped taking her birth control and had begun taking prenatal vitamins, they both wanted to make love as much, and as often, as possible.

"I can't remember when I was pregnant with Sammy," Savannah said quietly, her body curled into Bruce's body, wearing nothing but her new diamond ring. "So when I get pregnant again, it will feel like the first time."

Bruce ran his hand up and down her shoulder. "Does that upset you? That it will feel like the first time, I mean?"

She nodded before her words followed. "Yes. I'm sure it will. What was I like when I was pregnant with Sammy?"

Bruce laughed lightly, his eyes closed. "You were really grouchy. I mean *really* grouchy. But so frickin' cute. You didn't have to buy maternity clothes until the very end of your pregnancy, and that really ticked you off."

"I was mad because I wasn't *big* enough?" She lifted her head to look at him. "That's just flat-out weird.

"What else?" She prodded him.

"You craved marinated mushrooms and buttercream frosting."

"Oh—*God*. Yuck. That's disgusting! Together?"

"No. Thankfully."

She could tell Bruce was about to fall asleep—his voice was increasingly groggy and muffled, he wasn't holding up his end of the conversation, and his eyes had been closed for several minutes. But she had other things in mind. She ran her hand down his stomach and took his flaccid penis in her hands.

"Hmm." Her husband made an interested noise.

"Is it too late to make a withdrawal?" she asked him playfully.

He turned his head toward her on the pillow and kissed the top of her head, still not opening his eyes.

"No, ma'am. It's not."

Chapter Fourteen

"Oh, Lilly…" Savannah stared at her reflection in the full-length mirror. "It's incredible."

Lilly had been working tirelessly on her jingle-inspired vow renewal gown. The dress was made of white cloth and was heavily embellished with rows of silver metal cones and ornate flat-stitch bead work on the sleeves, all of which created lovely flower-shaped bursts of turquoise, red, magenta and yellow, with a wide belt cinching the waist. On the bottom hem, a row of fringe gave the long sheath dress a bit of interest around her calves.

Savannah shifted her hips side to side, and the dress made its own sort of music, like wind chimes in a gentle breeze.

"I feel strong in this dress," she told her mother-in-law. "Like I can face anything and survive."

Lilly had offered to make her a pair of matching moccasins, but Savannah wanted her outfit to represent all of her—she chose to wear a pair of cream cowgirl boots, hand-crafted, with a tapered high heel.

"I am so glad that you like it." Lilly smiled at her with her dark brown eyes.

"It's..." She felt herself start to choke up with emotion. Today she would marry the man of her dreams, her best friend, lover and father of her children—for a second time. "It's more than I could have ever expected. You are so talented."

Lilly hugged her, kissed her lovingly on the cheek, and then left the cabin to return to the main house to get ready for the ceremony. Her mother and her two sisters passed Lilly on her way out, and Savannah started to laugh by herself in the bedroom at the sound of her family's loud, excited voices filling the tall rafters of her log cabin.

Savannah walked down the hallway, swinging her hips so her jingle dress would jingle, and met the women in her life in the living room.

"What do you think?" She spun around to show off her outfit.

"Now, *that* is a dress!" Joy, in town for the weekend, ran over to her and gave her a big hug. "You look ah-maze-ing!"

"Oh, sweetheart." Carol started to cry. "I've never seen you look more beautiful."

"Here." Justine handed their mom a tissue.

"Better just hand her the box." Joy laughed.

Her mother and sisters shuffled her off to the bedroom so they could carefully remove the dress until after her hair and makeup were done.

"I'm *here*!" Jessie screamed, while at the same time slamming the front door. "Let's get this party started!"

Savannah was pampered and prepped by the women in her life. Joy slicked her hair back off her face and created a single, simple twist. With such an ornate, special dress, she wanted her hair and her makeup to be subtle.

Jessie, up on the latest in makeup trends, took care of making her face look youthful and dewy. By the time she was all dolled up, she hardly recognized herself in the mirror.

"I look like the woman Bruce will want to marry twice."

"You look like a woman my brother is gonna knock up tonight," Jessie said from her perch on their bathroom counter.

"Lord have mercy." Carol's peaches-and-cream complexion turned pink.

"Well…" Justine gave her a look of approval. "Let's go get you *renewed*, sis."

"What's goin' on with this stupid thing?" Bruce couldn't seem to get his silver-and-turquoise bolero tie, a gift from Lilly, to cooperate.

"Let me do it." Liam bent his knees a bit so he could take a closer look. "There."

Bruce turned to look at his reflection; he'd gotten married in jeans the first time around—this time, he was wearing a tuxedo. Savannah always wanted to see him in a tuxedo, and what better time than this ceremony to renew their commitment to each other. This was the day, a day long awaited, that he would dedicate his life, his heart and all of his days to Savannah.

"Well, this is as good as it's gonna get." Bruce shrugged. His recent haircut was a little too short for his liking, and the tuxedo made him feel like he couldn't much move his arms. Hopefully, Savannah would be impressed when she first saw him. That would make all of the discomfort worth it.

"Here." Colton came in with a couple of aspirin and a glass of water. "This'll help you feel better."

"Thanks, brother." Bruce took the aspirin gratefully. His frat brothers and his blood brothers had taken him out the night before, and his head felt like someone was hitting him in the temple with a ball hammer.

Savannah had warned him not to go out and get drunk with his brothers, and he hadn't really intended to do that. A couple hours into the evening, hopping from one old haunt to the next, all of the drinks his brothers were buying him had started to blend into one big drink. No, he hadn't gone out looking to get drunk, but he surely had achieved that goal.

"My wife is going to have my head on a stick if I show up looking like something the dog threw up."

"You're kinda jaundiced." Like a unicorn, Shane was making a rare family appearance. Bruce was glad to see him, but he smelled strongly of marijuana. Lilly and Jock would not be pleased.

"Thanks, bro." Bruce had noticed that his skin was an odd shade of yellow. "'Preciate it."

A loud burp followed those words; why—*why*—had he indulged last night? If Savannah sensed how sick he felt, he was going to begin their marriage reboot with a seriously ticked-off wife.

"You ready to head out?" Liam came out of the bathroom, dressed now in his tuxedo. Liam had been his best man during their wedding ceremony; it meant a lot to have him standing beside him for the vow renewal.

"Let's do this." Bruce had to fake it to make it, and he would. Savannah was counting on him.

Bruce walked up the path to the porch of Story Mansion, and was greeted by his friends and his family awaiting the start of the ceremony. He entered the mansion with so much history and so many of his own memories. The building had been restored to its early 1900 glory—with wide-plank wood floors and thick, unpainted crown molding—and the air smelled of wood polish and fresh paint.

"Mom." Bruce hugged Lilly, who had chosen to dress in a traditional ceremonial Chippewa-Cree gown and moccasins, with her silver-streaked hair deliberately styled into two long braids.

"Son." Lilly pressed her cheek to his. This was their way.

With Liam standing beside him, somewhere down the hall, an antique grandfather clock chimed four times. It was time for Bruce to see his bride—it was time.

Bruce heard his wife approaching before he saw her; the jingle dress foretold her arrival. At the entrance to the turret room, Savannah stood between her father and her mother.

"Damn…" Bruce said under his breath. "That's my wife."

The moment he laid eyes on his wife, wearing an ornate jingle dress made by his mother's talented hands, thoughts of his acid stomach and his pounding head disappeared into the recesses of his mind. All he could think of was the ethereal, angelic, powerful, badass woman who was his bride.

Savannah kissed her father and her mother, and then walked the short distance to him on her own. Her dress jingled charmingly with every step she took toward him. Her smiling eyes were on his, holding him with the look of unadulterated love.

He took several steps to her, reached out for her hand and walked with her, together, the rest of the way to the spot where they would, once again, pledge their lives to each other. They'd opted to write their own vows, just their words, without a pastor.

Liam took his seat after he hugged Savannah, and then it was just the two of them, facing each other, hand in hand.

"You look handsome." Savannah smiled up at him with a gentle, sweet, accepting smile.

"You are beautiful."

This was the moment—it was time, in front of God and all of his friends and family, to tell Savannah how much she was loved by him.

"Savannah. My beautiful, brilliant wife. I love you, a little bit more every day. I stand before you now, a lucky man, a blessed man, because of your love in my life. I have promised to love you, in sickness and health, for richer and poorer, until death us do part. I reaffirm that vow to you now. I promise you that I intend to spend the rest of my days on earth being worthy of your love."

Jessie sneaked forward and pushed a handkerchief into Savannah's hand. Savannah laughed, which broke a little bit of the tension in the room, and carefully dabbed the tears from her eyes, trying valiantly not to smear her makeup.

"Thank you." She gave her sister-in-law a quick sideways glance.

"Bruce," Savannah began, a catch in her throat that she had to clear before she continued. "I am so proud to be your wife. You are my best friend, the love of my life. You have my heart, Bruce—my whole heart. My life doesn't work without you. I vow to always love you, to always be by your side, no matter what comes our way." Savannah held his gaze and repeated, "No matter what comes our way."

Bruce took her face in his hands and sealed their vows with a kiss. Savannah laughed through fresh tears and wiped her lip gloss from his lips.

"I love you, Bruce," she said. "So very much."

Their friends and family were clapping loudly, cat-calling and whistling. Bruce barely heard them.

"I love you more."

They took pictures inside the mansion and on the grounds surrounding the historical home. Then the entire party of friends and family headed back to Sugar Creek for a Montana-style shindig. They had a band, a dance floor put down, and plenty of food and drinks. They requested that, instead of gifts, their attendees contributed money to the GoFundMe page that Savannah had started for Sammy Smiles—the foundation that she was determined to create in their son's memory.

"Here." Jock opened up his son's jacket and slipped an envelope into the inside pocket. His father rested his hand on top of the jacket, then gave him one single pat on the chest. "That's for Samuel."

"Thank you," he told his father. "It means the world to Savannah."

He'd managed to lose his wife shortly after they arrived back at the ranch, but he found her near the stage speaking to his younger brother, Shane.

Bruce shook his brother's hand. "I'm glad you came."

"Shane's going to play for us later," Savannah told him.

"Everyone'd really like that." He put his arm around his wife's shoulder. "I'm going to steal her for now."

Bruce led his bride out onto the dance floor, and spun her around until she walked into his embrace.

"Are you happy?" he asked her as they danced slow even though the music was fast.

"So happy." She rested her head on his chest.

They danced and drank and ate until midnight arrived, and Shane sat down on the piano bench; her favorite brother spoke in a low voice, in between puffs on a cigarette, to the band. After a minute, he adjusted the microphone and asked for everyone's attention.

Bruce and Savannah stood next to the stage, their arms circling each other.

"Most of you know that I don't do covers." Shane spoke in a raspy voice as the crowd gathered around the stage. "But this here's Savannah's favorite song, so I'm gonna play it for you folks right now."

Shane's hands on the keyboard, her troubled, talented brother-in-law said, "I love you, Savannah. Bruce."

As they stood, wrapped in each other's arms, their

friends and family all around, Shane began to play the piano and sing, in that haunting, rough, damaged-deep-in-his-soul voice, Eric Clapton's "Wonderful Tonight."

The crowd was mesmerized by Shane's rendition of a classic song; everyone was so quiet until he took his hands off the keys and put the half-smoked cigarette burning on the edge of the piano back into his mouth.

"Thank you," Shane said before he stood up. "Take care of each other."

Before they could catch him and say thank-you for the song, Shane disappeared into the crowd, and undoubtedly returned to his garage apartment, his safe zone, back in town.

Savannah tried to stifle a yawn, but Bruce felt as tired as she looked at this point. This day had been incredible, but the planning of such a big event had been exhausting for them both.

"We need to go to bed, my love. We have an early flight and a long journey."

She nodded her head in agreement. They began to make the rounds, saying good-night and thanking everyone who had been such an important part of their day. They had one last champagne toast with their guests, then they turned in with their dog pack. With his help, Savannah carefully took off her dress and hung it in a protective garment bag.

He came up behind her, brushed her hair off her neck and kissed the warm, sweet-smelling skin he'd uncovered.

"You looked wonderful tonight," he told her, repeating the words of her favorite song.

She turned in his arms and held on to him, her head on his chest, her arms wrapped tightly around his body.

"I love you more than words can say, Bruce."

He took her face in his hands, his eyes sweeping the lovely features. "That makes me the luckiest man in Montana, my love. The luckiest man."

"I can't believe we went to bed without fooling around on our vow renewal day." Savannah brought him a cup of coffee while he packed the last toiletries into his carry-on bag.

"Don't you worry your pretty little head about that." Bruce took a sip of the coffee. "We're going to more than make up for it on our trip."

"When are you going to tell me where we're going?"

"I already gave you a hint."

"A ridiculous hint."

He laughed. "You won't need a bathing suit, but you can bring one if you want. That's a great clue."

"No." She frowned at him playfully. "It's not."

They both took turns hugging and kissing their dogs before they dropped them off at the main house. They headed to the airport and that was when Savannah finally got to find out where Bruce had been planning, for a long time now, to take her for their vow renewal honeymoon.

"Oh. My. God!" Savannah grabbed his arm and pushed it back and forth excitedly. "Fiji? You're taking me to *Fiji*?"

"That's where you always wanted to go, isn't it?"

"Are you trying to make me fall in love with you all over again, Mr. Brand?"

Bruce gave her a quick kiss on the lips. "You'd better believe it."

* * *

It was a long day of traveling, and she had never been much of an airplane person. The seats were too cramped; there were too many people coughing. She was more concerned about the germs recycling throughout the cabin than she was of crashing, oddly enough. But by the time they were close enough to Fiji to see those legendary sapphire-and-turquoise blue waters, Savannah forgot about her germ concern and just focused on all of the amazing adventures she was going to have with her husband in the most amazing paradise on the planet.

Bruce had booked a private bungalow on Turtle Island. They would have access to their own private beach, opportunities to hike, bike, snorkel, surf, sunbathe in the nude and lounge in their own hot tub.

"We have to get couples massages at the spa." Savannah pointed to a picture in the dog-eared brochure she had been reading and rereading to pass the time on the plane.

"I don't like people touching my feet." Bruce gave a little shake of his head. "Can I keep my boots on?"

Savannah smacked him with the brochure. "When in Fiji."

They took a pontoon plane for the final leg of the journey to the five-hundred-acre privately owned Fijian island called Turtle Island, which was one of twenty volcanic islands in the western division of Fiji. They were going to be in paradise for two glorious weeks, and because the island was privately owned, they would have the run of it, and the utmost privacy on the beach dedicated for their bungalow. Bruce wasn't a fan of the idea, but she fully intended to get naked on the beach. She had always wanted to frolic on the beach in her birthday suit; this might be her one and only opportunity to have access to a totally private beach.

"This. Is. Amazing! Look at this place!"

They were shown to their accommodations by their own private butler, or Bure Mama, who would take care of their every need during their stay. Their villa, named the Ratu Mara Bure for a former Fiji president, was a thatched, vaulted-roof bungalow, hand-constructed from hardwood indigenous to the island by local artisans; the Ratu Mara was designed for luxury and complete privacy. Only one of fourteen tucked away in the tropical foliage with a view of their own completely private slice of white-sand beach, it was better than she had imagined. The pictures in the brochure, as beautifully done as they were, did not, *could* not do the real magic of Turtle Island justice. The native hardwood gave off a sweet scent that mingled with the salty breeze blowing in from the beach. The first thing she did after she hugged and kissed her husband for finding them the perfect spot to celebrate their marriage reboot, was yank off her boots and socks and run out to the beach.

"Come with me!" she called to Bruce.

Her husband sat down on a chaise lounge chair on their private deck, removed his boots and socks and followed her out to the beach.

Savannah tilted her head back, suddenly not feeling the least bit fatigued from the nearly twelve-hour plane ride, reached out her arms and spun around in the sand.

"I am so happy!"

Bruce scooped her up and continued to spin her.

They both ended up dizzy and laughing, sitting on the beach.

"We are in paradise together," she said in amazement.

"Yes, we are."

Savannah linked her arm with her husband's and dug her toes into the white, sugary sand. "You know I'm going to sunbathe on this beach in the altogether, don't you?"

Bruce squinted his eyes against the sun. "I know."

"I think you should get naked with me—let it all hang out."

"I think that's a solid 'no.'" Her husband's answer was swift. "All of my altogether will be neatly tucked away in proper attire."

Savannah jumped up, started to walk down to the water's edge and called out to him, "You know what, Brand? You can be a real prude."

Bruce followed her, scooped her up in his arms and began to run toward the water.

"Are you ready to get wet?"

Savannah squealed, kicked her legs and laughed and wrapped her arms around his neck. She wanted to make sure that if she ended up in the water, Bruce ended up in the water with her.

Her husband carried her into the water, turned around so his back was to the water and sank down with her still in his arms. Wet, fully clothed, they wrapped their arms around each other and kissed the water from their lips.

Savannah felt her husband's arousal, so hard, so fast. She wrapped her legs around his hips, and pressed her groin to his.

"Okay—we need to either, one, go back to our villa—" she licked the salty water from his neck and nibbled his ear "—or, make love to me right here, right now."

Chapter Fifteen

They did consummate their vow renewal that night, in the balmy air drifting into their bure while they bound their bodies together and loved each other as an expression of their deep and abiding connection. And then they slept. Nothing had ever felt so peaceful, being lulled to sleep in their king-sized bed, with a rhythmic breeze brushing over their bodies bringing a scent of tropical flowers, growing wild all around the bure, mingled with the fresh, salty smell of the water of the Pacific Rim.

Savannah rolled over onto her back, bringing one of her three pillows with her. She blinked her eyes several times, trying to adjust them to the bright light being brought into the villa by the late-morning sun.

"What time is it?" Her voice sounded a little raspy, and she prayed that she was just tired from the past months of her life instead of experiencing the first sign of an "airplane cold."

Bruce was sitting at the built-in desk, looking at his laptop. "Eleven-fifteen."

"Oh, my God," She yawned loudly, stretched and then turned on her side and snuggled back into the mattress and pillows. "I can't believe I slept that long. When did you get up?"

Her husband had yet to turn toward her, his attention still mainly on the computer screen.

"Around nine. I went for a walk around the island."

"Did you eat?"

He nodded.

"Well…" She yawned again. "I'm starving."

Another nod.

This *would not* do! They were *literally* in paradise—her husband was going to unplug from technology while they were there. Savannah threw back the covers, forced herself to get her body moving as she swung her legs out of bed. Naked, she walked over to where Bruce was sitting, gave him a hug and a kiss on the cheek, before she reached over his shoulder, slammed the laptop shut and then took it.

"Hold up!" Bruce finally turned to look at her. "I was answering an email."

"No," she said forcefully, holding the laptop behind her back. "We are in *Fiji*! You need to stop working on things that can keep for two weeks and focus all of your attention on what really matters."

As if noticing for the first time that she was standing naked before him, Bruce's eyes swept over her body, lingering on her breasts, the curve of her waist, and the small patch of hair at the spot where her thighs met.

"What's that?" Bruce's slightly narrowed, sexually interested gaze was back on her eyes.

"Me." Savannah laughed. She clutched the laptop to her chest, spun around and ran to the other side of the bed.

Bruce always loved a good chase, and he easily caught her near the bed and pulled the laptop out of her hands—but instead of taking the computer back to the desk, he put it on the night table and took her to bed instead.

Her pushed her back onto the mattress playfully; one breast he massaged in a way he knew she enjoyed, while he began to kiss the other breast, taking the nipple into his mouth.

Laughing, Savannah escaped from his grasp. "You've got to feed me first, Brand. I need energy to keep up with you!"

Their Bure Mama made sure she had a breakfast fit for a queen brought to the villa. Savannah feasted on passion fruit, guavas, star fruit and papayas. She drank two large cups of coffee, and then she felt ready to get up and enjoy the natural gifts of Turtle Island.

Dressed in a modest bikini, Savannah handed her husband a bottle of sunscreen. He was dressed in a T-shirt, bathing suit trunks and his standard boots had been replaced with a pair of flip-flops.

"You do me, and then I'll do you."

Living in Montana, even during the summer months, there were places on their bodies that just didn't see the light of day. They both had superpale legs and stomachs, while their necks and arms were a shade or two darker.

"We have to really work hard not to get burned," she

told him while he rubbed coconut-scented sunscreen on her back, her derriere and her shoulders.

They went down to their private beach, which made it seem like they were the only two humans in the Garden of Eden. The Bure Mama had a two-person lounge chair brought to their private beach at their request.

"Oh, Bruce." Savannah sighed, her eyes closed, the sun on her face. "Thank you."

In response, her husband took her hand and squeezed her fingers, his version of "you're welcome." Their first full day on the South Sea island paradise was perfection; they relaxed, vacillating between the lounge chair and the cooling sea-foam-green and turquoise-blue water. Every second of that first day was theirs; no schedule, no reminders of the past, no stress. Just the two of them, together, in what had to be one of the most beautiful places on the planet.

After a day at the beach, they took showers and got dressed for a surprise planned by Bruce. Feeling more free and sensual on this remote South Sea island than she had at any other time in her life, Savannah slipped into a lightweight minidress with spaghetti straps. Her legs had been turned gold with a pink undertone, but it didn't hurt. She opted to go commando beneath her dress and as she turned around in front of the mirror, making the filmy skirt of her dress float away from her body, she felt so sexy. She hoped Bruce agreed.

Hand in hand, they walked down to the water's edge of the island's Blue Lagoon, a cove protected from the waves, and that was when she saw a pontoon floating in the calm water, with a table for two, lit only by lanterns lining the boat.

"Is that for us?" Savannah squeezed her husband's hand in excitement.

"Yes." Bruce sounded proud of himself for keeping the secret—and for pleasing her.

A boat carried them to the pontoon; their food would also be brought to them by the same boat. Together, by the light of the lanterns, they feasted on seafood and vegetables picked that day from the island's garden. They filled their bellies with Pacific green lobster, cooked to perfection, and caught a nice buzz from the sweet red wine.

Their empty plates had been removed, and now they sat at their table with a 360-degree water view, drinking a last glass of wine.

"I will never forget this, Bruce," she whispered, feeling like the space was too sacred to speak in a full voice.

"You deserve this, my love." They touched glasses one last time. "Here's to second chances."

"Yes," she agreed softly. "To second chances."

They walked back to their villa from the Blue Lagoon, and once again, they were completely alone. Savannah had kicked off her sandals and was dangling them from two fingers, swinging them as they walked the beach. Hand in hand, they strolled along the water's edge, with the only light given off by the nearly full moon hanging in the clear night sky.

They reached the part of the beach directly in front of their villa.

"Let's get a towel and sit on the beach," she suggested.

She was glad that her rancher, who was typically

set in his ways as far as extracurricular activities, was being more open to her ideas than usual. Bruce put on his swim trunks, just in case they wanted to get into the water, and picked up a couple of towels for them.

Savannah chose a spot close enough to the water to enjoy the sound of the gentle waves rolling to shore, but far enough away that they wouldn't get wet if they chose to stay dry. Perhaps it was the dreamlike, mystic charm of the island, or perhaps it was the fact that she was in a place where her wildest desires were possible, but Savannah felt like she couldn't put off the experience of being her natural self in this place that was raw and wild in a way that she had never known before. Savannah stood up and pulled her dress over her head and dropped it onto the towel at her feet.

She closed her eyes, stretched her arms high above her head, her naked flesh completely exposed to the elements. Empowered and free. These were the two words that came to mind as she stood, unclothed, with the soft ocean breeze brushing over her breasts, her thighs, her face.

Bruce was quiet beside her; he didn't approve, but he wasn't going to try to stop her. This was one of her bucket list items; he knew her well enough to know that she knew her own mind, and she followed her own heart.

"Bruce!" She stepped off the towel and sank her toes into the cool, damp sand. "You should try this!"

"I'll live vicariously through you, my love." He had leaned back on his elbow and was admiring the view of her naked body in the moonlight.

"You'd love it." She spun around, her arms open wide. "I love you."

* * *

One of the most memorable moments of his life, he was certain of it, was watching his wife, naked as the day she was born, wearing only her heart-shaped diamond and a smile, frolicking on their Fijian beach. This trip had set him back a pretty penny, but it was worth everything he had spent and more. Money could not buy the happiness on Savannah's face; she was like a kid in a proverbial candy store. She wanted to taste everything, make friends with all of the Fijian people, drink as much as she could manage and experience every activity the island had to offer. She already had them scheduled for couples Lomi Lomi massages and Ulumu facials at the resort spa; she had also signed them up for snorkeling, a sunset cruise, windsurfing lessons and stand-up paddleboard lessons. He'd rather not tackle any of those activities, but he wanted to please Savannah. He wanted to make her smile and then keep her smiling. So he'd had to hang up his cowboy hat and put up his cowboy boots, and learn how to step out of his Montana rancher box.

"You're beautiful!" he called out to Savannah, who was currently executing rather impressive naked cartwheels and handstands.

He was always turned on by his wife's naked body; this moment was no different. Bruce had to shift his position to make the erection in his swim trunks a little less annoying. There was no way the hard-on was going away; he couldn't keep his eyes off Savannah. Her sun-kissed flesh in the moonlight, her hair blowing wildly around her pretty face, her breasts bouncing enticingly with every step she took.

Bruce stood up and walked over to Savannah, who

was standing at the water's edge, letting the ocean lap over her bare feet.

From behind, he wrapped his arms around her body and kissed her sweet-smelling neck.

Savannah reached up and put her hands on his arms, leaning her body back. "Hi."

"Hi."

Bruce, unable to wait a minute longer to have her, lifted her into his arms and carried her back to the towel. He laid her down on her back, lightly running his hand over her breasts, her stomach, until his fingers were nested between her thighs.

"Hmm." Savannah arched her back and tilted her hips upward toward his hand. "Yes, please."

Bruce then did something he swore he wouldn't do—he untied his swimming trunks and stripped them off. The more he watched his wife playing on the beach, her naked body glowing in the yellow light, the more he wanted to make love to her right here, on this secluded spot.

"You're so handsome." Savannah admired him through heavy-lidded eyes.

He lay down beside her, leaned on one elbow so he could hover just above her, and kissed her with all of the pent-up passion he felt. She reached between them to wrap her fingers around his hard penis; he reached between them so he could slip his fingers in her hot, slick center.

She stretched for him, pulling him forward, signaling that she was ready for more—that she needed more. Quietly, their breaths mingling as they gently kissed each other's lips, Bruce guided himself into her body, joining them as one being. Buried all the way inside of his wife, he lifted himself up, his elbows locked so he could watch her face. Every little movement of hips made her gasp.

"Is this what you wanted?" he asked her, their eyes locked in the moonlight.

"Yes." She gasped again, reaching for him, pulling him downward so he would give her the weight of his body.

They moved together, adopting the rolling rhythm of the ocean, each giving the other as much pleasure as they received. She came first, her cry of ecstasy caught by the breeze.

"I feel you," Savannah whispered into his ear, sending a shiver down his spine. "I feel you."

Those sensual whispers sent him over the edge; he thrust deep inside of her and exploded with a primal scream, unlike any sound he'd ever made during love-making in his life.

Savannah had her legs wrapped around his back as he let her take his weight, for just a minute, while he caught his breath. Holding on to her, he rolled their bodies so she was on top of him, her head on his chest, his nose breathing in the coconut scent in her hair.

"That was amazing." Savannah laughed, her fingers buried in his chest hair.

"Agreed."

They stayed on the beach, curled in each other's arms, until they were both so tired that they feared falling asleep there. Groggy and satiated, they ambled back to their villa, rinsed the sugary sand off their bodies and then climbed, completely spent, into the canopy king-sized bed.

* * *

"Well?" Savannah was staring at him like a cat watching a fishbowl.

"What do you want me to say?" he asked her.

They had just had their Lomi Lomi massages, considered to be an ancient healing massage, a living Aloha, first practiced in Hawaii.

"Did you *like* it?"

Bruce was glad to be dressed again; he wanted to get the heck out of the Vonu Spa.

Savannah's face was glowing from her facial, and she seemed to be perfectly languid and relaxed by the Lomi Lomi.

Now outside of the spa and far away from any ears that could be offended by what he was about to say, Bruce said in a harsh whisper, "They double teamed me!"

Savannah laughed, her head thrown back, her eyes twinkling at his obvious distress and discomfort.

"Four hands. *Four* hands!" He hadn't really been all that thrilled with two strange hands massaging him; his wife had been very strategic about *not* telling him that there would be *four* strange hands involved in the Lomi Lomi.

"They touched my feet! Both of them."

"Both of your feet? Or both women?"

"Both!" he snapped. "It felt like an assault!"

Savannah kept on laughing; she grabbed his hand and swung their arms.

"You'll be fine," she said with a teasing glint in her eyes. "It was good for you."

"Says who?"

It took several tropical fruit drinks and a lunch of

freshly caught fish to help him recover from his "healing" massage. After lunch, they did something that he had been wanting to do: visit the island's black volcanic cliffs. They took a tour of the cliffs, snapping copious amounts of pictures to post to social media so their friends and family could share in their adventure. After the volcanic cliffs, and now being one week into their two-week vacation, Savannah was starting to crave the company of their fellow Turtle Islanders. They got cleaned up from the day and dressed for the group dinner provided by the resort every night. This would be their first group dinner, and Savannah was beaming with excitement.

"They are going to have native music and dancers perform for us," she told him. "I can't wait. Aren't you excited?"

He raised his eyebrows at his wife, who seemingly could get excited about the smallest of things. "I can't wait."

She rolled her eyes at his lack of enthusiasm, which she had to accept as part of who he was, gripped his arm with her hands and bumped her shoulder into his. "Don't worry. You're gonna love it. I promise."

"Look," he said, only half joking, "after that assault you called a massage earlier, I am going to approach all of the activities you plan for us with caution."

At the group dinner, they were seated next to another couple, two people they had met briefly on a walk along the path through the lush island jungle.

"Hey!" Savannah smiled at the familiar faces, always quick to make a new friend. "We meet again!"

The woman was tall, over six feet at least, slender,

and undeniably beautiful; her features were subtle and balanced, her mouth full and colored a deep red—her skin was the color of light brown, and she wore her raven curls in a loose Afro which added a lovely frame to her pretty face.

With a British accent, the woman greeted them as they joined her and her companion at the table.

"I'm Ivory," she said, introducing herself. "And this is my husband, Miguel."

After the introductions and ordering the food, Savannah started small talk with Ivory and found out that she was a model and a budding fashion designer.

Ivory touched her husband's shoulder. "My husband is my biggest supporter. He picks me up when my chin's dragging on the ground."

"I'd love to see some of your designs," Savannah said to the model. "I love fashion."

Ivory stood up and modeled the boldly patterned sundress. "This is one of mine."

Savannah's eyes lit up. "My sister, Joy—she's the tall one—would look amazing in that dress."

"Tell her to visit my website." Ivory sat down and asked her husband, "Do you have any of my cards, love?"

Miguel, a quiet man much like Bruce, pulled a card from his wallet and handed it to her. Savannah looked at the card before tucking it into her pocket.

"Where are the two of you from?"

"Montana," Savannah told Ivory. "Bruce's family owns a ranch outside of Bozeman."

"I've been to Montana," the British model told them. "One of my best friends is from Montana."

"Small world…" Savannah interjected.

"She's an incredible painter. Maybe you've heard of her?" Ivory continued. "Jordan Brand? Well, Jordan Sterling now."

Savannah was rendered temporarily speechless, and she felt Bruce stiffen next to her. Their branch of the Brand family discussed the other Brand branches so infrequently that she often forgot that they existed.

Not sure exactly how to handle this, Savannah decided to just speak their truth. "Jordan is actually our cousin...mine by marriage"

"You're joking!" Ivory's brown-black eyes opened wider for a split second. "I just saw Jordan last week— she was just at our wedding!"

Chapter Sixteen

The rest of the dinner was filled with small talk, but Savannah was actually glad when the dancers began to perform. After discovering Ivory's connection to their estranged extended family, the rest of this meal felt a bit awkward and strained. In order to salvage the evening and keep Bruce at the table, Savannah quickly shifted the conversation away from the Bent Tree Ranch Brands, out of Helena, Montana, back to Ivory's designing career.

Now back at their villa, Savannah and Bruce both sank down into the hot tub with a bottle of champagne and assorted tropical fruits with melted chocolate for dipping.

"I can't believe that out of every island on the planet, we ended up on a Fijian island with a good friend of your cousin Jordan. How does that even happen?"

Bruce dipped a piece of papaya in the chocolate and held it up for her to eat.

"Hmm," she said between chews. "So good."

Her husband popped a chocolate-covered star fruit into his mouth. "Beats the hell out of me. But when she called us the 'bad Brands,' I had a real hard time holding on to my table manners."

She moved her arms in the bubbling hot water. "I know. How did we become the bad Brands—if Jock's brother hadn't been so greedy after your grandpa died, we'd all probably still be a whole family, don't you think?"

Bruce poured a glass of champagne for her, but she shook her head.

"No, thanks."

"You didn't drink yesterday—you didn't have wine with your dinner. What's going on?"

Savannah drifted over to him, a secretive smile on her face. "Do you remember how worried I was about getting my period while we were here?"

He studied her face carefully. "Yes."

His wife stood up in the hot tub, water rolling down her breasts to her puckered nipples in the most tantalizing way.

"Well—" she ran her hands over her stomach "—I missed my period.

Now he was looking at her stomach—had he planted a baby inside of her?

"I brought two early-detection pregnancy tests," she told him. "If I *am* pregnant, we'll know tomorrow before breakfast."

Bruce wanted so badly for his seed to take hold in his wife's womb. Every time they made love, every time he climaxed, he prayed that this would be the moment when they made another baby together. And he knew that Savannah felt the same way; they had been having sex like hormonal teenagers on this trip. Whenever he wanted it, she wanted it, too; whenever she wanted it, he gave it to her.

He put his empty champagne glass down, leaned his head down to lick the water from her nipples, his hand splayed across her stomach.

"God, I pray you're pregnant, Savannah."

His wife moved onto his lap, their slick bodies coming together so naturally. "I have prayed to God every day to give me your child, Bruce. I want another child with you so badly."

"We aren't going to stop trying until it happens." He dropped gentle kisses on her lips, her cheeks, her eyes. "I promise you that."

When they got too hot from the hot tub, they rinsed off with cold water in their shower, dried themselves, and then got into bed. Quietly, no words were needed, they began to make love again. Savannah rolled onto her stomach and then lifted up on to her knees, offering herself to him. Bruce leaned forward, massaging her back, her hips, and then reaching beneath her body to massage her breasts. He entered her from behind, loving the little gasp she made as he controlled the rhythm and the depth. Holding on to her curvy hips, he thrust forward; he knew the minute he touched her cervix because Savannah began to push back, moaning, writhing her hips, begging for him to come inside her. This was the shortest lovemaking session they had on their trip—it was so quiet, so quick, his climax so intense that it bordered on painful. Spent, he pulled his beloved wife into his arms, pulled the covers over their bodies. Somewhere deep inside, in a place that was as intangible as it was mysterious, Bruce felt that this was the night—this was the moment—that he had given Savannah another child.

They spent the last week in paradise trying to work their way through Savannah's extensive checklist of activities. The morning that his wife had taken a pregnancy test, and it had come back negative, Savannah's spirits slumped. Bruce had made it his mission to lift her spirits and to remind her that they had only been trying for a short time. And wouldn't it be even more special if they could trace the moment of conception back to this amazing island?

They spent the last day on their private beach, lounging, floating in the clear water and doing their best to soak in those last precious moments of their time in Fiji. That night, their last night, they packed up their belongings and then had a romantic last dinner for two on their patio.

"Well, let's make one last toast." Savannah held up her glass of water.

Even though she hadn't gotten the news that she had wanted, and she wasn't in fact pregnant, his wife had decided to stop drinking alcohol to prepare for pregnancy.

"To us, my love." Bruce touched his glass to hers. "Thank you for being my wife."

She smiled, pleased. "I love you."

He took a sip of his wine; he'd discovered on this trip that he actually preferred it to beer.

"I love you more."

After dinner, they took one last walk on the beach. The sky, now that the moon was such a small sliver, was bursting with twinkling white stars.

"Do you think that we'll ever come back here?" his wife asked—he heard a sadness in her voice that their time on the island was coming to end.

"I don't know." This trip had been a once-in-a-lifetime visit that had come with a hefty price tag. He didn't begrudge the expense, but they did have a Montana ranch to run back home, and that wasn't cheap, either.

"Even if we never get to come back—" she tucked her hand into the crook of his arm "—this was such a blessing to be able to come here even once."

That was the moment when they shared a last kiss, on the beach, in the salty air, with the sparkling stars of Fiji twinkling in the cobalt-blue night sky.

Bruce had loved the trip to Fiji, but he was sure glad to be back at Sugar Creek Ranch. Montana was still his idea of paradise. He was back in his jeans and his T-shirts, his cowboy hat and his boots. He'd had his fill of seafood and tropical fruit; he was happy to have grits and eggs on his plate in the morning, and steak and potatoes on his plate at night. Savannah loved the ranch as he did, but he also knew that the transition from Fiji back to Montana had taken her a bit longer.

"Hey," Savannah greeted him when he got done with the day's work. She was sitting cross-legged on their bed, as always surrounded by their canine family members, with her laptop open in front of her.

He gave her a quick peck on the lips, wanting to get in the shower and wash the sweat and grime off his skin.

"I want to show you something when you get out of the shower," she told him.

"Okay."

On the way to the shower, he picked up a pair of Savannah's jeans and a bra.

"Love, why can't you seem to get your clothes near the hamper?" Bruce asked, tossing the dirty clothes into the hamper in their closet.

"Didn't I?" his wife asked distractedly.

Bruce chuckled, half out of disbelief, half out of acceptance. One of the minor prices he would have to pay for being married to Savannah was her chronic inability to get her clothes in the hamper.

He showered, shaved and then joined his family on the bed.

Savannah smiled at him and turned the computer screen so he could see it. It was her GoFundMe page for the Sammy Smiles foundation.

"Is that accurate?" He looked at the large bank of money on the page.

"Yes," she said, her voice emotional. "Our friends and family *and* people who have visited my page out of interest or because they have lost a child themselves to household drownings. One hundred thousand dollars, Bruce. *One hundred thousand.* We have more than enough to get off to a great start."

He leaned over and kissed her lips. "I'm so proud of you."

"Thank you. I'm actually pretty proud of me, too."

* * *

She wanted to say thanks to her friends and family for their generous contributions to Sammy Smiles. So Savannah decided to organize a party as a way of expressing her gratitude but to also talk about next steps. Now that she had more than enough money to set up a nonprofit organization and begin to put the donations to work to save lives, she had to figure out what the heck to do. She had an idea, she had a passion, but she wasn't sure how to best use the money that had been entrusted to her. The truth of it was, she had the money and the idea, and zero experience running a nonprofit.

Even though she didn't have an idea about how to run an organization, she was pretty talented at throwing a fabulous, memorable party. While Bruce spent his days working the ranch, Savannah threw herself into planning an event to unveil the logo design and the website she was having built for Sammy Smiles. The best place she could think to hold the event was Sugar Creek Ranch. Jock and Lilly were always gracious hosts, there was enough space for their guests and the beauty of the swath of land that was Sugar Creek was undeniable.

"Oh, thank you, Dad!" Savannah threw her arms around Jock's neck and kissed him hard on the cheek. "I promise we'll pay for everything, and we'll clean up after ourselves."

"It's for Sammy," Jock said gruffly. Jock had loved that little boy so much; Jock's $25,000 check had gone a long way to get them to that $100,000 mark.

That night, Savannah filled her husband in on the details of the first official Sammy Smiles event.

"It seems like it's all pulling together real nicely," her husband said.

"It really is," she agreed.

After a moment of silence, she posed a question that had been on her mind. "Let me ask you something."

Bruce didn't look up from the game he was playing on his phone. She poked his leg with her toe. "Bruce."

"What?"

"Would you please look up from your game for one second, please?" She knew that she drove him crazy when she didn't pick up her clothes or left the toothpaste cap off the tube, but he drove her just as nuts with his Angry Bird games.

"I'm looking at you."

"I hope it didn't hurt too much," she teased him with a heavy dose of sarcasm.

"Not too much."

"Brat," she retorted. "I really want your advice."

Now he was really looking at her and listening.

"Do you think I should go back to school to learn how to run a nonprofit?"

Bruce thought for a moment. "If you want. Do you think you can handle that and having a child?"

"Tons of women do." She shrugged. "Why can't I?"

"Then I say go for it."

"Really?"

"Really."

Whether he was just placating her so he could get back to his game playing, or if he sincerely thought it was a good idea, didn't really matter. She had asked, he had answered, and she was now positive that she was going to go back to school in order to acquire the skills she needed to run Sammy Smiles and have the foundation have the biggest impact.

"How did you talk Dad into a party this soon?" Jessie, ever pretty and full of energy, asked her.

"I think he was willing because it's for Sammy Smiles."

"I think he was willing because *you* asked," Jessie shot back. "Who's that?"

Savannah looked over to where Jessie was pointing. "That's one of Bruce's SAE brothers."

"Hello, frat boy." Jessie trilled her tongue.

"He's way too old for you, Jessie."

"I only want to play a little, Savannah. Don't be such a killjoy."

There really was no talking Jessie out of anything she was determined to do, and Bruce's fraternity brother didn't stand a chance if Jessie decided to hook him.

Almost everyone who'd RSVP'd showed; the night, a clear, cloudless evening, cooler now that it was fall, was filled with dancing and laughter and eating and catching up. She showed everyone her pictures from Turtle Island, still missing those warm waters and the freedom of making love on the beach, as she scrolled through photos.

"Dance with me." Bruce held out his hand to her.

"Go with him," her friend Deb told her. "We'll catch up some more later."

Her husband led her out onto the dance floor, spun

her into his arms and smiled down at her with appreciative eyes.

"You sure know how to put together one hell of a shindig, Mrs. Brand."

"Everyone seems to be having a good time, don't they?"

"They sure do."

Sometimes, Savannah still had difficulty synthesizing the Savannah before the accident, the one who had lost over three years of memories that never returned, with the Savannah she was now. She still ran into Leroy and Kerri on occasion, but the impact of seeing them was hardly noticeable.

"What are you thinking about?" Bruce interrupted her private thoughts.

"Oh." She shook her head and gave him a little smile. "It's silly. Sometimes I still try to remember something, anything from those lost years."

Her husband's concerned eyes swept her face. "I don't want you to hurt over that anymore, my love."

She tilted her head back so she could look at him with all the love she felt in her eyes. "I don't hurt anymore, Bruce. I have you. I have all of this. I have Sammy Smiles."

The music stopped, they stopped dancing and Bruce kissed her, as he always did, on the lips.

"It's time to make some announcements," Savannah told her husband.

Bruce had his arm around her shoulders; in a low voice meant for her ears only, he asked, "Are you ready for this?"

She leaned back against him, her head touching his shoulder briefly. "I've been ready."

They both climbed the stairs to the stage; Savannah stood behind the microphone, now adjusted for her shorter height, while Bruce stood beside her, ever her support system.

"Good evening!" Savannah greeted everyone at the event. "Is everyone having a great time tonight?"

All of those friendly faces of her family and her dearest friends made her feel the swell of love and kindness she was sending to them reflected right back to her.

"First, I want to say thank-you for all of your generosity. Because of you, Sammy Smiles has been officially registered as a tax-exempt nonprofit organization!"

The crowd cheered and clapped for her; on a large screen behind her, a picture of their sweet son, Samuel, appeared, and the cheering and the clapping grew louder, became more intense.

She had promised herself that she would get through the speech without crying; she had promised herself. But the minute she looked over her shoulder and encountered the larger-than-life face and smile of the son she had lost, the tears wouldn't be denied. The picture she'd selected for this night, and for the logo of Sammy Smiles, was the very first picture she'd seen of her son after the accident. It was the first memory she had of Samuel.

"There's my angel," she said, her eyes lingering on her son's face a moment longer. "Sammy's life, his sweet soul and his incredible smile will live on because of all of you. Sammy's life will never be forgotten, and because Sammy lived, because Sammy smiled, I hope that not one more parent will have to suffer as we have.

And, even though there are still so many memories missing from my mind, the love in my heart for my precious little boy knows no boundaries."

After Savannah unveiled the new Sammy Smiles logo and website, she reached for Bruce's hand and waited for the rowdy, enthusiastic attendees to quiet down.

"Bruce and I have learned that no matter how deep your pain, no matter how large your loss, life does indeed go on."

She glanced up at her husband.

"It is possible to come back from the edge of the abyss. It is possible to forgive and heal and feel joy again."

Bruce squeezed her hand reassuringly as she continued.

"And we are living proof, a testimony to God's grace, that we can stand before you tonight, stronger in our marriage than ever before, and proudly share with all of you that we are, in fact, pregnant."

The shouts of surprise and joy filled Savannah's heart; how could one woman get so lucky twice in one lifetime?

"That's one hell of a souvenir!" someone yelled from the crowd.

"You're damn right it is!" Bruce agreed.

Hand on her stomach, Savannah smiled out at her friends and family. "I believe in my heart that Sammy will be watching over his little brother or little sister from heaven, and I…" She paused as tears of both sadness and joy continued to flow down her cheeks. "I take comfort in that." After the announcements were over, Bruce hopped off the stage and reached back for her. She bent her knees and let her husband swing her down.

Her husband wiped the tears from her cheeks. "Do you have any idea how happy you've made me, my love?"

"Only as happy as you've made me." She leaned into his body, her arms around him, her face tilted up. "I love you."

Bruce, her handsome, strong Montana man, held her face in his hands, his deep blue eyes so full of love for her and their unborn child.

"My beautiful wife," Bruce whispered against her lips, "You know I love you more."

* * * * *

Don't miss the next book in the
BRANDS OF MONTANA *series, coming in*
August 2018 from Mills & Boon Cherish!

And catch up with the entire Brand family:

THANKFUL FOR YOU
MEET ME AT THE CHAPEL
HIGH COUNTRY BABY
HIGH COUNTRY CHRISTMAS

Available now wherever Mills & Boon Cherish
books and ebooks are sold!

MILLS & BOON®

Cherish™

EXPERIENCE THE ULTIMATE RUSH OF FALLING IN LOVE

A sneak peek at next month's titles...

In stores from 7th September 2017:

- **Whisked Away by Her Sicilian Boss** – Rebecca Winters *and* **The Maverick's Return** – Marie Ferrarella
- **The Sheikh's Pregnant Bride** – Jessica Gilmore *and* **A Conard County Courtship** – Rachel Lee

In stores from 5th October 2017:

- **A Proposal from the Italian Count** – Lucy Gordon *and* **Garrett Bravo's Runaway Bride** – Christine Rimmer
- **Claiming His Secret Royal Heir** – Nina Milne *and* **Do You Take This Baby?** – Wendy Warren

---

Just can't wait?
Buy our books online before they hit the shops!
www.millsandboon.co.uk

Also available as eBooks.

MILLS & BOON®

EXCLUSIVE EXTRACT

Crown Prince Frederick of Lycander needs a wife
and an heir, and discovering he has a secret son with
beautiful supermodel Sunita makes him determined
to claim both!

Read on for a sneak preview of
CLAIMING HIS SECRET HEIR

'You have a baby?'

Frederick's hazel eyes widened in puzzlement, a small
frown creasing his brow as he took another step into her
sanctum. His gaze rested on each and every item of Amil's.

'Yes.' The word was a whisper, all Sunita could
manage as her tummy hollowed and she grasped the
door jamb with lifeless fingers.

'How old?' Each syllable was ice cold, edged with
glass and she nearly flinched. No, she would not be
intimidated. Not here. Not now. What was done was
done, and, rightly or wrongly, she knew if she could
turn back time she would make the same decision.

'Girl or boy?'

'Boy.' Each question, each answer brought them
closer and closer to the inevitable and her brain wouldn't
function. Instead, all she could focus on was his face,
the dawn of emotion – wonder, anger, fear and surely
hope too? That last was so unexpected that it jolted her
into further words. 'His name is Amil.'

'Amil,' he repeated. He took another step forward and instinctively she moved as well, as if to protect the life she had built, putting herself between him and her home. 'Is he mine?'

For an instant it was if the world went out of focus. She could almost see a line being drawn in the sands of time – this was the instant that separated before and after. For one brief instant she nearly took the coward's route, wondered if he would swallow the lie that Amil was Sam's. Then realised she could not, would not do that. 'Yes. He is yours. Amil is your son.'

Now she understood the origins of a deafening silence. This one trolled the room, echoed in her ears until she wanted to shout. Instead she waited, saw his body freeze, saw the gamut of emotion cross his face, watched as it settled into an anger so ice cold a shiver rippled her skin. Panic twisted her insides – the die had been cast and she knew now that whatever happened, life would never be the same.

Don't miss
CLAIMING HIS SECRET HEIR
by Nina Milne

Available October 2017
www.millsandboon.co.uk

MILLS & BOON®

Why shop at millsandboon.co.uk?

Each year, thousands of romance readers
find their perfect read at millsandboon.co.uk.
That's because we're passionate about
bringing you the very best romantic fiction.
Here are some of the advantages of
shopping at www.millsandboon.co.uk:

* **Get new books first**—you'll be able to buy
  your favourite books one month before they
  hit the shops

* **Get exclusive discounts**—you'll also be
  able to buy our specially created monthly
  collections, with up to 50% off the RRP

* **Find your favourite authors**—latest news,
  interviews and new releases for all your
  favourite authors and series on our website,
  plus ideas for what to try next

* **Join in**—once you've bought your favourite
  books, don't forget to register with us to rate,
  review and join in the discussions

Visit **www.millsandboon.co.uk**
for all this and more today!

Join Britain's BIGGEST Romance Book Club

- **EXCLUSIVE offers every month**

- **FREE delivery direct to your door**

- **NEVER MISS a title**

- **EARN Bonus Book points**

Call Customer Services
0844 844 1358*

or visit
millsandboon.co.uk/subscriptions